UNDER SHŌKO'S BED

Under Shōko's Bed

M. HARMON WILKINSON

ISBN 978-1-954362-00-0 (Hardcover)
ISBN 978-1-954362-01-7 (Paperback)
ISBN 978-1-954362-02-4 (Ebook)
ISBN 978-1-954362-03-1 (Audiobook)

FIRST EDITION

Cover design: Laura Duffy
Interior design: Karen Minster
Published by M. Harmon Wilkinson
www.mharmonwilkinson.com

For S, too far away,
and for my wife, who never left me

Japanese Content and Pronunciation

Translations of all Japanese words and phrases are given after the main text. Units of measure (metric or US customary) depend on the point of view. English place-names are used if they are common (e.g., *Tokyo* rather than the Romanized Japanese *Tōkyō*).

Japanese pronunciation is relatively simple. There are five vowel sounds: a - father, i - eat, u - moon, e - bed, o - alone. A line over a vowel merely lengthens the time it is held (e.g., the first *o* in *Shōko* is held about twice as long as the second). The Japanese *r* has no English equivalent but is somewhere between *d* and *r*. It is similar to a Spanish *r* but without the trill. Finally, all syllables receive the same emphasis (i.e., no accented syllables).

Dialogue of characters speaking Japanese occasionally includes the word *Sir*. One would rarely use such a term in Japanese, but it expresses the same feeling as humble and honorific verb forms in the Japanese language that have no English equivalent, as well as other, sometimes subtle differences in word choice that reflect the speaker's rank or position relative to the listener.

I

Stray

野良猫

Sunday, 5 July 2009

1

STABBING JAGGED AND SLOW, DESOLATION HAD WORKED IN SO DEEP that he was now, at his core, pain itself. He imagined having done it, his body tumbling downstream in the chill water, limbs dangling loose, an empty bag, altogether careless—unless agony follows you when you die. He shuddered. Of all the horrid reflections that had grated away his sanity in the last three days, that thought may have been the worst. If only he could drown body and spirit, self-awareness slipping out in a trail of bubbles; or better yet, just blink off and be gone.

He lay motionless on the hardwood floor, his soul dripping out into a gradually expanding puddle beneath him. Through a window to the west and another to the south over her bed streamed the last direct sunlight. Against the air conditioner's breeze, the sunbeams' warmth gave the floor a baked feeling that pulled his eyes closed. But bleak thoughts, too real, stared back at him in disgust, so he opened his eyes and let them roam the floor. The low sun showed every scant speck of dust in high relief. It was a house pet's perspective that would surely prick less tidy people into pledges to clean more thoroughly and frequently, which they never do. Witless people, making vows they can't keep.

He wasn't sure when his benefactress would return, if that mattered at all. Even if he'd found a place to stay the night, what did he amount to anymore? Lying on the floor, as small as he could be, nearly lifeless, he barely cast a shadow despite the sun's low angle.

He shifted his gaze around her room. Between exposed structural wooden posts, the walls were fiberboard, rough and a little sparkly. The ceiling was smooth, unstained cedar panels. The furniture appeared to be European, not Japanese. Her single bed looked soft, its pillows and cotton print bedspread all pastel yellows and blues, tranquilly mated. It was unusually high off the floor, but its shadows held only a pair of shallow boxes.

Can you tell something about a woman by the space under her bed? Not that he'd seen underneath many women's beds. Dark, private, hardly glimpsed by happenstance, it was a place to put things away, but not too far; totems she dared not display, yet could never discard; perhaps even secret treasures. The space under this bed was vaguely sad, as if her past was too meager to fill it. Could *his* have? Was there anything he could claim? The faithless woman had owned him so completely that every object, every memory, seemed bound to her, the one who abandoned him. Anyway, he would stay the night, but this one would not own him. No one would ever own him again.

He closed his eyes but saw the traitor sauntering away, oblivious to his devotion, thick, gluey, now splattered like slowly cooling tar on a road waiting for gravel to be spread. So he stared at the oddly clean floor. As the time crept by, it wasn't the sparsity of dust that fascinated him, though, but its uniform distribution. There was no buildup anywhere— even under the bed, where people always miss spots, if they sweep at all. But a length of loosely wound red yarn was all that was out of place there. This one was obviously thorough, but the cleanliness hinted at ... training, regularity, duty? So why on a whim bring home a stray? Whatever her reason, at least for now, he would rather be here than the levee, or that empty apartment.

He was lost in the dust again when the bright spot on the floor vanished. He lifted his head and yawned, but his stretch was abbreviated by a deep ache in his back, followed by the hollow where his insides used to be. The warmth gone, he wanted somewhere he wouldn't be seen, a safe place, small, completely his. So, struggling with each movement against the weight of a life better ended, he crawled under the bed as far as he could, turned to face out, and stared; first at the expanse of the floor, legs of the table and chairs rising like perfectly sheer pinnacles of an alien landscape; then at the yarn, a forgotten scrap like him. He yearned to have it wind through his mind until his entire existence was the mental creation and keeping of that intricate coil of red.

It was good to have moved. His darkness was returning. His magical yarn woefully short for a cocoon, he took comfort in the shadowed closeness under the bed. It was a space clearly delimited, wholly without connections. He was done with them. They pull you, rip you, and finally dismember you—or you tear them—one way or another, everything ends in pain. Inevitably near, how painful would his end be?

He was bearing that question into his shell of a world when the door slid open, the light turned on, and feet came padding quietly into the room. He watched her walk briefly here and there. Then she sat, her feet tucked back under the chair. In his mind, he traced them, following the gentle curve of her arches into toes curled up against the floor. He was playing with the subtle range of colors reflected from the soft, smooth soles when, with the simplest grace, she crossed her feet at the ankles, and hushed though it was, his breath escaped in an audible sigh.

He could stay tonight, perhaps longer, in this dark place, clean and undemanding, with those soft feet. Maybe soft feet stay.

ALTHOUGH SHŌKO had never lived overseas, neighbors knew that she used to speak English in her job in Tokyo. In early June, a month ago, two of them asked her to tutor their middle schoolers. She had time Sunday mornings, so she agreed, although she refused to take any money. The girls had midyear exams coming up before the summer break, so today Shōko earned tomatoes, cucumbers, and a small watermelon from their families' gardens with a particularly long session. Though she was laughing with the girls as they slipped their shoes on in the *genkan* and waved goodbye, she was tired. It was a clear day in an especially wet rainy season, though, so prodded by the sun, Shōko ventured out for a simple picnic in the shade of the riverside locust trees.

He had joined most of her Sunday picnics or riverside strolls since she started them nearly two months ago. Today, though, she was already on her way home, walking along the path atop the levee, before she found him sitting alone. He was staring blankly at the river as if it were flowing through his own head. Over the last few weeks, she had witnessed with growing concern his deterioration, like a cardboard box left wilting in the rain, but he had never been this haggard. Wondering whether he was hungry, she offered him an *o-nigiri*, but he showed no interest in the rice ball. She tried to lift his spirits with a gentle voice, but though she broke his communion with the river, his eyes stayed mostly on the ground. He occasionally looked at someone walking by, but only a few times at Shōko, and only at her feet. Still, she sat with him, and as an hour spun into two, he lifted his gaze. She tried a few times to get him to move, without success, so they sat, silently watching the people and looking out at the river, still swollen from yesterday's rain. Eventually, home duties had been calling so long that, worried though she was, she whispered a final encouragement, touched her hand to his back, and got up to leave.

Shōko was halfway home when, sensing a pursuer, she looked back in alarm, but it was just him, following half a block behind. As the adrenaline rush faded, she slackened her pace, unsure of what to do. It was strangely beguiling to see him trailing after her, trying not to be obvious, but not enough to hide from view. Might she keep him for the night? Her parents would more than disapprove, but did they have to know?

The idea of taking him in was so peculiar that she wondered with a wan smile whether it was a first step to becoming a *neko obasan*, the neighborhood madwoman with a hundred cats. Did he want to stay? Realizing it was her intent but perhaps not his, the eccentricity of it stunned Shōko all the more. As she walked on, though, thoughts circling in uncertain spirals, she saw the same thing every time she glanced back: him, still a half block behind, feigning nonchalance, oddly endearing, hopelessly pathetic. So, when she reached the house, she motioned to him to catch up, then encouraged him with a smile to accompany her up the short path through the rhododendrons to the front door and into the *genkan*.

The kitchen, living room, bathroom, and her parents' small bedrooms were on the first floor. Upstairs were only Shōko's room and a spare room used for storage. It took an expectant, reassuring look back from the stairs before he followed her up. Once inside, she slid the bedroom door closed behind him, and while she set her purse and hat on the table, he tarried near the door and took in the space.

The room brightened as sunlight suddenly illuminated the curtains. She thought natural light might be cheery and stepped over to the window, took hold of the curtains, but hesitated, rubbing the familiar calico-print cotton between her fingers. She picked out this fabric when she was seventeen. Most of the color had faded in the thirty-five years since. She looked down at her hands, at the age that showed in them, and watched her fingers tremble.

I can open the curtains. It's been long enough.

She clasped the fabric firmly to stop from shaking.

I can.

Still, she stared at the sunlit cloth for a long minute before she squared her shoulders, drew back the curtains, and let in the sun for him. It was the first time she had opened them since returning home seven months ago.

Shōko smiled at him as he walked over to the window, but he did not look out, or at her. His eyes were on the floor. There they remained as he sat, then lay down, all in such perfect stillness that it left her with goose bumps, as if she were witnessing a spirit linger for a few final moments before flight.

She had to make dinner for her parents, though, so she left him there on the floor. The sunset was fading before she returned with a bowl of rice and roast fish, only to find the room empty. She sat at the table. Should she go out and search for him? But then she heard a soft sigh from under the bed. She knelt and looked. There he lay, the light reflecting in his green-gray eyes. Apparently, that was where he wanted to be, so she set the food down in the space he had chosen as his home for the night.

She could hear the faint sound of him eating. It lifted her spirits. It had been a very long time since she had cared for anything she felt was her own. It was just for this one night, of course; any more and her parents would surely find him and be angry. Shōko didn't quite feel like a boarder, but her childhood sense of ownership had dulled over the twenty-five years since she last lived here, a dismal few months of abject dejection after her divorce. Secretly harboring him tonight was disrespectful, but she focused on the charity, compartmentalizing and choosing the contented space with him and the compassion he aroused. Shōko knew full well that bundling him off to the nearby *kōban* would be the reasonable, responsible thing to do. The officer at the neighborhood police box took care of minor questions and troubles all the time. But she ignored reason. Unfathomable though it was, she wanted this bond. At least for tonight, he belonged to her.

The evening proceeded in perfect silence until bedtime. She changed into pajamas when she went downstairs for her evening bath. Having slid something soft for him to lie on under the bed, all that remained was to turn off the light, and tonight for the first time since she could remember, to say good night within the confines of her room. She spoke in English: "Good night, my tired friend. I hope you sleep well."

He was soon asleep, but Shōko lay awake in the bed above him long after, resting in the rhythm of his breathing, grieving the dreams that had outrun her, and wondering whether fate had contrived to show one on the horizon after so long.

2

HE LAY CURLED UP AGAINST THE WALL, HIS FACE HIDDEN.

"I think you are awake now," Shōko said.

He had to leave with her. Last night she was here to watch over him. What if her parents found him? Faced with walking him to the street and saying goodbye, though, she wavered. It would be tantamount to sending him back to the river, to that levee where she had stood, twenty-six years ago, facing the same choice she feared he was contemplating yesterday. At least here under the bed, even by himself all day, he could feel welcome and wanted.

She stood and checked her purse. She looked at her watch. It was past time to leave, and she was never late.

She thought of his eyes looking back at her from beneath the bed yesterday.

Shōko closed her eyes and sighed. In the surfeit of anger and resentment she sat in each day like a pool of winter slush, he was sunshine.

She checked her watch once more, then knelt by the bed and said, again in English, "My friend, I hope you are resting here today. I leave foods for you. Please be quiet. My parents don't know you stay here and too loud noises could be scaring them. You may leave anytime. I just want you being comfortable."

Shōko walked briskly through a light rain, an umbrella in her left hand and, as always, a phone clutched in her right. She kept to the middle of the empty neighborhood streets in the few blocks to the *kōban*, where she took comfort and eased her pace. Bowing to the police officer standing in the doorway as she passed, she turned and headed up the large thoroughfare that was her safest route downtown. She paused at the bus stop but decided to save the money and walk. It was not a big city, and it only took twenty minutes, passing another *kōban* and the main police station, before she would turn and hurry the final blocks.

Shōko's steps stayed quick as she picked her way between the puddles. She wore the older of her two pairs of shoes. They were well-worn, but she was hoping to keep them from the cobbler at least into autumn. Her uniform, a skirt of baby-blue polyester gabardine and an ill-fitting matching vest, was immune to the weather, but she was careful to keep her white blouse dry. Though she hated wearing a uniform just as she had in high school, at least it spared her the humiliation of asking her parents for money to buy clothes.

A block past the second *kōban*, though, thoughts of him under the bed disappeared as a sudden premonition seized her. She twisted her head in a frantic search, but there was no one. She tried to tell herself that her tormentor wasn't really there, like countless times before. But a vise was crushing her chest and her skin crawled at the thought of him close enough to see her. She turned and stepped back toward the *kōban* as she forced herself to breathe. Her second step was tentative—and she leapt to the curb and waved frantically for a taxi.

3

HE HEARD THE RAIN STOP, BUT FITFULLY WAKING AND SLEEPING, HE saw afternoon sunshine on the curtains only briefly. Through the long hours, his thoughts and dreams were a caustic obsession: the inhumanity of his abandonment, despair at the anguish that would be his existence until the day he died, and grief that he was not already dead. He heard the river's constant beckoning, cold, dark, infinitely deep, but he was too exhausted to move. Unsure whether time was passing or had stopped altogether, he was so tired when awake and slept so poorly that it was difficult to tell them apart. All he could do was lie there and wonder at how vivid and awful his dreams could be, while reality was a nightmare, totally surreal.

In one of his brief periods out from under the bed, he looked out the window at the dense, gray sky. With the rain, the river would be high again today. It would take only minutes to walk there, and once in the water, one short, final minute before the panic passed, then the pain, then the world.

He stared at the clouds. . . .

It would take too much effort to walk that far and finish himself, so he sat on the floor. He would do it, though. Hour upon hour of torment, knowing it would only stretch into days and weeks and a lifetime of pain; no one could endure it.

He closed his eyes to take the measure of his despair, but somehow thought of those soft feet walking through the door. In his imagination she smiled, then said:

"I am glad you are better enough to come out into the bedroom. We can walk outside."

Shaking his head, he silently responded, "Not today."

"But you were thinking about it a minute ago."

He was quiet.

"What you need now is someone for talking. That is it, more than anything. Or we can walk, sit, whatever you need. You are not alone."

"I'll always be—"

"No," she interrupted his thought. "Maybe always from now you have a lonely place deep inside. You think I don't have? Everyone has, I think. That does not mean you are alone."

He looked at the door.

"Don't do that," she said.

"Why wait? To relive her leaving me a hundred times a day? To make the stabbing persist? To somehow savor the feel of the blade?"

"I don't ask for you waiting forever, just today. See me again when I get home. We can go out. It will not be dark yet."

He sat silently.

"Yes," she said softly in his mind.

" 'Yes' what?"

"Yes, it is worth pain for afternoon to see me again."

He hung his head.

"You may wait under my bed, but you must see me."

4

SHŌKO SPENT HER DAYS HOPING THAT MINDLESS DRUDGERY WAS not the actual cause of dementia. In Tokyo, she had handled English-language correspondence and customs compliance for a midsize trading company. The work required vigilance and constant learning, and she had spent much of each day on the phone in English. In contrast, today she was entering data into electronic files that were unindexed and therefore would probably never be used.

The monotony left Shōko's mind free to vacillate between how best to extract her guest from beneath the bed and get him out the door today, and how she might keep him until she found him a safe, stable place to land. She realized that he might already be gone, and she shook her head countless times to free herself from the vision of him walking to the river in the rain. Yet the pitiful movie played out every time she imagined ushering him out the door, so on she dithered. It was midafternoon before she realized that despite all her concerns, she had yet to shake off a vision of what might happen if she let him stay.

———

IT WAS STILL MISTING on her way home, so Shōko held her umbrella loosely, a grocery bag hanging from her arm. As she walked along the levee path, she listened to the soggy crunch of her shoes on the rough asphalt and noted the progress of the weeds in the cracks. She began taking this path home regularly only a couple of weeks ago. It still wasn't an option in the morning, when she took comfort in the police presence on her way to work. Her departure from the house would be much more predictable than the timing of her afternoon or evening return. And there were others on the path later in the day. Despite them being strangers, she was safer with people in sight.

Most days she heard birds, but the air today was full of the churning sound of the river that made a great arc around her neighborhood. Its main channel, thirty meters wide and three meters deep, was near the far levee. The river was high today, enough to overrun the shallow channels that meandered closer to this bank, though it still did not fill the entire river bottom. She often thought of the river as her life: swift, steady, its serpentine channels a seemingly endless braid, no repetition quite the same, but repetitions, nonetheless. It was going somewhere, but only to the ocean, which amounted to oblivion for the river. Looking into the future at fifty-two, childless, back living with her parents, was a fatalistic journey. Her trips into memory were worse, though. Her failed marriages, both short-lived, one ending in divorce and the other without hope or desire for reconciliation, draped her in such shame at her ridiculous choices that she hid from the memories, though they still stalked her. Myriad other decisions, dense with regret, begged, "What if I'd . . . ?" in an existence that promised no joy. So, though Shōko longed for more, she invariably focused on the current, a daily routine of helping her parents and meticulously doing her job, her river flowing still and steady, resolutely channeled, levees just a waste of dirt.

Shōko opened the door and shouted, "*Tadaima!*" She didn't like to shout so loud, but her parents would not consider hearing aids; her mother insisted her hearing was fine and her father said he enjoyed the quiet. Shōko was about to shout out again even louder when she heard her mother call back from the living room, "*O-kaeri-nasai!*"

Shōko stepped up out of her shoes, artlessly aligned in the *genkan*, picked them up, and stowed them in the shoe cabinet. She deposited the groceries in the kitchen before returning to the front hall. Turning toward the stairs, though, she stopped, lifted her eyes to her room, and listened.

The house was perfectly still. Her parents were probably reading.

As she climbed the stairs, it seemed like there were more of them today. Her heart was racing by the time she got to her room. Stairs never winded her, but her chest felt tight, so she stopped at her bedroom door and took a deep breath.

He shouldn't be there. It will be simpler if he's gone.

Her fingers on the door, Shōko paused for one last breath, as if readying herself for a doctor's needle, before she slid it open. She glanced about as she walked to the table in the middle of the room and set down her purse. Nothing appeared out of place. The food was untouched. So was he . . . ?

He shouldn't be there. And I shouldn't care either way.

Stop caring!

She dropped to her knees and looked. He was there! And ignoring the foreboding that gripped her at the sound of her heart pounding exultantly in her ears, she smiled and said, "Hello, old friend. Are you comfortable still?"

SHŌKO GAVE UP READING and dropped her book on the bed. She listened intently for any sound, but there was only the faint ping of rain on the roof and the languid splashing of puddles beneath the eaves.

Preoccupied with his eyes under her bed, she'd read only a few pages, yet still had dallied long enough that dinner was late. She was setting out the dishes as her parents sat down.

"Did you buy the fish fresh today?" asked her mother.

"I always do," replied Shōko politely as she set a small bowl of rice in front of her mother. As she did the same for her father, he looked up and caught her eye. She paused as he held her gaze. It was only a second, and he did not smile or change his expression, but there was appreciation in his eyes. Thankfulness showed back in her own for the moment before she sat, they all said, "*Itadakimasu*," and turned their attention to the food.

They ate silently. Her father was a quiet man, and Shōko was thinking of the eyes under her bed. She thought of her father's, too, and whether she would ever see appreciation in another's eyes.

Shōko's mother broke the stillness: "I saw him today."

Shōko froze.

Her father frowned. "I told you not to say anything."

"But she should know."

"If you really saw him, yes, but not a single one of your sightings has turned out to be true. You worry her needlessly."

Shōko rested her hand on the table, the ends of her chopsticks shoved under the lip of the plate to keep them from shaking.

Her mother chewed slowly. "The rice is a bit dry, isn't it?"

Shōko dropped her chopsticks, pressed her hands to her eyes, and ran from the room.

At the stairs, she stopped short and looked up at her door.

No, he can't see me like this.

She spun and faced the front door, but the thought of what could be outside made her quake so violently that she dropped to the floor. There she knelt, her face in her hands, curled up so her forehead nearly touched the floor, trembling.

Her father knelt behind her. "We haven't seen him for four months."

Shōko nodded.

"Whoever your mother saw, it wasn't him. Every time, he's shown himself. Remember, he wants only to terrorize you. He can't do that if he stays hidden."

She whispered to the floor, "I know."

He placed his hand on her back before he took her by the shoulders and gently pulled her upright. He remained behind her, both of them kneeling.

"Keep in mind that the times he's come, it's unlikely he saw any sign of you. He's not even sure you're here. Forget him. He's given up."

He handed Shōko his handkerchief and she wiped her eyes.

"You should eat."

She nodded again, but it was a few more minutes before she was back at the table, eating in silence.

5

WHEN THE ALARM WOKE HIM TUESDAY MORNING, HE FOUND HIMSELF halfway out from his hiding place. He pushed back under the bed until he reached the wall, where he took solace in his near invisibility. In the darkness it was easy to imagine his presence as a secret even from the one person who knew he was here.

He fell asleep again but woke to the sound of breakfast being placed on the floor beside the bed. Still pressed against the wall, he hesitated but soon gave in to hunger and moved. He lay there watching her dress as he ate. Why was a woman this kind and beautiful alone? The question tarried, even as she said goodbye.

He did not sleep as much as yesterday. As the hours dragged by, he counted, first his breaths, then the sparkles in the wallboard, and time and again, how long the false-hearted one had owned him. Tallied in years, in days, in seconds, each total left him at the same moment, the swift slice that gutted him. He didn't need a thumb to count the four empty days since. He struggled to evacuate his mind, simply to stare—at the bottom of the bed, the floor, the curtains, the walls—until he could see the textures of this new box even with his eyes closed. This was his space to lie in, beached. Here the sand would parch and his skin crack and bleed as he waited, not for the return of the one who forsook him, but for the weightlessness that would come as he shriveled into nothing.

"Hurts go away," came his friend's imagined voice from the bed above him.

"Only if you let them," he said silently.

"So do."

He was still.

"You are choosing this pain?" she asked.

"Deserving."

"Why?"

After a long pause he said, "I did nothing to stop her."

After a full minute she said, "I leaved foods for you, like yesterday. You can eat something, or at least take a drink."

His eyes went to the water. It looked cool, and he was thirsty.

"When I get home, I am happy to see you took a drink."

He did not move.

"You know you don't really dry up and disappear. You just get more thirsty."

He was quiet.

"Take a drink. I will sit with you while you go back to sleep."

6

SHŌKO DID NOT EVEN PUT HER PURSE ON THE TABLE BEFORE SHE knelt and checked under the bed. He did not move at all as she looked at him, but his eyes were open and he met her gaze steadily. She smiled at him for a few seconds, without speaking, then stood and turned on the air conditioner. Catching sight of her smile in the mirror, though, she checked herself sharply.

Shōko opened the curtains and took a long look out the window to the west. It was cloudy, but she was warm, as if the sun were gleaming directly into her face.

But it was a brisk walk. And the room is hot. I should turn on the air conditioner before I leave tomorrow.

She surveyed the room. It appeared he spent a second full day under the bed, languishing at best, food again untouched. At least he had a good drink today. Despite the eye contact, though, he looked more ragged than yesterday, which was worse than Sunday. He needed more from her than safe harbor, and there was a limit even to that. She had to draw him out while there was still time.

Shōko pressed her handkerchief to her face as she considered what to say. She rejected a dozen openings before she said, "I hope you were relaxing today. Did you go out? I guess no. It was raining again today." She stopped and listened.

Nothing.

Arching her back and dropping her head back, she sighed. *There has to be something besides the weather.* She pulled a T-shirt and jeans from her dresser, then stared at the bed as she unbuttoned her vest, waiting for inspiration.

Fine, weather again. "I like sunshine days. They make me happy since I was a little girl." She frowned as she paused. "You know I am the only child in my family. I lived in this house long ago. At ten years age we moved to this house. I was excited to have my own room."

She slipped off her blouse, worked her arms through the T-shirt's sleeves, and pulled it on over her head. "We went to a circus the summer after we moved here. I loved the big cats. They were so strong but moved in a soft way. So I wanted to be the animal trainer for a circus. Then my parents gave to me a kitten. I loved her so much. She was American Shorthair like you." Shōko laughed. "Remember I named her Yuki, 'snow,' because she was all white? Then I wanted to be the veterinarian and care for animals. I had many friends, but Yuki-*chan* was my best friend. I think maybe you know Yuki, yes? When I graduated high school and went to art college in Tokyo, I miss her, so after first year I took her with me. That was my best time of my life. Did you know that?"

Shōko lay on the bed and told him more snippets of her childhood, all inconsequential, merely keeping him company. At length, she checked her watch. "Oh, I must cook!" Hurrying from the room, she had the door nearly closed before she saw he had moved. His face was almost in the light.

HE STAYED CLOSE to the bed's edge all evening. Shōko talked to him a few times but got no response. During her bath, though, she had an idea. Back upstairs, she sat on the floor next to the bed. She checked whether his eyes were open before she said, "I brought something to show you." She laid an old family photo album on the floor, the last pictures of herself that she had in her possession. She leafed through the pages, then lay down on her stomach. He was still near the edge of the bed, so she slid the open album close to him and said, "This is me with my friends in last year of high school." She let him look, pulled it out, flipped the page, and slipped it under the bed again. "This is my cat, Yuki." Another page. "This is painting that won highest award at prefecture high school art competition."

She was about to pull the album out and turn the page when she thought she saw movement. She waited, and as she watched, he reached out and touched the picture of her painting.

They both lay on the floor, perfectly still, for the next couple of minutes before he began to stir. As he moved toward the edge of the bed, Shōko sat up. He sat in front of her on the floor and she gave him a wide grin. "Will you be sitting with me in my room from now?"

To her surprise, though, he got up, stretched, walked to the door, and after poking his head out and listening, disappeared. Shōko was so astonished that, by the time she rose and looked out the door, he was nowhere to be seen. Suddenly she was showered with needling doubts. She was letting him hide out as if a few days rest or some silly childhood stories would cure him? She should have taken him to a hospital, not home. What if someone was looking for him? She should walk him to the *kōban*. The police would know what to do.

Did she have to do it *tonight*, though? She imagined the look on his face, beyond pathetic, when she turned him over to the police. As she stealthily led him out of the house, she would see a moment of surprise before bewilderment, brief resistance, and eventually, resignation. As they neared the *kōban*, she imagined him looking at her for the last time, his eyes mourning her betrayal. Sitting with him and rubbing his back on the way to the hospital, would she even exist to him any longer? Finally, imagining the midnight stillness of the hospital, seeing his sullen eyes seemingly asleep even as he stared straight ahead, she made reacquaintance with despair, intimate and true.

Hearing the door open, she cast her anxious eyes to his, and he hurried to her. She held him, too tight, but he just leaned into her, and she paused, looking up at the ceiling, until she could speak again. "You look so clean. I am glad you washed."

7

LOOKING OUT AT THE ROOM, HE SQUINTED AT THE FULL DAYLIGHT. Counting the days made today . . . Wednesday. She opened the curtains before she left this morning, and despite the heavy clouds that he could see out the window, the room was brighter than the previous two days.

His brief distraction from reality now over, though, he was stranded again with thoughts that inclined predictably to the one who left him. And before feet could come padding into his imagination and a soothing voice turn his eyes away, he watched anew the three agonizing days that had driven him to the levee. Reliving his abandonment, a tangible darkness folded around him like a thick blanket that offered no softness or warmth, only unbearable mass. Smothered under its infinite weight, he lay under the bed, unable to move, unable even to scream out his desperation. He knew he would never escape. This misery beyond all expression would be his as long as he lived.

He ached to disappear, to forget her frigid gaze that chilled him even now, days after the disloyal one left. If only the weight would crush him into nothing.

Then, oddly, it did. He viewed himself from across the room: nothing but a thick scattering of dust under the bed. As he gazed with wonder at the peaceful scene, he imagined his friend breezing in and chatting to him. He made out the concern on her face when he didn't respond and saw her kneel by the bed to check on him, then press her forehead to the floor in grief.

His weight evaporated. Altogether innocent, she had shown him nothing but loving concern!

Claustrophobia overwhelmed him. He scrambled out into the room. And shivering in the cold from the air conditioner, he stared at the blanket under the bed.

———

THERE WASN'T MUCH to see in the bedroom. There was a short book-case next to her high bed, a square table in the center of the room with a small flat-screen television and two chairs, and a dresser and large wardrobe against the far wall. The rest of the room was open space. In his mind, she said:

"There is another room next to mine."

"What's in there?"

"How can I know? I am only imaginary friend. Go look; I don't stop you."

Her room was at the head of the stairs and easily visible from below, so he hurried the few silent steps to the other room. It was smaller, just storage for a kerosene heater, *futon*, a wardrobe, and lots of boxes.

She got me out of her room for this?

Self-satisfied, she said, "I like you up and moving."

"You want me out of your hair."

She replied with emotion in her voice, "If I want you gone away, I take you outside on the first morning."

His own emotion would surface if he responded, so he was quiet.

He was about to step back into the hall when he heard footsteps. He could tell where her parents were if they were talking, their voices were so loud, but the footsteps took him by surprise. Hurriedly pushing the door to, he left it open just a crack. Peering out, he saw a small woman with mostly silver hair climbing the stairs. *Her mother.* They even looked alike, except that Shōko stood straighter.

"*Ōi! Bāsan, doko sa itta?*" a man called from downstairs.

It must be her father. Does she usually ignore him? Or maybe she can't hear him and I don't have to be as quiet as I thought.

The call came again, louder: "*Ōi! Bāsan, in no ga?*"

This time, her mother heard. "*Hāi,*" she yelled and started back down. As soon as she was out of sight, he stole back into the bedroom and secreted himself under the bed.

Twenty minutes later, though, he was tired of hiding. Besides, he wanted to look in the closet. The door slid open to reveal boxes of various sizes, neatly stacked. *"As I expected,"* he said to her in his mind. *"Everything has a place. So, how long will you let me have the space under—"*

Footsteps again, close! How did her mother get upstairs so silently? There wasn't even time to scurry under the bed. At the last moment, he noticed the bedding she had stripped that morning, and he slipped under it.

Peeking out, he watched the door slide open. The old woman shuffled to the center of the room, bent her tiny frame, and knelt on the floor, not six feet away. She set down the cloth she was carrying, pulled a sewing box from under the table, and started taking things out, placing them in her lap. *"Nan da be, Shōko. Hari doko sa oitan da be?"*

"What did she say?"

"You want to know? Learn more Japanese," answered imaginary Shōko.

Shōko's mother dug through what seemed like the entire box before she sounded happy: *"Atta!"* After repacking the box, though, she stayed. And lying there as still as he could be, fearful that even his breathing might give him away, he watched as she picked up her cloth and sewed.

"TADAIMA!" Shōko called as she stepped into the *genkan* and slid the front door closed.

"O-kaeri-nasai!" came her mother's call, and Shōko, frozen midstep, blanched as she raised her eyes to her open bedroom door.

Shōko hurriedly kicked off her shoes and sprinted up the steps. In a loud voice, she asked her mother, "Is everything—" She stopped in the doorway. "You're sewing?"

"I couldn't find a needle."

Shōko glanced around the room, her heart racing, as her mother went on, "You know you forgot to turn off the air conditioner when you—"

As she heard her stop short, Shōko's eyes shot to her mother, who said in alarm, "You're soaked! Did you forget your umbrella?"

"I was wet through from sweat before I ever left the office."

"But why?"

Shōko forced her eyes away from the bed. "It was raining, so they never turned on the air-conditioning." Looking under the bed would only prompt her mother to do the same. Shōko felt her mother's expectant stare, though, so shrilly imitating the owner's voice and looking down her nose, Shōko said, "Come now, let's not be wasteful. The rain will surely keep things pleasant enough."

"Shōko-*chan*, don't speak rudely of your employer."

"Who fled the heat midmorning and never returned. My clothes felt like cling wrap all day." With the owner gone, of course, someone could have inconspicuously flicked the switch, but no one did.

"No matter," said her mother as she folded up her sewing. "I'll go draw a bath for you right now."

Shōko helped her mother up off the floor and listened patiently to her all-too-familiar synopsis as she shuffled out of the room: "It's sad that a woman like you can't find a better job. You must have talent, and all that experience from your years in Tokyo. But I suppose we have to settle for what's available when we get too old to change companies. What a pity you didn't come home after college. Then you would never have had those awful experiences. Such wicked men. Shameful. But sometimes we have to accept that our lives are what they are and not hope for more, don't we? Acceptance brings peace, doesn't it? Yes, it does." Shōko could have reminded her mother that she strongly favored both marriages, but there was nothing to gain by it.

Shōko watched her down the first few stairs before she closed the door and dropped to her knees.

Gone!

Just as panic began to twist like an enormous screw into her chest, though, she saw movement under the pile of sheets in front of the closet. She dissolved into laughter as his head came poking out.

SHŌKO LAY ON HER BED, chuckling at a game show full of people famous for one thing or another, some simply for being famous. During a break, she rolled over and checked to see whether he was visible. One foot barely protruded.

If only she had something special to lure him out.

Maybe a treat?

Excited to find something he'd like, she popped off the bed, knelt briefly, and said, "I get a dessert for us."

Foraging through the kitchen, she settled on fruit, but as she looked at the four bowls, she wanted it to be more special. Although she had never tried it, she knew something he might enjoy, so after surprising her parents with cut peaches, she dressed up the remaining two bowls.

Back in her room, Shōko set two identical dishes on the floor so he would see it was "their" treat, but she slid neither under the bed. "I cut peaches for us and put on top . . . *hoippu kurīmu-tte nan te iu no . . .*? Whipped cream? It is American dessert, I think." She sat by the bed and asked, "Will you sit with me?"

She waited a minute before she took a spoonful.

Whipped cream on peaches, so odd . . . but smooth. Nice!

She heard movement and looked down.

Trying to stay detached as she watched him emerge for a second evening in a row was akin to stuffing a litter of puppies into a shoebox, but somehow Shōko managed. It wasn't long before she could talk. She chatted as they ate. Then, to her surprise, he was willing to sit next to her on the bed and watch television. Finally, he lay down. She thought it might help if she showed him affection, but as she scratched behind his ear, he moved and laid his head in her lap.

Shōko's eyes shot to the door—but it would be cruel to push him away. And he was warm—

No! Her life was a simple hut, ways of thinking and feeling and behaving woven reed by reed. Well patched—some big ones this year—it was holding up against the storms, but a misstep in an attachment too strong could beat it flat.

Still, he needed this, and she might not have a second chance, so she rested her hand on his back, just affectionate. Circumstances might be beyond her control, but not her feelings. If she was indifferent to him staying, he could not mutilate her by leaving. No love equaled no abandonment—and no relationships, with all their abuse and humiliation.

8

AFTER THE ALARM, SHŌKO RUBBED HIS HEAD AND HE OPENED HIS EYES to her grin. "Good morning. It is Thursday. Are you *genki*?" She brought him breakfast and he ate under the bed. But he fell asleep again as she prepared to go and missed her leaving.

When he eventually awoke, it was to an eerie, muted morning light and dead silence. He crawled out from beneath the bed and stretched. He made a few slow, noiseless circles around her room and ended up by her bed. It looked comfortable. He could feel Shōko saying:

"You may sit or lie down."

"Presumptuous, don't you think?"

"But we sat together last night."

"The real you invited me."

"Or we can take a walk. It is not raining," said the imaginary Shōko.

He could venture out, briefly at least. It would be dangerous—he might be seen by Shōko's parents—but he was willing to risk it.

Imaginary Shōko led the way downstairs, but he had to open the front door himself. As he stepped outside, the thick heat, despite lowering clouds that looked about to burst, surprised him. He reminded himself that it was July now and by some calendars the dog days of summer had already begun. She beckoned to him from the street, so he quietly slid the door closed and stepped through the rhododendrons. When he reached the street, though, she was suddenly gone from his imagination. There was no one to beckon him safely to the left, a world unexplored, so he stared to the right, those few short blocks where he followed her home four days ago, and the river. The levee was too far to see, but he was there in his mind already, and he watched, oblivious to time, as the muddy water roiled past. He felt heavier, as if his feet would never move again.

He looked back at the door to her house, his refuge, and watched it recede as he stood alone in the street in the dull, ashen light.

There was a flash of lightning followed closely by thunder. He cast his eyes to the clouds above and a gigantic raindrop slammed into his head. Another splattered on his back, and as he ran for the house, a million more crashed all around him.

Standing under the eaves, mostly dry, he waited for the rain to let up. He lacked the patience of his demons, though, and after fifteen minutes, he went inside and dragged himself back up the stairs to her room—still silently, for fear of Shōko's parents.

Curled up on her bed, listening to the rain beat on the roof, he slipped back through the days. He clutched for his memory of last night, but too late: he was already in last Friday, and six days ago, Shōko was not there.

Passive, invisible, he imagined the perfidious woman packing. She was thorough, and soon her only trace was the hollowness she left, empty drawers and hangers, like footprints in sand. She rolled her bags down the hall. He ran to block her path, but the walls disappeared, and she walked around him. On she went as the building disappeared, then her bags. He needed to stop, just let her go, but he followed, frantically calling.

His tears were wetting Shōko's pillow, so he dropped onto the floor, crawled to the farthest point in the room, and lay down in the corner, his face inches from the wall, hard, blank. There he remained for the rest of the day. No kind tête-à-tête came to his rescue. He briefly slept, but through the rest of the long hours, he lay in absolute stillness as the same few desolate thoughts replayed endlessly in his now one-dimensional mind. Though he longed to make Death's acquaintance, he lacked the will to find him. All he could do was hurt. If only the reaper of souls were inclined to take first those who welcome him.

THE RAIN STOPPED before Shōko started home. Looking for the birds she heard singing in the trees by the levee path, she soon forgot the cares of the day. She walked up her street in a cheery bubble, smiling as she anticipated seeing her friend as tranquil as last night—but she was knocked to the floor by the ball of agony she found in the corner by her closet. "What happened?" she asked over and over, but he stayed still as a stone, staring at the wall.

She pressed herself against him and stroked his head and back. She kept it up, whispering soft words, holding him. At length, she had to prepare dinner, but she soon returned and held him close once again. She shortened her bath as well, and there was no painfully loud television with her parents, no reading on the bed, no special dessert. She simply sat on the floor, trying her best to comfort him. And ever so slowly, he uncurled until he was lying somewhat comfortably on the hardwood.

It was past bedtime, and Shōko was leaning on the wall, emotionally exhausted but satisfied with her evening's work. This was the fifth night of his one-night stay, though, and she could no longer ignore the ridiculousness of trying to care for—

He rolled over, and for a moment, his green-gray eyes stared straight into hers. Crouching close to him on the floor, she hugged him tight.

She faced a quandary, however. He still needed her close. She could sleep there next to him, but she wanted him up off the floor. Was he ready, though? Shōko rested her head on the wall and looked at her bed as she ran her fingers over his hair, short and smooth.

Finally, leaning down close, she whispered, "Come to the bed. We should sleep."

She stood and tugged on him. He moved.

She took a step and waited. He got up.

She took another step; he followed, and she would have clapped for joy were it not so pitiful. She got him comfortable on the bed, climbed in next to him, and held him.

He fell quickly to sleep, but she embraced him long after, stroking the velvety hair behind his ear and thinking how strange he was. So mercurial, would he ever be stable? She could hardly say he was any stranger than the men she knew. Men are so like cats, no matter the outward temperament. Yet here she lay with this unhinged stray, emotionally snagged, and all by her own invitation. She may as well have beckoned an injured jaguar, for men and cats are without loyalty, and love to the point of loyalty was her deepest, most punishing need. It was a need she ignored—and when she couldn't, she flailed it—but through all the abuse it stayed with her, year after year. It was a lasting gift from her first husband, wrapped in the memory of his final farewell, void of any regret or guilt—or even any mention yet of divorce—self-serving and unapologetic to the end, before he walked to the car and drove away, his lover at his side. Shōko packed and left him that day, and she never saw him again.

So why hadn't she kept her vow never to become entangled again? True, her second marriage was not for love, but that was more indictment than consolation. She had subjected herself to a man without even love's blindness as an excuse, hoping that it would grow into something deeper; she shuddered anew at the thought.

But then came the memory of her last day with her second husband, of her frantic escape, followed by flashes of him close again, near enough to touch her. It was mere seconds of idle thought, but all too potent. Now shivering, she held her stray, this emotional land mine, like a life preserver. Peacefully still, warm, soft, he would not maim her tonight. She could deal with the danger he posed tomorrow.

Or the next day. Whenever.

9

WHEN HER ALARM SOUNDED FRIDAY MORNING, HE WAS UNDER THE bed again. He vaguely remembered moving there in the night. Now it was confining, though, so he freed himself and stretched, then sat on the bed and gazed out the window at the world glistening in the morning light. She had tapped the alarm and gone back to sleep. When it rang again, she seemed amused to find him sitting there looking at her. She patted his leg, then sat up and gave him a brief hug. "You look well today." He felt well too, better than he had for a long time.

All too soon, she dressed and said goodbye. Today, though, his loneliness was tolerable. Curiosity took hold again. The two shallow boxes that had been concealed under the bed now stood stacked at its foot. Though he hoped for her sake they held a fascinating treasure, he expected to find sweaters, or more likely, papers.

He slid the boxes out into the room, lifted the lid off the top one—and let it drop in astonishment. Mostly papers, yes, but these were special indeed, mementos of her high school and college days, treasures from someone who loved her. He looked through them, careful not to damage anything, as thoughts of Shōko percolated into the room until he was steeped in them.

An hour later he was still sitting, staring at the box, but finally he opened the one underneath. It held more of the same papers, but also photos, even older. Underneath were pencils, charcoal and pastel sticks, and other old art supplies, including sketchbooks, though only the top two had any drawings.

He lay down next to the boxes, took a pencil in his mouth, and bit softly at the blunt end as he stared up through the window at the hazy morning sky. If only he could do something for her, a gesture as generous and tender as she deserved. He had an idea, although he was not sure he could do it well enough anymore.

He watched a great, cottony cloud blow slowly past.

Why had there been no imaginary conversation as he looked at the boxes? Now, as he considered what to do for her, still she was silent in his mind.

Is she hoping I'll do it?

He bit down harder on the pencil.

Or is my imagined Shōko quiet as I inch closer to the real her?

The thought sent a warm tingling up his back and neck.

He turned the pencil and bit down again.

It would please her.

10

AS SHŌKO WAS WALKING HOME ON THE LEVEE PATH, A YOUNG couple approached from the other direction, holding hands. Shōko looked away.

Such a public display, imposing their private feelings on everyone: it's untoward. No one would ever see someone my age holding—

No, no one would see Shōko holding anyone's hand, ever.

She slowed down as her mind searched back. She and her girlfriends often held hands when she was growing up, but a hand held in romance . . . one boy, when she was twenty-two.

Shōko turned and watched the couple walking away. She looked at the low sun dazzling white and gold in the river and thought of her patient's tenacity, holding on to sanity, on to her.

Shōko's arms swung with more energy as she started walking again.

After her shock the previous afternoon, Shōko tried to temper her anticipation as she climbed the stairs and opened her bedroom door. She stepped back in dismay, though, at the sight of the boxes on the floor. They were out next to the bed, unstacked, so he must have opened them. She knelt and looked under the bed. There he was, gazing back at her. She stared at him for a long time before she said, "Hello," though the boxes begged for more.

Shōko could conjure nothing more to say. She could not just stand there, though, so she stepped over to her dresser and began changing her clothes. It took her ten minutes to choose a loose summer blouse and a pair of shorts, and all the while the boxes tugged at her. In the end, though, there was not a thing to do, so she stacked the boxes on the table.

She stared at the bed's shadow.

Something must need attention downstairs.

AFTER COOKING, Shōko spent the evening searching for things that needed cleaning. In the brief time she spent in her room, he never emerged from his hiding place. She talked to him, always in her happiest voice, but with no response. Finally, soaking in her evening bath, exhausted, she decided that she had to say something. So when she went back upstairs, after checking a few words in her dictionary, she stood facing the bed and tried to approach it directly, as an American would:

"I see you explored today. You found some boxes, I think." She paused. "You know those are special. I could never throw away."

She waited, her hands, clasped together, pressed to her lips. "I hope you are not upset when you see them. I cherish them. They are my most special things."

There was still no response. She took a timid step toward the bed. "I hope you will come out."

Again, she waited. In a soft, pleading voice she said, "Please, come out. Please."

She studied the darkness under the bed, helplessly hoping her words would suffice, her arms now crossed over her chest, her fingers digging into her shoulders. There were more words, years of them, but tied to memories so pure, so intense, that even their edges were painful. So she waited, fearing that those boxes had crushed his nascent recovery, wondering how she could have let this happen, and sensing with awful foreboding that tragedy was at hand for them both.

She heard the softest of sounds. In the shadow under the bed she glimpsed . . . paper?

She bent down. It almost looked like one of her old sketchbooks.

As she watched, though, he pushed it out a little farther, then into plain view—and her shock was so complete that she was unable to move, unable to speak. There in realistic detail, perfectly shaded, composed with delicate balance that infused it with a soft energy, was a rendering in pencil of her room as it would appear from under the bed, light streaming onto the floor, illuminating feet crossed at the ankles, sitting at the table.

How did he . . . ?

She didn't even pick it up. She just stood and stared—and cried. It never occurred to her to try to stop, silent tears of joy and longing and regret and hope all welling up in her eyes at once and spilling out onto her cheeks.

As through a stream she saw his hand emerge, still holding the pencil, chewed on the end as his always were. He pulled himself out from under the bed, picked up the sketchbook, and placed it on top of the boxes on her table, boxes that held art supplies and her only mementos of him.

"Shōko, don't cry. Please don't cry." And taking her gently by the shoulders, he pulled her close and kissed her eyes.

"Oh, David, it is like so long ago. . . . "

II

Stripes

縞、あるいは鞭打ち

11

On this quiet, leisurely Saturday morning, Shōko watched over the top of her book as David sharpened the pencil with a small knife, every motion deft and smooth. In the last half hour, she had turned all of three pages. The pencil's scratching made reading impossible: not the noise, but the pleasure of David drawing. She sat half reclining at the head of the bed, a book poised as if reading, pretending to be unaware he was sketching her. He sat at the foot of the bed, ostensibly drawing the view out the window over the bed. She blushed when she first realized what he was doing, but he was out of his musty den, engaged, acting like a normal person, and for that, she could bear the self-consciousness.

Shōko observed with growing fascination, first through furtive glances and then with some difficulty by keeping her eyes trained on the top of a page and concentrating on him in her peripheral vision. Now and again he would pause to assess the drawing, running his hand through his short, thinning hair. His concentration showed in the intensity of his eyes, his strong jaw set hard beneath a close-trimmed, graying beard, even in the tautness of his skin that made him look younger than his fifty-two years. When drawing, though, his hand was in constant motion; and not only his hand or even his arm, but often his whole body, slim and tall, as if in a subtle dance. There was no discernible rhythm, but still it was beautiful. She had never seen anyone so consumed by drawing—and drawing *her*. So she swathed herself in it, a warm, plush robe, so soft that it was no wonder she drifted. . . .

"Hey, you probably need to wake up," came a voice, deep, almost whispered, and oddly outside herself.

"I was dreaming?"

"A pleasant one, I hope."

Eyes closed again, she held a pillow to her chest. "I saw a dream that Yuki came back, but big, shiny like silk, and all black, with gold spots in the light. Then I saw it is not Yuki, it is male, and I said, 'David?' and a leopard sat up and looked at me."

"Did I eat you?"

"No," she answered into the pillow.

"Did I at least bite you or chase you around?"

"No." She opened her eyes. "You were nice leopard, but scary. You rub your back on me and knock me down."

"Sorry."

"So I found a scarf to dress you up like I dressed Yuki to play sometimes when I was little, pretty red scarf. My hands were shaking so much when I tie it on your neck. But then you looked bright and happy, like Christmas."

David laughed and Shōko hugged her pillow tighter as she smiled softly. She didn't tell him that by the time he woke her, she was a cat too, small and snow-white. She had crawled into the scarf to rest, snuggled to his neck as if bound to him by the supple red swath.

David stepped to the door and asked, "Is it safe?"

"Yes. My parents are out, but back maybe in one hour."

It took her a minute, but Shōko sat up and checked the clock: 9:12. She needed to get busy. Before gathering up the laundry, though, she looked at the drawing. It was her from the waist up, more detailed than she had imagined, especially her face and her hands, which were amazingly life-like. Shōko had always found hands the most difficult to draw: astoundingly complicated, yet so familiar that the slightest misrepresentation left them looking painfully deformed. Even Rembrandt had little use for them. As much as David's talent awed her, though, it was his vision that held her eyes fast. Was that how he saw her or was it the pencil in his hand, some technical artifact, that made her look softer and younger? It was remarkable how spirited she appeared, even sitting with a book. She was almost more alive on the paper than she felt in real life, as if he drew the Shōko he used to know, the one he'd drawn in college.

At the sound of David's foot at the top of the stairs, she dropped the sketchbook and faced the door. As he entered the room, she announced with mock authority, "It is laundry time. Wear *yukata* again," and she picked up her old summer-weight cotton *kimono* and held it out to him.

David made an uncomfortable face. "Yours again?"

"I can't find guest *yukata* still. Maybe *Otōsan,* my father, uses it. And this is good and lovely *yukata.* So pretty light pink with tiny purple *hamanashi* flowers pattern."

"Uh-huh."

"You are lucky I share such beautiful *yukata!*" Remembering the leopard, though, she did not push her playful authority too far as she held the *yukata* out again. "Please change now." And Shōko turned her back as David obediently undressed.

When she heard the phone ring downstairs, though, Shōko's eyes shot to the door.

David covered up. "Do you need to get that?"

Shōko stood still, staring at the door. "No, calls to home phone are not for me."

As Shōko hung the whites on the clothesline in the backyard, she kept David's shirt and underwear inconspicuous in case her mother looked outside. She hated sneaking—it made her feel like a naughty child—but looking up at her window and seeing him sitting there drawing, she smiled at her accomplishment. As much as it moved her to have him this close, though, he had to go back to his own apartment. Now that she had him back on his feet, it was time to take a step. Staying here too long would only make things more difficult for him. And if her parents found him, her impropriety would appall them. But as her thoughts nibbled at the question of why she let him stay so long already, she emphatically snapped the last clothespin onto the line and went to busy herself elsewhere.

No matter the task, though, throughout the morning, thoughts of David surrounded her like soap bubbles. She popped each delicate sphere before it got close enough to reflect a woman teetering on the brink of love. She did it most often by questioning where to go from here, and she decided that today would be a good day for David to go home. She didn't have to go to work, so she could go with him to his apartment, get him settled, perhaps shop with him and cook something. Then they could spend all of Sunday together. She could even bring him to the house and introduce him to her parents; no more sneaking. Then on Monday, hopefully, he could go back to work.

Shōko knocked once to keep David from panicking, then slid the door open to find him lying on the bed. "You take a nap?"

"Just a rest. I'm not used to drawing. My hand gets tired."

"*Ā, sō ne.*"

She smiled as he sat up. It was such a change, even since yesterday, and looking at him it was easy to see the boy she—

Shōko turned and busied herself putting her clothes away. "I was thinking...."

"Mm-hmm."

"Maybe we go out today."

"Out?"

"Yes, you are here in my room many days, so bored, maybe. We can take a walk, go to your apartment, and—"

Glancing back over her shoulder, she saw she had erased his smile with a single swipe. There was darkness in his eyes, now half-shut, and he was bending over, arms pulled close, like a sea anemone abandoned by the tide. She sprang to the bed and sat tight against him, pushing her shoulder up into him and hugging his arm, forcing it away from his chest. She spoke in a soft voice, "But we don't have to. I think maybe you don't want to go. *Sō?*"

David straightened up and nodded.

She gave a reassuring smile. "Okay. You may stay longer."

Soon she felt him relax. "You feel better?"

"Yes, sorry."

"No 'sorry.' All is good. Leaving . . . you are not ready. We try maybe in . . . two days?"

He nodded slightly, and she held his arm tighter and leaned her head on his shoulder. After a minute, he said, "I just . . . I don't know how to explain it."

"It is okay. I know," she whispered. She wasn't brave enough to go back yet either.

12

HE WAS GLAD SHŌKO DIDN'T WASH HIS CLOTHES EVERY DAY; HE FELT silly wearing nothing but her flower-print *yukata*. She went out to do the day's shopping while his clothes were still on the line, though. So he sat by the window again and lost himself in shading his drawing from that morning, adding depth and luster until the page appeared as if projected from his mind. Whether it was the page or his mind that more came to resemble the other as he worked was of little consequence. This world, this one sheet of paper, he could transform into whatever he wanted, and if his desire evolved, all the more creative the experience.

It was a powerful feeling, small as it was, after the weeks of impotence, failure, and abandonment that had driven him to the levee. Looking back on it now, it was obvious he should never have left Micron. He had serious misgivings even when he made the choice. It was his wife's influence, of course. So many of the decisions in his life were mostly hers. And this one was easy for her: going on fifty-two years old, this was his last chance for a big step in his career. Plus, she hated Boise: too cold, too boring, too far from family and her consulting clients. With their two children grown, there was no reason to stay in Idaho any longer. She loved the West Coast and was excited about Portland, so he took the job at Star Micro.

A few weeks in, though, David got a new assignment with a new boss, Paul Salazar. Paul described the job in glowing terms, superlatives gushing out in such a stream that David knew when the other shoe dropped, it would crash through the floor. Finally, Paul got to the location. "So, the part turning me green wishing I was in your shoes is where you're headed. You'll lead our only foreign joint venture. David, you're going to Japan."

David asked, "Where in Japan?"

"What difference does that make?" asked Paul, sounding peeved. Then he said, with what looked like a forced smile, "Up north someplace. Fujitsu chip fabrication plant, marvelously quaint town, you'll *love* it. Let me see. . . ." And after a few seconds, Paul named the one city in northern Japan that meant anything, Shōko's hometown.

Paul talked about how the previous manager looked left as he was about to step into the street, as one would in America, and strode right out in front of a car. Paul laughed as he explained that "it was one of those little toy cars you can barely fit one person into, you know, like they all drive over there. You should've seen the car; it was totaled." Paul's laughter at something so appalling put David off, but he was too distracted to say anything. As Paul droned on, David did not raise a single real objection. He let Paul lead him to the slaughterhouse without even tugging on the rope, almost as if he was drugged.

In the talks that followed, David learned that the project in Japan was Star Micro's first attempt at anything but custom logic, etching circuits into a chip to create electronic "machines." The new chip was too complex for that, so they turned to David's specialty, embedded systems. Instead of hardwiring everything, software would handle parts of the system. It would run on a special processor etched into the chip. But while the embedded system worked in simulation, the actual chips were failing. Paul told him little more, though, and David suspected that Paul did not understand the problems himself. David didn't find out until he got to Japan that the last manager's accident broke both his legs, both his arms, and his jaw. It was two more weeks before David took it as an omen.

David spent the first week in Japan meeting people, having them explain their responsibilities, the project's troubles, and their ideas for solutions. Language problems came up first, complaints that everything took twice as long as it should, but they could do little about that. Luckily, the senior manager from the Star Micro side, Leon, spoke Japanese well enough, and the two top Fujitsu managers, Itō and Takahara, had each lived in America for a few years and had good English.

The language problems were minor, however, compared to the chip design. With no experience in embedded systems, Star Micro had to buy the design for the embedded processor, a "map" of its circuits, its "intellectual property." Everyone in Japan agreed the IP they got was inferior, but worse yet, it was three generations out of date. Circuits now were smaller, more tightly packed, than the map was made to handle.

One day after he'd been there a couple of weeks, having spent the earliest morning hours emotionally preparing himself to play the leader in front of his top lieutenants, David gathered Leon, Itō, and Takahara to confer with Paul over a speakerphone.

"You've got Paul!" blared his voice from the speaker as if they had won the lottery.

"Hi, Paul."

"Oh, David. Hey, I don't have a lot of time. I need to get to my son's soccer game."

"Yeah, I remember those days. They sure go by fast."

"Yes, David, I know you're older than me. Why did you call?"

David forced a smile to make his voice sound more positive: "First, thanks for sitting down with us to talk about the problems here."

"Us?"

"Oh, sorry. I've got Leon here."

"Hi, Paul."

No response.

"And Itō-*san* and Takahara-*san*."

"Hello, Paul-*san*."

Silence.

"Paul?"

"David, I don't do conference calls without prior notification."

"You didn't know I was calling?"

Paul didn't respond at once, but finally said, "Anyway, give it to me quick. How are things coming?"

"Well, there are integration issues, but we've traced most of the problems back to the IP for the embedded processor. Paul, the IP is junk."

Leon looked at David with dismay, mouthed, "No!" and hastily scribbled, "Paul chose the IP!"

David bowed his head and rubbed his temples, waiting for Paul to say something rather than trying to wriggle out of the embarrassment like a sycophant.

Paul said, "I'm sure we agree our first focus should be the production process, since the chip works fine in simulation."

David looked at the others and exhaled slowly. "It's odd it doesn't work like the simulation. Makes me think it's time to back up and take another look at how the simulation was—"

"Just another sign of process problems."

Itō was at the edge of his seat by now, scowling at the aspersions on Fujitsu's production skills. He enunciated into the speakerphone, "Failures are systemic, not random. That means design flaw."

Paul was silent but finally said, "We need to talk, David, just you and me."

David sat back with a frown. Leon looked sympathetic, but Itō shook his head as he closed the door.

"Okay, go ahead," said David.

"I expect results and I expect compliance! If I say it's—"

"Every process check is normal, Paul, every single one! It's not a bunch of interns here calling at the first sign of trouble. It's a design flaw, it's in the IP, and it's not going to magically right itself. With this IP, the chip's not coming in on time, if ever."

"Unacceptable!"

"I agree. I'll find IP that gives the smoothest transition, but—"

"No."

"No?"

"Right."

David was lost. "What?"

"No, the problem is not the IP. It's in the production process."

"So you've said, and we're testing that too, but—"

"Good."

"*But* we have capable people here who say the IP's unworkable and I won't ignore them."

Paul was quiet before he said, "You want to muck around in the IP? Fine. You're supposably the expert, right? But I stuck my neck out on a limb for you, so be warned: I'll have no choice but to hold you responsible for any delays."

"Which means . . . ?"

"Just what it sounds like." Paul hung up.

David stared at the phone. *What in the world . . . ?*

The others echoed his sentiment as he related the outcome of the call. "I don't get it," said Leon. "Having chosen the IP, he should be supersensitive to problems, because they reflect on him."

David sighed.

Leon drummed his pen on the table. "There's plenty of IP out there tested and proven, just drop it into place, but he had to go for something synthesized and hopelessly obsolete."

David said, "Proven IP is big money. Synthesized is cheap, obsolete's even cheaper, and his aim is to make this the most profitable chip Star Micro has ever produced."

"*If* it's ever produced. Why assume shrinking the circuits so extremely would work?"

"I don't know, Leon; I'm not an idiot."

They all chuckled.

"You know," said Leon, "Paul wasn't this bad on the last project. But he had a lot closer supervision then."

"You think he's just run amok on this?" asked David.

"He wouldn't be the first. And he does love taking risks. It's actually one of his strengths, when the risks aren't crazy. But he's young—younger than me, even. He's never had this much responsibility before. I'm afraid he's floundering," said Leon.

David stood, but having just been cut off at the knees by Paul, he felt like he was floundering too. Still, despite doubting his own leadership, he tried to project confidence. "Okay, Paul wants more tests for problems in the production process. Takahara-*san*, every test you can think of."

Takahara nodded.

"He swears it's not the IP, but we'll recheck everything."

Nods all around.

"And Leon, I want you to find out everything there is to know about the simulation that went into this design."

13

SHŌKO'S SHOPPING BAGS WERE NOT HEAVY, BUT SHE DRIPPED IN THE heat as she plodded home along the levee path. Squinting in the afternoon sunshine, she lifted her gaze to the river. It was her favorite place, the one thing that always seemed fresh and vital in a town where nothing changed. Today, though, its meandering flow led her to reflect on life and how few mistakes it takes to hollow it out like a blown egg, leaving a person so fragile that an errant touch could cave her in completely. Thinking back to the move home after her first marriage, Shōko turned and walked backward for a few steps. The prominent buildings in the center of town were new since then. The years since the economic bubble burst in the early 1990s, though, had produced little besides the big Fujitsu factory on the outskirts of town. The weather was certainly different that December evening in 1982, twenty-seven years ago. The river was frozen over in the third day of a weeklong ice storm that still served as the local benchmark for winter pain. She had always thought it apropos to the end of a marriage, if she could even have called it that.

It was a month later that Shōko stared at the icy water until her feet were numb and, in the end, decided to go on living. She stayed cold for years, though, turning down dates or even talks over coffee. Yet, somehow, she was foolish enough to end up in a second failed marriage, and last December she carried her luggage out of the station into the bite of another winter evening. She saw her breath illuminated by the familiar downtown lights as she dragged her nearly fifty-two years like so many sandbags behind her and wished she were lying under a train's wheels instead. The plan was to stay for a few weeks before finding a hiding place in Tokyo, but her parents needed someone, and being "single," she did her duty and stayed.

Duty...

Shōko stopped and watched a cormorant swimming low in the lazy flow of the river's deepest channel. It dove suddenly but reappeared a second later with nothing to show for its effort.

If I were a river, would I naturally flow into the sea, or would I do it out of duty?

Or would she rebel and flow *up* the valley? From all corners of the world people would flock to see the amazing Shōko River rush up over mountains, dance in the sky, and burst into colors. Or would rebellion bring only floods and misery to anyone luckless enough to live along her banks?

14

CONSUMED BY DRAWING AGAIN, DAVID WAS FINE AFTER SHŌKO LEFT, but eventually, too tired to maintain the control he demanded, he lay down to rest. It started innocently enough, considering his next drawing and whether to ask Shōko to pose, which took him to thoughts of her kindness, all sanguine until the idea flipped on its head: *What if I lose Shōko too?*

He shook off the thought.

But if I did...?

David tried again to shake it off, but the hook was set. So, too agitated to lie still and too tired to draw, David paced, his steps smooth and silent, and before long, the loosely tied sash fell and the *yukata* streamed out behind him like a cape.

He could not lose Shōko. She was all that held back the darkness.

In one of his turns, though, he glimpsed the river out the window—

He turned away, to his sketch of Shōko, but his mind leapt to his wife. He had sacrificed his deepest desires for her. He had yielded as she pushed, cajoled, and loved him into the man he was today—and the mess he was in—*and this crippling depression. She left me*! Standing still now, he thought again of his last day with her, and her words, chillingly final. How long had she planned the divorce in secret before she left?

Her lawyer called while she was still on the plane.

David stared at his hands clamped on the edges of the table, as the world blurred, then disappeared, his focus drawing down ever tighter onto himself. Bent over the table, he was spiraling toward another day of agony under the bed. His anger was already turning to self-pity, which would soon become self-loathing, darkening through shades to black, his mind growing sluggish as it caramelized over the heat and slowly charred. It all followed step-by-step, a recipe for self-destruction, unless someone took it off the stove—

"*Tadaima!*"

By the time Shōko entered the room, David was already returning to himself, somber as he still was. It was hard to stay indignant as he raced to tie her pink *yukata* closed. And the sash was too long! He finally wrapped it around himself twice and sat on the bed. He was fingering a loose red thread on the *yukata*'s sleeve when she walked in and chirped, "Hello, my friend."

David showed her a smile and affected a happy tone: "Hi. Did you have a good shopping trip?"

"Oh yes. You will be so happy of my shopping," she said and dumped the contents of a large bag onto the bed next to him. "Clothes for you! Now you will not be pretty girl in pink *yukata*." She picked up something light blue. "Now you have pajamas. Not pink, sorry." She chuckled. "And T-shirts, shorts, socks, towel handkerchief for hot summer days now, and . . . *ētto* . . . *otoko no pantsu-tte* . . . underpants?" and her face showed a slight blush.

"Shōko, you shouldn't be buying me things."

"Why not? You buy things for me."

"Not recently."

Shōko shrugged.

"Anyway, thank you. I appreciate it." There was a smaller bag too, and he picked it up. "What's this?"

"Oh, things for washing."

He looked through it. "No comb?"

"You need comb? But hair is so short and on top not so much—" She saw his exaggerated look of pain. "You tease me again! Be nice or I make you wear *yukata* more."

Shōko turned around while David slipped off the *yukata* and began tearing cellophane and removing tags.

"It took longer than you thought," he said.

"Yes, shopping took much time, and I walk slow to home."

"Everything okay?"

She hesitated, and she sounded different when she answered. He realized that her voice today had been younger, almost girlish, but he heard her adult voice now: "I remember things."

"Sad things?"

She was briefly silent before she said, "Yes, sad."

It was obviously an unpleasant memory. Should he drop it? Still, she brought it up, and it might help if she opened up to someone. "You know, you can talk to me about anything. Even sad things."

For a long time, Shōko was quiet. At length, still looking away, she said, "I was thinking about my first marriage."

"Oh." He paused, then said, his smile gone, "I'm sorry. I suppose some hurts never completely heal."

"No, it was long ago. You know I married first time at twenty-five, but only a few months."

"What happened?"

She shrugged. "His mother thought I will be a good wife, but she did not know her son."

"So, it was an arranged marriage?"

"Yes. My mother was afraid I will be Christmas cake."

It sounded as if she was smiling, but he wasn't sure. "I don't understand."

"On December twenty-six, no one wants to buy, right? She thinks I should marry while I am twenty-five."

David pursed his lips and nodded his head.

Shōko's voice was serious, though, as she went on: "His mother was from countryside. His older brother married so fashionable girl and she spends too much money. So his mother does not want to let the younger brother choose. She thought a girl from countryside will be a best wife."

"This city's not big, but I'd hardly call this countryside."

"Everyplace outside Tokyo is countryside," she said, and again he heard the smile. The next words were so quiet, though, that David barely heard them: "But he wanted someone else."

David waited.

"He loved a girl at his company, but his parents did not like her. So he married me, but keeps her still. From the beginning, even before, he has mistress."

"Shōko . . ."

"No one should be mistress or have mistress. Husband should be . . . *seijitsu-tte* . . . true?"

David answered softly, "Wives too."

Shōko nodded.

They were silent as David slipped on one of the T-shirts.

"I'm dressed. You may turn around now."

Shōko turned to face him, he worked his mouth into a sympathetic smile, and she smiled in return. Then she spun him around. "It fits! You are tall so I choose extra-large shirt, but you are not so big and I worry extra is too large, but it is perfect."

"Yes, everything fits well. I should pay for all this. I have cash in—"

"No, they are just Uniqlo things, not so expensive."

"More than I deserve."

As Shōko picked up wrappers, David looked around the room awkwardly and finally asked, "May I ask what happened in your second marriage?"

It was an ill-considered attempt to pull her closer, but he cringed even as the last words slipped out. Shōko's smile vanished and her chin crinkled up, as when she was deep in thought or worried. She hesitated, then seemed about to speak and stopped again. Finally, she said, "Already it is time to make dinner. My parents will be hungry." And with a strained smile, she left.

15

SHŌKO POURED ALL HER CONCENTRATION INTO THE *SEN-GIRI* ("thousand-cut") cabbage. If she counted, slicing thin, how enormous a pile would she make with a thousand actual cuts?

From the start, my voice, my demeanor, could not have been clearer: I don't want to talk about it. But he asks anyway. So I think, Maybe I should tell him. His loss is so fresh; it might help if he understands some of mine. Then just when I think it might've helped, he asks for more! How can he be so—

Shōko stopped cutting. It was not rude or unfeeling by David's way of thinking, whatever that was. In fact, his tone was quite caring, as if he was trying to be solicitous of her feelings with his intrusive questions. It was . . . alien!

She closed her eyes and took a deep breath before she went back to cutting.

Overreacting to cultural differences is childish. Besides, he's too pitiful to be angry with.

Frustrated, maybe.

Even annoyed.

Still, it was nothing compared to what her husbands did. Shōko's chopping echoed out into the hall as she thought of a day, a month into her first marriage. She was chopping *sen-giri* cabbage in the shiny, modern kitchen of the unconscionably expensive condominium that her husband's parents bought them in a central Tokyo high-rise. It was for a meal she ate alone after his phone call. Work would keep him late and he planned to stay at a hotel near the office. That was the first night, the first of dozens of nights, that Shōko spent alone before she got an appalling, sickening phone call. Her husband had a lover, and it was the lover's husband sharing the news that Shōko's husband was cheating on her. The marriage had lasted six months.

After all the nights alone, though, at age fifty, a year and a half ago, she married again. Her second marriage lasted twice as long as her first, just under a year. Now she scowled. *Better to eat alone than to listen to Masaru play the food critic.* Taking the knife in her fist and using both hands, she stabbed it through the head of cabbage and into the cutting board so deep that it stuck fast. *Better to starve than to endure that for another day!*

There were ample hints before Shōko married him that her second husband was not what she thought, if only she had paid attention. She would always feel a burning shame that the marriage, with all its degradation and misery, was a needless mistake. What was so tragic in turning fifty that could have led her to obsess so on the prospect of growing old alone? Her savings were steadily growing. She had friends. A man in the house was as likely to become a burden as a help.

Masaru did not offer the financial security her first husband had. In fact, his immediate resources were meager. But he was an only child and his family was well enough off. And his expressions of love, while appropriately discreet, were determined and seemed altogether sincere. She soon discovered that they both loved to read, and their talks opened books to her as if for the first time. More than anything, though, it might have been his laugh—he loved to laugh—and a laugh in the house is never a burden.

Eyes closed and head hanging, Shōko leaned on the counter for a while before she worked the knife point out of the cutting board.

How could a laugh so effusive roll out of him, altogether natural, as if from the bouncing of his heart? How could any joy at all escape from a man so consumed with himself?

Although Shōko still marveled at her cluelessness during their short engagement, one thing about Masaru that she could not have foreseen was his reaction to her cooking; she never cooked for him before they were married, and he never acted like that in a restaurant or his mother's home. The first time was the day they returned early from their honeymoon trip (for work, he said, although later she realized he simply didn't want to pay for the final two days). They got back late in the afternoon and were both tired, but this was the first meal she would prepare for him and she wanted it to be special. Everyone raved about her *tempura*, so she went to the supermarket and got prawns, fillet of *kisu*, vegetables—carrots, bell peppers, lotus root, *shītake* mushrooms, *kabocha* pumpkin—and fresh cooking oil, eggs, and rice. With the table set and the ingredients all cut and laid out, she put the oil on to heat and started on the batter. She whipped an egg, added water chilled almost to freezing, and stirred in flour light and quick so the batter wouldn't get sticky. The oil reached 180°C as she finished the batter and she started frying immediately, never letting the temperature vary more than a few degrees. When the *kabocha* was almost finished, she put everything else on the table and called, "Dinner is ready!"

This was the first time she noticed it, but she soon found she could hear his footsteps from anywhere in the house. She wondered how years of such a tromping gait had not left his joints in ruin. Masaru entered the dining room. Without a greeting or comment of any kind about the meal, he dropped his heavy frame unsteadily into his chair, and Shōko realized with surprise that he had been drinking. Without waiting for Shoko to sit, barely even mumbling the obligatory *"Itadakimasu,"* Masaru picked up his prawn, and just before dipping it, groused, "I don't like grated radish," and purposely knocked over his dipping bowl.

Shōko was appalled. She grabbed a towel and ran from the kitchen to clean it up, then refilled his bowl, this time with only *tentsuyu* sauce, and rushed back to pluck the *kabocha* from the pan; at which point, having yet to glance in her direction, Masaru said, "And the grated radish?"

She kept her eyes on the pan lest he see her ire and said politely, "But you said you don't like it."

"Don't like *that much*, but it needs *some*. Get it over here!"

From the kitchen, she scowled at him. "What's wrong with you? Are you drunk?"

But when he turned to her, eyes bulging, she shrank back.

"*Never* speak to me that way again!"

Too stunned to speak, she did as he asked, then hurried to serve the *kabocha*, and sat—only to stare in disbelief. Masaru was eating like a hyena in a feeding frenzy. *Tempura* is a delicate dish, to be savored, but he barely had time to chew. Food spilled out of his mouth and he shoved it back in as if he was packing sausages!

By the time Shōko overcame her astonishment and poured beer into his glass, his food was almost gone. She was still pouring when he tossed his chopsticks onto his plate, empty except for the carrot and bell pepper, which sat untouched. He waited impatiently, then grabbed the glass out of her hand and guzzled most of it. Shōko looked away and tried to focus on her food. She picked up her *kisu* and raised it to her mouth—

"You will not eat while I am speaking to you."

Shōko looked up, unable to believe he had said it, but offered no provocation. If he had something to say about dinner, she could take the time to listen—besides, if she spoke, she might lash out at him—so she lowered her chopsticks and waited.

"What kind of rice was that?"

"*Akita Komachi*, as I always—"

"You will use *Koshihikari. Uonuma-san Koshihikari.* Can't you taste the difference? Even if you can't, you should've known by the price that it's the best."

"I like the taste of *Akita Ko*—"

He banged his fist on the table so hard that the dishes jumped. "You're questioning me? You? How dare you question me? I am a university professor!"

Shocked, but too defiant to let it pass, Shōko said, "Yes, but you are a professor of literature."

She could see the veins in his forehead as he yelled back at her, "I am an expert—an expert!—on the influence of Victorian literature on Meiji literature. Two areas of literature! You don't even understand how remarkable that makes me!"

So, if turn-of-the-last-century literature is so important and you're so remarkable, why aren't you at one of the big national universities?

But Shōko, though fuming, was too proper to say it.

"How could I have married someone so uneducated? My wife is an idiot!"

Then to prove she was an idiot, he grilled her knowledge of rice varieties. While neither was an expert, Shōko knew more than Masaru and could have proved it, but to what end? She wanted it over. So she looked for an opening and, trying to reach a positive note, brought up the part of the meal he seemed to have liked: "I hope you enjoyed the *tempura.*"

He sneered, "I could barely eat it. The vegetables you chose were disgusting."

She blinked. "I'm sorry. What do you like?"

"Use sweet potato, not bell pepper. I hate bell pepper. And why so many vegetables at all?"

His attitude was vile, but his preference would be easy to accommodate. "Next time I can use sweet potato . . . and perhaps more shellfish, if you would like that. And I don't have to cook bell peppers"—she looked at his plate—"or carrots for you. I can just cook those for myself—"

"No!" He slammed the table again, this time the shock knocking over his empty glass. "There will never be a bell pepper in this house again. And carrots only grated in salad." And in a low, ominous tone, he said, "When I tell you what I want, that's the way you make it, for me and for yourself. You are my wife, and my likes and dislikes are now your likes and dislikes. Am I understood?"

Shōko's cheeks were as flushed as if he'd physically slapped her. She stared at him, reviewing the day for a slight that could warrant this rebuke. But her reflection was ill timed. Every muscle in his face seemed to tense up, his eyes narrowing into menacing slits. He rose out of his chair, leaned over the table, and hissed at her through clenched teeth, as if fighting to control his rage: "You will apologize, *now*, and you will *never* commit such an offense again. *Am I understood?*"

Shōko could see the tension now in his whole body. She bowed respectfully and said, "I am very sorry the *tempura* was not to your liking."

"'Not to your liking, *Danna-sama.*'"

Danna-sama? He wanted her to call him "Master"? She cooed it at him as he wanted during sex on the honeymoon, but that wasn't just role-playing? He wanted—?

No!

Never!

So she sat, head bowed, while he castigated her, until his screaming was so high-pitched that he sounded like a little girl and seemed on the verge of leaping across the table and striking her. Curled down into her chair, protecting her face with her hands, she said, "I'm sorry," countless times, though never "*Danna-sama,*" so her apologies did nothing to stem his tirade. In his most commanding tone he declared that he deserved better, he expected better, and he would put up with nothing less.

Shōko was trembling by the time Masaru stood and threw away what he hadn't eaten. She told him not to bother, that she would take care of everything, but he didn't acknowledge her. She apologized again and promised to try her best to please him. But he made a great show of dumping the rice from the rice cooker into the trash. He followed that with the food in Shōko's dishes, except her prawn, which he ate as he stormed away. He had eaten for three minutes, spouted commands and criticism for twenty, and left her with nothing to eat, not even that first bite that never made it into her mouth.

It took Shōko days to calm down, but in the end, she thought it best to let it go. She rejected the popular idea that things said while drunk must be forgiven, but she could look past a single indiscretion, however atrocious. And her promise to do her best for him was not in vain. She was determined to do her duty and make her second marriage work, and she could easily adjust her cooking if that was all it took to create a comfortable life with Masaru.

Shōko watched the next day, but Masaru had only a single beer in the afternoon. She also let him rest, for he was surely tired the day before. He wanted expensive, so she went to a rice-specialty store and got the highest-priced *Uonuma-san Koshihikari* they had, then left the bag out in the kitchen until she was sure he had seen it. There was no mention of the rice that night, no demand to be called *"Danna-sama,"* no complaints at all. Except for eating like a pig, he was perfectly pleasant.

Two weeks later, though, he threw Shōko's food away again, and again a few days after that. It happened often enough that Shōko started keeping notes, searching for a trigger or pattern, but his rants were entirely random. Shōko took to eating while she was cooking, but the frequency of his tirades increased and she stopped even that, her appetite gone, as every meal became a minefield.

As the weeks passed, Masaru's robust laugh was replaced ever more by shouting, or on good days, disdainful sneers. His criticism quickly spread beyond food, and Shōko came to realize that there would never be any recognition of an attractive outfit or a joke told well or a thoughtful gift. Masaru criticized. It was his calling in life.

At least he didn't often demand sex, and after a couple of months, except for the rarest of occasions, it stopped altogether. She had learned from her first marriage the pathology of a cheating husband, and Masaru showed no signs, but his apathy was odd. During the first weeks of their marriage he bragged of his prowess and past conquests (and Shōko had herself tested for venereal diseases), but Shōko found little joy in him. He belittled her for it and claimed that she was physically inadequate—and after her first husband's scorn ("You lie there, sexless, like a frozen tuna!"), she worried it might be true. But no sexual pleasure would have been worth the price of being that close to him. (She solved the mystery of his libido weeks later when she heard odd noises on the computer late at night and walked in on him pleasuring himself to a pornographic video.)

As Shōko's hopes deflated, she channeled her pluckiness into a stout-hearted determination not to become a two-time loser. Struggling to keep the marriage afloat, she adjusted, acquiesced, and one by one jettisoned her pleasures, interests, preferences, and opinions. Still, their last few months together counted only a handful of days that Masaru failed to insult or ridicule her in some way. She laughed some of it off and ignored more of it, telling herself it amounted to nothing, but only the toughest shell could have deflected it all. As her dreams sank, her pluck was swamped along with them. Facing no resistance, Masaru pressed all the harder. He criticized *everything* and with relentless brutality. Despite persistent threats, the abuse never turned physical, but bruises on the soul are just as real, and bruise after bruise after bruise eventually leaves a scar. With those scars Masaru crippled her. She was smaller, thinner, more of a shadow sometimes than a person. One could almost have seen her growing more transparent month by month.

She couldn't slip off the smile that was her cloak and show David those scars, her private disgrace. How could she admit she lived with Masaru's abuse for almost a year, making it all possible? But marrying him in the first place, marrying so badly a second time—if only she could cut the shame of it into a thousand little slices.

16

TEN DAYS AFTER HIS FIRST PHONE CALL, DAVID SENT CONCLUSIVE evidence that the chip's design was flawed, not the production process, to both Paul and Paul's boss, but Paul was unmoved: "So there's problems. Work around them."

Nothing sapped David's self-confidence like conflicts, but he projected a brave front: "It would take forever, if it's even possible. We're already eighteen weeks behind."

"And how far behind when you arrived?"

"Probably fourteen."

"So in three weeks, you've accomplished less than nothing."

As a joke, Leon had glued a picture of Paul to an old foam mouse pad and handed it to David before the phone call. David stabbed it with a red pen now as he said, "A normal disruption for a leadership transition. The real issue is that we'll only drop further behind as long as we're saddled with this lame IP. It's a bad circuit design."

"We paid a reputable vendor a lot of money for it."

"For a processor IP, it was a pittance."

"I gave you a perfectly workable chip."

"It never even had a complete simulation done, one of all the circuits."

"Of course, it did!"

"Then why can't we find documentation of it?"

"We have customers waiting for this."

"In other words, you—" David stopped himself. "It was too big a rush to push the simulation that far."

"How dare you try to pass the buck up the line to me!"

David pounded his fist softly on the table. "I'm not putting names on anything. My only aim is to get a working chip."

"What about events during fabrication?"

"What, like a power outage?"

"Yeah, they could be hiding something like that."

Paul was grasping at straws, but still, David was glad Itō did not hear the accusation. "It's Japan, Paul; there are no outages. Besides, that's monitored."

"But who does the monitoring? Are our people involved?"

"It's a joint venture; they're all 'our people.' And this is senseless. Everything points to a design flaw. We can't trust the simulation, because a complete one was never done. It's the IP. It's broken. We need a new one."

"So you want to redo the simulation now."

"What? No. Not without new IP."

"Fine, redo it. Waste your time."

"You want us to re-simulate with the current IP?"

"Sounds like that's what you want, and there's customers waiting, so you better get it finished by yesterday. But anything you find, mark my words, is gonna be a lot to do about nothing, minor enough to fix with software workarounds."

It was like reasoning with an ass.

"How'd it go?" asked Leon.

"How do you think?"

"Still he refuse to believe bad IP, even after tests?" asked Itō.

"He can't refute the test results, so he's ignoring them."

"You can call other people?" asked Takahara.

David nodded as he tried to hide his anxiety. He had not been at the company long enough to know the various managers. If cold phone calls were required, though, he had no choice but to try to find the right people. "I'll call today, but Paul insists management in Portland is squarely behind him. He challenged me to redo the simulation, a complete one, and swears we can fix whatever we find with software workarounds. I agree what Paul's asking for is a waste of time and money. I'll find someone higher in Portland who can make this decision, but in the meantime, we get more evidence, do the simulation as fast as possible. We're still running tests anyway."

Leon looked resigned, Takahara dejected, and Itō irked. David could not handle Paul, and everyone was paying the price.

17

DAVID WAS SKETCHING HER AGAIN. WHY DID HE TRY TO HIDE IT? HE was terrible at concealing what he was doing, or even thinking. He was playing you-don't-know-I'm-sketching-you, though, so Shōko relaxed and played I-don't-know-I'm-being-sketched, unconcerned with who was winning. People on television were playing too, a word game, and being tossed in a pit of flour when they lost. Shōko couldn't help laughing along.

But then she remembered sitting in Masaru's living room on a Saturday night, laughing at this same show, when he walked in and turned off the television. He dropped heavily into his chair with a huge manuscript he'd been working on for years before they met. He looked at her solemnly.

"Are you all right?" she asked.

"This is the manuscript for my book, or books. It will have to be more than one volume, probably three."

"Three? Oh my. Yes, you've been working hard on it. Is something wrong?"

"It is finished."

"Finished? That's wonderful!"

He should have beamed, but his voice stayed somber: "It's ground-breaking work. It needs to be published immediately."

"Yes, of course."

"But the usual publishing houses are too slow."

"But they'll surely recognize its value."

"What do they know about literature? This is my big step. These ideas are so important, my academic standing will be incontrovertible. I'll be able to work at any university I choose."

"Oh, that would be wonderful."

"So you see the importance of publishing right away."

Shōko's smile evaporated as a queasy feeling spread up from her stomach. "Yes..."

"I'm happy you've pledged your support."

She dug her fingernails into the arms of the chair.

"We'll use our savings to cover the publishing costs."

Masaru had no savings, though his mother was well-heeled. Shōko stayed quiet waiting for details, but Masaru said nothing more. After a few seconds, she asked, "So, you will contact your mother . . . tomorrow?"

"Mother? You really are a sponge, aren't you? No, *our* savings."

"My retirement account?" Shōko asked, aghast.

"Oh, don't worry, we'll sell the books for much more and the money will be back in our account in only a few months."

"But it's awfully risky, don't you think? Especially at our age."

"Nonsense!"

And nonsense it was. She should have walked out, but her shame at the prospect of a second divorce held sway as he burned through her savings with his cockamamie books.

Hearing David's pencil scratching away, she looked over at him. At least David had an attractive facade. Was that any indication of what he was underneath, though?

Just then, David glanced up, their eyes met, and he looked like a child caught stealing candy. He quickly looked away to continue the ruse that he wasn't drawing her, even as he blushed full red.

18

IT WAS EARLY IN THE RAINY SEASON, THE MIDDLE OF MAY, EIGHT weeks ago, when David first walked the levee path. Fuji-Star was the perfect storm: alone, nothing to fill his time except his sinking project, and Paul refusing to back him, yet hanging the responsibility for the project around his neck like an anchor chain. Leon told David that he looked as if he could use more sleep. What he needed was emotional support, and his wife was not scheduled to arrive in Japan for another week, if she did not delay her trip yet again.

Morale at Fuji-Star was flagging. The computer simulation uncovered so many problems that the engineers looked like zombies, new setbacks sparking nothing more than stunned silence. Eventually, even the most optimistic agreed that the chip was too broken to fix. It needed a complete revision that would add three million dollars to the budget. Once again, it was up to David to get agreement from Portland. Though his previous calls to Paul's boss had been met coolly, David went over Paul's head once again. He took hours to prepare, and the call was painful from the first hello, but David explained the problems succinctly, illustrating each with its most shocking example. It took ten minutes, and through it all there wasn't a single word of response. In fact, there was silence after David finished.

"Are you there?" David asked.

"Uh-huh."

"A complete revision."

"We heard you."

David waited a few more seconds. "It has implications for our relationship with Fujitsu. Bill Dietrich put the joint venture together, right?"

"Yes, and we talk to him. Everyone in Portland is well aware of the state of the project."

"We have a talented team here. They've really pulled together. With new processor IP we can start immediately."

It was Paul's icy voice that came back: "David, I told you from the start there wouldn't be new IP."

"Hi, Paul. I'm not sure when you came in, but—"

"I heard enough. So you're telling us it's impossible?"

"I'm telling you it's highly unlikely that a reliable solution even exists, and all the less likely that it can be programmed within any reasonably expanded project time frame."

"But you as much as said you don't know how to fix it. It's all hit-and-miss with you. You don't have the revision worked out."

"Of course we don't, Paul. That's a whole new chip!"

"So you're a 'no solution' guy demanding that we abandon my perfectly good design and an IP we've poured months of time and money into. Have you got some savior complex or something? Getting the project on track won't get you enough attention? You have to redo the whole thing from scratch?"

"Excuse me?"

Paul told David, "Look, Reese, we're late for a meeting."

Why did Paul switch to my last name? David asked, "Okay, so you talk to people there and get back about the new IP when?"

"What? Reese, don't you listen? The decision is made. You have an IP. Get it working."

"You're joking, right?" David was losing control.

"Another crack like that and I won't just yank you off the project, I'll fire your ass. And people have had enough of the bitchy emails, so don't start in on phone calls to the corner offices. We don't work that way at Star Micro. It's my chip and you go through me, period."

David searched for anything that would move them closer to a solution, but all he wanted to do was strangle Paul. After a few seconds of silence, Paul said, "Good, you're finally listening instead of talking. If your simulation found problems, they're yours to fix using software. That's my answer."

David paced while the others entered the conference room and sat. As he recounted the phone call, he could see their thoughts on their faces: second-guessing, reproof, and dismay. He was leading them nowhere, and they knew it. He needed to get away, if only for a few hours, but all he knew were his apartment, where he would stew alone, and this chip plant. To drive for as long as he needed would leave him irretrievably lost.

So David went for a walk. No destination in mind, he turned right at the front gate of the factory, toward the river. When he came to the levee, although it was grown over with a knee-deep mat of inkberry and kudzu, he climbed it. He found that there was a pedestrian/bike path on top, so he started walking aimlessly toward town. The river was swollen from the rain, the water roiling brown and angry, but compared to what he had left, it was sublime. He stopped and listened to a flock of *mejiro* in the branches above him discussing the day's events. Even as his anger receded, though, there was no hope in its place. Quitting was the only immediate escape, but if he resigned himself to failure, he had no idea how long it would dog him. Besides, he chafed at losing to Paul. He could endure a few more weeks if he could just come up with a makeshift direction that would keep the team motivated until people in Portland woke up and realized it was pointless. Then they could kill the project and he could go home, job intact, or they could give him new IP and he could start on a new chip. His ideas ranged from the unworkable to the absurd, though, so on he walked.

He was all the way into town when he saw a woman, just over medium height and quite trim, walking toward him, but he was too preoccupied to pay attention. He was puzzled as she slowed and stared at him, but he smiled politely and bowed his head, not focusing on her face. A couple of steps past her, though, he heard the voice that changed everything: "David?"

19

IT WAS SATURDAY, DAVID'S SEVENTH NIGHT UNDER THE BED. HE LAY on his back on the *futon* that Shōko had slid under the bed for him that first night, listening to her breathing softly in the world above him. David envied her ordered life and her calm, restful soul, especially at night. He took comfort knowing she was there to talk to, even when they were silent, but if sleep found her first, loneliness wafted into his little space, and in its wake, a weighty darkness. The mistakes in his life were uncountable; and if sleep took too long, cowering there in shame before the man he should have become, the steamroller eventually caught him. Other times, lacking the will for the struggle, it was as if something had him by the neck, jamming him down deeper, push by push, through the shattered remains of his life. He let it push, despite the unbearable, slicing pain, and as the earth closed in around him, all light and hope were extinguished. Sleep, for the night or forever, was the only thing that could stop the torment.

Once he escaped into sleep, though, the morning would bring light. The desire for another day with Shōko would push into him like a corkscrew and draw him out from under the bed, leaving behind the blackness with an almost audible pop. Then he could lose himself in drawing again. As long as he was lost, he was fine: time would slow as he considered compositions, permutations of forms, subtle hues, with no sense he ever had to stop. But when it came to shading, the play of light and shadow, the brilliance of a point reflecting, then time halted altogether. As the shape and luster of the scene emerged from the paper, as the drawing gained mass, somehow the weight in it lifted him. He forgot to eat, forgot to move, forgot to think.

Why did evenings have to end? If only he could turn the clock back and share the time with Shōko again and again, living in perpetual twilight. He thought back over their seven evenings, particularly the last two. They didn't talk much; they mostly just sat and enjoyed being together. He drew while she read—or she held a book; the pages rarely turned. The times she knew he was drawing her, she was self-conscious, but she never asked him to stop. Why was she being so kind, letting him stay, feeding him, and now even clothing him? When she went out, she always left lunch for him, plus a basket of snacks and drinks. She brought him rice, *miso* soup, and some other tasty thing for breakfast each morning. (Except once when she brought fetid, slimy, fermented soybeans.) In the evening she brought a large plate of whatever they had for dinner. He was concerned, but Shōko assured him that no one would notice extra helpings, because she did all the shopping and cooking. She laughed when she said the only thing that required caution was bringing it upstairs, because her mother would disapprove of her sneaking food off to her room.

How much more so a man under her bed? He almost smiled, but he was too close to unconsciousness.

20

"I'D NEVER LET YOU LEAVE ME. I'D PUT YOU IN YOUR GRAVE BEFORE I let you shame me the way you shamed your first husband." Shōko could feel the malice in his threats even when he wasn't there. She looked at her trembling hands and cursed Masaru for his viciousness and herself for not leaving sooner.

She tried to calm herself, telling herself that it was still morning; he wouldn't be back for hours.

But if he came home now, he'd see. He checked her room all the time. He'd see the suitcase, and he'd kill her.

"Don't worry, you're safe with me. Come to bed."

Shōko whirled around to see—David? In his new pajamas? But it was Masaru's house. Looking down, she saw she was wearing pajamas too.

"Shōko," came David's voice, soft and deep.

David. It was the most natural thing in the world, and she smiled shyly now at his bidding. She so wanted to feel his warmth, but too bashful to face him, she turned away as she slipped into the bed. Soon, though, he put his arms around her and pulled her close. She gave in to the narcotic euphoria of his body pressed tightly to hers.

But then she heard a door slam downstairs—footsteps loud on the stairs—the door splintered and flew off its hinges! Masaru stood in the doorway but a moment, chest heaving in rage, before he lifted her chopping knife over his head and charged.

Shōko did the only thing she could, rolling onto David to protect him. She felt the blade pierce her back, and then Masaru's full weight forcing the air out of her lungs as he pushed it into her. Time slowed to a crawl, her only sensation the crushing pressure. When it stopped, she lifted herself in slow motion. David was looking in horror at her chest. There was a wide slit in her pajamas at her right breast, surrounded by an expanding circle of blood. Seeing a glint of metal through the slit, she realized the blade went all the way through her. She was going to die. It was a moment of sublime calm as she realized this was how her life would end.

Then the slow motion was over. She felt the knife moving inside her, scraping against her rib as Masaru pulled it out. And rolling off David, seeing the knife already flying down at her throat, she screamed—

IT WAS NOT YET four a.m. and the levee path was deserted. David and Shōko walked close together, near enough that their hands sometimes brushed together and her shoulder bumped into his arm.

He'd had to get her outside. She just lay there, shaking, unable to speak, tears streaming from her eyes. He thought if he could get her walking it might calm her down, so he grabbed her shorts, got them onto her legs, stood her up, and pulled them up over her short pajamas. He got his own shorts on, and grabbing his shoes, he took her hand and led her down the stairs. In the *genkan* he put sandals on her feet and then pulled her out into the night air, away from that room, that bed, and whatever terror had seized her.

He held her hand as they walked silently to the levee and climbed it, stepping through the *hirugao*, their sleeping blossoms closed like tubes of silk crepe. It was a long walk down the path before he felt the tension leave her, and eventually she stopped quaking and seemed to return to herself, though still silent. Only then did he let go of her hand. They were well beyond where David had ever walked. "Shōko, should we turn around and head back?"

Her reply was a simple "*Un*," and they started back, all in silence, except for the crickets chirping. As they walked along, her gait showed more energy, enough that David dared ask, "Shōko, what happened? What did you dream?"

She moved closer for a few steps before she took his arm and hugged it tight. After a couple of minutes, she spoke: "Sometimes I have a bad dream, same bad dream. Tonight is not a first time."

He kissed her head. "What dream?"

"I dream my husband is killing me. I am packing to run away. He comes into my room." She paused, and there was a tremor in her voice when she went on, "He stabs me with a big knife. I feel it cut deep into me so many times." With the last words, she started to cry.

David stopped and turned her to face him, but as he wrapped his arms around her, she broke down completely. So he held her tight as she soaked his pajamas with her tears.

They stood there for a long time, the cool night breeze ruffling Shōko's short hair, while David rubbed her back and whispered reassurance. The river reflected the growing light in the eastern sky before Shōko finally calmed down enough, though still sobbing, to speak haltingly, "I am sorry. I should not cry . . . with you. I don't want to show weak . . . childish side of me. And I worry . . . you become sad from my crying."

"You worry too much. Show every side of you. I adore them all. Okay?"

She nodded almost imperceptibly.

"Shōko, stop me if I shouldn't ask this, but . . . did he hit you?"

She shook her head, her face still pressed into his chest. "No, he only said he will. It is better if he hit me . . . then I leave him sooner. But he never hit me, so I did not leave . . . for so long!"

David held her as she choked and cried harder. Eventually, he took her hand and started her walking again, and in a few minutes, she was able to speak. "He said cruel things every day. Everything I do is wrong. He hates what I cook. The house is never clean. Everything is bad. Still, I try to be a good wife, but it was too terrible, and I ran away to here. He said so many times he will kill me if I leave. I hided in my room here and did not even turn on light. I never left the house. One day he came, asked where am I and screamed at my parents. *Okāsan*, my mother, called the police, and they took him away. But sometimes *Otōsan* saw him in front of our house, or in our garden, or down the street watching with"—she held her hands to her eyes like tubes—"like two telescopes for eyes. So *Okāsan* called the police many times, until they even know her voice. Now it is four months since he came, but I am always afraid he comes back."

"He won't hurt you."

"It was different before we married. He acted enough like a gentleman. His friend was at my company and made excuse to have us in the same place so many times. Then he said Masaru wants to date me. He was not good-looking, but he was thinking of me all the time. And he was quiet and liked to laugh and I thought he will be a nice man, maybe even like my father, and take care of me in old age life."

Shōko started sobbing again. "But after we married, he was so mean and selfish, every day, until I was so tired of so much selfish."

David put his arm around her shoulder. She was near breaking down again. "It got worse more and more. So I said we need marriage counselor. . . . He said no, but I pushed. We went only two times before he yelled and walked out. Then counselor told me, 'Don't try to save this marriage. He is crazy. You should divorce him.' . . . I was a shock!"

David stopped and held her, and again Shōko pushed her face hard against his chest. Her voice was even more ragged as she said, "He does not like my body and says . . . get surgery for bigger breasts. I refuse . . . and he was so angry . . . did not speak for days. He did not like color of my skin . . . says I am too brown, not so pink . . . so calls me '*dojin*.'"

"*Dojin?*"

"*Kanji* are 'dirt' and 'person' and means . . . I can't say."

He held her tighter.

"He is university professor. I graduated from college . . . but he says art college is not enough . . . he must educate me. So he gives me books to read, and . . . I must do homework, and he writes scores . . . with red pen."

Shōko was crying uncontrollably now and David was on the verge of tears.

"If score is too low . . . I must do again . . . and again. Oh, David, I am so ashamed. I did not tell him no!"

He lowered his head and pressed his face into her hair.

She could barely speak. "He yells at me . . . call him '*Danna-sama*.' Long ago wife said . . . for 'husband,' but nowadays it means 'master' . . . so I will not say. I tell myself no! Never! For so long . . . I will not say . . . and he screams . . . *so much!*" She stopped, gasping, her voice now the tiniest whisper. "But after months . . . I did it! . . . I said it to him!"

David's tears were wetting Shōko's hair, so he looked away as he folded his arms around her shoulders and head. He blinked the tears away, took deep breaths, and even tried to distract himself by watching the sunrise, but the pain he held in his arms was too profound. In the end, there was nothing to do but hold her tight as they both cried; and so the sun found them as it peeked through the clouds.

21

DAVID WOKE UP SUNDAY MORNING UNCOMFORTABLY WARM. SHŌKO lay next to him on the bed, sleeping soundly. They didn't talk much after her breakdown on the levee. She eventually stopped crying, and they watched swallows play in the air currents over the river before he walked her home. He stayed with her in the kitchen as she made breakfast for her parents, who weren't up yet. Afterward they sat on Shōko's bed and he held her again, all in perfect silence, until she fell asleep. He laid her down, slipped into the space between her and the wall, wrapped her in his arms from behind, and held her close. Soon he was asleep too.

Awake now, he lay still. She deserved her peace, this soft soul who soothed his pain, all the while silently bearing her own crushing hurt and shame. Long ago, David had described Shōko—innocent, trusting, able to see the good in anyone—to his wife, and her reaction stunned him: "She hardly seems your type, David. She sounds kind of mousy." In fact, Shōko was anything but. She simply needed a protector—perhaps everyone does—and Shōko's should have been him. He could have saved her from all that pain if he had just—

"David?" came the sleepiest of whispers.

He lifted himself onto one elbow, looked down at her eyes, still closed, and stroked her hair as he whispered, "Hey, sleepy thing, you gonna wake up?"

"*Iya.*"

"Okay, you rest."

"*Un.*" She pushed her head back against his arm.

David kept stroking her hair, and she was asleep again in a few seconds. He kissed her head and looked down on her, the muted morning light illuminating her face, tranquil, tragic, exquisite; not that she would be acclaimed as a stunning beauty—she never had been—but her face had a classic oval shape with delicate features. Her hair, black with just a bit of gray, and her skin, smooth but without all the tautness of youth, made her precise age hard to guess, though she looked younger than she was. He knew he was biased, so often seeing the Shōko of his college days in the way she moved, how she talked, or sometimes just as she sat, unaware of his gaze. And when she laughed, her mouth politely covered by her hand but the light gleaming from her eyes even as they drew up into little crescents, nearly closed, she became the Shōko he knew so long ago.

The impact of their first meeting at the levee surprised him: such an emotional jolt, even after thirty years, that it wiped clean every thought but her. Each ensuing meeting did the same. He lost two umbrellas, a hat, and a pair of sunglasses before she started running him through a checklist each time they parted. Even as he stopped misplacing things, though, the exhilaration continued, wondrously complicated, but there was no point in resisting.

Altogether beautiful . . .

He had to draw this.

David separated himself from Shōko with the utmost care, lifted himself off the bed, and after teetering like an acrobat—she would have laughed out loud—he set a foot on the floor. He noiselessly pushed a chair up next to the bed to be as close as possible. The sketch would be just the side of her face, an ear, her disheveled hair gracing her cheek, and the sadness he saw in her eyes even as she slept. Opening the sketchbook to the next clean page, he took the pencil from his mouth and studied her. He knew he had little time before she would awake, so he roughed in her features in preparation for shading, where he would add detail. As he looked at the sketch, though, it needed something more. . . .

The color of her face! Who could have seen the blush in her cheeks, the soft, warm glow of her skin, the color of milk caramel, and called her "dirt"? This perfect color—

He could start over in one of the pastel sketchbooks!

He dropped to the floor and pulled out her art supplies. He opened the wooden-boxed set and was pleased to find they were in good shape, although the choice of flesh tones was meager. They were soft, not good for fine details, but excellent for shading, and perfect for a dreamy sketch like this.

David worked meticulously, but fast. On the gray paper, he sketched her features with a white pencil, added dark outlines in charcoal where there would be shadow edges, then began with the colors. Darks came first, shadows of brown, purple, green, and crimson, followed by the warmer tones of her face, carefully blended. He wished he had a full set of two hundred colors instead of this simple set of thirty, and he smiled: the artist inside him was hungry.

Subtle highlights completed her cheek, nose, lips. But now, the final, most complicated piece—

"David?"

"Mm-hmm."

"What are you doing?"

He didn't answer.

"*Nani?*"

He waited another couple of seconds before he said, "Just shading your ear."

She opened her eyes and rolled them at him before she closed them again and lay still.

"How you doing?"

"So sleepy," she mumbled into the pillow.

David went on drawing for a minute before he spoke again. "You're pretty too."

"You finish shading an ear?"

"Almost. Why?"

"Because I might hit you now."

"Just a sec."

David used the black pastel stick to finish her hair around her ear and add a few stray strands across her face, then added the final highlights in white.

"Done!" he announced with satisfaction. Whereupon Shōko sat up and lifted her pillow over her head, grinning, ready to swing.

David lay the sketch pad and the box of pastels on the table, then sat on the bed next to her. He looked at her skeptically. "You really gonna hit me?"

She shook her head as she lowered the pillow and touched it to his face, then smiled at him softly and leaned back against the wall.

How could anyone have mistreated a woman this meek?

"What time is it?"

"Let's see. . . ." He checked the alarm clock. "Eight eighteen."

"Oh! I must get ready. English girls will be here at nine."

"Girls from England?"

"No, middle school girls who study English."

"Here?"

"Yes, to compare with you, maybe my English is like a bug, but to compare with them, I am the English goddess."

David smiled and Shōko turned him toward the bed while she changed out of her pajamas, but it seemed to David that she was taking longer than usual. When she let him turn back around, he saw she'd turned the sketchbook to face her.

22

THE DAY DAVID FIRST HAPPENED UPON SHŌKO ON THE LEVEE, SEVEN weeks before he followed her home, he was too lost in thought to recognize her.

"David?"

He stopped and looked back at her blankly—and she smiled.

"Shōko?"

"Bikkuri!"

"Shōko? It's really you?" He stepped toward her, arms open wide to hug her, but she pulled back shyly. "Oh, sorry."

"No, I am sorry. I am too shy for hug here."

"Which I should have remembered." David smiled.

"You came back to Japan?"

"A month and a half ago. I'm working at Fujitsu-Star Microchips, up the river," and he pointed toward the plant, though it was far out of sight.

"*Sugoi!* This is unbelievable!"

He was beaming. "I knew this was your hometown. But I didn't keep the envelopes from your letters and I couldn't remember your address. So my first day at Fuji-Star I asked my assistant whether there was some way to find you, but I didn't know what your last name is now or your parents' first names. She said Kawasaki is a common name and it wouldn't be easy to find the right family. So I was going to get someone to track you down—but here you are! This is . . . miraculous!"

"Here I am." She grinned back.

"So what's your last name now?"

She just smiled at first but finally said, "I use Kawasaki still."

They talked for half an hour before Shōko looked at her watch and told him she needed to rush. So they arranged to meet at noon the next day, Saturday, in the same place. He watched her go, then looked for landmarks, making sure he could relocate the most important spot in all of Japan.

He arrived the next day a few minutes before noon to find her already there, carrying a large bag.

"I bring lunch. You like to have a picnic?"

She seemed almost nervous at first, but he didn't realize until now that she had been afraid of her stalking husband. In fact, the day they met was only the third time she'd taken the levee path home. As they ate, though, she relaxed and warmed to the conversation, and soon her ready laugh was flooding him with memories.

He would have stayed longer, but she had to leave after a couple of hours. He could still remember her walking away in her pale yellow sundress and wide straw hat, little arms swinging. They met again the next Tuesday, then Sunday, and on they went, meeting at least once a week over the next two months.

Looking back, David wondered what Shōko felt in those weeks as he told her about the project. He gave her snapshots as it disintegrated and his days devolved into adjudication between competing camps of the damned, unable to reach a consensus on any fix because the whole chip was beyond repair. Yet he hung on, hoping for someone to wake up in Portland and replace Paul, or at least approve new IP, so he could stay in Japan. Shōko must have known he was brightened by having her there, but she also had to watch helplessly as he grew dimmer week by week.

It was a week before Shōko saved him that day on the levee that David found out just how hopeless the project was. "David-*san*, we finish the test and it is what you suspected," said Takahara gravely.

"What?" asked Leon.

"A race condition," said David.

"*What?*"

Takahara nodded.

"I heard about them in school, but I've never actually seen one," said Leon.

"You never work with IP so bad as this," said Itō.

David sat slumped in his chair. "There are two different circuits that lead to the same point. The correct circuit completes first about ninety percent of the time."

Leon stared at him, mouth agape.

"There could be others."

"Other race conditions? This is insane!"

David bowed his head. Everyone was quiet.

Calmer, Leon asked, "So, what do we do?"

David sat and pressed his hands to his face. He said, "Everyone, please sit."

Itō, Takahara, and Leon took their seats, and David breathed deeply as he dialed.

"You've got Paul!"

"Hi, Paul. I have everyone together again."

"Another doomsday prediction?" asked Paul with a laugh.

David scowled at the phone and took another deep breath, letting Paul sit and wait before he said, "Paul, the processor has a race condition."

Paul was silent for a long time before he said, "That's for you and me to discuss."

"It's been a group effort. I think it's helpful to have everyone here."

"You're wrong," replied Paul, and he hung up.

Their frustration was palpable as the others left the room. David fumed. How was he to command any respect from his people if he could not even get Paul to talk to them? Or perhaps that was Paul's intention all along.

At first, David could not force himself to make the second call to Paul. In the end, he affected a capable facade, just barely, and did it. At least it was short. It ended with strict orders that David not divulge anything, but thoroughly dispirited, he told the others anyway. Paul was no longer claiming that the Japanese were poor manufacturers, but he was convinced they were incompetent designers. He was looking at moving the design work to Bangalore, outsourcing it to the company he used for the IP. Itō, though silent, could hardly conceal his indignation. His group was under attack, his competence as their leader impugned, and David could not stop it. David was the project's linchpin. He had failed everyone.

David knew the chip would never go to India. Paul would let it languish while he shuttered the joint venture to hide his mismanagement. Then he'd try to resurrect it as a new project with new IP. David's increasingly frantic phone calls over the next week, though, played into Paul's hands perfectly. Paul had been poisoning the well since David's first call in April: David was Chicken Little trying to tell everyone the sky was falling; the Japanese programmers were bunglers; and in their latest debacle, to Paul's dismay, they had created a race condition.

Shōko showed increasing concern as the weeks went by. David learned that "fiction," "spin," and "scapegoat" have all been transliterated into Japanese. Her reaction to the India news was that Paul had created nothing short of institutional psychosis. David's wife finally arrived in late May and was ignorant he had met Shōko only days before. (There's no need to ratchet the tension any tighter by telling her I've reconnected with an old friend.) As weeks went by, she began telling him the same thing as Shōko, though more pointedly and without the Japanese lessons. David was determined to make the project viable and keep it here, but they both urged him to just turn his back on it, return to America, and save himself. Neither knew what David himself had yet to realize: his reason for staying in Japan had little to do with the chip, his pride, or his career. Besides, even desperate and despondent as he was becoming, no office frustration, no project failure, could completely break him. Computer chips aren't that intimate. It took a wife to do that.

23

AFTER ENGLISH TUTORING, SHŌKO WALKED DOWNTOWN TO BUY A gift for a woman in the office who was expecting a baby girl. She picked a dress with a big sunflower print. It had a yellow sash with matching bloomers and booties and a ribbon for the baby's hair, what she would have chosen for her own baby.

Shōko was anxious to get back home to David, so she did not take the time to have it wrapped. But walking home on the levee path, against the river's steady flow, her brisk pace slowed. Of all the unexpected turns her life had taken, not having children was the regret that jabbed most painfully. She tried to squirm away, telling herself that she simply had not been blessed with that. She could have been, though, with a few different choices. But Shōko stopped the argument there: it was irrelevant; that possibility was gone now. The next thought, though, while hardly new, left her standing still, staring at the river. *How would it have felt to be the center of a man's life, or even to have a man do something just for me?*

As she thought about it, she realized she had felt it briefly, but those days were half a lifetime ago.

DAVID SAT at the table finishing his lunch as Shōko wrapped the gift box in decorative pink paper.

"What's in there?"

"A gift I buyed—bought—today, for someone in my office. Soon she will have a baby."

"I thought Japanese stores were famous for gift wrapping."

"Yes, but it was a hurry today."

"A hurry?"

David thought he saw embarrassment on her face, but she said only, "The store was crowded." She was silent as she finished the folding and taping.

"May I ask for your finger to hold a ribbon?" she asked, looking over and smiling at him.

That smile that changes everything.

David obediently stood.

Shōko pulled a spool of pink ribbon from the bag on the table. She wrapped the ribbon around the package once and then, taking his long, slender finger in her smaller, even more slender fingers, she placed it.

Despite holding her hand for so long last night, David blushed. She was too close. He stifled the urge to reach out to her.

Maybe if we talk, I can calm down.

Shōko's ear was inches from his lips, so he kept his voice soft: "Pink paper and pink ribbon. It's pretty. I'm sure she'll love it."

"I hope so," she replied in her girlish voice as she taped it. She pulled a spool of thinner ribbon from the bag. "Red will make it prettier," she said, her eyes fixed on the task. She wrapped a length of shiny, red ribbon around the box, then took David's finger again to secure it in place.

As he stood next to her, watching her work, lending a finger to hold a satin ribbon, apart from the overwhelming desire he felt, it occurred to him how much a couple's relationship is defined by the most insignificant things they do. Time with Shōko was changing him, her soft spirit calling up a tenderness for something outside himself. He could feel the difference between today and yesterday, today and a week ago. He looked down at her hair, thick but soft, lustrous, too short to cover the nape of her lissome neck where it disappeared into her shirt.

Shōko opened the scissors and curled the ribbons daintily with the blade. After tugging on the curls to check the tension, she put down the scissors, and for the first time since David stood to help her, she looked up at him. "It is done," she said, almost whispering.

Mute now, he gazed down at her neck, gracefully outstretched; at her lips, lusciously soft, full, natural pink with only a hint of lipstick; at her deep brown eyes, melting him like chocolate forgotten in a hot car.

She blinked, but her eyes stayed on his. "David..." Her mouth was slightly open.

"Mm-hmm."

She closed her mouth and looked down. "You told me a few weeks ago that you are not painting now."

At the question, David looked away, and Shōko stepped back and sat. Thinking of his last painting, he retreated a step too. Had it been four years? And it was only occasional for ten years before that.

Four years with no painting at all. How?

Still, it was not as if he had wanted or planned to stop. Life turns like that. It just happened.

He frowned. *No, it had help.*

"David?"

"Sorry." He took a seat in the other chair. "I guess... no, I haven't painted in a long time."

"What paints did you use?"

"Egg tempera, mostly."

"*Iya da.* Bad egg smell is so bad."

"It's true it's troublesome, but you can make such subtle colors. I also used oils a lot."

"Oil paint smell so bad too."

"Yes, but it dries slowly enough that you can mix colors on the canvas to get a softer look, a perfect gradation of color."

"Grada . . . ?"

"Gradation. A series of small changes."

Shōko laughed. "*Guradēshon! Jojo ni henka suru koto ne. Sō datta wa ne!*"

It was impossible not to laugh with her, even though he didn't know what she said.

"I used acrylics sometimes, too, never for figures, but for abstracts, even landscapes. Why do you ask?"

Shōko was picking up her purse. She looked . . . distressed? Or at least flustered.

"You're going somewhere?"

She nodded. "I remember I forgot a thing."

She was gone before he could say goodbye.

SHŌKO WAS hot enough that she took a taxi downtown instead of walking. She wiped her neck, eyes closed, and leaned forward into the air conditioner's current.

Maybe he didn't see—he's American, after all—but I was fumbling with the tape like a child!

Today they should have been friends again, no matter how intimate they were last night. She could not lose her heart to a man, even one like David. But standing close was like having him next to her in the bed. His face so near, his eyes peering inside her, it was the leopard again. And if he had bent down the slightest bit . . .

Yet David too near was not what shrank the room so close she couldn't breathe. In fact, they were sitting across the table from each other. He said, "gradation," she laughed, and he lit up. And it dawned on her that when she laughed, or even smiled, he *always* lit up.

24

DAVID OPENED THE BOX OF PASTELS AND BEGAN ADDING THE VERDANT greens that inundate a Japanese summer. As the paper changed into a rough picture of the garden, it soaked in David's thoughts like a sponge. He saw things differently than he had a week ago. He could feel textures with his eyes. His sense of sight was becoming compositional, the way it was when he was younger. The juxtaposition of light and shadow was almost like a drug in the way it bent his mind around objects. As the colors played together in his head, they turned into temperas and oils.

He remembered painting the nude that won him "best of show" at the student exhibition his senior year at Cooper Union. Standing before the easel, palette and brushes in hand, the feeling of the brush on the canvas, the elation as his vision appeared—

"If you loved it so much, why did you stop?"

His wife's question was no more than imagined, but despite his determination to ignore her, it was enough to stop his drawing.

"Answer me. Why? You got enough praise. You won almost every award the school had to offer."

David stared at his drawing, even as the conversation continued in his head.

"It was the talk of a show at Peter Blum that did you in. You know it was. You've admitted it to me any number of times."

"I was bogged down, that was all."

"You were falling apart, David. You're desperate to believe that you would have gotten over it, but face it, you were a basket case."

"My parents, all the faculty, everyone said to make a career of it, except you. There was that hint of derision in your face when you wanted something and I was busy painting, as if I was flaky."

"C'mon, David, you know I loved your paintings. You were the greatest painter I'd ever seen. I married that painter!"

It was true. She had loved his paintings. In the beginning, she had even loved him painting her, yielding in total abandon as he posed her nude. Now he saw her lying in front of him, her perfect face, the sensuous curves of her naked body, her skin like cream. He could have painted it a hundred times, more, without ever losing his wonder for it. He had spent thousands of hours at the easel while she posed, begging her to sit longer, oblivious to her pain and boredom, lost in her skin and the paint. Over a dozen years, he painted her thirty-four times, but over that same time and more, she changed, and she changed him. He kept painting, even as he went back to school, trying to graduate again and start a new career before he passed his early thirties—the career that was now in tatters— but he painted less each year.

Was it her mere modicum of interest, the way she treated it as an imposition—or a hobby, as if he was collecting thimbles or something— or did he simply lose the will? *Why didn't I paint her a hundred times?*

25

"YOU FOUND WHAT YOU FORGOT?"

Shōko nodded

"Almost two hours. Must've been hard to find."

She smiled. "No, not so hard."

David stood back, hands on his hips, and studied her. "Go ahead, tell me."

"Tell you what?" Her smile broadened.

"Whatever you're so excited about."

"I am excited? You know me so well?"

As he folded his arms and smiled back, she stepped to the door and took a large flat bag and another smaller bag from the hall.

"Shōko, what did you . . . ?"

"David is a painter. Painter needs paints!"

"But Shōko—"

"Shh. First you look." She grinned as she held the large bag out to him.

David smiled with resignation, took it from her, and looked inside: two canvas boards and a paper palette. He stared at them for several long seconds before he looked up at her broad smile. She handed him the smaller bag: brushes, painting knives, paint, media, a water bottle, and disposable plastic cups for mixing. The only thing missing was an easel.

"Oh, I have old easel here from college time. Or if you need portable, I can bring tomorrow. I saw easel with legs that are . . . can be long or short, like camera tripod. And this time you don't sneak money into my wallet like yesterday you did it for clothes."

David looked down as he blushed.

"And acrylic is not your favorite, but oil is too strong smell for bedroom, I think." She seemed to be done, then blurted out, "And only F-size canvas boards in a store, no P or M. Sorry again." She remembered something else in her excitement and spoke so suddenly that David almost laughed at the staccato effect: "And I have so many rags for you. I know you need rags." She was almost bouncing on her toes.

"Shōko—" He stopped short, looking into her eyes. He looked at the supplies, and back at her. "Thank you."

She said nothing in response to his thanks. She just met his gaze, smiling, blushing, before she said, "It is time to cook. *Okāsan* will scold if dinner is late," and she was gone again.

David stood, shoulders bowed, hands in his pockets, and stared at the door for a long time. He looked around the room at Shōko's few possessions. He would repay her; not today, given her insistence just now, but eventually.

Still, painting . . .

He emptied the contents of the larger bag onto the bed. She had apologized for bringing only F-size boards, but he didn't even know what he might paint, so the aspect ratio didn't matter at this point. Canvas boards would also be easier to work with in a confined space like this. They were even pre-gessoed, though not to the smoothness he would have used for a figure.

He dumped out the second bag. The dozen brushes were good, stiff hog hair. Shōko's art training showed in the trowel-like painting knives, something the uninitiated would never have considered. She also knew to get a disposable paper palette: acrylics dry so fast it's easier to tear the used sheet from the pad than to use solvents to clean up. She got large tubes of primary colors and smaller ones of secondary colors. There was fluid for thinning and gel for thickening. She supplied everything he would need to paint again.

Every single thing.

"So, what subject will captivate you enough to carry you all the way to completion?" came his wife's voice from over his shoulder. "Or is this going to join the untold boxes of unfinished paintings in the basement?"

He sat on the bed and stared at the supplies.

"Even if you can somehow finish it, as emotionally frail as you are, the result will disappoint you. You know your best work. There's no way to pick up a brush after four years and be brilliant, as if not a day has gone by. As whatever it is materializes on the canvas, mediocre, burning out all desire to finish, what will Shōko say?"

"You have no right to say her name."

He imagined her shrug. "When you can't finish, even if she stays silent, you'll see dismay in her eyes."

"And her disappointment if I don't paint?" said David softly, but to himself, not the one who abandoned him. In fact, she disappeared as he picked up the big tube of Quinacridone Crimson and turned it, twisting the cap on and off. He squeezed the tiniest bit out onto his finger, blood red.

26

IT WAS AFTER MIDNIGHT, BUT TRAPPED IN A MAZE OF THOUGHTS OF having a man under her bed, Shōko couldn't sleep. David was awake, too; she could hear him moving. More than that, she couldn't hear his sleeping breathing. Although comforted by his presence, unused to sleeping with another person in the room, she was not sleeping quite as well since he arrived. Even when she was married, she had her own room. The last time she shared a room was—

She frowned at the thought: the *futon* on the floor of her father's room after she ran away. He insisted when she told him of Masaru's threats. And the last time before that—

She cringed: her honeymoon with Masaru. And before that—

Her honeymoon with her first husband? She sat up, held the pillow tight to her face, and screamed into it, then got up and started to pace.

David poked his head out. "You okay?

"Yes, but I can't sleep."

"Neither can I."

"I am sorry. Do I make you be awake?"

"No, no, you never keep me up." David crawled out from beneath the bed.

"Maybe space is too tight for you. We can move the *futon* to here." She walked over and stood in front of the closet.

"No, don't! It's . . . fine under the bed. Cozy." He paused. "It's safer too. No one can walk in and find me in the night."

"Oh, safe, yes." But how did he have to contort himself to turn over under there? Still, somehow, he had enough room to do it.

Shōko sat on the bed. David sat too. She smiled at the irony: he stayed for the space under a bed that she bought as a declaration of independence as she gave up on ever finding a man worth loving. Her antique French bedroom furniture was a present to herself for her fortieth birthday.

"I suppose we could take a walk or something," said David.

"It is late."

"Yeah, but neither of us is going to sleep, and the time lying awake is . . . thoughts come that are . . ."

Shōko looked at him with concern for a few moments before she said, "Maybe a walk is good." She hopped up. "Okay, we change clothes."

They each gathered clothes and then turned away from each other and changed.

"Where shall we walk? The river?" David asked as he dressed.

"We walked someplace else ever?"

"No."

"Then I show you this neighborhood. But we don't want neighbors to say 'Oh, Shōko has new husband!' so we must be so quiet and imbis . . . imbuis—"

"Invisible."

"Yes, imbvuisabul. Is that right?"

"Not quite."

Shōko kept practicing under her breath as she dressed.

After silently slipping out of the house, they headed left, away from the river, and turned at the first corner. As Shōko led David through the narrow streets, did he notice how often she chose the direction with fewer lights? But he seemed satisfied just to be out in the cool night air. Shōko spoke in a hushed voice as they strolled along, telling him about the people who lived in the houses they passed: interesting memories, funny little stories, and at one house even a bit of salacious gossip. After a few blocks, though, Shōko didn't know who lived in any of the houses. She pointed out a *nemu* tree and explained that it closed its flowers and leaves at night as if sleeping. She laughed when David plucked a leaf, caressed her arm with it, and asked whether its sleepiness would rub off. There were only a few more explanations along the way before both fell silent, walking close together like last night.

Once Shōko stopped talking, she found it hard to pay attention to what they were passing. The tingling when their arms touched made her shiver. David even asked once whether she was cold! She was mortified: it was a cool night, but he must have known that wasn't it.

As they walked on, Shōko felt herself shrinking. She was taller than average for a Japanese woman, but the top of her head barely reached past David's chin. His stride was so long she could not begin to match it, yet her pace was pulled toward his, leaving her feeling like a child pattering along next to him. There was something else, though, more than just his size. Some of it could have been the way he moved, lithe and strong, the same thing that drew her eyes to animals at the zoo or the circus when she was a child.

While Shōko's memory of the big circus cats was a happy one, it also called to mind fragments of her leopard dream from yesterday morning. It left her feeling not just smaller, but vulnerable. She glanced up at David, but shivered again and looked away, hoping he did not see.

———

IN FACT, David had seen only bits of the last several blocks. The walk was not the escape from his thoughts that he had hoped. Now he was far away, wandering about in his painting, the wife who left him, and whether he could ever resemble the man he used to be.

27

AS DAVID LAY BENEATH THE BED, UNABLE TO SLIP BACK INTO SLEEP after waking at first light, his mind was lost in painting. *His wife lay in front of him, demurely posed for one of her first nudes. She was the most beautiful woman he'd ever painted. She had a perfectly proportioned face; so much so that it was difficult to determine her most striking feature. Some, including David, would say it was her large eyes, a light, limpid, gold-flecked brown. Most, though, were captivated by her smile, impossibly broad and bright even before her lips parted and showed her glistening teeth. Her deep brunette hair was long and full. She was slender but shapely, and just tall enough to look David in the eye in her highest heels. She had spent so long posing for this painting that he could still remember every detail.*

He was losing himself again in the smoothness of her skin when he imagined her saying, "David, stop."

"Stop what?"

"Painting, David. Stop painting."

"What's wrong?"

"It's gone on too long."

"We can stop for a while. Or call it a day and work more tomorrow."

"No, David. No painting today, none tomorrow, none ever."

"But there's so much interest in my work. I only need a couple more standout pieces and they'll set up the gallery show."

"This is one of those standouts?"

"It's the best I've ever done."

She got up off the bed, slipped on a thin satin robe, walked over, and said, "Baby, look at it."

David's eyes lingered on her for a second before he turned—

The canvas was blank! There were no highlights of her skin, no colors worked together with patient care, no subtle hues reflecting up from deeper layers. He looked down at the palette in his hand, perfectly clean. So were the brushes.

"Sorry, David, but it wasn't meant to be."

David imagined the studio: the easels, the walls, the shelves. He watched as the figures, portraits, landscapes, and abstractions of an entire artistic career flowed down the canvases and boards, dripped off the bottom edges, and evaporated. There was not even a trace to stain the floor. Years of work—not just years elapsed, but hours that totaled into years—gone.

"David, don't act so surprised. You didn't think the paintings would last after your talent faded, did you? I know it must hurt terribly, but be strong and face it."

David pushed her away. He grabbed a tube of paint, opened it, and held it to the palette as he squeezed hard.

Nothing came out.

He tried another.

Nothing.

He stepped back and stared at her idyllic form framed by the now-blank studio as she smiled and held her arms out to him.

David scrambled out from under the bed. Sitting on the floor, knees held tight to his chest, damp with sweat, he could still see the empty canvases.

He stood and looked at the brand-new acrylics on Shōko's table. He took a step back, chilled at the humiliation of being a "former" painter, dissipated, exhausted, his talent bleached away by too many years in the withering sun of an ordinary life. He looked at Shōko and imagined her waking, going through her morning routine, talking to him excitedly about painting. Could he look into her cheery face and have that conversation, unable to return the slightest hope? When she got home, expecting to see paint on one of the boards, how could he shatter the faith of the one person who still believed in him? It would be better to die.

He sat on the floor and buried his face in his hands. His family and career were already gone. Now realizing he would never recreate the softness of skin with paint, never see a sheet of canvas transformed into a living person, *never* paint again—it was a waking death. The core of his being was on fire, incinerated as he sat, alone.

No one could endure this!

28

SHŌKO AWOKE SHAKING. AFRAID TO KEEP HER EYES CLOSED, SHE looked at the ceiling.

It's already light. And it's my room, in my house.

But the dream was so vivid that she dared not look across the room. Again, she had been with David and again Masaru kicked in the door. But when she rolled onto David to shield him, what lay beneath her was three times David's size. It was striped white and black, with a gigantic head and a visage so vicious—pale yellow eyes glowering behind heavy brows, enormous mouth open, with teeth as long as her fingers bared in pure malice—far beyond warning, it was the face of death assured. Not hers, though: the tiger was looking past her, at the door.

She looked toward Masaru in disbelief, only to see him raise the knife over his head. He should have been running for his life! Instead, he charged. The blood stopped in her veins, her heart crushed in her chest, as David opened his mouth as wide as her head and roared so loud she had to press her hands to her ears to stop the pain. She opened her mouth to scream—but nothing came out. She watched David rise and spring. He caught Masaru's neck in his jaws, the momentum of his enormous body not just stopping Masaru's charge, but jerking him backward, lifting him off his feet. As they fell, there was a sickening cracking sound before they slammed into the floor, Masaru flat on his back with David on top. She looked for any sign that Masaru might still be alive, but when David rose, Masaru hung limp from his jaws. David shook him, and the last of the air escaped Masaru's lungs with a hissing, gurgling sound, before David dropped the lifeless body on the floor. Still David waited, tense, unmoving, as a pool of blood grew around Masaru's neck.

When Masaru didn't move, ever so slowly, blood dripping from his mouth, David turned his gaze from her dead husband to Shōko. She held her breath, waiting for him to look away, but as he growled so deep and heavy it rumbled in Shōko's chest, his eyes stayed fixed, unblinking, staring into her soul. Yes, she had thought of Masaru dead countless times, but not like this! Still, the tiger stared, and trembling in her sweat-soaked pajamas, frozen in abject terror, barely breathing, Shōko stared back into the eyes of the killer that slept beneath her bed.

Even now, awake, irrational as it was, she feared Masaru might be there. Would she be more frightened by the sight of him alive or freshly killed? The thought gave her goose bumps. She needed to see David—even sleeping, it didn't matter—but she felt as if she were lying atop a wild animal's den.

But it's David; the sight of him should calm me!

Her heart was pounding so hard it felt as if her whole chest was beating. Still, she had to see him. She took a deep breath, slipped to the floor, and looked—

Where is he?

She leaned on the bed. *He's downstairs using the toilet, and I don't need to check on that.* She switched off the alarm clock and sat on the bed with her hands in her lap.

Close your eyes and just sit.

But her legs were still shaking.

Breathe more. Don't go downstairs. Calm down. Wait.

Shōko checked the whole first floor, even peeking into her parents' rooms. She ran back upstairs and checked the spare room.

When he disappeared before, everything turned out fine. It's the same now. He's just out . . . doing something.

Like what?

No, don't feel that! He'll reappear soon enough.

Shōko sat at the table in her room and ran through what they did yesterday and the day before, looking for any clues. *Were the paints too much? He seemed pleased, but maybe he felt pressured. Maybe he doesn't want to paint anymore.*

But he didn't say he didn't want to paint.

But he didn't say he did! Why did I get him the paints? I knew he was fragile. Things I can't even understand sink him with no warning at all.

All she could do was wait, though, and waiting meant more worrying and she would only end up frantic, so she went downstairs and turned her mind to preparing breakfast. She worked fast so that thoughts of David would have less time to squeeze in, but it was a lost cause: breakfast took no thought at all.

If it was the paints, if he's gone and I'm alone—

I'm altogether too upset. It's idiotic to be so wrapped up in a man, and one who's sick. I need to take him home. Or to the police?

No need for that. We've done nothing wrong; or illegal, anyway. But home, definitely. It's two days since we talked about it, so today—

Wait! If he left for good, would he take his sketchbook?

She ran from the kitchen and was halfway up the stairs when she heard the front door quietly slide open. She stopped, her hand squeezing the life out of the railing, and turned.

David!

He was out—painting?

She blinked, gave him the briefest of smiles, and ran upstairs.

Even as her eyes stayed glued to her day planner, Shōko watched David enter the room and set down yesterday's shopping bag he must have used to carry the paint and brushes. Still, he held the canvas board, keeping it turned away from her. He took a step toward the bed. "Want to see?"

She pressed her fingers against the planner to keep them from trembling as she waited the couple of seconds that would lend an air of calm, and when she looked up, she nodded. David set the board on the table and turned it to reveal a sunrise over the river. The river was only sketched in, the tall cedars on the far levee barely outlined in deep green, with space left empty for the feathery bamboo thickets in front. But there were parts of the sky that were more developed. The brilliance of the coming morning burst from the blackness of night as if heaven itself had cracked open. His sketches were moving, but they were nothing like this. He was so—

Why do I have no words?

He was waiting for her to speak. She wasn't looking at his face, but she could feel his apprehension. She searched for praise as high as he deserved, but it took her a full minute to find something she thought she could get out without choking up. She turned her gaze from the painting to David. He was looking into her eyes, his face creased with worry—

How can I speak now? David needed it, though, so she forced herself: "It is so beautiful paint—"

David's reaction finished her. She turned away, hoping to lose herself in the morning routine, but David talked excitedly: "You know, I wasn't sure I could do it. I mean, there was a time, in the night, when I thought painting would be too . . . that it had been too long. But when I got to the river there was a *perfect* sunrise just waiting for me, as if it was fated!" He paused, then went on more subdued: "I might not have tried," his voice wavered, "but I couldn't very well let those new acrylics go to waste, could I?" and he fell silent too.

Shōko walked over and squeezed his hand.

How is it possible for his talent to gleam this brightly even as he is still too fragile to go home?

Silly question; Van Gogh was much sicker. But David was so different only three days ago!

She chanced another look at the painting.

He captured the sunrise with such drama. It's just paint!

And with that thought, not looking at David again, she hurried downstairs.

Breakfast with her parents got Shōko back under control, and soon it was time to go, so she finished putting herself together, then walked over to David and said, "I am so impressed your painting. It is such a dramatic sunrise. You have talent that—"

Why did I even try to talk?

She squeezed his hand and left.

She was at the river before she noticed a tiny dot of red on the cuff of her sleeve. It must have gotten there when she took his hand. She got out a tissue and wiped it off, but she knew that acrylic paint has to be washed out at once or it's there to stay. She would have to change her shirt. She turned back toward the house—

No, no, no. It's just a little stain. Perhaps no one will notice.

The weather was clear and unusually hot. Was the rainy season finally over? Walking along the levee path, Shōko slowed to listen to birds singing as everything began to bake in the morning sun. She looked at the stiff *susuki* grass near the river bottom, nearly two meters high, standing motionless for lack of the slightest breeze. The river was low, and the clear water called to her playfully. It invited her to skip down the levee stairs, cross the narrow gravelly stretch to the shallow channel, kick off her shoes, and dip her feet into the frigid flow. But ever stalwart, she walked into the glaring sunshine, off to do her duty for the company.

Sweat was rolling down her back, though, and she slowed. . . .

29

SHŌKO WAS LATE TO WORK FOR THE FIRST TIME, BUT NO ONE ASKED for an explanation—or where her nylons were, or why the bottom of her skirt was wet. And as the day went on, no one commented on the paperwork piling up on her desk. She couldn't concentrate. At first it was remembering the water. It was so cold she almost screamed when she first stepped in. She thought of how she giggled as it tickled her naked legs, and how she stood there until her toes were nearly numb, wondering what a woman is supposed to do when she falls in love with the man under her bed. Such an impossible love was bound to break her heart. Reason screamed at her, "Fool! Wake up!" but all she could do was smile. Ignoring Reason, she played in the water, and to her surprise, Reason quieted down.

Long before her skirt dried, though, memories of her morning wading were replaced with images of David, and he kept coming back, thanking her for the paints, showing her the canvas board, beaming. She didn't even need the spot of red on her sleeve as a reminder; her eyes would close, and the scene would play all by itself. She heard the front door opening behind her, saw the sunshine stream in with him, and realized that he'd been out painting. She saw the diffuse morning light that filled her room, and the way it shone on his head as he leaned over to set down the painting supplies; poor thinning hair, David hated it, but he was adorable. She heard his voice, deep and quiet—always quiet for fear of her parents hearing—and excited. He affected nonchalance, but his eyes betrayed his pride. She watched his beautiful, slender fingers, stained with paint, turning the board around. Tension filled the room as she stared at it, her thoughts devoid of words.

It was what she saw next, though, that pushed in deepest. Again, it was in his eyes: a need, almost a hunger. She didn't understand it at first—and she couldn't remember her exact words—but when she told him the painting was beautiful, his reaction! As that part of the scene played it sent shivers from behind her knees up through the small of her back and shooting into her arms and neck, every time. She watched as her simple praise lit him like a beacon. That was when she realized, when her throat closed tight: he painted it for her.

III

Searching

搜索

30

THE RINGING PHONE WOKE HER FROM A SOUND SLEEP. "HELLO."

"Mrs. Reese? Kelly?"

At her name, she rose like bubbles to the surface. "Yes."

"This is Paul Salazar, David's boss. We had dinner a few months ago after David joined the project."

"Yeah. Yes, I remember." She was awake enough to recognize the name of the man who'd upended her whole life.

"I was wondering if David's left the country."

"What? Which country?"

"Japan, Kelly. I'm calling from Japan. Can you tell me whether or not David has left Japan?"

"I . . . don't think so. . . . I left him there when I came back to America a week and a half ago."

"So he hasn't gone home to Portland?"

"No," she said, sleepy and bewildered.

"I got here Thursday night. David was supposed to meet me Friday, and he stood me up. Turns out he hasn't shown up for a week and no one knows where he is. I figured he was taking time off or was sick or something, but I've been waiting two days since then and not a word from him. Anyway, I thought you could tell me what's going on."

Kelly sat up, eyes wide, in the dark.

31

ŌBUCHI, SUPERVISOR OF DETECTIVES, CALLED THE MORNING ASSEM-bly to order. It was Monday, so he asked for thorough case recaps before he introduced a new one: "We have a missing person."

There were some muffled groans, but it was mostly quiet chatter as he put David Reese's picture on the screen.

"As you can see, the individual is a foreigner. American manager of a joint project at the Fujitsu microchip plant. His wife faxed the search application, and the company filed it last night with this photo. Fifty-two years old, one hundred eighty centimeters, seventy-two kilograms. Thinning brown hair, beard, both graying and cut short. Lives in Ōmachi ni-chōme off Urayama-dōri. No one has seen him at work or in his neighborhood for a full week and they suspect he's been the victim of a crime. Immigration has no record of him leaving the country. Kikuchi and Nakagawa are assigned full-time. Please give them whatever cooperation they request.

"A foreigner should not be hard to spot in this town. I don't want to waste much time on a case like this, but since it's a foreigner, it's not a normal missing persons situation. Procedure demands the same extra level of search as for a criminal like the *yakuza*. And Tokyo will be watching. The last thing any of us needs is for this to blow up into an international incident."

A MIDDLE-AGED OFFICER from the local *kōban* showed Detectives Kikuchi and Nakagawa that David's car was in its parking space, then escorted them to the apartment where the landlord was waiting. The detectives showed her the faxed form with Kelly's signature that gave them permission to enter and search the apartment. She unlocked the door and held it open while the detectives donned white gloves.

Kikuchi removed his shoes in the *genkan* and entered, followed by Nakagawa and the landlord. She stood in the living room as the detectives worked their way through the two-bedroom apartment. Nakagawa, a young, new detective, was impressed by its size, exceptionally large by local standards. "This is a nice place."

The landlord bowed appreciatively, and Kikuchi said, "Yes. I worked on the case of the last American; you know, the guy who walked in front of the car. His apartment was big too."

There was nothing out of place, no trace of home invasion, plenty of food in the refrigerator, although some was spoiled, and not even a day's worth of dirty dishes in the sink.

"Here's his phone," said Nakagawa from the kitchen.

"I was afraid we'd find it here. He wasn't answering."

"There must be fifty missed calls," said Nakagawa as his thumb flew over the buttons. "And no calls answered or made since seven twenty-three p.m. on the third, ten days ago."

"So much for any hopes this would end today."

Nakagawa put the phone in a plastic bag. "No contact for ten days before anyone called us. Can you believe it? Lonely guy."

"I don't know, some people handle it all right," said Kikuchi, and Nakagawa detected a trace of the loneliness he so often felt from his partner. Kikuchi went on: "But the first seventy-two hours are key. Ten days suggests he isn't going to be found unharmed," and then more ominously, "or alive. Look at this."

Nakagawa walked over to the dining room table and saw a pen and a blank sheet of paper with a wedding ring placed on it. "No words, just the ring as punctuation. Should I bag it?"

"No, leave it where it is. But get a photo."

Nakagawa worked his way through the bedroom as Kikuchi watched. "Clothes all neatly put away, except for a few days of dirty clothing in the hamper. Luggage is still here."

"As if he stepped out and he'll be back any minute," mused Kikuchi.

"He's married, so where are her clothes? And there's no makeup or anything in the bathroom."

"She's in America. She's supposed to fly over within the next couple of days. But look at that empty section of the closet." Kikuchi checked the dresser. "Two of these upper drawers are empty too. He wasn't alone until recently."

"I'll make a note to ask during interviews at the company."

Kikuchi checked the boxes in the closet. He handed Nakagawa a sketchbook and looked through the unmarked manila envelopes that were with it.

Nakagawa leafed through the sketchbook. "If he did these, he's extraordinary."

"Anything useful?"

"Looks like it's all sketches of the same girl, but I see no names or notes anywhere. These cityscape backgrounds look maybe like Tokyo. They're old though. Look at the cars in this one."

Kikuchi chuckled. "Ancient. That was my first car."

"What's in the envelopes?"

"Letters, in English, all from the same Japanese woman; see the handwriting? Thin paper, airmail, but no envelopes, only the letters. Hopefully there's a name or address somewhere. Bag them and we'll take them with us."

"Yes, sir."

They made their way out of the apartment, double-checking things as they went. As Nakagawa sealed the door, the local officer asked, "Is it good or bad that you're out that fast?"

Kikuchi frowned. "In this case, bad. We've got his phone, a day planner with only a few notes, and a notebook PC, which could have clues, but we'll have to crack his password first."

Nakagawa picked up the evidence bag and turned to the landlord. "Do you know whether he had a bicycle?"

"A bicycle?" She thought briefly. "No, he didn't."

Kikuchi told her, "Do not allow anyone into the apartment, and please call us immediately if anyone comes by."

"I will."

He told the local officer, "Check the building every day. Also, your officers should finish their canvass of the neighborhood today. You have enough copies of his picture?"

"Yes, sir."

After polite thanks and bowing all around, the detectives got into their car. The local officer and the landlord waited until the car started to move and everyone gave one final bow.

Nakagawa drove along silently. Kikuchi's disappointment was obvious. Would McDonald's make him feel better? Kikuchi loved their french fries. It was not quite noon, but interviews at the company would likely take the entire afternoon.

Suddenly Kikuchi blurted out, "A bicycle?"

"I thought it was another way to get out of town."

"Then why didn't you ask whether he had a boat?"

"I'm sorry. I will next time."

Kikuchi looked askance at him.

Nakagawa continued in mock solemnity: "Or scads of helium balloons."

"Impudent kid."

Nakagawa smiled. They drove on in silence for a minute before he quietly said, "Rollerblades."

"Oh, shut up."

32

KELLY PHONED DAVID EVERY HALF HOUR AFTER PAUL'S CALL, BUT THE intervals shortened until she was looking at the clock every five minutes for permission to try again. She jumped out of her chair when she finally got through—only to discover after a long conversation in frightfully poor English that a detective had David's phone.

Kelly hung up, leaned back in her chair, and stared at the phone. The few times she had called after returning to America, David never picked up. She assumed he was too angry to talk. At first, she was relieved. She did not want another fight, and until David was ready to listen to reason and consider putting an end to that hopeless project, there was nothing to talk about. Her greatest fear was that he would ask her to come back to Japan. What point would there have been in that? She was useless to him there. It was weird after feeling his need all too desperately in the weeks of daily talks before she could join him there. She tried her best to shore up his confidence and make him feel her tenderness, too far away, but the project was a total snafu. In her six weeks in Japan, she had not been able to brighten a single day. Besides, Melissa's baby, their first grandchild, was due in early September.

Still, going this long without contact wasn't like David at all; he could get angry, but he didn't stay that way. He had been acting strangely, though. She had never seen him that consumed by anything, except his art.

In the last weeks before I left Japan, he was awfully down, though. It was similar to his mood twelve years ago when he'd been diagnosed with depression. He was on medication for two years to pull out of that.

Could he be depressed again? He was awfully self-absorbed, even selfish. He wasn't like that normally. Should I have found him a doctor instead of leaving? Oh, what have I done?

She drew her legs up into the chair and hugged her knees. If she had recognized the signs, she would never have left.

No, I shouldn't have left, regardless.

She got up from her desk, walked over to the long wall of windows in her office in their Portland home, and looked out at the neighboring field and the hills in the distance. She gathered her long hair and mindlessly twisted it.

David had been healthy for years, though. Plus, if it was a full-blown relapse, he would have been bedridden before she ever left; the project was a disaster from the start.

So, what is this, David being petulant?

Kelly turned away from the window and looked at the large self-portrait of David on the opposite wall.

He's probably cooling off somewhere. That would explain him leaving his phone, so no one could contact him. Not telling anyone he was leaving was dumb, but dumb was not out of character if he was upset. He was brilliant, but such a scatterbrain, as distractible as a butterfly, flitting from one brightly colored flower to the next—especially with his art, inspiration demanding that he dab away at one painting or another, or worse yet, make another canvas. He finished most of them, eventually—and they were wonderful—but how many boxes of unfinished paintings were there in the basement?

Still, perhaps her worries about his career at Micron were overblown.

Turning back to the window, Kelly scowled at the murder of crows lined up on the backyard fence.

No, he had gotten as far as a technical expert could go, and it showed. He was slowing down, losing his motivation, being that butterfly again. Besides, plenty of times he had wondered aloud to her whether line management would offer more sense of accomplishment. If only they had kept him in America, it would have worked out perfectly, but they had to give him a foreign assignment—and Japan, of all places.

Kelly took a Diet Pepsi from the tiny refrigerator in the office but paused as she was about to open it. After a long look, she put it back and headed for the old refrigerator in the garage where they stashed the regular Pepsi. She opened a bottle, watched the wispy fog curl up out of the top, and leaning back on the fridge, she guzzled the sweet cola until her eyes teared up. Catching her breath, she took another drink and stared at David's Acura roadster. She stepped over to it, opened the door, slipped into the driver's seat, and set the Pepsi bottle on the garage floor. She took hold of the steering wheel but had to point her toes to touch the pedals. A deep breath was disappointing: it smelled like a car, not him. Twisting her hair again, she hung her head.

David came home for lunch unexpectedly on Kelly's last day in Japan. She hadn't planned to leave, but with the blowup that afternoon, there was no way she could stay.

She hung her head and said softly, "No, David, that's enough. I don't want to hear anymore. I hate it here. I've had it."

David said, "All you do is complain. As much as I loathe that chip, I hate coming home to you even more."

"I can't stand this. I've told you what to do with that chip; you don't listen to a word. But this is so much bigger. It's our whole relationship here in Japan. I'm sick of it."

Seemingly unable to contain his anger, he strode back and forth. "You're burying me. You know it and you do it anyway."

"You buried yourself! The whole joint venture with Fujitsu was going down the drain from the start. It couldn't have been managed any worse. On the Richter scale of project screwups, this is a ten. Maybe eleven! Even *you* can't make a project like this recover!"

David was seething. "You're not helping. You never have. I've gotten nothing from you since the day you arrived. You might as well have stayed jet-lagged these whole six weeks—or never have come. I'd rather be alone."

Kelly threw her head back and let out a single guffaw. "You know how long I've been here? That's a surprise! If you want help, then let me! Why don't you look for another job? I'm powerless here. There's no way I can help. It's a lost cause. Has been from before you ever arrived."

"I needed you and you abandoned me!"

She tried to make him see: "And you didn't abandon me? We've been a couple here? When? Tell me one day we've done anything together like a married couple. With this chip in your head, there's no room for me."

"You abandoned me before you even got here. We were supposed to come to Japan together! But heaven forbid one of your clients might miss you for a week or two."

Kelly gave up in disgust. "I'm leaving. I'm just—I'm leaving! You—you make me so angry! I can't live with it. I'm out of here." Kelly went into the bedroom and opened the closet where they kept their luggage. "We should get out of this mess; just go back to America. Why can't you recognize there is no fixing it?"

David just yelled, "You bail on me when my project doesn't pan out."

She pulled a dresser drawer, it stuck, she jerked it harder, and it popped out, dumping T-shirts on the floor. She glared at David. "That's ridiculous. You wanted this! And I didn't choose this project. Why didn't you refuse it?"

"I wish I could ever count on you."

Kelly was beside herself. "I hate you! I hate this whole situation!"

"So you're leaving, even though you know I can't—

"I'm done with this fight! It's over!" she yelled with finality.

David glowered at her, then turned and stormed out of the apartment.

Now Kelly thought, *David was sinking, and I may well have pushed him the rest of the way under!*

Leaving was supposed to be a statement: the project was wrong-headed, and she couldn't sit by and watch. Without her there to stabilize David, though, what if his ridiculous need to succeed dissolved, and facing failure, he caved in?

What a mean, stupid move, and what an utter disaster! If I'm such a loyal wife, why didn't I consider his feelings more? I should have known that leaving would backfire.

So was David off gallivanting around Japan? When he got back, there would be unimaginable trouble. *He never was much good at seeing consequences.*

But I am. So why didn't I see this? How could I have been so cold when I left? I never treated David like that before. What was it about Japan?

Curled up in the little red NSX roadster, David's Japanese lover, Kelly thought of their last ride before he left for Japan, her heart in her throat as he took corners at twice the speed limit. She remembered the garage door closing, the beauty of his eyes as he gazed at her, and the gentleness of his touch in the dark.

Where would David have chosen as a hideaway in America? As she considered it, her hair now twisted into a taut brunette rope, a vague, ominous fear stole up behind her. In all the troubles David had faced in their twenty-seven years together, she could not remember a single time when stress drove him to escape out of town.

33

"REESE HAS NO PLACES HE LIKES TO GO, NO HOBBIES, NO FRIENDS?" asked Detective Nakagawa.

"No anything. Just work and his wife," answered Itō.

"You knew his wife left?"

"Not until after he disappeared."

The veteran Detective Kikuchi asked, "Would you say he's doing a good job?"

"As well as can be expected under the circumstances."

The detectives looked at him quizzically.

"The project was in trouble before he ever arrived. He's done an outstanding job of figuring out what's wrong. Unfortunately, the problems are systemic. It needs a total redesign, but the Americans won't consider it. They've been pressing him to fix it but tying his hands. And he doesn't have the political skills to cut through it."

"Pressure. Heavy?" asked Kikuchi.

"Very."

"Unbearable?"

"I don't know; depends on the person."

"And Reese? Can he bear a lot?"

Itō was quiet. "No," he finally said. "He isn't weak, he bore up reasonably well, but I think everyone could see him wearing down. And not all the pressure was real. He thought we were angry that he couldn't get the American side to cooperate, and it's true he could've handled things better, but his boss is impossible. Someone with connections could've worked around him, but David's new. It's just an unfortunate situation."

"Feeling such pressure, could he have done something rash?"

"Such as?"

"Oh, for example, run away or kill himself."

Itō thought about it. "He left early sometimes, maybe once a week, but after two or three hours he'd be back. So running away . . . unlikely, but possible, I guess. Killing himself? I never saw him that despondent. But the last few weeks he didn't have the same energy. He was being crushed."

"Who's running things with him gone?"

"His boss, Paul Salazar, who's here now from America. You talk to him next, I think. We would've contacted you a week sooner, but Paul insisted everything was fine. It was weird; he seemed almost relieved that David wasn't here. But it doesn't matter who's in charge at this point; we need to scrap the chip and that decision may be in the works. Anyway, I've been trying to explain to Paul why the chip can't be fixed, but he keeps talking about moving the project to India."

"India?"

Itō nodded, then shook his head in disgust.

———

"I didn't really like the idea of using David for the project, but he was all I had. I guess I should've spent more time over here, but I had no idea he was that unstable. Mentally, I mean."

Paul smiled as Kikuchi waited for the translation. The company arranged to have a translator, but Kikuchi hated how it slowed things down and threw off his rhythm. "Unstable?"

"Obviously. I mean, he ruins the project and then disappears, leaving everyone else to pick up the bag."

"He did a poor job?"

"Disaster's more like it. I arrived last week hoping to make up the slack, but he's shot this thing in the foot and everywhere else. The guy looked fine on paper. We'd just hired him, and people were saying, 'Give him a chance.' But he was totally unrealistic, constantly complaining, trying to blame other people for his failures. He wasn't a team player, and like the Japanese, at Star Micro, we're huge believers in teamwork."

"Where do you think he might be?"

"Now that's the question, isn't it?"

Kikuchi didn't wait for the translation. "Yes, that's the question. You have answer?"

Paul looked taken aback. "Of course not. I've got no idea. A loser who misrepresents himself like that could do almost anything. Of course, I hope he's not hurt or anything. My guess is he's out on a long drunk somewhere."

After working through a translator with Paul, Kikuchi was relieved to discover that Leon could speak passable Japanese.

"We've heard the project has problems."

"Whatever you heard, make it two or three times or more."

"That bad?"

"Yes, yes, and the problems were before David. They are not his. To fix things, we must write software. David is very good, it is his specialty, but there are so many problems. So the software has gotten very big, too big for the chip's memory. So it has to run in cycles, in pieces, so it is slow, much too slow. The only solution is to redesign the whole chip. But Paul, you just talked to, will not allow it. The chip is a lost cause and David knew it. He was trying to tell executives—"

"People would've been in trouble?" interrupted Nakagawa.

"Yes."

"Serious enough to lose their jobs, ruin their careers?"

"Probably."

"Who would've feared such revelations?"

"More than anyone, Paul."

"Anyone in Japan?"

"No, no, David protected people here. He is not always so organized, and he is too much of an engineer and not enough of a manager. He fixes problems himself instead of having the team fix them, but he takes pressure on himself to protect his people. He felt so much pressure all the time. He even told me he feels pressure from us, disappointment and blame. I told him no, we support him, but as the weeks went by, he looked more and more tired."

Kikuchi asked Leon a confirming question: "So, the only one who might have felt threatened did not arrive in Japan until after Reese disappeared."

"Yes."

Kikuchi took over again from there. "Did he drink?"

"Never."

"People say you knew him best. You're sure? Never?"

"I have never seen him drink alcohol. And at home: no beer, wine, nothing. He drank grapefruit juice."

"Where did he like to go?"

"Nowhere. He had no time. I would call with questions in the night, on weekends; he was always here or at home. And he did not talk about going anywhere. He does not even have a camera. Can you believe it? He goes abroad without a camera?"

Kikuchi smiled. "Hard to believe for Japanese, isn't it?"

Leon nodded.

"Would you say he was depressed?"

Leon didn't know that word, but the translator helped out.

Leon smiled and said, "He missed his car."

Kikuchi gave him a serious look.

"Sorry, no." But then he stopped and thought about it. "Perhaps. Kelly, his wife, left that Friday, the last day he was seen. He got home, and she said take her to the station, she is leaving. After that, I talked to him on the phone. He sounded . . . tired, I think."

"He had a good marriage?"

"I think so. He did not talk so much about it. I met Kelly many times. She always had a happy voice and said good things to him, but he told me she was not as happy as she seemed. She was bored and could not adjust to life here. She wanted David to go back to America. He was excited when she was coming to Japan, but she was so miserable that soon he was very sad."

"Is it possible he became suicidal when she left?"

"Suicide? David? I do not want to think that. The David I first met in April? No, he could not. The David I talked to after his wife left? I don't know, but I don't think so."

"Anything else to add?"

"Please say nothing, but I told him long ago he should quit."

"Why didn't he?"

"I don't know. I never understood that."

THE SUN HAD SET and the last light was nearly gone before the detectives finished the interviews and expressed their thanks to the managing director of the company. They did all but the first few separately, so as Kikuchi dropped himself into the passenger's seat, he asked Nakagawa, "Did you learn anything helpful?"

Nakagawa sat in the driver's seat, stretching his neck as he looked through his notes. "Not a thing. I got confirmation of things we heard together from Itō, Takahara and the top Americans—not so much Paul Salazar—but they all agreed Reese is a wonderfully pleasant person, everyone likes him, all that."

"What about suicide?"

"A couple of people said he got more subdued over the last month, and he wasn't the same the last few days, but no one was prepared to say he was that far gone."

"Understandable. Who wants to admit they saw someone slipping away? Did they confirm he never drank?"

"Yes, no one could remember him ever taking a drink."

"Same results from the Americans, but no one said he looked sad, just 'Nice guy,' 'Smart guy,' 'Nice guy,' 'We're so worried.'"

"Oh, the secretary! She wondered whether he's an alcoholic."

"Why?"

"Every time people went out, he'd order fruit juice or ginger ale or something like that. So, looking back on it, she thought he might be alcoholic because recovering alcoholics never drink."

"Did he say he used to drink or he quit?"

"No, it was just that he never drank. She said he seemed blue at the end and wondered whether he might be lying drunk in a park somewhere. She seemed quite concerned."

Kikuchi rubbed his forehead. "Not drinking doesn't mean someone's an alcoholic. It's probably a medical condition, or his religion, or he just doesn't like the stuff."

"Yes, sir, I know."

Kikuchi cocked his head to the side and looked over at the young detective, but it wasn't worth any more discussion.

"Oh, she told me one other thing, though it's not much."

"He loves *sushi*, so he might have signed on to a tuna boat?"

Nakagawa smiled. "No, sir, it might actually be useful. When I asked about women, female callers and such, she remembered that his first day here he asked her to find someone, an old friend from college."

"A woman?"

"Yes, but don't get your hopes up. She thinks the family name might have been Kawashima, but isn't sure, and she couldn't remember the first name at all."

"She didn't find her?"

"He didn't mention it again, so she never looked."

"You're right; it's not much." Kikuchi sighed and rubbed his forehead again. "Okay, he's not at home or work and no one can suggest any other place to look. So, first thing in the morning, you take the train stations. In this town they should remember a foreigner, especially one with a beard. And have the station masters send us copies of all the security camera tapes since he disappeared. Have them rush the first three days. I'll work the buses and taxi companies."

"What about his bank and credit cards?"

"Probably waiting for us. I put in the request this morning."

34

DAVID COULD NOT SEE THE CLOCK, BUT HE KNEW MONDAY MUST have given way to Tuesday. Shōko was long asleep in the bed above him, and in the solitary darkness of his imagination, David found Kelly sitting on the floor, leaning on Shōko's bed.

"I came to Japan for you—

"Two months late," interrupted David.

"But I came. So why didn't you treat me better? The chip was a goner from day one; more hours would hardly save it."

"Fuji-Star was—

"A black hole, and all you could do was stare at the nothingness as it ripped you apart."

"I would have made it up to you."

"When? Week after week alone. Any bit of intimacy—finding a good restaurant together, anything—would have done it for me. You had all of Japan you could have shown me. In my six weeks here, we never even took a weekend trip to Tokyo or Kyoto."

Why had he been so wrapped up in himself here? Having fun, that's what he would have done with the girl who followed his class around the museum week after week. Kelly swept him right off his feet; not that he was hard to sweep. She was different from his other friends, the only person he knew back then who was grounded. She was realistic, uncomplicated, and imperturbable, when his other friends were so tied in knots, they couldn't decide what paints to use. It was more than that, though. She was in motion; and too exhilarated merely to watch, he wanted to go along. Mostly it was a fantastic journey too, until Japan.

David waited through the first weeks in Japan with anticipation, but then Kelly pushed back her trip by a week, then two more days, then ten, and more. When she finally arrived after two months, the project had him strung so tight he could have snapped over anything. All it took was Kelly sleeping through three days of jet lag; by the time she was awake, the edge to his excitement was gone. Though he couldn't believe he'd been that easily frustrated, in less than a month, her frustration outstripped his. She was ready to pull the plug, and over breakfast one morning, organizational conflict being her consulting specialty, she tried an intervention:

"A reasonable professional stuck in an unreasonable position looks for another job. Everyone knows it's easier to find a job when you still have one, and the way Paul is acting, either he'll fire you or the project will fail and they'll fire you all. So call everyone you know and find a highly probable landing spot, either permanent or temporary. Talk to the same people about a consulting gig too. And call Jim, and perhaps Marci and Ravi, and see whether you can get a visiting professorship for a year."

"Kelly—"

"David, I'm serious! Once you have options, call Paul. Tell him he's put you in a situation where success is highly unlikely and if he wants you to fix it, then you require three things. Pick the three biggest stumbling blocks; more than three and he'll forget. Tell him the solution requires those things and either he gives you the resources and authority to fix it or you're leaving; you didn't build the ship and you feel no obligation to go down with it. Make it clear empty promises won't keep you on board. If he fires you or doesn't give you what you need, so what? You keep telling me it's going to fail."

"Kelly, there's so much more to it than—"

"No, there isn't and you know it! Or fine, if you want to try to work through it, then use the Japanese programmers' culture against them:

work them sixteen hours a day, seven days a week; and real work, not hanging out in restaurants until all hours. If you can't crack the whip, then find a lieutenant who can do all that macho Japanese shouting. Be imperious and intimidate them into compliance. In the short term, intimidation is an effective technique. You're senior here, so act like it!"

That was where he walked out. He could never do something like that. She should have known better than to even suggest it.

And if he had never taken that walk weeks before, never run into Shōko again, how would Kelly's counsel have sounded then? And how did he fray things to where she would even consider such advice? That wasn't the Kelly he married. Perhaps life with him poisoned her.

Was the poison her resentment, though, or his? How different would things have been if he had never stopped painting? It was not the sole stress with Kelly, but he always resented it. The bitterness was unfounded, though. He was the one who stopped painting. It wasn't as if she demanded it. At her urging, he gave up painting as a career, and later he acceded and stopped painting nudes, but if she had asked him to give up painting altogether—

I never would have, and so she never demanded. She was more subtle.

David set his jaw hard even as he sighed. So, if she were here today, would he announce that he would paint anything he chose?

At that moment, though, he could see Kelly's face as if she were lying next to him, wounded, dismayed, the sorrow all too real. To confess his resentment and smudge out the smile of the woman he loved so desperately: was painting that important?

David pressed his arm to his eyes as he remembered walking into the apartment that Friday eleven days ago. Uncharacteristically, he had gone home for lunch. When he arrived, Kelly was on the phone. David heard her say with what sounded like exasperation, "Just tell him he'll hear from my attorney. End it. No conversation required," before she hung up the phone.

"What was that?" asked David.

Kelly glared at the phone. "Nothing." Then under her breath he thought he heard her say, "Or nothing you need to know about yet."

"Tell me."

She sighed and let her head drop back as she closed her eyes. "Oh, David, haven't we fought enough? I hate what we've become. I've had it with you."

"And I'm tired of these complaints. As much as I loathe that chip, some days I dread coming home."

She wheeled toward him, glaring. "I can't stand this. I've told you what you can do with that chip. But this is so much bigger. It's our whole relationship. I'm sick of it."

David began to pace in consternation. "You're burying me. You know I can't breathe, and you do it anyway."

"You buried yourself! The whole joint venture with Fujitsu is going down the drain. You couldn't have managed it any worse. On the Richter scale of your screwups, this is a ten. Maybe eleven! You'll never recover with this project."

David tried to keep his voice calm and measured despite his anger. "Why can't you help? I've gotten nothing from you these whole six weeks."

She laughed in derision. "You actually know how long I've been here? I'm in shock! And you want help? Why don't you simply quit like I told you? There's no way anyone can help. You've turned this into a lost cause."

He looked at the sofa. Sitting would be calmer, but he couldn't. "I needed you and you abandoned me!"

"And you didn't abandon *me*? What, we've been a couple? When? Tell me one day—one hour—we've acted like a married couple! With this chip in your head, there's no room for me!"

"You abandoned me before you ever arrived! We were supposed to come to Japan together!"

She shook her fists at him. "I'm leaving. I'm just—I'm leaving you! You make me so angry! I can't live with it. I'm done with you." Kelly stormed into the bedroom and pulled her suitcase out of the closet. "I'm getting out, back to America. Why can't you recognize there's no fixing us?"

David yelled after her. "You bail on me when things don't pan out."

She pulled a dresser drawer open, but too far, and it fell to the floor. She looked at David in rage. "You're ridiculous. I didn't choose your project. It's all your fault for not refusing it in the first place!"

"I wish I could have counted on you this whole time."

"I hate you! I hate this whole relationship!"

David growled in fury. "So you're leaving me, when you know I can't go on alone."

She screamed, "I don't care! I'm done with you! It's over!"

At that point, David walked out.

When he returned home that evening, though, he found Kelly waiting for him, bags packed.

"I'm ready to go. Will you give me a lift to the station?"

"You're really leaving?"

"I told you I was. What's the surprise?"

"Oh, no surprise. Just . . ."

She waited for an answer, but as he looked at her standing by her bags, he knew nothing he said would change her mind. And at that moment, he didn't want her to stay. He needed freedom from those eyes, that shone disappointment on him like floodlights of darkness, blotting out all warmth, filling his mind with oblivion. She was the one who fixed things, without fail. She was the one who held the universe together, who made his sun rise each day, who drew it across the sky. But she did not rescue him a single time in her six weeks in Japan. She could not fix him, and he hated her for it.

As he started the car that Friday, he looked over at her briefly, avoiding her eyes. He had always loved her long, slim legs; she walked with such grace and confidence; but he would never see those legs again, or those hands, or any part of her. He would never touch her, hold her, or hear her whisper his name in love. Nothing showed on his face, but inside, he rent his clothes and wailed. He was incorporeal, existing solely for her, a being of tender, desperate energy. But then he looked at her again, into her squelching eyes, and everything he was faded away, dissipated, leaving nothing more than static. He knew life would be impossible without her. She knew it, too, and she didn't care. He left her at the station without a word, just took her bags from the car, set them on the sidewalk, and drove away, never making eye contact again.

Back in the apartment, he stared at the river, within easy sight of the living room window, but with her lawyer's call—before her plane had even landed—his suicidal thoughts gained gravitas. Kelly and he had talked about suicide before, when they went to see the BASE jumpers at the bridge in Twin Falls. She brought it up: "How many people have ended it all from this bridge?"

"Yeah, but I wouldn't use the bridge. It's too dramatic. I'd just bind my hands and feet and use the river." Morbid as it was, they talked about it in some detail, how drowning brought brief panic, but then calm before the end.

So, late that Sunday morning, needing the pain to stop, he sat to write her a final farewell. He looked at the paper for hours before he took off his wedding ring, placed it on the paper, locked the door, and went to do what she had to have expected. Welcoming the coming rest, the nothingness, he was calm as he climbed the levee. When he saw the river running high and fast, though, he staggered at the reality of losing all the remaining years he should have spent with her. Grief pushed aside anger and even hopelessness, and he fell to the ground and cried.

Now in the blackness under the bed, David could see Kelly's eyes filled with disgust, and he started to sob. She didn't love him anymore. His companion and strength for half his life wanted nothing to do with him. He almost convulsed as he curled up, and his head and knees banged hard into the bed.

It was only a moment before he felt Shōko's hand gripping his shoulder, tugging. She pulled him onto the bed, lay him down, and held him from behind. He felt her breath warm on his neck. He lay there, silent, as the heat of her body spread down his back all the way to his thighs, melting the memories, then the pain, then him, until he disappeared into her.

SO "PEACHES AND CREAM" is supposed to be just cream poured over sliced peaches.

Shōko took another bite and closed her eyes. *Decadently rich.*

She wasn't sure what time it was, but she guessed three a.m. They were in the back of the garden behind the house, sitting in their pajamas on a bench by a gardenia tree, gazing at the quarter moon rising over the rooftop. Her parents' bedrooms were only a few meters away, so they ate in silence. Their only communication was her shoulder pressed softly into his arm and their thighs lying gently against each other like rolls of socks in a drawer.

As Shōko took another bite, she saw luminous eyes at the edge of the garden. She knew many of the cats that lived nearby, but not this one. She tossed it a slice of peach, but it scurried away.

So skittish. Like David? He didn't run, though; he was just... unhinged. Making a life with a man who wakes shaking and grief-stricken under the bed...

But how many times had she woken up screaming? And even if there was something medically wrong with David, he was depressed, not schizophrenic or psychotic or something. *It's not easy, but lots of people recover from that completely.*

Then what, though? Anyone could see he still loved his wife, even someone as lovestruck—

She winced.

But if he wants to stay...

THE MOON would take eight more days to wane. How many cycles had it made over his lifetime, waxing slice by slice, right to left, before the night retrieved them, leaving nothing but a hole in the drapery of stars? It wasn't even half a cycle since he followed Shōko home. Would he ever be able to leave her? She cared so deeply.

Did she love him, though? She was probably just being kind to a sick old friend. If she loved him, she would have said something, wouldn't she?

Perhaps. And would he stay?

Staying would mean leaving a lot behind.

But Shōko was too warm and close to count that cost now.

David moved his foot, so their calves also touched.

THE RICHNESS of the peaches, the scent of the gardenia blossoms, sweet and thick, and the warmth in Shōko's entire leg, now spreading into her stomach and back—she looked up and tried to just focus on the moon. Westerners said there was a face in the moon, but all she could see was the rabbit that her father showed her when she was little.

Anyway, who cares whether David's a little shaky mentally? Not me. And who cares whether he's married—or whether I'm married?

Maybe me.

Later, though, not tonight.

35

SHŌKO GLANCED BACK OVER HER SHOULDER AND SAW DAVID SITTING on the bed, turned away as he was each morning while she changed out of her pajamas. That first morning, eight days ago, when he was too dispirited to move, she was already undressed before she realized he might be watching her. She instinctively covered herself and looked at the bed, but she couldn't see his face, so even if he was looking, he couldn't see much past her knees.

When she came home from work that first day, though, she had faced the problem again. The idea of changing in front of David made her blanch, but running off to the spare room would only show she was uncomfortable having him there. At the thought of him on the levee, she decided not to cover up. It was shockingly improper, but if she acted at ease with him, maybe he would come out from under the bed. Besides, he wasn't going to look. Still, Shōko had kept her back turned. She also averted her eyes if she had to face his direction: if he was looking, eye contact would only humiliate them both.

That first evening, too sick to leave his hiding place, David had turned away. The next morning, though, he was near the edge of the bed and could see much more than her knees. She had felt his eyes on her as she began to unbutton her pajamas. She stopped, got out the clothes she would need, and looked at the door. But she thought again of what he might do to himself if he left. She turned away, took a deep breath, took off her pajamas, laid them over the back of the chair, and dressed. Even with her back to him, though, it had been horrible. Always demure, she had not even let her husbands watch.

That was the one time, as far as she knew, that he ever peeked. Still, she supposed preparation and speed made things easier for them both. Talking also helped defuse the tension, so this morning as she laid her pajamas on the chair, seeing the sketchbook on the table, she asked, "Why did you stop painting?"

No sooner were the words out than she stopped dead. *What an asinine question. I'm more aware of people's feelings than that!*

The moment dragged on as she stood there, nearly naked.

It's being undressed: it makes me stupid!

She finally picked up her bra and slipped it over her arms.

Say something, David, even the simplest answer. I don't need anything elaborate; I just need—she fumbled with her bra—*my bra hooked!*

"It was taking a lot of time."

Shōko let out a sigh as she reached back for her blouse.

Wait—*that's no reason to stop painting.* "A lot of time?"

"That's what she said."

"*Ā, sō ka?*"

"I did spend a lot of time on it. I was more a painter than an engineer in the early years. I suppose I spent more time on the job, but in my mind, I was a painter. She was right about that."

"So you stopped?" She was facing him now, watching for any sign she had upset his delicate equilibrium. Realizing she was still just holding her blouse, Shōko slipped an arm in.

"At the end, I was doing abstracts—and landscapes, some—not what I really wanted to paint."

She slipped her other arm into the blouse. "What did you really wanted to paint?"

She reached for the first button, her shirt still hanging open. Seeing movement, she glanced up—

David had stood and was looking directly at her.

Shōko stood absolutely still, fingers frozen, cognition fled. She felt naked, as if standing in her underwear, blouse open, in the middle of Shibuya Crossing with the pedestrian light about to turn green. It felt like hundreds of people on every corner were looking at her, with thousands more watching on the giant screens above.

Shōko, still frozen in full blush, stared back at David as she saw him break eye contact and look at her body—a single, eternal second—before he gazed again at her face.

She opened her mouth, but it was seconds more before, voice quavering, she said, "You wanted ... ?"

David didn't reply. He smiled shyly, walked to the window, and looked out. Shōko watched him, fingers still trembling on the same button, wondering what to say, what to do—until, finally, she realized she should button her blouse.

36

KELLY LOOKED AT HER UNPACKED SUITCASE AND THE AIRLINE TICKET lying next to it on the bed. She had gasped when the travel agent told her how much a next-day, open-ended trip to Japan would cost, but she would have paid any price to find David.

Kelly looked at the painting that hung on the bedroom wall, their daughter Melissa holding her baby brother Ben. Gazing at that painting always brought such peace.

So where could he be?

She walked into the library-office and went through the old sketchbooks for the ones from David's time in Japan. She didn't know the last time she had looked at any of them, but she remembered seeing sketches of old farmhouses.

David always talked of Japan as such an extraordinary place. Kelly suspected the girl he knew, whatever her name was, had a lot to do with it. David said it hadn't developed into anything, but Kelly always knew there was more to it than David would admit. His reverence for the culture and esteem for the people suggested something significant happened to him there. Just mention Japan and his whole mood changed.

A Japan sketchbook! Kelly took it out and checked the next one, and the next, all numbered, thirteen, except number twelve was missing. She sat on the sofa and looked through the first one. It started with cityscapes, doubtless Tokyo, mostly rough, but lots of finished ones, a few stunningly good. Did David ever show her these? There were people, temples, Tokyo at night, a girl . . . lots of sketches of a girl, but no notes on the backs like the other finished sketches. She checked the other books until she found rural sketches: mountains, rice fields, farmhouses, people . . . that same girl.

Kelly started over, caressing the edges of the pages as she leafed through the books.

Why doesn't he draw anymore? And when did he stop?

Book thirteen ended with more sketches of the girl, intimate, sitting on a bed, holding a cat, the last one with Chinese characters—and a note on the back: "Shōko relaxes on our last day."

Shōko, with a little line over the first *o*.

At least she has clothes on.

37

AS THE AFTERNOON BAKED, SHŌKO WISHED SHE WERE ANYWHERE but her sweaty office. All day, look something up, write a note, answer the phone—if she lost her concentration for the briefest moment, the heat dragged her back to the bedroom where she stood, mostly undressed, dying, as David looked at her. Yet she longed to be there, comforted by his presence, reassured that he was not lying broken under her bed.

Now as she closed her eyes and wiped her neck with a terrycloth handkerchief, David's stare replayed itself yet again. She squirmed in her chair, for this time, deeper than that morning's distress, she had a yearning to be touched she had not felt since—

Eyes still closed, she pressed the handkerchief to her blushing face as the scene burst upon her. She was twenty-two years old, sitting on her bed in her college apartment, jeans off, shirt undone, and though not completely open, it was obvious she had nothing on underneath. Even more than seeing it, though, she could feel it, the mortification as she held Yuki in her lap, wishing Yuki were bigger, enough that Yuki's soft white fur could cover her—for sitting on her roommate's bed, sketching her and Yuki, was David.

It was David's last day in Japan before returning to America. After lunch, when Shōko asked what he would like to do, he said he just wanted to be with her, someplace quiet where they could talk. Her roommate was at work, so she took him to her apartment. They held hands almost all the way there. She sat on the bed with Yuki and David sat on the other bed and sketched her. They talked and laughed as he drew, and when he showed her the finished sketch, she teased him about how badly he drew the *kanji* for her name. He was embarrassed, surprisingly so, and she was sorry. She suggested that he do a second sketch—but when he told her what he wanted, she was dumbstruck. Lying on her stomach would be relatively modest for a nude, but there was no way! Yet she wanted desperately to please him. She couldn't undress, though, not all the way.

David started to explain that he needed something intimate to capture their feelings, but Shōko put her fingers to his lips to stop him. Why did he have to say everything? She looked up at him, and finally he seemed to understand something without words, though he looked as if he might reach out and unbutton her shirt. So she put her hands on his waist and turned him around until she was ready.

Shōko had never experienced anything erotic before, and even without being naked, it was painful from beginning to end. It was not just the embarrassment of being undressed with a man for the first time, but the awful confusion of being so excited by it. There was a tingling that wouldn't stop and the constant wish that David would come closer. It terrified her. It would have been impossible without Yuki-*chan*. The softness of her fur somehow made it bearable. It was not until much later that she remembered more subtle feelings from that day that had been drowned in the embarrassment and the heat. Even after two marriages, it remained the most intimate experience of her life. Underneath the racing heartbeat and the wild, tangled thoughts was a profound calm; not that she was supposed to be undressed—she never felt that—but that she was meant to be with David, to play out this scene countless times over a whole lifetime—

The blush left her as Shōko opened her eyes and stared dumbfounded at her desk. How could she have been oblivious to it all these years? How had she never recognized the gravity of that day in all she had experienced and become? *That second sketch!*—that surprised her ever after by showing none of the inferno that nearly consumed her; that David tore carefully from the sketchbook and gave to her; that she laid away, treasured all these years in the box under her bed—their intimacy as he sketched her that day remade her. Those two hours on the bed, almost totally undressed, being adored by him, feeling as if they were touching even when he was sitting across the room: she spent most of the last thirty years alone because she never felt that again.

It took David one afternoon to change her life completely.

Shōko wiped the sweat from her neck.

What would he do to her this time?

38

DETECTIVE KIKUCHI TOOK A SEAT NEXT TO THE YOUNGER NAKAGAWA IN the video room and said, "The interviews are all finished, and no one remembers seeing him or any other foreigner. How many hours of tape have you gotten through?"

"It's almost all digital files now, not videotape."

Kikuchi frowned at him.

"Sorry, sir. Hours . . . the whole team? At regular speed . . . maybe six hundred? I hate to imagine how long this would take if we couldn't speed up the video."

"And if you were looking for someone who blended in."

"We're done with the first three days he was missing, all the key places where there wasn't a clerk, driver, or anyone else who would have seen him. The rest could take weeks."

"The likelihood you'll see him after day three is low. We can work on the rest when there are no other leads."

"We have other leads?"

"No."

Nakagawa slumped back in his chair. "Did they find anything in the letters from his apartment?"

"They're still reading. They go from 1973 to 1981, well over a hundred, all in English, and long too. Yet there's nothing specific enough to identify her: names are all first names; trips and events, like high school graduation, always have key information missing; even the signatures: just an *S*. She's local, though. She mentioned places here in town and the autumn festival. And there are things in with the letters: a protection amulet from a local shrine, and photos—a girl, a cat, things like that—with local backgrounds. Other things aren't local, though: photos in Tokyo and Kyoto, cherry blossoms pressed in a pamphlet from a Wyeth exhibition at one of the big Tokyo museums—"

"Wyeth?"

Kikuchi looked at him with a mix of disdain and sympathy. "You've never been to a museum, have you?"

"I went to the Manga Museum in Kyoto."

Kikuchi shook his head and Nakagawa smiled. "What if we check the pictures against old school yearbooks?"

"Interesting idea," said Kikuchi. "I wish we had a picture of her in a uniform, so we'd know which school. We could start with the local ones, though, and others that were the most popular back then. That's probably twenty or so. Still, picking her out won't be easy. The pictures with the letters aren't clear at all, none are closeups, and they're all big smiles, not the somber shots in yearbooks. You can make out her hairstyle best of all; it looks like Miki from the Candies, but back then every girl had her hair cut like the Candies."

"You're sure it's the Candies, not Pink Lady?"

Kikuchi scowled. "They were cute."

"Sorry, sir."

"And Pink Lady was later."

Nakagawa laughed out loud.

"Anyway, even if we focus on *S* names, that's a huge number of girls. But the woman who's working through the college-era letters said it's obvious she loved him."

"You think she's the one he asked his secretary to find?"

"I'd put money on it."

Nakagawa was quiet for a few seconds before he asked, "Do you think it might be worthwhile to canvass the entertainment district, hostess bars and such?"

"Do places in Yūrakuchō even allow foreigners? Besides, everyone except that secretary who suspected he was alcoholic agreed he didn't drink."

"Yes, but I thought it might be worth it to take a couple of officers and just show his picture around."

"I'm sure you did. When did you want to do it?"

Nakagawa shrugged. "Soon. Maybe even tonight."

"Whatever. Before you and your friends are too drunk to see straight, get the high school picture search organized."

39

DAVID WAS IN THE NATIONAL GALLERY OF ART IN WASHINGTON, DC, but it made no sense. This was a museum field trip for the class he taught at Cooper Union after he returned from Amsterdam, but that was in New York City, not Washington. And while this room should have held the National Gallery's collection, all the paintings were from other museums. There were works by John Steuart Curry and Thomas Hart Benton that he was certain belonged at the Whitney, a Grant Wood that should have been at Reynolda House, and the half dozen by Andrew Wyeth had been collected by an apparel manufacturer in Japan.

A crowd of young people had gathered around David, but none were students he recognized. He had to start, though, because there was no ceiling or roof, and dark gray clouds threatened to drench the entire gallery. So he walked them over to the painting by Grant Wood. He explained how his representational style contrasted with the period's growing abstractionism and that Wood was part of a regionalist trend in American painting at the time, his subjects taken from the Iowa countryside that was his home and—

David's attention was suddenly consumed with a gorgeous young woman at the back of the group, and the students began to fade and disappear. David stared at her, sure she was not a student, and sure they had never met. At the same time, he knew they were about to meet, because they first met in a museum when she followed his group as he discussed early twentieth-century American painters.

"Where's American Gothic *on display?" asked a girl in front taking copious notes.*

"It's on permanent display at the Art Institute of Chica—"

More of the class faded to nothing.

"So, isn't it odd that Wood caricatured a farm couple if this was his whole world?"

"It's been said the woman is not the farmer's wife, but his spinster daughter, and the original is a sympathetic portrayal. You lose a lot in a reproduction, like the lively green stripes in his shirt, the delicate flower pattern of her smock, and her cameo."

Students disappeared, fading away, second by second as David spoke. "The painting was controversial, though. Many thought it was a parody. But look at all of Wood's work; this landscape, for example, where you see farms laid out over softly rounded hills like blocks in a patchwork quilt. He respected and loved the people of Iowa; their lifestyles, work, and crafts."

The girl in front, the only student left, was writing furiously, paper spooling from her hand to fill the floor below. "A father and—"

The beautiful girl stepped up to take the last student's place, with the father and daughter from American Gothic *now standing stoically behind her, dressed as Polonius and Ophelia.*

"And now will I evaporate?" David asked.

"Would you like to?" she responded with a coy smile.

"Not just yet."

But suddenly she looked serious, older too, and the pair from the painting were dressed all in white. "You wanted to disappear a week ago," Kelly said.

"You left me."

"I had to."

"Why?"

"I told you before I left."

"Tell me again."

"There isn't time. It's morning."

"But—"

"Shh. Not everyone leaves. Shōko never will, no matter what she might say. Now open your eyes."

David let the shivers of his dream pass. He often woke at first light in Japan. Now, as he had each morning since he started drawing, he put his feet against the wall and pushed himself out from under the bed, taking pains not to touch it for fear he might wake Shōko. The *futon* slid out with him, so he pushed it back into place. It was too early yet to put it away and be up for the day.

David got his sketchbook and charcoal pencils and sat next to the bed, close to her face. Was it proper to do something while she slept that would otherwise discomfit her so? She would only be uneasy, though. She would not complain that it was wrong per se, so if he could do it without the discomfort, it must be all right. It didn't matter, though: right or wrong, he had to capture the moment.

It was a charcoal sketch of Shōko's face, from the middle of her forehead to her chin. He did a light compositional sketch in graphite, then took a soft charcoal pencil and outlined her major features, all effortless, as if the light from her face shone into his eyes and flowed through him and out of his hand onto the paper.

David was shading her eyes, putting roundness into her eyelids, capturing the gentle arc of her eyebrows, when he realized he was no longer drawing. It sometimes happened when he concentrated on her in the quiet: he drowned in her. How he longed to do this in paint! He imagined the subtle olives of her skin overpainted in beiges and browns and pinks, with blues and deep greens and purples in the shadows. He would paint her shy, but alluring—or better yet, asleep, where her innocence and sensuality coexisted altogether naturally. The lighting ... dawn, perhaps kissed by the first sunlight, although that would require a different room.

Gazing at Shōko so serene, overcome with her grace, David's thoughts slowed and stopped, leaving only the urge to lean closer.

When just days ago I wanted to disappear?

It had only been a dream, all the students disappearing, but the thought sobered him.

David busied himself again with blending the shading of her eyes. After final work with a highlight pencil, he put away the sketchbook. Then he touched his finger ever so lightly to Shōko's lips before he slid back under the bed. Perhaps he could sleep a little more before the alarm forced her awake and out the door, leaving him alone again.

40

ŌBUCHI, THE DETECTIVES' SUPERVISOR, GOT TO DAVID'S CASE TOWARD the end of the morning assembly. "Kikuchi, where are we on the missing foreigner?"

"Still no solid leads. No evidence of foul play at his apartment. His car was there. So was his phone. No activity on his credit card or cash card. We should receive activity reports on his American credit cards today. The neighborhood canvass yielded nothing. We've checked train stations, buses, taxis, hotels, hospitals; even Yūrakuchō." Kikuchi glanced at Nakagawa, who shook his head, bleary-eyed. "No one remembers seeing him, and he wasn't on any security camera recordings for his first three days missing."

"Drugs?"

"No one ever even saw him take a drink. And no beer, wine, or liquor in the apartment. Not even a corkscrew."

"Mistress?"

"Nothing to suggest it. No unusual calls at work or on his phone, and the handset logs match the phone company's; he wasn't deleting calls or messages to hide anything. No unusual credit card activity before he disappeared, no emails, no rumors."

"Suicide?"

"Possible. Coworkers said he was under considerable stress and a few said he was not handling it well, although no one was willing to say he seemed suicidal. His wife left him and went back to America. That was the last day anyone saw him. And in the apartment"—he paused—"we found his wedding ring on the table on top of a blank piece of paper."

There was a scattering of ominous sighs before Ōbuchi spoke and everyone was silent: "Anything else?"

"He talked to his secretary about locating an old college friend from here. She thinks the last name could have been Kawashima. She told him it would be difficult, and he never mentioned it again. But we found years of letters from a local girl, first initial *S*, and some pictures. We're gathering yearbooks from high schools to find a match. We also wondered whether it might be worthwhile canvassing everyone with a *Kawa* or *Shima* family name who has lived in the area for over twenty years, with special attention paid to *S* names."

Ōbuchi waited for any comments before he said, "That's hundreds of households, possibly thousands."

"If we cover not only longtime residents, but all those with a woman over fifty, yes, probably thousands."

Ōbuchi waited again. "Very well, I'll get the *kōban* officers started on it. Thank you. Next case. . . ."

41

DAVID GATHERED THE BRUSHES AND PAINTING KNIVES AND PUT THEM in a jar of water, but his hands were a mess. Shōko thought it was too dangerous for him to be downstairs cleaning brushes, so she cleaned them that first morning he'd painted, the day before yesterday. Since then, he let the brushes soak and she cleaned them at night. He could use rags to get most of the paint off his hands, but he dreaded getting paint on any of Shōko's things. Besides, he would only need a few minutes to scrub his hands and refill the jar, so he stole down the stairs to the bathroom.

The arrangement was typical for Japan. The toilet was in a tiny room with a small sink. A separate room nearby had a larger sink with the family's toothbrushes and such, and a washing machine. Through a door from that room was the bath. Since it was Shōko who did the laundry and everyone bathed at night, David felt secure as he closed the door to the bath and quickly washed.

Climbing the stairs, though, David heard noises from the second floor.

Shōko's mother? Did she get up there that fast, or was she already upstairs when I came down? How does she move so quietly?

No matter, he needed to hide. As he reached the bottom of the stairs and turned toward the bathroom, though, he saw the door at the end of the hall opening: *her father!*

He glanced at the kitchen—*far too dangerous*—before he jumped into the *genkan* and hurried out the front door. He couldn't just stand barefoot outside the door with a jar of paintbrushes, though, so he scampered around the side of the house and parked himself behind a big bush.

FEELING IN PARTICULARLY good spirits, Shōko's mother headed upstairs to satisfy herself that all was well in the house. She checked the storage room first, making sure nothing was mildewing in the summer heat. She opened Shōko's door and was irked that Shōko left her air conditioner on again, but when she went in to turn it off, she found Shōko's easel—and a painting!

When did Shōko start painting again? And why didn't she say anything? It's quite a change of style from her old paintings, but even unfinished, it's beautiful!

Shōko's mother heard a call from downstairs. She headed for the stairs, but the front door slid closed just as she was starting down. She got down the stairs as quickly as she could, slipped on sandals in the *genkan*, opened the door, and called out, "Yes!"

The police officer, who had mounted his bicycle and was about to ride away, bowed and hurried back to the door. "Please excuse the intrusion, Kawasaki-*san*. I'm Murakami, from the *kōban*."

"Oh, Officer Murakami! You are always so helpful to us."

"No, no, we just try to do our duty. Have you had any more trouble with your daughter's husband?"

"Come in, Officer Murakami. Come inside and I'll get you a cool drink."

"Thank you, not today. No more trouble from Ōta-*san*?"

"No. I thought maybe I saw him last week, but I don't see well anymore. He called last month and screamed that he's paying taxes for Shōko and if he's paying for her, he has the right to know where she is. He said her duty is to return home at once and we are the worst people in the world and so many ugly things. We still worry he might do something crazy. He has caused us such terrible trouble and we're sorry we've had to call you so many times."

"Please do not hesitate. That's what we're here for."

"Thank you so much."

"I have another question—"

"Oh, did you find out whether we can do anything about her credit card?"

"I talked with your daughter about it a few weeks ago. She has already canceled the card, and I'm afraid that Ōta-*san* did not do anything illegal when he ran her credit account up to the limit. He is still legally her husband, and he had a card for the account. She can contact a lawyer, but it's unlikely anything can be done."

"Oh no. That's terrible!"

"Yes. So unfortunate. Excuse me, but there's another reason I came today."

"Oh?"

"There is a missing foreigner." He showed her a picture. "We're trying to find anyone who might know something. He had a friend in college from here and he might have tried to contact her. They think her last name was Kawashima and her first name started with an *S*. We're checking similar names too. She would be about the same age as Shōko-*san*. Did she have any foreign friends in college?"

"Shōko? Foreign friends?" She thought for a few seconds. "She had an American pen pal. He came to Japan when she was in college. But no foreigner has called the house. I'm sure she hasn't been out socializing. With all the threats from her husband, she spends her evenings here at home."

"I see. Perhaps you could ask her when she returns tonight."

"Certainly."

"Thank you very much."

"Thank you, Officer Murakami. You are such a help to us."

"As you are to us, Kawasaki-*san*. Good day."

"Take care. Good day."

DAVID WAS admiring the blossoms on the enormous hydrangea bush that hid him from view. Hydrangeas had been in bloom for nearly a month. David never saw them growing wild before and was amazed in Japan to find them covering riverbanks and even vacant lots. He saw every color from baby blue to deep purple, but these lacecap blooms were such a startling electric blue he almost wondered whether they glowed in the dark.

He was about to try going back inside when he heard someone arrive on a bicycle, so he sat silently. A minute later, it sounded like the visitor was about to leave, but then David heard Shōko's mother call out to him. He waited, unable to hear well, waiting for something that sounded like end-of-conversation tones. Finally, they were saying goodbye, and as he heard the bicycle move, he peeked out.

A police officer. More trouble with Shōko's husband?

David watched him ride away before he picked up the jar, moved quickly to the front door, and quietly slid it open. He didn't hear anything, so he hurried inside. He was afraid he might leave footprints, but getting out of sight was more important than a little dirt. Still, he stopped for a moment on the stairs, looked back, and sighed in relief that he had not dirtied the floor.

As he turned to dart up the stairs, though, he saw that Shōko's door was open. He proceeded carefully, afraid that Shōko's mother was in the room. As he peeked in, he saw her sitting at the table with her back to the door, looking at the painting. David slipped over to the other side of the doorway so he could escape into the spare room when she got up to leave, but she just sat there, so he stepped into the spare room to wait.

David sat by the door, basking in Shōko's mother's appreciation. He thought of works that brought him admiration, even acclaim, and one in particular, although the recognition was private. Melissa was six and Ben was one. He could remember her face as she delighted in the finished painting, a dreamy, soft tempera of her holding her sleeping baby brother, caressing his face. She saw it take shape, so it wasn't a surprise, but somehow the idea that it was finished had her bubbling over with glee: "I like it, Daddy. No, no, Daddy, I *love* it!"

"I'm glad, sweetheart. That's the way I see the two of you."

She smiled even bigger and started bouncing. "Can we show Mommy now?"

"Yes, kiddo, we can. Why don't you go get her?"

She tore out of the room yelling, "Happy birthday, Mommy!"

David hurriedly tidied up and began wiping his hands. The painting was a gift for Kelly, and for six weeks he had banned her from the studio. It took marathon sessions to get it done in time, but Melissa was a trooper, wanting it done for Mommy's birthday as much as David.

He heard them coming, Melissa running ahead, then back to Kelly, then ahead, back and forth, as Kelly was obviously moving too slowly. He laughed out loud and turned to greet his wife as she stepped into the room—and stopped in her tracks, her mouth hanging open. That was what he lived for! It was as if she had sparked a white-hot sun inside his chest. She was holding little Ben, barely asleep, and she finally bent over and gave him to Melissa. As she raised her hands to her face, the tears poured out. She tried to speak but gave up. A few minutes later, she tried again but "Oh, David . . ." was all she could get out.

He stood wiping his hands, proud and profoundly touched for having struck her dumb.

"David, it's . . ."

He walked over to her and she was about to hug him, but he stopped her and stripped off his smock. She grabbed it from him, tossed it aside, and held him tight.

Now, alone in the spare room, he could almost feel her as he had so many years ago, pressed to his chest, his elbows holding her close as he kept his paint-stained hands away from her clothes. "Oh, Kelly . . . ," David whispered, before he bit his lip and leaned his head against the wall.

SHŌKO SLID the front door open. "*Tadaima!*"

"*O-kaeri-nasai!*" called out her mother with more excitement than usual. She shuffled out to the *genkan*. "Shōko!"

Shōko smiled back at her beaming mother. "*Okāsan*, did something happen?"

"You never told me you started painting again!"

"Painting?"

"It's beautiful!"

Shōko's hands closed tighter on the grocery bags. She glanced up at the door to her room. "I'm so glad you like—"

"I do! When did you start again?"

This is painful! I hate lying! And how did David avoid being seen?

Shōko blinked. "I . . . did not paint it."

"*E?*"

"A close friend did it."

"So, your friend was painting here?"

I need to end this! "Was painting it out on the levee. You recognize the scene, right? Isn't it fun to catch up with an old friend? Anyway, was in a hurry today and this was a close place to let it dry, so . . ." Not a lie per se, but Shōko felt a sting in the back of her neck and had to force herself not to look away.

"Ah, I see. I guess that's why there weren't any paintbrushes in your room. Yes, of course. I'm glad you could meet your friend. Please introduce me when she comes to get the painting."

Shōko murmured in agreement, smiled, and turned toward the kitchen.

"Oh, Shōko . . ."

"Yes?"

Her mother was silent for a few seconds. "There was something I was supposed to ask you." More silence. "Oh, I hate being old. I'm sure I'll remember later."

"Tell me when you do."

When Shōko checked under the bed, she laughed. David had the blanket in front of himself in case her mother came back.

"Don't worry, it is safe now."

"Hi," he said as he slid out.

Shōko stood and looked at the painting, letting her admiration show. "It gets better each day. I am proud of you."

David smiled, then turned away from her toward the painting.

Were those few words too much? But he needed to hear them. "How many more days to finish?"

Still turned away, David shrugged and held up two fingers.

He would regain control soon enough. Maybe she could help, though: "*Okāsan* told me she likes your painting so much."

David nodded. "She looked at it for a long time today."

"Where were you?"

"Downstairs washing my hands."

Shōko laughed. "She wanted me to be the artist, but I said it is my friend's. She wants to meet you, but only one problem."

"Oh? Only one?"

"Yes. She thinks you are a girl. I must find very tall dress." She covered her mouth with her hand as she laughed.

42

DETECTIVES KIKUCHI AND NAKAGAWA LEANED FORWARD WITH THEIR elbows on the counter, quietly talking, waiting for their *ramen*.

"Do you think we're close to finishing?" asked Nakagawa.

"Soon, but there's more we should do. And the wife hasn't even arrived yet."

"What do you think the chances are we'll find him?"

"I don't know. Pick a number close to zero."

"You think he killed himself."

"He comes to Japan, trouble at work, wife leaves him, despondent, suicide."

"All very possible. . . ."

"What? Say it."

"It's just that . . . Americans aren't as willing to kill themselves as Japanese."

"Hmm. . . . Is that true?"

"I read that the suicide rate in America is half of Japan's."

"Hmm."

The cook put two large bowls on the shelf that separated the kitchen from the counter where the detectives sat. Nakagawa took Kikuchi's *ramen* and placed it in front of him, then reached up and got his own. Each broke apart his disposable chopsticks, said, *"Itadakimasu,"* and started slurping the noodles.

After a minute, Kikuchi said, "Not killing themselves, that's true for business failure, family shame, and such. But mental illness—some cases of severe depression—can kill anybody, even people who think suicide will send them to burn in hell forever, like Christians. My wife was Christian and one of her church friends killed herself."

"I suppose so."

It was a few more minutes before Nakagawa said, "Of course, I can see how it could be suicide. . . ."

"But . . . ?"

"Where's the body? There has to be a body someplace, doesn't there? Even if it was in a spot no one would look, the smell should've prompted a call days ago."

"So he either did it someplace else, or the body was moved."

"You think someone might have moved his body?"

"Not some*one* as much as some*thing*."

"The river?"

Kikuchi nodded.

Nakagawa looked down at his bowl.

"But . . . ?" asked Kikuchi again.

"I'm sorry, sir. If he used the river, then he drowns, he sinks, he bloats, he floats, right? Shouldn't someone have noticed a corpse bobbing in the water by now?"

"Not if the body was carried all the way to the ocean. With all this rain, the river's been high. And an ebbing tide could've taken him right out to sea. He's been eaten by now for all we know."

"For someone who doesn't like coincidences, things would have to be perfect for—"

"No, depending on the conditions, it can take a body a long time to float up to the surface. He could be trapped under a rock or log or tangled in weeds."

They were nearly finished before Nakagawa spoke again. "I was just thinking. . . ."

"What?"

"Rather than the river, what if he's in the mountains?"

Kikuchi gave him a dubious look.

"Hanging from a tree or something."

"Unlikely. That's very Japanese. Americans are scared of hanging. No, they often use pills, although they don't do research beforehand, so most of them fail. But they have all sorts of ways of succeeding that you rarely see here. They shut the garage with the car running, or jump off a building, or get in a shootout with police."

"A shootout?"

"I read it in a novel. Guy can't pull the trigger himself, so he gets into an armed standoff with police and starts firing so the police have no choice but to shoot him."

"So willing to push problems onto other people."

"As this has been pushed onto us. Stupid American, why didn't he just get on a plane and go home? Anyway, if he's in the mountains, we could search for weeks and never find him. Someone said he liked to take walks on the levee path. With nothing else to go on, that points to the river."

"I see." Nakagawa waited a few seconds. "Should we canvass the areas close to the river in case anyone saw him?"

"We've done everything else. It's a logical next step. Another task for the *kōban* officers, I suppose."

"Oh, I've gotten word back from every *kōban* about the Kawashima canvass. Nothing."

"Everything with this case turns into nothing. Have we been able to match S to any high school pictures?"

"Pictures from the local high schools came this afternoon. They'll start checking them in the morning."

Nakagawa looked as if he wanted to say something more, so Kikuchi asked, "Any other thoughts?"

"Okay, odd idea, but could someone have taken him in? I mean, do you think he could be staying with someone?"

"Like a stray cat?"

"Not a real possibility, is it?"

Kikuchi didn't respond. He just stayed quiet until it was clear everything had been said. "Hey, thanks for telling me about this place. Great *rāmen*."

"I'm happy you enjoyed it."

They stood, called out, "*Gochisō-san!*" and walked to the register to pay their bills.

43

KELLY GOT NO SLEEP DURING THE ELEVEN-HOUR FLIGHT FROM PORTLAND. Her anxiety must have shown, too, because after snaking through the lines at immigration and finally picking up her single bag, they took her aside for a thorough customs screening. As she stepped through the security doors into Narita Airport's bustling arrivals lobby, her clothes rumpled and her hair twisted into a tight spiral over one shoulder, the reality of her return to Japan settled onto her, oppressive and sticky. She felt none of the anticipation or relief that everyone else exuded. The airport, the lights, the people: everything looked gray. And she had hours left to go.

She asked for directions to the Japan Railway ticket office. There she bought tickets for the Narita Express to Tokyo and the Shinkansen and local trains that would take her back to a city she had hoped never to see again. She exchanged dollars for yen, rented a phone, and finally made her way down the escalators to the train platforms on the basement level.

Kelly frowned when she saw that the few seats on the platform were all occupied.

How long is this trip going to take?

If only I could sleep.

44

IT WAS TIME FOR BED, BUT NEITHER SHŌKO NOR DAVID WAS READY to sleep. So, with the lights off, David sketched a tree framed by the west-facing window, illuminated by the garden lights.

"Shōko, what kind of tree is this?"

"*Kaki.*"

"And what's that?"

"In English? I don't know. Small orange fruit in the fall."

"Oranges?"

"No, that is *orenji.*" She got her electronic dictionary from the table. "Pe·ru·shi·mon."

"Per what?"

"Pershi— Oh, you are bad! *Kaki!*"

David laughed. "Sorry, I like the way it sounds. Say it again: 'persimmon.'"

"*Kaki.*"

He laughed again. "I don't think I've ever eaten a *kaki.*"

"Never? They are tasty. Dried too. But not ripe until fall, so you must wait."

"I'd love that," said David as he continued sketching.

Shōko gazed at him. He could not imagine how beautiful it would be when the first snows piled up on the dark branches. The whole scene would become a study in black and white, save for the few bright orange *kaki*, too high in the tree to pick, that would still cling stubbornly to the branches.

Long before the snows or even the autumn leaves, though, David would have to face life and all the trouble he was in head-on—wife, job, everything—and Shōko was not at all sure he could handle it. He seemed happy and capable when she was here, but he was not well, just dependent, and she had no idea how long it might take for him to stand alone.

45

EXPECTING TO STAY AT THE APARTMENT, KELLY WAS SURPRISED WHEN she arrived at almost midnight to find it sealed with police tape. There was also a sticker over the lock. She knew better than to tear it off even if she couldn't read it. Exhausted, she rested her head on the door for a minute, summoning the energy to make the day one step longer. She sat on the doorstep, opened her suitcase, and changed into her running shoes.

The taxi was already gone, and she did not know how to phone for another, so she decided to wheel her suitcase the two blocks to a major street and wait for one to drive along. Everything except bars and restaurants had been closed for hours, but taxis would be hunting people to ferry home from their evening socializing. After a few minutes with few cars and no taxis, though, Kelly looked up and down the street: no restaurants or bars, so no taxis. She sighed slowly and deeply. There was a 7-Eleven convenience store half a block away. It would be odd to ask the staff to make a phone call for her, but at midnight, streets deserted, it wasn't as if they would have anything else to do.

"*Irasshaimase!*" called out the man behind the counter as the automatic door slid open. Turning around, though, he seemed shocked to see a foreigner dragging her suitcase behind her. When she approached the counter, he looked nervous.

Do I look that dreadful?

Then she realized he was probably just afraid of having to speak English with her. He greeted her with an anxious smile. "*Irasshaimase. Ētto . . . Nihongo wa . . . ?*"

Kelly smiled and spoke slowly, "I need a cab to a hotel. Can you help me?"

He looked at her as if she were from Mars. As he stared at her, Kelly saw the tension building until, crossing his arms in an *X* and shaking his head, he said, "English, no, no."

So English is a no-no. Sorry, guy, truly, but that's my only option. I'm afraid you'll have to cooperate. She gave him her most reassuring smile, bent down slightly to make herself shorter, and approached it one phrase at a time, slower, louder, and without articles. "I · need · cab."

Again, Martian.

"I · go · hotel." She cocked her head to the side and put her hands under her head, palms together, in what she hoped was the universal sign for sleep.

"*Hoteru? Hoteru ni ikun desu ka?*"

"Yes, *hoteru!*" Understanding achieved! "You · call · cab?"

"*Yūkōkyā-tte nan darō . . . ?*" he said to himself, still staring at her, eyes wide.

She searched for another word. "Taxi?" She held her fists out and moved them as if steering a car. "Taxi?"

"*Takushī desu ka? Hoteru e no takushī?*" Then he added in thickly accented almost-English, "You go *hoteru, takushī?*"

"Yes, *hai*, please. Thank you."

The taxi soon arrived, and Kelly fell instantly asleep in the back seat. She was disoriented when the driver woke her at a hotel across the street from the train station she had left almost an hour before. The whole trip had been one big circle.

46

SHŌKO LAY IN BED LISTENING TO THE CRICKETS OUTSIDE. THEY WERE loud, though, so she got up, closed the window, and turned on the air conditioner. As she lay down again, she could hear David's breathing. It was so much slower than hers that it pulled back on her, stilling her. It made it no easier to sleep but was comforting nonetheless, affirming that she was not alone.

She got up, retrieved another pillow from the closet, not for her head but to hold, as she used to hold Yuki when she couldn't sleep, and sat at the table. She picked up a sketchbook and thumbed forward from the back.

There was the *kaki* tree; what a complicated drawing. And herself sleeping. When? The one when she woke up Sunday morning was in pastels. This was charcoal, and just her face. The shading made her look . . . soft. It was beautiful.

She turned the page and found another picture of herself sleeping, this time the whole bed. She was lying on her back, her arm up over her head. Next, she was sleeping on her stomach, then a closeup of her sleeping face. She leafed through it faster. How many of her sleeping? Every one? Not quite, but almost.

She checked random pages. *When did he do these? Does he draw all through the night?* She imagined David sketching her as she slept. If it were anyone else, it would have been creepy, but she could not help smiling tenderly at the thought of David watching over her.

There was another sketchbook on the table. She recognized the first drawing: her feet tucked under the chair. *Five days ago.* Next was her reading, the garden, her room, then sketches of her on the bed, and finally her sleeping. He must have done these first, before he started the other sketchbook.

She sat on the bed, opened the curtains to get more light and leafed through the two books in chronological order. It was not until midway through the second sketchbook, though, that it dawned on her what happened when she was dressing yesterday morning and she asked David what he wanted to paint. When he stood and gazed on her as if he was seeing right through her scant clothing; as he took in her face, his eyes so earnest, then glanced down at her body and back to her face—that look, punctuated with a shy, tender smile before he looked away—that was his answer.

IV

If Only We Had Fur

毛皮があったなら

47

DAVID WAS USED TO THE MORNING ROUTINE. HE WOULD HEAR THE
alarm and Shōko turning it off. If he wasn't facing out, he would roll over,
not wanting to miss the sight of her feet landing silent as two tiny pillows
on the floor. She would sit while gravity drained the sleep out of her, then
head downstairs to make breakfast. Meanwhile, thoughts of her would
swaddle him warm and close, and he would slip back into sleep until she
returned.

Today, though, there were no post-alarm feet. David slid out from
under the bed and stood. Shōko lay on her back, arms spread on either
side, breathing deeply. He gazed at the graceful curve from her forehead
to her nose, the gentle arc where her neck met her shoulder, and the curl
of her fingers holding a dream as she slept. He thought how much she
deserved this rest. It was a Thursday morning, though, and she had to go
to work, so he sat close by her and gently stroked her hair.

She turned to him, eyes half-open, and smiled. He continued playing
with her hair, and after a minute, she stretched and looked at him as if
she had something important to say.

"*Nē . . . ,*" she began.

"*Nani?*"

"Oh, your Japanese is so good!" she said, half teasing. "*Nē*, why do you
paint landscape and abstract mostly?"

"You mean why not bowls of fruit and stuff?" He brushed her hair
away from her face with his finger. "Maybe I don't like bowls of fruit and
stuff."

"You like bowls of peaches." She smiled.

"Mm-hmm, I do."

"No, I ask why you don't paint people?"

"I dunno." He tucked her hair behind her ear. "Because I haven't got a model?"

"If that is all you need, I could be a model."

David sat back for a moment, then put his hand on the pillow, leaned closer, and took in her face. Shōko was smiling softly when he began, but as the seconds went by her smile disappeared and her chin crinkled up. Finally, he asked, "How much of you would I get to paint?"

Shōko kept her worried face for a few seconds before she replied, "Maybe an ear."

He pursed his lips and nodded. "Tempting, but I'd rather paint all of you."

"Both ears?"

"Toes too."

She looked into his eyes with a contentment that made him blush. He turned away and scanned the room. "We have a problem, though. The room's too small."

She turned her head and looked across the room.

"Say you're sitting on the bed. You know the other side of the room isn't far enough to see all of you at a glance. Even if it was, I'd need another few meters to stand back and take in both you and the canvas from a distance."

"*Sō ne.*"

"I'd love to capture you right here in this room, though. It has a lot of..." He looked around the room again. "After these last few days, it's..." David smiled before he bit his lip, still looking away.

"Maybe this room is big enough to paint not all of me."

After a few seconds, he looked at her eyes again. "True."

"You will need more paints, I think. I can buy paints and a small canvas today."

"I don't know the names of the colors I'll need; I haven't bought any for so long. We could check on the Internet, though."

Shōko frowned. "I don't have a computer. I had one at home before, but..." She was quiet for a few moments. "But this is not last chance for more paints. A store is close to my office. I will ask for the Liquitex color chart today."

"Actually . . . I don't think acrylics are up to the task."

"Up to . . . ?"

"For this painting, oil would be better."

"But the smell!"

"There are odorless media to use for the underpainting, and after that, linseed oil, which isn't too strong."

"*Sō?*"

"To finish it quickly, though, instead of odorless I should use a quick-drying medium, and siccatives are smelly."

Shōko looked worried.

"We can open the windows if it gets to be too much for you. With two windows we should get a draft. And we can put the painting in the next room at night."

"But problem is parents, not me. They don't hear well, but noses are still . . . *nan te iu kana* . . . effective?"

"Oh, true, the smell will fill the whole house, even with the windows open."

"Acrylic is not good?"

"To make it you, to capture the luster of your skin, we need oils."

"But if they smell it!"

"Can you tell them you're painting?"

"I don't want to lie."

They looked at each other for a minute before Shōko said, "Maybe just a few days and then you can be happy to go to work again? We finish painting in weeks after that?"

"Go back to Fuji-Star?" David frowned. "I doubt I have a job to go back to. But if I recover as much in the next week as I have in the last one . . ." He paused. "Hey, can you say a friend is painting it?"

"They ask, 'Why here?'"

"And if your friend's painting you here, they'll want to meet me." David frowned again. "What's 'stuck' in Japanese?"

"*Komaru.*"

"We're really komaru-ed."

"No, say '*komatta*' and then '*nā*.'"

"*Komatta nā.*"

"*Sō ne.*"

Again, they were silent.

"Or maybe before you use oil paint you need time for . . . *te-narashi -tte* . . . train a hand?"

"Rehabilitation?"

"*Un.* Maybe first charcoal or watercolor."

"That's . . . a great idea, actually. I need to do a series of studies before I start the painting anyway."

"What do you use for those?"

"I think pastels. And last of all, one or two in oil."

"You need more pastels?"

"I do."

"I can pick up what you need," said Shōko as she sat up, eyes fairly sparkling in the morning light. "So what kind of painting do you think?"

"Well, if we do studies first and paint later, we could make it bigger. If we can eventually find a studio big enough to do the painting, that is."

"Your apartment maybe?"

David winced in spite of himself.

"Sorry."

"No, you're right. It would be perfect. The bedroom connects to the living room through big double doors. Open those and we'd have the width of the two rooms together as studio space."

"Are you ready to go maybe?"

David sat back for a while before he shook his head.

"Maybe in one week?"

He shrugged, but looking at her eyes, she deserved to smile, so he grinned and said, "Maybe sooner."

"So, for now, we do studies for more than a face?"

"Mm-hmm. I think I'd like to try something intimate."

"Like what?"

"You lying on the bed sleeping or something like that?"

Shōko gave him a single nod, as if it was exactly the answer she expected.

48

DAVID DID ROUGH COMPOSITIONAL DRAWINGS FOR MOST OF THE morning, looking back periodically at sketches from the last few days, and at one in particular. Shōko lay on her back, one arm over her head, the other having pulled off the covers. He felt her sultry and uninhibited, uncovering herself to the world, to life, to him. Yet she had an air of purity and innocence. It was as if she was wholly unaware of her tantalizing sexuality. (Given her age, though, he suspected she exuded less than his own desires projected).

As his ideas jelled, the sketches became larger and more detailed, with one pose he especially liked: Shōko curled up, an animal at rest. Next would come something rendered, however roughly, and David faced the question of what he would have her wear. A nude would be the most dramatic, though it would be difficult to keep the viewer from losing sight of her innocence. Still, the idea excited him, so he started on another sketch.

Nothing ignited David's artistic passion like the female form. In its proportions, flowing curves, inherent sensuality, and symbolic meaning, there was nothing as sublime. He could manipulate contour, texture, color, luminosity, softness, what the subject reveals and conceals, what she makes one feel; it was perfect. There were periods when he painted female figures almost exclusively, mostly nudes, but he had never done one of someone he knew this well; except Kelly, but they were married, so that was different.

He wasn't sure how different it had been for Kelly, though. Most of her nudes were in the first few years they were married. She was less willing to pose as time passed and stopped altogether when Melissa was six. What was so awful about being walked in on by a six-year-old? Mom sitting naked on a bed wasn't something Melissa normally saw, but it might have been a tender moment if Kelly hadn't screamed and made Melissa hysterical. There must have been more to Kelly's discomfort than that one incident, but she never posed nude again.

Apart from the first few, though, Kelly had always been uncomfortable; so much so that she was difficult to paint. He could feel the tension in his arm and hand, the motion of the brush less fluid. It was stultifying to create something less than it should have been. Kelly's was the most perfect form he had ever seen, though, so with time after each letdown he tried again. Early on, he still used other models, but as his day job demanded more of his time, it was difficult to arrange sitting times. Besides, even with her frustrating inhibition, Kelly moved him more than any other woman. At the end, she was his only nude model, until she refused.

David did more detailed sketches in charcoal of how he imagined Shōko might look nude, including one finely rendered, and by late morning he had her pose basically set. She was lying on her side, curled up in a way that was not overtly sexual, the sheet draped low over her hip and part of her legs. It was stunning, he had to admit as he propped the sketchbook up on the table and stood back to study it. What would Shōko think, though? They painted a nude together in a class when he was an exchange student. Their styles were different, but it was fascinating watching each other's visions appear on the canvases. Having done nudes, male and female, Shōko knew that capturing one in a painting was a completely objectifying process. Even with an acquaintance the painting became quite impersonal. Still, Shōko was the painter, not the one sitting there naked.

David had wondered before what the model must feel, but now he stood, looked at himself in the mirror, and imagined someone looking him over—and over and over and over.

Unpleasant, even dressed.

He turned around and looked.

Very unpleasant.

But if Shōko asked?

I'm not very tight skinned anymore. No "love handles," but I've seen guys my age take their shirts off in movies, and even for the best, it's sad.

Still, he knew he could never refuse her.

She could refuse him, though. The idea would surely shock her and might rattle her so deeply that their delicate balance would never recover. He would be out from under her bed, gone from her room, her house . . . her life?

No, she's an artist. I can broach the idea.

But what if she somehow agreed, and then the actual sitting turned out to be more embarrassing than she had imagined? What if she was stiff and tense, or worse, mortified like the day before yesterday when he looked at her while she was dressing? No, it was too dangerous.

Besides, he could hardly claim that his interest was purely artistic.

David fingered the corner of the next page in the sketchbook. He had always loved the feel of drawing paper: not smooth and flimsy like the paper in an office, but substantial, rough enough to have character.

So what do I have her wear?

49

KELLY AWOKE WHEN THE HOUSEKEEPING STAFF OPENED HER DOOR. She'd set the time for the alarm last night, but somehow failed to turn it on. Her appointment at the police station was half an hour ago! She took a two-minute shower, threw her suitcase on the bed, and pulled out a simple skirt and blouse. She ran one pair of nylons in her rush to get them on, so she was more careful with the next pair. Any makeup would have to go on in the taxi. She grabbed her purse and headed downstairs.

Thankfully, the hotel's people had better English than the guy at the convenience store last night, and they got her a taxi to the police station. When Kelly arrived, an hour late, a uniformed officer greeted her, bowing low. The officer asked whether she was Mrs. Reese, then expressed condolence and escorted her upstairs to a large room with an array of identical desks, all facing the front of the room. The officer bowed again, asked Kelly to wait and said something to a young woman in the front row. She hurried to the back of the room where there was a single desk behind all the others. She bowed to the man, said something, they both glanced over at Kelly, and then they bowed to each other. The woman hurried off to another desk as special-desk-man stood and picked up some papers. The bowing and glancing at Kelly were repeated by a man one row ahead of special-desk-man, and he was on his feet and headed in Kelly's direction.

The three of them arrived together and the two men bowed to Kelly. Desk-in-front-man spoke, "Good morning, Mrs. Reese. My name is Kikuchi. I am detective in charge your husband's case. This is Ōbuchi, supervisor of detectives."

Special-desk-man bowed. "Thank you for come today."

Kelly bowed mechanically, doing her best to match the form and depth of the bows she was receiving. She said, "I'm terribly sorry to be so tardy. I arrived late last night, and my alarm did not go off."

"Please come we talk," said Kikuchi, and he escorted Kelly to a glassed-in alcove on the side of the room. Once seated, Kikuchi expressed condolence with the same words the officer downstairs had used. She thanked him for his concern, and he explained the situation: the last trace of David, where they had searched, the lack of any evidence he left town, or was in town—the lack of evidence, period. It took over an hour, as Kelly often had to ask him to repeat things and he was constantly looking up words with his electronic dictionary. She wished there was someone with better English, or a translator, but it wasn't Tokyo and she assumed he was the best they had. Kelly told herself his skill as an investigator was more important than his English ability.

As the explanation droned on, though, Kelly grew apprehensive over how little they knew. They had proceeded logically enough, but she wasn't sure they were still looking. Her hands were on the table at the start. But she forced herself to relax them so many times she eventually gave up, put them in her lap, and just tried to keep the wringing motions from showing. Each bit of explanation knotted the muscles in her neck and shoulders tighter.

Finally, Kikuchi asked, "Do you know place your husband might be?"

"No, I don't. I wish I did. I would have told you."

"There is place he likes to go?"

"He's only been in Japan for three months. He knows no places to go, unless someone at Chip Star told him. We didn't go anyplace special while I was here."

Kikuchi looked puzzled. "Chip Star?"

"The company."

"Ah, Fujitsu-Star Microchips. Yes. But Fuji-Star person do not know where is your husband." He looked at his notes for a moment, then continued, "You leave your husband?"

"I left Japan two weeks ago, not David."

"Good marriage? He is happy?"

"Our relationship was strained lately, and no, he was not very happy. Neither was I. He was even less happy when I left."

"Your husband has depression you return to America?"

She did not respond except to frown.

"Some Fuji-Star person say he has bad emotional condition. It gets— got worse, very much. Then you return to America and he is gone."

"David was upset I left, but . . ."

"Bad depression?"

"What are you suggesting?"

"To say is bad thing, but please understand. He did not leave a city, but no one can see him in a city," said Kikuchi. He added in a grave voice, "Maybe because he is suicide."

"Impossible!"

Kikuchi looked at Ōbuchi, who had been sitting, arms crossed and stone-faced, through the entire meeting, but Ōbuchi did nothing more than raise an eyebrow.

"You said your marriage is stained."

Kelly almost corrected him, but "stained" was close enough. Besides, if she did, he would look it up in his electronic dictionary, whose batteries might give out any minute. "It hasn't been easy since David came to Japan."

"Your husband is away late in night?"

"Yes, David worked long hours."

"Maybe late night is not work?"

"Not work?"

Kikuchi looked uncomfortable. "Maybe he has a mistress?"

Kelly knew this must be a standard line of questioning, but it riled her, nonetheless. "You keep saying 'your husband,' as if he doesn't have a name. It's David. And no, he's not sleeping with another woman; he's not that kind of man."

As Kikuchi drew back, Kelly stopped herself. She looked down at her hands, red from all the rubbing, and laid them flat in her lap for a few seconds. She looked up and studied the peeling paint on the wall behind the supervisor of detectives. She was waiting for the looseness in her arms, legs, and especially her neck, the steely detachment she used in serious negotiations, but it wasn't coming. Nevertheless, she was able to calm down enough to tell Kikuchi, "I'm sorry to speak sharply. I know you don't know David, but please believe me, I do. So you can forget that whole line of questioning. He was not having an affair."

Should she say something more? But after a few seconds, Kikuchi said, "Your—*ētto* . . . David has college friend, Japanese woman?"

"He came as an exchange student in college, yes. There was a girl he was close to."

"She was from this city?"

"Excuse me?"

"Her name was Kawashima, and she was from this city?"

"I think her name was . . ." Kelly closed her eyes and tried to recall the sketch . . . a girl on a bed . . . but the name was gone. She sighed before she quietly said, "I don't remember."

Kikuchi frowned. "It started with *S*?"

"I think so."

"You know he asked the secretary to find her?"

"No, I didn't know that."

"When he comes to Japan, first day."

Kelly made no response.

"He does not talk about her?"

"No."

"You know he has many old letters from girl of *S* name?"

"Letters?"

"Yes."

After a few seconds, she asked, "May I see them?"

Kikuchi went to get them and returned with a stack of letters so thick that Kelly's eyes widened and her jaw went slack. She looked through them, hands trembling ever so slightly, as he continued, "Marriage is stained. He looks for old college friend, old girlfriend. You think affair?"

Though cowed by the letters, Kelly's eyes narrowed. "No, I do *not* think affair!"

"I see. . . ."

Kikuchi said something frustrated-sounding to Ōbuchi, and Ōbuchi sighed and said something back. Their speech was different from the hotel staff, guttural sounds that were more like grunts than words, almost monotone, their lips hardly moving. Kelly had no idea how anyone could understand it, but then Kikuchi closed the folder and gathered his papers, and she realized it was an end-of-interview discussion.

Ōbuchi said, "Thank you for come today," and stood.

"Excuse me, but I don't think we're done," said Kelly.

"Excuse me?" asked Kikuchi.

"I don't think we're done," she said again, slower. "I have questions."

"Oh yes, of course," Kikuchi said and looked at Ōbuchi, who sat back down.

"What are you doing now to find David?"

"Now we are looking, yes."

"Yes, but what are you doing, specifically?"

"Yes, what are we doing? We are looking at recordings from security camera many hours."

"Do you have anyone out looking for him? I mean, you said he must still be here in the city, right?"

Kikuchi looked bewildered, so Kelly repeated it more simply and slowly until he seemed to understand.

"Today, many officers talk to people near river. Your—David likes to walk on river path. We ask anyone to see him, ask all home and business. Show his picture. Ask people on path too."

"So the only place you're looking is on the path?"

"Yes, we are looking on the path."

"No place else?"

Kikuchi glanced at Ōbuchi, then sat back in his chair and bowed his head. When he finally looked at her again, Kelly read concern on his face and his voice was softer: "Mrs. Reese, David is missing. We know you are upset very much. Terrible thing. Very terrible and we feel you hurt very much."

Kelly stared at them, silent, desolate.

Kikuchi was quiet, as if gauging whether Kelly was ready to continue. "Mrs. Reese, if we have any place to look, we look. Any place. Please understand we look no other place, because we have no other place. David is gone and no clue. None. Without clue, we cannot look any place."

Kelly looked out through the glass at the large room. As frustrating as it was talking to Kikuchi, she wanted another question to ask. This was her sole task for the day, for the entire trip, her only part in the search for David. But there was nothing more to say.

Everyone sat in silence.

Finally, Ōbuchi spoke, "Mrs. Reese, where do you stay?"

"Washington Hotel. The apartment is sealed."

There was a short exchange in Japanese before Ōbuchi turned back to Kelly and said, "Detective Kikuchi drive you to apartment now. You stay. He call, morning, night, tell a situation. If you are worry, question, you call number," and he glanced at Kikuchi, who took out a piece of paper and wrote his name and phone numbers for her.

"Thank you," said Kelly as she searched her purse for the little courtesy pack of tissues the taxi driver gave her that morning. "May we get my suitcase from the hotel?"

Kikuchi answered, "Yes, of course," as he and Ōbuchi stood.

Kelly, looking at the pile of letters, was slower to rise. "May I take these with me?"

"No, now we use them anymore."

Kelly gave a slight nod, picked up her purse, and they stepped to the door. Before Kikuchi opened it, though, Kelly extended her hand to him. He took it loosely and started a handshake, but Kelly held his hand firmly and looked into his eyes until he returned her gaze. "Please," she said and her voice cracked so badly she had to whisper the rest: "Please, find David."

Kikuchi made as much of a bow as was possible with her standing so close, then looked into her eyes again. "Mrs. Reese, we do everything. If we do not find David, he cannot be found."

Kelly silently mouthed, "Thank you," and Kikuchi opened the door and led her to the front of the room, where there was a final round of bowing and polite farewells.

They were both quiet as Kikuchi drove her first to the hotel and then to the apartment. He took the seal off the door and after more bowing, left to tell the landlord that Kelly would be staying in the apartment.

Exhausted, Kelly slipped her shoes off in the entryway, the *"genkan"* David had called it, but before she did anything else, she searched the apartment for David; pointless, but she had to do it. Sadly, it took only seconds. She rolled her bag to the sweltering living room, turned on the air conditioner and collapsed on the sofa under its cool flow.

Lying there looking out the window at the hazy blue sky, she whispered, "David, David, what in the world have you done?"

She bounced her legs nervously.

I never should have gone home—

Kelly sat up board straight.

Home? Home was always wherever David was. Had she waited all those weeks before she could finally join him, but then somehow left her heart behind in Portland? She was excited about coming to Japan, though—not that she ever thought it was a good idea—but David was so enthusiastic that she couldn't help but get caught up in it. That excitement carried her through some difficult preparations. She temporarily had to shutter her thriving, one-person conflict management consulting practice. That meant rushing projects and getting all her clients to accept a "sabbatical" of up to six months. She and David also had to find trustworthy people to take care of the house and a hundred other things.

As it all fell into place, Kelly read about Japan and realized that she was embarking on an adventure. She could experience another culture as more than a tourist, get serious about running again, study a foreign language, possibly even write the book she was always promising herself. Most of all, though, she would have time with David. With Ben now gone to college, it was time they got closer again, and this would be the perfect chance. If David needed help with his project, she would be there for him. Or it might be relatively easy, and they could take a little time to play. Either way, they could return to America as if from a honeymoon.

It was not long, though, before her dream faded. Two of her consulting clients held her back, and the company sent David to Japan two weeks early. So, for seven weeks, their wonderful closeness turned out to be text chat and once-a-day video calls over the Internet, where she watched his excitement over the project evaporate after only two weeks. He was moody, irritable, and uninterested in any aspect of their normal lives. As frustration consumed him, she did her best to buoy him up, but he was too far away.

Kelly had never been away from David for that long, and she was never so lonely in her life—until she got to Japan. David was trapped in an irrational, almost maniacal obsession to keep his project going, even though he was the one who had proved—to everyone but Paul—that the chip was impossible to fix. So Kelly ended up sitting alone with nothing to do. David told her that foreigners in Japan don't hire personal translators. So she was deaf, dumb, illiterate, and trapped in an apartment barely bigger than her kitchen and family room back in Portland. She was unable to wander off the main streets for fear of getting lost in a city so drab that nothing stood out as a landmark. There was probably nothing to see anyway. She had never felt so miserable, useless, or neglected. She was shocked at her lack of motivation to do *anything*. She couldn't get out of bed, had no appetite, and had to train a mental shotgun on herself to complete even the smallest tasks. Normally, David would have been solicitous, but his ridiculous project was killing them both. So after a few weeks she wondered aloud if it might not be best for him to quit, but he refused to even consider it. Finally, chafed by her chains long enough, she packed her things and left.

He must have known the awful things I said weren't true, though. It was the frustration and isolation I hated, not him.

Still, after all that anger . . .

Kelly stamped her foot, stood, and glanced around the room for something to do. She checked the bedroom. It was clean, and the bed was neatly made—

But that's how I made it up the day I left. David never slept in it?

She opened the closet. It had not changed since she packed.

She pulled open the dresser drawers. Everything was exactly as she had left it, as if David never came home from the station.

She paced, her hands clenched.

I have to calm down.

She got a glass of water in the kitchen and sipped it as she walked into the dining room, where she saw a piece of paper on the table—

50

AS SOON AS IT WAS LUNCHTIME, SHŌKO GRABBED HER PURSE AND hurried the four blocks to Art World. The name made her laugh, because it was one of the smallest art supply stores she had ever seen. Still, they crammed an incredible inventory into their tiny space. There was a surprisingly wide variety of pastels, and she looked them over carefully before she chose the largest set they had, ninety Rembrandt soft sticks. Although it was a portrait assortment, she also looked at flesh tones in the store's open stock but ended up choosing only a few extra shades of white. She also got a box of three dozen hard pastel sticks and in rapid succession added a kneadable eraser, brushes, sponges and other blending tools, and a can of spray fixative.

David wanted a larger sketchbook, and on her way to get it, she stopped to peruse the oil paints. She knew what David meant this morning about oil paints and skin. The professor in her figure painting class in college taught them that oil paints dry to form a chemical structure like glass. Light penetrates even the most opaque upper layers and reflects the colors in the layers below. He showed them how veins can show through in oils as well as they do through real skin, and how different under-layer colors can change the whole feeling of the painting.

Setting her shopping basket down next to the register, Shōko was concerned that she might not have enough cash to buy it all. She counted, including what David gave her that morning when he emptied his wallet, but as the total grew on the register's display, she saw she would be short.

"Excuse me, it seems that—I'm terribly embarrassed—but I don't think I have enough cash."

"Oh, we accept credit cards."

She bowed her head as she sighed. *Masaru.*

"I'm afraid I'll have to go to an ATM. Could you hold these for me, and I'll pick them up on my way home this evening?"

Shōko stopped at the bank on her way back to her office. She already had one shop in mind to visit that evening, and after that and picking up the pastels, she wanted to get back home as quickly as possible.

51

AT THE SIGHT OF DAVID'S RING ON THE TABLE, KELLY DROPPED THE glass she was holding. It shattered on the wood floor, leaving her stranded, barefoot, and eyes too full of tears to see the shards. She wiped her eyes and wiped them again, before she gave up, crouched down, and just bawled. Wherever David had disappeared, he went without her. Even at his lowest points, he had never pushed her this far away.

But he'll come back.

He will.

Her tears dripped onto the floor.

It's a ring he left, not me.

Still the tears flowed. She stood, wiped her eyes again, and tipped her face toward the ceiling, but the tears were rolling toward her ears, so she looked down and let them fall.

What am I supposed to do now? I don't know how to find you; how to find anything in this country!

What could David have been thinking? Was he sick? Angry?

She knew she had to be patient. He would be back. Soon. She needed to stay cool somehow and not worry.

He has to know I love him. He can't be leaving me—

But she left him. If it hurt this much, no wonder he was angry enough to leave his ring behind.

But I didn't leave him, I left Japan. And he hasn't left me, he's left the apartment. I can't feel abandoned just because David took a little trip without telling me.

But he brought that Japanese woman's letters with him. What if he was with her?

Impossible. All he had in his head was that godforsaken chip.

But what if by leaving Japan Kelly knocked David just far enough off balance, made him just crazy enough, to travel to wherever his old girl-friend was?

And do what, go out to dinner with the woman and her husband, or meet her children, or grandchildren?

Kelly folded her arms in front of her and glowered out the window at Japan.

Action. I need to do something, even if I can't look for him.

There was a chair within reach, so Kelly pulled it closer and stepped up onto it. She could now reach a second chair, and she moved it toward the kitchen and stepped onto it. She moved the first chair, repeating the process, creating leapfrog-style stepping-stones, until she was free. She ended up stepping on a sliver of glass at the end, but her soles were leathery enough to take it.

Kelly swept up the broken glass, wiped the floor to make sure she got it all, and busied herself unpacking her suitcase. She was done in minutes, so she cleaned out the refrigerator.

She took out the garbage.

She spent a half hour in a hot shower.

As she was drying off, her phone rang. She answered tentatively, not knowing if it was the police, someone from Fuji-Star, or a call to her American phone number which she had just set up to ring through to Japan. "Hello."

"Kelly! I'm glad I caught you. This is Brett Westling of Hayes and Lethbridge—"

"I've told you that any communication should be with my lawyer."

"I have a new proposal."

"No! How many times have you called and how many times have I told you to work with my counsel? And how many times that the sale is final, finished—that it's *over*? Do I need to contact the bar association about you?"

"No, no need. I am sure your counsel will find the offer of interest. I'll contact her straightaway."

Kelly hung up the phone with an exasperated sigh. One month after they closed the sale of their home in Boise, the family who bought it exploded into a sudden and acrimonious divorce. Kelly had taken dozens of calls from Westling, the husband's lawyer, who was dreaming up endless schemes to negate the sale. Even though she had been telling him for weeks that she and David had a lawyer and all his contact should go through her, Westling still insisted on calling Kelly. Kelly was glad she had been the one to answer all his calls. The last thing David needed was news of problems with the Boise house. Besides, their lawyer assured Kelly that the contract was airtight. David would not need to know until the whole mess was over.

Kelly found herself staring out the window again. So she dressed in running clothes, grabbed her phone and keys, and headed out into the afternoon heat. Before long, she was on the levee path. It was her favorite place to run, but it felt different today. She kept looking for police as she ran along. She frowned that the police had to tell her this was David's favorite place to walk. She looked at things—the tiny stores in the neighborhoods next to the levee, the meandering river channels, all the engineering that went into its passage through town—and wondered what David thought when he saw those same things on his strolls.

Kelly also watched the people as she ran along—watched them watching her—and at a child's exclamation of surprise, she glowered again. *Letting her child point like that and not saying a thing about it, how rude! Don't Japanese mothers teach their children any manners? But the adults aren't much better. It's as if they've never seen a woman running. I get stares here running or not, though. If I'd stayed, perhaps I'd be used to it by—*

A pair of high school boys looked her up and down as she passed.

When will David come to his senses? This is insane!

And what if that's exactly it, and he's lying in some hotel room too depressed to move, or sleeping in a park somewhere?

Kelly slowed as a wave of fear lapped over her, before she imagined David homeless. What a ludicrous idea!

How hard could it be to find a tall, bearded foreigner in Japan? Either they weren't really looking, or they were wrong about him not leaving town. Who was looking anywhere else? They needed to take this seriously. There must be someone to talk to about this, some way to get things moving, people jumping into action—

The American embassy!

52

SHŌKO IN CHARCOAL, AND LATER, PASTEL, FILLED DAVID'S AFTERNOON. He explored more poses, more facial expressions, her hair, but the problem of what to have her wear, or not wear, dogged him. He tried ideas of her napping in casual clothes, but nothing felt intimate enough.

Pajamas? They're intimate. People don't go walking around in them. Except for surgeons.

A few pajama sketches later, though, David still thought about a nude. Skin was simply magical: no fabric could begin to match its softness or subtle color variations, especially the marvelous way it glows, so softly, in any light. And fabric can't *feel*.

But a few more nude sketches, including one that was finely rendered, left David no closer to solving his problem.

Maybe something with less fabric . . . like what she had on under her pajamas? He had seen them come off, though. With nothing but short panties, she might as well be nude.

But he could add a camisole.

The detailed pastel of Shōko in camisole and panties took longer than David expected. For texture, he decided on plain cotton to help mute the sexuality. More difficult, though, was adding her pain. He did it subtly, contorting her body and adding tension in her hands. The figure showed an intriguing question: must someone both innocent and sensual inevitably find pain? Finally, he combined all the elements into a detailed pastel rendering. His best sketch of the day, it would make a great painting.

As he sat back, though, he thought of Kelly. She often wore camisoles, and David imagined her undressing. He watched as she coyly stripped off her clothes piece by piece. He remembered posing her for her first nude, how embarrassed she was. It was the only time he had ever made love to a woman he was painting.

David picked up the smaller sketchbook and reviewed his morning's work, trying to fill his head with Shōko, his savior, his muse, his dearest . . .

"Can't find the word?" he imagined Kelly asking.

He didn't respond.

"You always were better with pictures than words. Better with numbers than words too."

"I suppose."

Kelly laughed softly in his mind. "Give up. English is hopelessly ill-equipped to cover the range from friendship to love—"

"No matter, I don't even know what I feel for—"

"Yes you do, perfectly well. You just don't want to deal with the consequences of admitting that you—"

"Stop it."

"Why? It's better than thinking about me, isn't it?"

David was silent.

But it was a different voice that came back to him: "No, thinking of Kelly is like staring into the eyes of death itself."

David had heard that voice only once before, the night Kelly left him. David was shocked at the timing of the phone call. Her lawyer called while she was still on the plane! The man had stated his name, Brett Westling, his firm, Hayes and Lethbridge, and then, "We have not met, of course. You were already in Japan when I first spoke with Mrs. Reese here in Portland, who has been trying to work things out, and I recognize has put forth a great deal of effort. And I really must stress what an effort she has invested over the last couple of months in trying to reach an amicable outcome. But with her phone call today informing me that she, in her words, 'is sick of dealing with the whole situation and you can tell him to just go and screw himself. Because I'm done with this crap, and I mean done! As in final! Finished! No charitable sort of forgiveness or legal reconciliation! For the last time, *it's over!*' I am afraid that I must inform you that your—"

David had hung up on him, but remembering that voice, ponderous, precise, unequivocal as God raining ruination to end all time, David could feel himself being crushed again. Darkness filled the air, a cloud of ash hurtling down, choking him, reawakening the river's pull. He could see it in his mind, swallowing him, the chill water numbing all pain forever.

But today, even weak as he felt, David didn't want to be the river's. So he chose his weapons, Shōko's pastels and a sketchbook, and went to try to face it. He paused at the bedroom door, though. He expected to be back before Shōko got home, but he remembered her distress last week when he headed downstairs to bathe and she thought he had left. He stepped back to the table, wrote the briefest of notes, and placed it underneath her phone.

David was surprised to see a police car parked down the street from Shōko's house. He stopped and peered through the window. No shotgun in the front, no barrier between the front and back seats, it was so wee and innocuous that it seemed elven compared to American police cars.

As curious as David was, though, he turned and walked on. His confidence was swelling. He had a river to conquer.

THE OFFICER showed Shōko's neighbor a picture of David and asked, "So you have not seen this foreigner?"

"Oh no, I'm sure I'd remember seeing a foreigner in the neighborhood. What did he do?"

"He's simply missing and we're trying to locate him. He often took walks on the levee path, so we're contacting people in the neighborhoods along the river."

"Oh, I see. I walk there sometimes, but I've never seen him."

Shōko's house was next, and her mother was surprised at police visits two days in a row. "Officer Murakami was here only yesterday."

"Oh, was he? Today, we're contacting everyone who lives near the river—"

"Is there a problem with the levee? Are we in danger?"

"No, no, everything's fine. We're trying to find someone. Have you seen this foreigner in the neighborhood?" he asked and showed her the picture. "He often walked on the levee path."

"Oh, the picture Officer Murakami showed me yesterday. No, I haven't seen him. I don't get out much anymore."

53

SHŌKO GAVE LITTLE THOUGHT TO WHY A POLICE CAR WAS PARKED up the street. She skipped up the stairs and into her room with a cheery "Hello!" But there was no response, just a note: "Back soon, D."

With my phone! I went all day without realizing I didn't have it with me!

Shōko picked up her phone, checked for calls or messages, and was about to put it back down on the note, when she noticed that underneath the note was a sketchbook.

I should wait. He's probably looking forward to seeing my reaction.

She set her phone down next to it.

But I already waited all day.

She closed her eyes and felt the air-conditioning on her face.

It would be ill-mannered to look without permission.

She rubbed her fingers over the cover.

At all of them, yes, but I could peek at a few before I change clothes.

Shōko opened the sketchbook and flipped through several pages. She recognized a few of the first sketches, but then she came to new material and she slowed. The sketches were rough, which she expected, but she was surprised at the number. Each page had as many as a dozen small sketches, various poses viewed from different angles, recognizable as female figures, nothing more.

Shōko leafed through the pages ever more slowly as the sketches, while still lacking detail, began to be more developed. He was focusing in on a few poses, her arms and legs curled, as if she were a question mark. It was fascinating to see his ideas progress—

As she turned the page, her hand froze. The sketch was her—rough as it was, it had her face—and she was nude!

Oh, David!

She turned the page. The next was nude too. And another. There were a few in pajamas, but then more nudes!

Oh no! This is in charcoal and not rough at all. He spent time blending the shading. Even my hands are detailed. And I'm naked!

And the next page—blank?

This is his final sketch!

Shōko dropped the sketchbook on the bed and stared at her naked, sleeping self as her hands drew up into fists.

As little as I had on, I didn't sit nude for him even when I was in college, and now I'm over fifty! How could he so much as imagine that I'd be willing to pose without clothes? What indication have I ever given that I could sit naked for—

But she *had* indicated it, every day! She had stripped almost naked each morning, and again when she got home from work—twice a day for how many days now, eleven?—bludgeoning her modesty each time, smothering her distress lest a hint of imposition wake David to just how insane he was acting.

Shōko wrapped her arms around herself tightly as she tried to think. *Maybe I could just laugh, treat the idea as if it were nothing, and he'll understand that it's too much and propose something else. But as fragile as David is . . .*

She imagined him holding the sketchbook, shamefaced.

And what if her mask cracked, and he saw her abashed? How many steps would he retreat?

She sat on the bed as the vision descended of David curled into a ball underneath it, then worse: no David at all. As thoughts pressed onto her of him leaving, she tried to imagine him returning to his apartment, a good thing. But panic had her by the hair, jerking her head around. It forced her to follow him down the bank of the levee, to stand with him on the river's edge, to watch him as he inched into the river's flow, summoning the final will.

No! He wouldn't!

But he could slip away again, back under the bed, unable to move. It could set him back weeks.

Shōko walked over to the mirror.

Would I go that far to keep him from relapsing? If he asks, can I, truly?

She looked up at the ceiling, shaking the tension out of her hands.

So, if I did, somehow, if I could—if I can—what will he see?

Shōko stared at herself in the mirror, trying to judge objectively whether she was pretty enough. Her hands clenched again, and she turned and took a step toward the bedroom door.

No, I have to do this.

She sighed. *I have to.*

It took a minute, but she stepped up close to the mirror. She knew every line in her face, having hated each from the day it first appeared. She had watched over the years as her skin slackened and her cheeks began to sag. The skin over her eyes sagged, too; and her neck—everywhere—like the sweater she threw out last month because it had no shape anymore.

What if I smile?

That's even worse! I look every bit my age, plus five? ten? I can't be con-sidering this!

She covered her face with her hands.

Oh, my hands!

She had been careful not to get too much sun ever since she was young, but still she could see the beginnings of age spots. She looked at the skin on her arms. The texture was old-people skin; squeeze it and it crinkled. She remembered before the last honeymoon trying on an old swimsuit she hadn't used in years. As she pulled it on, the elastic in the fabric disintegrated, the strands shattering into dust.

Shōko was shivering, but the point was to be undressed, so she took off her vest. She forced her fingers to undo the top button of her blouse, and another. As it opened, she saw the skin on her chest, smoother and softer than her face, but nothing like it was thirty years ago. She pulled her blouse open, but immediately closed it again.

Fifty-two!

She lifted her foot to stamp it but stopped. It would be childish. And she was not at all a child. She was—she glared at the mirror—matronly.

Seeing anything more meant removing more than her vest, and she had to bully herself into it. She turned away from the mirror as she pulled off her blouse. She unbuttoned and unzipped her skirt and let it drop to the floor.

With a deep sigh, she looked at herself again. The flesh on her arms didn't hang limp. In fact, they were firm. Her stomach was still trim, though not flat as it once was. Below that, she would have to take off her pantyhose. With her eyes shut tight, she stood as tall as she could, then opened them again. She was roundish below her navel. Turning sideways to check showed the same thing.

She tried to think of David as she beat her fists on her hips.

If I lie on my back, looking up, my stomach might seem flatter.

She faced the mirror again. She had a waist, not as well-defined as it used to be, but she knew plenty of younger women who had none. Her hips did not make her the least bit pear-shaped. She turned to the side again, then around as far as she could and looked over her shoulder.

This is hopeless!

Despite the mounting disgust, she forced herself to go on. Her legs were well proportioned, not short like many women's, and in passable shape from walking. Still, they looked mushy.

She stepped back until she could see all of herself at a glance.

She was much the same woman she had always been. She wasn't fat; had gained no weight in thirty years, in fact, despite the increasing difficulty. But her body had settled; not that she was shorter, but her center of gravity was lower than it used to be. How different would her shape be if she had borne children? What physical price would she have paid not to be alone now; those parts of her never used, wasted?

As much as she hated it, she needed to finish, so she unhooked her bra, pulled it off, and dropped it onto the pile of clothes. She had never liked her small breasts. Neither of her husbands ever complimented them, not with words, not even with an appreciative look. After a bad bout of influenza pushed her weight dangerously low, Masaru sneered that they looked like "raisins on a washboard." Other men simply ignored them. She didn't want men to leer at them, but shouldn't someone at least glance sometime?

They don't sag, but so what? That doesn't make them worth noticing— or painting, to save for posterity, to frame and display on a wall, to be gazed at by strangers for the next hundred years.

She looked away as she saw herself frowning.

Maybe I could lie facedown, and they wouldn't show.

Shōko took another step back and looked at herself, naked down to her panties, as her heart slipped into her bowels.

So David's curious. Men are. But that's a wretched little gnat of desire that flits away at the first glimpse. Once he sees, he can't be inspired to paint this.

And what if he saw through to what she loathed, the aching disappointment inside? Were men repulsed when they saw women her age, knowing they were slowly going rancid? Her body felt desiccated, too-loose skin draped over the stringy remnants of a woman. She was in her midthirties when she first noticed it, her body falling behind in its daily refresh, outrun by the increasing pace of decay. How many of her forty-nine kilograms were left over from years past, the sludge of aging, sediment built up once the river was dammed?

If David wants this apple forgotten in the refrigerator too long, brown and dried-up . . .

Why can't people just have fur? Then we wouldn't need clothes, no one would ever be naked, and I wouldn't have to deal with this!

She picked up her bra. She watched in the mirror as the straps slid up onto the shoulders of a woman who bore almost no resemblance to the Shōko David had loved, stripped of youth, vitality, self-assurance, and certainly innocence. And if she could somehow give in to him, slip off her *yukata* and lie naked in front of him? It would be cringing, dying, hour upon hour of sheer mortification. Even if she could cope, at some point, lying there with nothing on, she would think of how little time she had spent naked in her life. As memories of her marriages deflated her like a day-old balloon, shriveled and pathetic, David would ask what was wrong. He would expect her to talk about it. As she lay there, unable to say a thing, in his worry he would try to cheer her. Then his sympathy would turn into pity as he saw her for what she was: stale, a wilted body and a withered soul, the most ridiculous and wretched castoff in the world.

Could he possibly want this?

Inconceivable as it was, this was what he drew, but why? What was so special about having her nude?

She got a shirt from the dresser, and as she glumly watched her skin disappearing button by button, she noticed a difference. More skin vanished as she slipped on her jeans. She tried to imagine greeting David. She forced a smile—and she saw it: faux Shōko, the calm and happy fiction she showed the world. Maybe it was skin's reality that fascinated David so. Sitting for him naked, though, hour after hour over days and weeks, he would see *everything*.

54

KELLY LOOKED OUT AT THE LIGHTS OF THE CITY FEEBLY REPLACING THE sun as it set.

It looks so peaceful.

She slipped off her pants.

Are you out there somewhere, hiding, escaping the stress I should have saved you from?

Before, she had always unraveled it for him. She was his haven, unshakable, unfailing—

And I left you.

She leaned on the window glass.

So what refuge were you left with in this country of . . . weirdness? People bow at telephones, David! They put tuna, corn, curry sauce, and mayonnaise on a crust and call it a pizza!

She closed her eyes tight and pounded her forehead with her hand.

Damn it, why didn't you just go back with me?

Kelly got a camisole from the dresser and tossed it on the bed. Back at the window, she watched the last rays of the sunset disappear as she unbuttoned her shirt. She reached back to unhook her bra—

David always offered. All these years and he never lost his excitement for undressing me.

She leaned again on the glass. What a gaily lit and miserable place. *And I didn't like Boise?* But they had to go where the semiconductors were. *Anyway, Portland's nice enough.*

Staying in New York would have been a dream.

But that show! Even his "forty" depression was not as daunting, and that required medication. He was just too mercurial to be a commercial success as an artist, jumping into the next painting with so many still unfinished.

He managed all right through shows in school and small galleries, though. What was it about that show? It was as if David's perfectionism and distractibility mated and spawned a monster. She watched him wrestle with it for almost two years. It was ghastly, stripping away his confidence with all the pain of being dismembered one joint at a time. Nothing was ever good enough. He would settle for nothing less than awing people, bringing them to tears, moving them so deeply that they were changed forever. It was no wonder he couldn't produce something that absurdly powerful. Watching failure get its claws into him was the most horrible thing she had ever seen. He was going dark, David, the one who glowed.

And you did, David, with such awesome beauty. But I saw darkness in your face even when you were painting!

She did not want to ask him to stop painting as a career. She struggled with it for months. But it got to the point where he wasn't painting at all. She fell in love with the man, not the painter. So she solved it for him: he would continue to paint, but start on another career. It would break the creative dam, eliminating the pressure to create masterpieces on cue. He could paint purely for art's sake, with no worries about finding a buyer for anything, ever.

And he refused, just like here.

What else could she do? She couldn't go on watching him destroy himself. So she begged him, knowing he would never be able to refuse her. And he went back to school and everything turned out fine.

So why didn't you listen this time? Why didn't you follow me back to America?

Why didn't I beg?

55

DAVID WAS VICTORIOUS IN HIS BATTLE WITH THE RIVER: ONE GRAND sketch in that frame of mind and the river was his. He considered doing a second, out of pure truculence, but it was time to go. Yet as he reached the top of the levee, he was arrested by a barrage of slender amber beams that had blown holes through the clouds and shone as luminous isles in Shōko's neighborhood.

He had to draw it.

The sun was glowing orange over the hills by the time David left the levee. Quietly opening Shōko's front door, he saw her shoes in the *genkan*. He could hear someone in the kitchen, and he wanted to peek in and smile at her, but her mother could be with her. So he picked up his shoes and hurried upstairs, where he found it sometimes pays to be less impetuous. "Shōko!" he said with quiet glee.

She glanced at him for the briefest moment before she looked away and responded flatly, "Hi."

"Is everything okay?"

"Yes." She smiled, but not her usual smile, and she quickly excused herself.

She soon brought his dinner, but instead of sitting with him while he ate, she said, "I must go wash dishes," and left.

David tried to draw while he waited for Shōko to return. He spent more of the time worrying there was some new problem with her psychopathic husband, although it was more likely a bad day at work.

Eventually, David needed to use the toilet. Shōko was in the bedroom when he got back. She did not acknowledge him when he came into the room, though, so David stood by the door, watching her, waiting. What could he say?

After a minute, Shōko looked over at him. He smiled. "I did a lot of sketches today."

She seemed to smile in response, but then she turned away.

David watched her for another minute before he asked, "Are you okay?"

She glanced at him, again with her odd smile, and nodded.

David relaxed as she turned and walked toward him, but she said, "Excuse me," and continued past him and out the door.

David stared at the door after it closed, but eventually he walked over to the table and sat in one of the chairs. He glanced around the room, unsure of what to do. He could not understand any of the shows on television, he had no book to read, there was no Internet, and Fuji-Star was no longer his problem. All he had here was drawing.

He looked down at his hand and flexed his fingers. They were sore from the day's work. He looked at the sketchbook and pastels, then back at his hands.

Something that would get him through the pain . . .

Fine. Another nude.

David lay in silence under the bed, dolefully exploring the texture of the wall in the blackness of the bed's shadow.

"You don't know for certain that she's going to ask you to leave," said Kelly in his mind.

"I've done something. I don't know what, but something. I've driven her away somehow."

"Not necessarily. It could be her husband again—or any of a hundred things—and you'll never know unless you talk to her."

"I'll tell her I'm well enough to go home. That way she won't have to ask me to—"

"No, talk to her!"

"You left me. She will too. It was only a matter of—"

He heard the quietest of footsteps on the stairs.

"Here she comes. Get out from under the bed."

David lay still.

"Now! Move!"

The door slid open, but Shōko left the light off. As David watched her walk silently to the bed, Kelly faded away.

Her feet stood close enough to touch.

He closed his eyes. Shōko wasn't moving.

David let out a sigh, slipped out of his hiding place, and stood. Facing Shōko, though, all he could think to say was, "Hi again."

"Hi," she whispered as she sat on the bed, but said nothing more.

"Shōko, I think . . ." David looked at her as she stared down at her lap, her shoulders bent low. He was silent for a minute before he tried again. "It seems like . . ."

She sat perfectly still.

David took a chair. "Shōko, what's bothering you?"

She refused to make eye contact. He took a deep breath as he tried to steel himself. *This will be more than just "It's time for you to go back to your own apartment."*

He waited as she sat there looking like she was trying not to cry, arms pressed tight to her chest, her head sinking.

He leaned forward and whispered, "Tell me."

She shielded her eyes from David with one hand, her arm still pressed close, as she stood, stepped to the table, and reached out with the other hand to touch one of the sketchbooks.

"The sketchbook?" David picked it up, and after turning on the light, led Shōko to the bed. He sat near enough that the mattress's sag brought them together, but as their legs touched, Shōko moved away.

"Shōko, talk to me. What's wrong?" he asked, his voice starting to break.

"I don't think I can . . ." Her mouth made a few more words, but there was no sound.

"Don't think you can what?"

Head bowed, she made a couple of false starts before she whispered, "Be a nude for you."

"Shōko, no! What made you think that?"

Barely audible, she whispered, "Sketches are all nude." She was on the verge of breaking down.

David leaned over close and asked softly, "Did you look at *all* the sketches?"

She nodded.

"You didn't see any that weren't nudes?"

She shook her head, stood up, and stepped away.

"Shōko, no, no, they're not all nude," and he got up and led her back to the bed. "Look with me."

David flipped through the sketches until he got to the detailed nude sketch. "You saw this."

Shōko nodded.

"Is this the last one you saw?"

She nodded again.

Because the afternoon's drawings are in the pastel sketchbook.

David sighed as he got up and put the sketchbook on the table. He picked up the pastel sketchbook, and sitting back down next to Shōko, he asked "Did you see any of these?"

She shook her head.

David opened the sketchbook and showed her pastel sketches with clothes, rough ones at first, then with more detail, followed by a few of her in pajamas.

"Lots of you with clothes," said David, and Shōko leaned over onto him and clung to his arm as he turned the pages. There were many underwear sketches, rough at first, then detailed studies—hands, arms, hips, and legs—and finally a richly rendered pastel of her sleeping demurely in camisole and panties. Shōko stayed quiet throughout, so after giving her a minute to take in the last sketch, David said, "See? You don't have to be nude."

"I was afraid . . . ," she said and paused. Then she whispered, "Afraid you want to paint nude *obasan*."

"What's that?"

"Old woman."

"You're not an old woman."

"I mistake. Middle-aged woman."

"Still, *not* how I see you."

But she looked cowed.

"Shōko, I care for you more—" After a long pause he said, "I see a beautiful woman and I want to paint her."

"Thank you," she whispered, head still bowed.

"But I want intimacy, the Shōko only I can see."

They were both silent for a few seconds.

"So you can't pose nude. That's okay; I never see you nude anyway. So . . . an intimate you . . ." He stopped and thought. "Okay, if it was a hot night—really hot—what would you wear to bed?"

"I wear pajamas."

"Yes, I know, but if it was really hot?"

"I put on air-con and wear pajamas."

"But if the air conditioner was broken?"

"I wear pajamas."

"You wouldn't wear just your underwear?"

"No."

"What if your pajamas were dirty?"

"I wear other pajamas."

"Okay, so what if *all* your pajamas were dirty?"

"I wash them."

David nodded slowly. "Then I guess we do pajamas."

"Okay."

"So, you'll sit for me in pajamas?"

Shōko looked into his eyes for a long second and nodded, then turned her eyes away.

David reached over and squeezed her leg and she touched his hand.

After a minute, she whispered, "Time to sleep, I think."

But he pulled her into his lap and held her instead.

V

Studies of a Snow-White Cat

白い猫の習作

56

KELLY'S DAYS AND NIGHTS WERE SO BACKWARD THAT SHE GAVE UP ON getting back to sleep. She watched the sun struggle and finally break free of the clouds over the eastern hills. The brightness now victorious, she got up and walked through the apartment hunting for something to occupy her thoughts besides "Perhaps today...," but minutes later she was back in the bedroom, circuit complete.

She looked through David's things in the dresser. She could remember where she bought almost every item. The closet was the same. It was good that David let her buy his clothes: it was beyond her how someone who could create such extraordinary works of art could have such an unimaginative, Levi's-and-T-shirts sense of fashion.

There was nothing left to look in but the boxes in the closet. David kept them for the trip back to America, and she could tell by lifting them they were empty, except—

The missing sketchbook number twelve. S's letters and a sketchbook.

So he brought some nostalgic keepsakes. So what?

Her meager excuse did nothing to soothe the sting, though. She stepped to the bed and sat, holding David's secret treasure. As she opened the sketchbook, she took a deep breath, although she measured its release, refusing to sigh.

Kelly had seen enough drawings in the sketchbooks at home to recognize the girl looking askance at her from the first page. The next, a more contemplative S, was so perfectly rendered that it seemed almost more a sculpture than a drawing. Next, S cleaning the lens of her camera, oddly a pastel in a sketchbook meant for pencil or charcoal, but astoundingly lively and warm. S sitting, standing, reading, laughing; her face over and over, her hands ... the back of her neck?

Nothing but S.

Every single page.

57

DAVID AWOKE UNDER THE BED TO SOMEONE TUGGING ON HIS PAJAMAS, though perhaps the least insistent tug he had ever felt. "David, it is morning. Will you be awake now?"

Eyes still closed, he answered, "If you want me to be."

"You can sleep more, but last night you said you want to see morning light."

"Oh yeah." David moved at Shōko's soft pull and was soon sitting in a chair across the room from the bed.

"Please lie down," he said, rubbing one eye that wasn't as awake as the other.

Shōko lay down on the bed in her pajamas. David sat with the pastel sketch pad and stared at her. He was only assessing the light, but she must have been embarrassed, because she closed her eyes after a few seconds. The window over Shōko's bed faced a little west of due south and would not catch direct sunlight for four more hours. He did a quick sketch, annotated with color swatches, before he asked Shōko to help him block the light from the other, west-facing window. "With light from a single window, the contrast and shadows will be more dramatic." It took a few minutes, but they found a box in the storage room that flattened into a workable shape.

Shōko returned to the bed and David did a quick pastel sketch of her there, followed by a detailed sketch of her face. The light was on the cool side and sufficiently diffuse that the shadows, while deep, were not stark; enough contrast to accent her contradictions, but soft enough to complement her innocence. The light would be steadily changing, though, and David's plan was to do a series of sketches devoted to lighting in brief interludes over the next two hours before Shōko had to leave for work.

Done for the moment, David walked over to the bed where Shōko lay curled up, hugging a pillow. She covered a yawn with the pillow as she uncoiled and then stretched her arms out as far as she could before she returned to holding the pillow.

"I got the first lighting sketch done," he said.

She lifted the pillow off her mouth just long enough to say, "*O-tsu-kare-sama.*"

"Can you sit again in about fifteen minutes?"

Shōko looked into his eyes and nodded. As he held her gaze, he saw the pillow inch higher until she said, "I will be right back," and slipped around him and off the bed.

David watched her as she headed for the bedroom door, her pajamas rumpled and her hair a mess, graceful steps with silent footfalls, so small, his oldest friend.

THE LAST CANVAS David had prepared for a nude figure was almost two years after Kelly refused to sit for him anymore. Although he suspected Kelly's aversion was not only to posing but to nudes in general, discussion might have meant compromise. So, in one of the stupidest decisions of his life, he hired a beautiful, young model without telling Kelly. He should have known Kelly would eventually find her posing. He answered Kelly's accusations with recrimination: she had left him no choice with her refusal to pose, and it wasn't as if he was having an affair. It sounded hollow even to him, though, and in the end, he was a deer in headlights: if it was such a proper thing to do, why had he kept it to himself?

Arguments over figure painting volleyed back and forth for three months, but unable to stand the tears, he finally made the promise that bleached much of the color out of his life. Things had been ordered and predictable ever since, but though Kelly might have taken comfort in a road running straight to a far horizon, David never had. Still, a person can adapt.

How would things have turned out if he had refused to give up painting as a career? The second year he was married, the morass of trying to finish the paintings for the Peter Blum show, was his darkest time as a painter. Mostly he had sat in his studio, too lost to paint; just sat, without even a brush in his hand, staring at half-finished works, his inspiration withered or misplaced somewhere. But then Kelly, her vision always clear, led him out of the fog, starting him back to school and into a new career. It had always awed him that she could not only see what she wanted, but somehow keep the vision, like a Polaroid photo clutched in her hand, inspiration to stay true until she saw it again in reality.

In fact, Kelly's pushing to give up nudes was not out of selfishness. Though figures were his most passionate artistic expression, that last one was not going well. His frustration at each distraction was like another grain of sand in a machine, grinding everything to a halt. Kelly saw the seeds of a devastating depressive episode, and she acted.

Now David kneaded the eraser with his fingers.

I gave up figures. For her.

He squeezed the eraser hard.

But I refused to abandon a hopelessly broken microchip.

He looked down at the sketch of Shōko asleep on the bed.

No, not a chip.

58

"BUT DAVID COULD BE SICK, OR EVEN SIGHTSEEING SOMEPLACE. WHY are you focusing only on the possibility he's dead?"

Detective Kikuchi responded, "It is a highest chance, but we check everything. Sick: we ask all hospitals of this prefecture and prefectures around; two sick foreigners only and no one is David. If he run away, then someone should saw him on train, bus, something, but no one saw him."

As deeply as it hurt, she had to ask, "What if he left in a car . . . with someone?"

"A woman? Maybe friend S?"

Kelly did not appreciate having it spelled out but: "Yes."

"Then to still be gone means they are gone for long time. Too long, I think." Kelly was quiet, so he continued, "Yesterday, we show his picture in home and business near river and hear one new thing."

Kelly perked up.

"Sunday, July fifth, twelve days before, someone saw him walk near the river. I am sorry, that is all. It is not a good clue."

Kelly deflated again.

"Without a good clue, we must think situation is very bad."

"I agree. I'm worried."

"So you think like us, maybe: David is not alive now."

"What? No! Please believe me, he couldn't have!"

"It is hard to accept—"

"No, it's impossible to accept! Understand David's not a quitter." Kikuchi looked puzzled, so Kelly slowed down and tried to explain, "Example: David enjoys running. Once, he was injured, but he ran a race anyway. He ran so hard that he fractured his leg, a stress fracture, but he finished the race! He never quits!"

Kikuchi just looked at her blankly.

Kelly strode back to the apartment with a scowl, but her anger was more at herself than Kikuchi. *What a failure!* She taught training programs in conflict resolution and negotiation, but today she failed to swing a single point her way. Yet, what was she supposed to say? She could have given dozens of examples, but he didn't want to listen. *Perhaps I should have kept talking, just taken up his whole day; perhaps then he would take this seriously.* But self-indulgence never accomplished anything. Besides, there were times David had given up on things.

Still, he wouldn't give up on life! He was awed by it, almost a child in his wonder at what he saw around himself. Although half the time Kelly could not see what was so amazing even after his explanation, those times she could were like God's own revelations. He brought her to tears that way so many times it was almost a running joke. More often, it was just his own weird excitement, but it was infectious! What words would convey to the police that he saw art in everything and loved life more than anyone she'd ever known? That was why she fell in love with him. In fact, she fell before she even knew his name, following his class around the museum week after week and daydreaming about the guy who saw beauty everywhere. A man like that couldn't possibly kill himself.

Kelly was nearly home when she tried to think of recent examples; they would be even more convincing. But an hour later, sitting in the apartment, she had yet to recall a single time since coming to his beloved Japan that David had stopped to share anything beautiful with her.

"KELLY!"

"Hi, Leon."

"Great to see you, except for the circumstances."

"Thanks. And thanks for taking time to meet me."

"My pleasure."

He escorted her to a small conference room.

"So how you doing?"

"I'm holding up okay," said Kelly as she sat.

"You always struck me as a strong one. So do the cops have any idea yet what's going on?"

"No, they think David killed himself. I don't know whether they're even looking. Makes me so angry!"

"Yeah, when they interviewed me on Monday, they asked whether he was suicidal."

Kelly regarded Leon earnestly before she asked, "Was he?"

"No, no," said Leon. He walked over to the window and looked out at the mountains. Still facing away, he answered, "You know he was down, though."

"I just wanted him out of here. It was killing him."

"I know. I don't understand why he was so dead set on keeping the project alive. And after we'd figured out it couldn't be fixed."

Kelly gave a long sigh before she leaned forward in her chair and said, "Leon, I know you're his friend; he depends on you and trusts you; and I know how friends protect each other, but I have to ask, so please tell me straight up—"

"Kelly, just ask. Whatever it is, I'll tell you."

"Was David seeing anybody here?"

"You mean, like a girl? No way. He wasn't inclined. And an affair would've taken serious time and concentration. He had none to spare—of either—zero. There was no room in his head for anything but this chip. You know that."

Kelly nodded, staring blankly, her head slightly bowed.

Leon took a seat next to her. "All those weeks, David and I were within spitting distance of each other, must've been at least twelve hours a day, and I mean the whole twelve hours. He talked about nothing but work, made no phone calls except work, and didn't get any. He didn't go out to restaurants or bars, except with people from the office, generally me." He chuckled. "Really, Kelly, he never went anywhere. Okay, once or twice a week he'd disappear for an hour or two, maybe three. I think he had to escape sometimes—me too—it's a lunatic asylum here. But as far as I know, he was just out taking walks, thinking about the project, because it always seemed like he'd come back with some new idea. Or it was like . . . I dunno . . . like the burnout wasn't as bad as before he left. Really, he was just out clearing his head. And after you got here, the hours he wasn't with me, he was with you. I know, because I seemed to have to call him every night, and he was always home."

Kelly smiled. "You called an awful lot. Perhaps it was an affair with you."

Leon laughed. "Hey, the only one he talked about was you."

She smiled briefly, but her face changed back to worry.

"He loves you. Don't doubt that."

"Thanks, I know." Looking down, she asked, "Did he know I love him?"

Leon leaned forward. "The project had him crazy, but he knew."

"And when I left for America, did he think I was leaving him?"

It took Leon a while to answer. "I don't know. I talked to him for a minute that night. To be honest, he was pretty down. I don't know how bad; he didn't want to talk about it. But what he told me was something like 'Kelly left' or words like that, not 'Kelly left *me*.'"

Both were silent until Leon said, "He should've quit."

Kelly nodded.

"The cops've only been looking since Monday, and it's Friday now? That's not long."

Kelly looked at her hands and fingered her wedding ring.

"Hey, I have to disappear into a meeting for a little while. There's a storm brewing. A bigwig from Portland coming in a few days, maybe. You want to stay here? That apartment must be awful lonely."

"Could I?"

"Sure."

"Thanks. I think I'll just sit for a while."

"Okay. I'll check in when my meeting's over. And hey, tonight you're having dinner at my place. Don't bother refusing, I won't hear it. Neither will Kuniko. You've met my wife, Kuniko, right?"

Kelly nodded. "Thanks, Leon, you're a sweetheart."

Leon smiled back at her on his way out. "Don't worry. David's too bright a star to disappear for long."

Yes, but before Japan, he didn't even disappear for an hour or two once or twice a week.

59

DETECTIVE KIKUCHI ASKED, "HOW'S THE YEARBOOK SEARCH COMING?"

His younger colleague Nakagawa answered, "We have thirty-two schools already."

"That's fast. I don't suppose they've found our S."

"No, but they have five candidates so far: a Kawashima—no, two— and a Kamishima, a Kawasaki, and a Kawahara; all born between 1955 and 1959; all *S* names. We've checked against the official household registry, and all are married. Only Kamishima lives here. They're following up on all five."

Kikuchi rubbed his eyes and Nakagawa asked, "How was the latest meeting with Reese-*san*?"

"Not good."

"She still insists he's alive?"

"She called the American embassy yesterday and said we aren't doing enough to find him."

Nakagawa's eyes widened.

"Prefectural headquarters got a call from the Ministry of Foreign Affairs this afternoon, followed by a call from the central office of the National Police Agency. Ōbuchi has suggested we find a way to 'deal more effectively with Reese-*san*, perhaps even convince her we're handling the case properly.'"

"Frankly, sir, I don't see how the pressure's supposed to help anything. You said yourself finding him would be a miracle. You think there's a chance they'll hang us out to dry?"

Staring straight ahead, Kikuchi sighed. "Another call to her embassy and they'll send an agent from their FBI."

Nakagawa looked at Kikuchi in silence for a long time before he asked, "So what do we do?"

"You wanted to search the mountains for Americans hanging from trees."

"A poor idea. I'm sorry."

"No, not entirely bad."

Nakagawa raised his eyebrows.

"Everyone agrees he must have killed himself, so I suggested to Ōbuchi we search for a body."

"In the mountains?"

Still staring, Kikuchi shook his head. "The river."

"That's a big job."

Kikuchi nodded once and looked over at Nakagawa. "Ōbuchi's committing the resources. We start at dawn to finish by sunset."

"You mean tomorrow?"

Kikuchi nodded again.

Nakagawa sat back in his chair and shook his head. "What a waste. If she'd just believe us . . ."

Kikuchi did not respond, and Nakagawa glanced up to see a "you need to learn something" look. The older detective held Nakagawa's eyes for a few seconds, as if making sure he had his attention, before he said, "She needs time."

"For . . . ?"

"She got here two nights ago, late. This is only her second day. It'll take longer."

"What will?"

Kikuchi said softly, "She knows he's dead."

It puzzled Nakagawa.

"In her heart, somewhere, she knows." He looked away. "Facing it takes time."

Nakagawa sat silently. Maybe the talk was right about Kikuchi having changed, that he got more serious and subdued as he watched his wife waste away over her last few months.

60

AS THEY STARTED ON DESSERT, CASTELLA CAKE AND RASPBERRIES, Kuniko asked, "How did you and David meet?"

Kelly looked down and smiled.

Leon laughed. "Oh, this is gonna be good."

Kelly picked up her fork and said, "I was working in New York. It was 1981, the year before I started my MBA—"

Leon asked, "You must have been so young. How did you ever get into business school?"

"I graduated from high school a year early, and then from college a year early too. I started my career at nineteen."

"Wow."

Kelly chewed quickly before she said, "Anyway, I turned twenty-four the fall I met David. He was teaching a class on twentieth-century American art at Cooper Union—"

"Wait, wait. David taught *art*?" asked Leon.

"Mm-hmm. Didn't he ever tell you? He's sold at least a hundred paintings. He's an extraordinary painter. You'd be shocked how good he is, awestruck."

"So when was this?"

"Before he got his double-E degree and started at Micron. Anyway, he was teaching this undergrad class, a big part of it was field trips to museums, mostly the Metropolitan, and I was there one day when his class came through. It sounded like a good free tour, so I tagged along in the back."

Leon chuckled.

"And he was gorgeous and smart and he mentioned where they would meet the next week, so . . ."

Leon laughed out loud and Kuniko covered her mouth as she chuckled.

Kelly grinned. "After three or four times, I got a copy of the syllabus for his class and attended every field trip."

They all laughed out loud.

"But the pressure of making it as a professional artist was too much. So he started designing chips, and he painted less as the years passed. He hasn't painted at all for probably five years."

"What did he paint?" asked Kuniko.

"For most of his career, figures mainly."

"Ooh."

"Exactly. In fact, there's one he did of me the first year we were married that would stop you in your tracks."

Leon and Kuniko laughed again.

"I had to put it away once the kids were big enough to know it was Mom nude on the wall. But even secreted away it's . . . special."

"It sounds romantic," said Kuniko.

Kelly laughed. "Oh, it was. You can't imagine—or perhaps you can."

They all laughed.

It wasn't until Kelly was home later that evening that she thought about the last nude they worked on. *Did he ever finish it? Was that the one when Melissa walked in and I got so embarrassed?*

61

SHŌKO LAY IN BED FOR TWENTY MINUTES BEFORE SHE WHISPERED, "Are you sleeping?"

"Not even close."

"I am not even close too."

"So what are you thinking about?"

"How did you start painting? You told me once long ago."

David laughed softly.

"You tell me again, please?"

His voice was soft and low. "Well, you knew my mom was a painter—I mean, as a hobby, a skilled amateur. I would watch her, and she would show me what to do. I was painting landscapes and stuff by the time I was in junior high."

"So you always love painting?"

"I enjoyed it. It was playing, sort of."

"When did you change to be serious?"

"She volunteered as a docent, a guide, at the Art Institute of Chicago. When I was little I would stay home with Miss Roselda, our house-keeper and nanny, when my mom was gone. Later I would go up with her and just wander around the museum. So, one day in the summer I was fourteen, I was in the American Modern Art section, looking at a painting by Wyeth. I looked at it for a long time, and then this guy started talking to me, asking what I thought. I don't remember what I said, something about the composition and the colors and I don't know. Anyway, every time I answered a question, he asked another, almost as if he was testing me. I eventually ran out of things to say. So he walked me over closer to the painting and explained how the brushwork creates this effect and that effect, capturing the way light reflects by using multiple layers of transparent color, the patience it takes to work in egg tempera, and lots of other stuff. It was amazing. I was a little self-conscious, because a crowd gathered to listen, but what he was telling me was so cool! Anyway, he must've gone on for thirty minutes. Finally, he saw someone in the crowd and said he had to go. Then he shook my hand and told me—I can still remember the words—'David, someone with your eyes must paint. You simply have no choice in the matter.' He left and then I saw my mom in the crowd, which was pretty big by then, and she walked up and gave me a hug and told me the guy was Andrew Wyeth."

"*Sugoi*! You never told that story!"

"Really? Sorry. Anyway, I got more serious after that, and you know I'd already decided to be a painter while we were still in high school."

"Yes, me too. All your paintings I saw are long ago, but I remember, and I can see Wyeth style a little. I saw his exhibition at National Museum of Modern Art in Tokyo when I was a high school student. I was very impressed. But you use brighter colors. His painting is more dark and sober."

"Somber."

"Somber, yes."

"Brighter? Oils maybe, but my temperas are more subdued. Still, my subjects are so different from his I doubt you'd see much influence now."

"Who else was inspiration?"

"For tempera technique, it was Wyeth. For oils, early on, British painters like the Pre-Raphaelite Brotherhood—"

"Pre-Raphaelites don't look like your painting."

"They were classical and mine are more modern, but my figures are realistic."

"Yes, I remember from college."

"But for oil, my biggest influence was Rembrandt. I got that two-year fellowship at the Rijksakademie in Amsterdam, and my technique got more refined. And I found other influences in Europe, like Bouguereau."

"I don't know Bouguereau."

"William-Adolphe Bouguereau, late nineteenth century, classical. You need to see what he did with skin. Oh, and you can! One of the big museums in Tokyo added a Bouguereau to its collection. I'd love to go see it."

A trip to Tokyo would be so fun! Shōko felt like hopping out of bed and lying on the floor to talk over the trip, but . . . no, it was not time yet to be making plans like that.

"But I'm not at all classical, except for the realism of my figures. I keep things simple, even abstract. It focuses you on the figure, and it allows more freedom. In that sense, think . . . maybe Gerhard Richter."

"Ah."

"Oh, and something I learned here in Japan: I like to focus the viewer on what isn't shown, the painting as a window into the viewer's own imagination. The painting points you toward emotion rather than making a scene of it."

Shōko almost laughed at the irony of David hiding the emotions in his paintings when he couldn't hide them in himself.

"So what about you? Tell me again how you started painting."

"I was in art club in school."

"Just a club? But you were a serious painter."

She laughed. "It was a serious club! Even junior high school, we painted so much. And other things too. We took club trip to Tokyo museums in . . . *chū-san wā* . . . 1971 and saw Marie Laurencin drawings and paintings at Isetan department store museum. So beautiful! I wanted to paint beautifully like that."

"You told me in college you studied Chagall."

"I like the . . . dreamish?"

"Dreamy."

"Dreamy feeling of Chagall. And I like impressionists. Japanese love impressionists more than realists, maybe. I like Seurat. His style is maybe dreamy too, a little."

"I can see you dreamy. So, should I paint you in my style or like a Chagall, or . . . Botero?"

"*Iya da*! I am not so big!"

They both laughed, then fell silent.

"Shōko?"

"*Nani?*"

"How are we going to go to sleep?"

"*Komatta nā.*"

After a minute of silence, Shōko said, "Close your eyes and imagine you are painting."

"Painting what?"

"I don't know. It is your imagination."

"So what will you imagine?"

She whispered back, "Anything I want."

The talk stopped before long, and Shōko's suggestion seemed to work on David. It was not as easy for Shōko, though, even after she kicked off her covers, for she was twenty-two years old, sitting on her bed in Tokyo, and it was warm.

62

IT WAS MIDNIGHT, KELLY WAS STILL JET-LAGGED, AND THE APARTMENT kept whispering, "*Where's David? It's your fault he's gone. Where's David? Everything you did was selfish. Where's David? The police aren't really looking.*" But when it said, "*You know, the police could be right,*" Kelly got dressed and left.

Strolling along the streets near the apartment, Kelly relished the cool night breeze. Was it safe to be out so late? But David said Japan was the safest place in the world.

I should head back, though. I'll never get sleepy out here.

Still, she didn't turn around. The apartment was spooky without David there. As she walked on, though, she thought of how boring it had been even when he was around. Before, there was always something to talk about or see or do: museums, restaurants, movies, shopping, friends, and more. Kelly thought about their first few years, each day a new page, plus everything to learn from each other's pages of the years before. They talked about everything, all the time. David told her things he learned, bounced ideas off her, worried aloud about work and family and art, asked how to deal with people—to the point that it was almost bothersome at times. She joked once, "It's a good thing you didn't marry that Japanese girlfriend of yours. The English burden might've killed the poor thing." But a month of interruptions now would be heaven.

Kelly stopped and listened. There were no traffic noises. Except for crickets, there were no sounds at all.

She turned and started back to the apartment.

So where are all the fireflies that David said Japan is supposed to be famous for?

Perhaps I should ask the detectives. They might have an inkling of where to search for missing insects.

"Hello."

"Hi, Melissa."

"Mom. I was just heading out the door. Is there any news?"

"No."

"Mom, you okay?"

Kelly didn't respond.

"You know, I was thinking about being late today. I do that, go in late sometimes, just for the lateness of it."

"No, you don't."

"Yeah, but I can. And you're more important. What's up?"

"I just can't sleep."

"The place is empty and silent and you're climbing the walls."

"The police have no idea what to do. It's as if he vanished. They're totally baffled."

"He'll turn up. As you said before, he's decompressing."

"But where?" Kelly's voice cracked.

"We have to be patient."

"The worst part is, I'm no help. I don't know a single place to search. I know him better than anyone, and I'm useless!"

"Mom, if there's one thing you will never be, it's useless."

"Here, I am."

Melissa was quiet.

"You really should go," said Kelly

"I'm pregnant, Mom, due in seven weeks. You really think anyone will give me grief about anything?"

"What did the doctor say yesterday?"

"All's peachy, except he says I'm not gaining enough weight."

"You should see the women here; they're tiny. I saw a pregnant woman yesterday, looked as if she was about to pop, but only her stomach. I swear, after she delivers, you'll never know she was pregnant."

"Thanks. Just what I needed to hear."

"Just saying, don't worry if you end up a little underweight."

"And don't you worry about Dad."

Kelly said softly, "That's not fair. Your worry's way easier."

"Hey, people like Dad don't just crumple up and blow away."

"I've been thinking about the way he sees art in everything around him. Do you remember the vacation we took when you were five? As we were driving, your dad explained how the atmosphere scatters light and makes the farther mountains look lighter. And he said artists in Japan captured it with nothing more than ink, because things are monochromatic that far away. That fall, you came skipping out of first grade with a watercolor painting: mountains, using only black paint, lighter as they went back."

Melissa chuckled. "Yeah, I remember that. With the possible exception of you, he's the most amazing person I've ever known. For the longest time, I thought I'd never get married; I could never find someone I could respect that much."

"But you found one."

Melissa's voice got softer too. "Yeah, I did."

Kelly was silent for a few seconds. "Hold on to him."

"I do. But if I let go for a second, he's still mine. And Dad's still yours. Don't be thinking you've lost him."

Kelly started to cry. "I was so cruel to him when I left."

"He loves you, Mom."

Kelly whispered, "I know."

"Just believe it. He loves you, and he's coming back."

"I miss him so much."

"Me too."

They were both silent, but eventually Kelly said in a calmer voice, "You should go."

"I don't need to."

"But you should. I'm okay. I'm even a little sleepy."

"But—"

"Go. I'm all right."

Melissa paused. "Call me tonight, okay? My tonight, I mean."

"I will. And Ben too."

"Love you. Get some sleep, 'kay?"

"Bye-bye, sweetie."

"Bye, Mom."

63

WHEN THE PREDAWN LIGHT WOKE HIM, DAVID TRIED TO LOSE HIMSELF in Shōko's breathing and sleep again. He had watched her sleep so many times as he sketched her, though, that he knew the way she curled up in the bed above him, where her arms likely were, even the angle of her neck. What showed on her face: placid unconsciousness, every muscle unwound; or the total contentment he had seen only a couple of times; or the most beguiling, shimmers of a dream's emotion? Of course, it could also be a drooly face or mashed-up-against-the-wall face or mouth-hanging-open-like-a-trophy-fish face. They were all Shōko and all endearing in their own ways, but still unworthy of a sketch.

It was no use trying to sleep, so he slipped out from under the bed—and what he saw sent pinpricks up his arms. It was new for her sleeping face, although he saw the expression every day when they joked or talked about happy things and she lost her usual self-consciousness. She was dreaming: the tiniest grin appeared now and then.

Oh, to see that dream—or be a part of it.

Maybe I am!

David smiled like an idiot for the next few minutes as he slipped on his clothes. Then he answered the insistent calls of the sparrows outside and set off on a brisk walk in the growing light.

He was soon at the river, but it was too early still for runners or dog walkers, so no one saw the anticipation oozing out of him. He had waited to paint Shōko his entire adult life. There wasn't time when they were together as students, so all he had were sketches. He had often considered turning one into a painting, but it would not have been her. The colors—the subtle gradations of her skin, the sheen of her hair—would never have been perfect unless he could see her as he painted, and so the years passed.

I painted Kelly, though. . . .

On a summer day like this, Kelly would have played in the sprinkler with the kids, acting like a teenager as they chased her around the backyard. Put Kelly anywhere near water, dress her in a swimsuit, and her laugh would bubble over until everyone was drunk with it.

Kelly's laugh carried her everywhere. David often accompanied her to dinners when her clients were in town. He would watch with fascination as she laughed and they smiled, she laughed again and they laughed, and soon, even clients she was meeting for the first time were regaling her with stories as if she were their dearest friend. They couldn't help but reveal intimate details of their lives and businesses to their new confidante. Kelly attracted people like bugs to a porch light. She made them smile; so much so that given enough time with her, their glow grew until they were lights too, and who doesn't want to shine?

It was the quiet times that David most cherished, though, like the feel of tiny fingers grabbing his lip and waking up to see Kelly smiling at him, all contentment and love, as she nursed Ben in bed in the dawn light; or the way she liked to lie with her head in his lap and read; or even how she leaned on him whenever they sat together; or the countless times she had succumbed to his voice, smooth and deep, as he read to her when she was tired. How many times had he carried her to bed asleep? When he set her gently down, how many times had she awakened and pulled him to her?

David stopped walking, looked down at the path, and kicked at the weeds. As he closed his eyes, he was holding her again. She was giggling as he undressed her. He was posing her.

David kicked the asphalt hard and gazed down the river toward the sunrise, but it was streaky and wet, so he closed his eyes again. If only they could have come to Japan at the same time. If he'd had her here from the start, maybe he would have shone.

David turned to start walking back but didn't.

He would never shine as brightly as he had in his years with her. Not even Shōko would understand him as Kelly had. And if she tried? Would she leave too, once she saw deep enough?

David opened his eyes to check his watch, but he couldn't read it. He wiped his face with his sleeve and looked again: 5:09. They were scheduled to start at 5:30. He looked down from the levee at Shōko's neighborhood. It was time to go back to her. He would . . . soon . . . when he could see again.

David eventually got himself walking. As he was about to turn off toward Shōko's house, he saw activity upstream. It looked like the police, many, with boats. A search? That was odd.

64

"YESTERDAY YOU SAID WHITE IS BEST," SAID SHŌKO.

"Mm-hmm, like your ones with the little blue pinstripes," said David.

"Is all white okay?"

"Yup, solid white would be . . . even better."

"Okay, I change fast."

As David slipped on the smock that Shōko bought yesterday, it surprised him to hear rustling paper behind him. When Shōko finished, he turned around to find her smiling at him in pure white pajamas, simple, long-sleeved, and comfortably loose.

"Wow!" He stared, and Shōko beamed—shyly, though, a small smile as she looked down, so Japanese.

He stepped closer and noticed large sheets of tissue paper and a bag and realized the pajamas were new. "Linen?"

She looked simultaneously pleased that he noticed the fabric and embarrassed that it mattered to her: *so* Japanese. "Really nice linen! Gorgeous, smooth, the texture will be perfect."

"I think silk would be too shiny."

"Yes, everything should be matte. Nothing shines but you."

Shōko closed her fingers over the ends of her sleeves and raised them to her face.

David said, "First let's move this table."

He stepped over to it and Shōko bounced along behind. They lifted it together and moved it over next to her dresser.

He smiled. "Now let's get you posed."

She stood behind him as he arranged the bedding. He pushed the bedspread down and toward the wall until a soft ridge of folds arced across the bed. He arranged the sheet, then the pillows, one large pillow lifted by two smaller ones placed against the head of the bed.

"Lie down."

Shōko did as ordered, lying on her back, straight as a board.

"We're not doing a funeral pose."

Shōko acted serious. "You pose me. I am your model."

"Okay, model-*san*, scoot up so your head's on the pillow."

He watched her move and then rolled her onto her right side, facing out. Shōko stayed pliable but taut, shifting with David's hands. He pushed her top leg toward her chest until her ankle rested on her thigh just above the other knee. Did Shōko realize she was staring at him? He tried not to look at her face for fear of embarrassing her. He brought her head forward, curling her up in the process, then took her right hand, pushed her sleeve up to her elbow and coiled her arm up around the top of her head.

As distracting as it was each time he touched her, it was exhilarating to be posing a model once again. She was becoming the serpentine undulation he had created in his head, every whit now in flesh, warm, breathing, and watching him from the bed.

He placed Shōko's left arm on her side, her hand draped in front of her, then paused to assess. The linen had transformed the scene: her hair shone a deeper, silkier black; her skin glowed warmer, creamy smooth; her body seemed to float above the deep blue of the sheets.

David pushed Shōko's left shoulder back and down, twisting her body so that her shoulders and hips were perpendicular, and she looked pained as she tried to stay in the pose.

"It's okay, don't try to hold it."

She closed her eyes for a moment, let her body go limp, and her shoulder lifted off the bed.

"That's it," he said and sat next to her. He reached out and took her face in his hands. She felt hot. Was he blushing too? He turned her head outward until it was midway between the angle of her hips and shoulders, then sat back, his hand resting on her hip, and gazed at her. Finally, David stood, formed his thumbs and index fingers into a rectangle, and viewed Shōko from various angles.

She said, "I thought you use a side view."

"Mm-hmm. But this is our chance to check other angles. You never know." He stopped and pulled her left pajama leg up to her knee, then stepped back across the room. The twist at her waist added just enough contortion without looking painful. Her body had a strong line; relaxed but structured; not posed, merely sleeping. "It's perfect."

———

65

IF KELLY GOT UP, SHE WOULD HAVE TO FACE ANOTHER DAY WITH nothing to do, so she didn't. Feeling aimless all day long was alien enough, but the driving need to search was rejoined ad nauseam by her inability to help. Time ticked by as if the gears of a giant clock were inexorably crushing her. The only proactive step she had taken since her arrival was calling the American embassy two days ago. Had she overreacted? But the people at the embassy took the whole situation quite seriously.

So what do I do today?

Kelly studied the ceiling before she rolled over and rubbed her hand over the empty expanse of bed next to her.

She got up, stepped over to the dresser, and opened one of the middle drawers. She stood staring into it for a minute before she pulled out a gray hooded sweatshirt, well-worn, with the beginnings of holes at the wrist seams, and crawled back into bed with it.

Nothing that smells like him, nothing that looks like him . . .

What I need is a painting—

Kelly sat up with a start at the sound of her phone ringing. "Hello? Uh . . . Mushi-mushi." *That can't be right.*

"Hello, Mrs. Reese. This is Kikuchi."

"Did you find something?"

"No, but today we search whole day, many police. Would you like to come and see? I come your apartment after one hour if you are ready."

"Yes, thank you. I'll be waiting."

"Then I see you in one hour—"

"Oh, sorry, before you go, where will you search?"

"Search is already starting since before five a.m."

"So early? Where?"

Kikuchi paused. "We search the river."

Kelly looked up at the ceiling in silence. "Okay, fine. I'll see you in an hour."

66

SHŌKO GOT UP, STRETCHED, AND WALKED OVER TO THE TABLE TO GAZE at David's first quick pastel. The composition fascinated her. Most of the page was herself curled up, her arms, body, and legs winding across the bed like a river. Above her the wall and window were disappearing into abstract shapes. Below her, the shadow under the bed flowed out and down the paper, turning crimson and finally almost black near the bottom.

She looked back at David, who was keeping his distance lest he get any pastel on her new pajamas, but she said nothing; she just smiled.

"Ready for another?"

She nodded.

Back in her pose, she waited for David to start, but he only stared at her.

"Am I pose right?"

"Mm-hmm." He looked at her for another minute. "It needs something . . . some other bit of color . . ."

Shōko watched, puzzled, as David looked around the room, then stared at her again, lost in thought. Finally, he walked up to the bed, dropped to his knees, and pulled a length of loosely wound red yarn from underneath it. She couldn't help but grin at his joy as he found the end and put it in her left hand, saying, "Here, hold this." He let the rest of it fall to the bed and, leaving a large loop in front of her, pulled the other end off the bed to the floor.

"Maybe tie on a finger?" Shōko asked.

"Oh, nice idea."

"Here," she said, indicating her little finger.

"It matters?"

She nodded, all in fun, or mostly.

"It's warm. Should we turn on the AC?" asked David.

"If you want. Control is on the table."

She watched David, distractingly attractive even just picking up the remote control and pointing it at the air conditioner. She lay there, hearing the beeps from the small unit high on the wall as David turned it on and set it. As the air hit her, a bead of sweat rolled down her back.

Shōko closed her eyes and relished the cool air on her damp skin. Under that calming breeze she could lie like this for a long time, perhaps even fall asleep. Maybe she already had. She opened her eyes lazily and watched as David moved the table closer to his chair. He settled himself, put the sketchbook in his lap, and searched the table for the right color to start. She watched him pick up a deep brown hard pastel stick and bounce it against his lip as he took her in from head to toe. Since he arrived, today was the first time he had posed her. In fact, the last time she modeled for him was in her college apartment. The pose was different, but his eyes were the same. So was the heat.

Another drop of sweat ran down her back.

Shōko had wondered whether it would happen again, but the heat, though raging, didn't come with the surprise it had when she was young. She was not sure whether it was secrets or a lack of them that made intimacy so enticing. But lying here, alone with David, open to each other and apart from the world, the room blurred, and her thoughts closed their eyes in bliss. It was everything she had longed for ever since that sketch so long ago, when she sat for him, almost completely undressed.

David was sitting in the chair across the room from the bed. Shōko stood wedged between him and the wall, resting her arms on his shoulders as he added the final highlights to her face. "Do I look so peaceful when I close my eyes?" she asked.

"Peaceful, but not quite like this."

"*Sō?*"

"I've done a few sketches of you while you slept."

Shōko smiled behind him. "Thank you for relax me. Will this be the light in a painting?"

"Something like this, very cool. That feels more tranquil, earlier in the morning, before anyone's supposed to be awake."

Shōko thought of the nightmares that woke her, screaming, and how different life would be with a man who saw her this serene. She leaned down and rested her chin on the top of David's head. "The cool light is nice."

67

KELLY WATCHED BOATS DRAG THE RIVER WHILE TEAMS WORKED THEIR way along the banks poking about with sticks in the weeds. All she could think was what they might have accomplished with this many hours spent searching for David alive. It wasn't long before she asked Detective Kikuchi to take her back to the apartment.

Solitary indignation was almost as bad, though, so Kelly drove to Fuji-Star again. It was Saturday, but Leon said during dinner last night that he would be in the office all day, along with almost everyone, and she should feel free to stop by.

Leon spent half an hour with her when she first arrived, mostly listening. His occasional reassurance and constant optimism calmed her enough that she accepted his invitation to stay for a while. Kelly didn't want to be alone, so she sat in the big open room that held everyone's desks, about forty in all. She took David's.

Leon gave Kelly a novel he had in his desk, and she was reading when Paul came in and startled her by booming, "Well, if it isn't Kelly Reese!"

He approached, arms open wide to hug her, but Kelly stayed in her seat and gave him a polite half smile. "Hello, Paul."

"Great to see you. You holding up okay? We're sure worried around here, all of us."

"I'm all right, thank you."

"Great. Great to hear that." He stood in silence for a few seconds. "So, hey, if there's anything we can do, or I can do, or whatever, to help, you know, just let me know. We'll do anything to find David."

"Thank you." Kelly turned her attention back to the book.

Paul stood there, though, and after a few more seconds, he said, "I . . . hate to disturb you there, but I'm . . . that's my desk while I'm here, so . . ." He looked at her apologetically, but expectantly.

Though no longer reading, Kelly kept her gaze on the book, letting the tension build before she looked Paul in the eye, her face emotionless. "No, it isn't."

"Excuse me?"

She was doing what she trained people never to do. "I said, 'No, it isn't.'"

She knew all types of people from her long career in conflict management, and although she had only spent a few hours with him months ago, David's descriptions were enough that she knew Paul's nature. Regardless of his relative abilities, as long as he was not with superiors, he barked and bluffed and insisted he was the alpha male. He would never let her affront pass.

"Sorry, Kelly, I really must insist. We've got a lot of work—"

"No. This is David's desk, not yours." Those sitting closest, Leon, Itō, Takahara, and a couple of others, were looking on in wonder, and she knew Paul could see it.

Paul smiled. "David can lend it to me now that I'm here doing his job."

"Don't you mean doing *your* job?"

"Excuse me?"

"Don't you mean you're doing the work you should have been doing all along as the manager of this project?"

Paul affected a laugh, then in a joking tone said, "C'mon, move it. We're far enough behind without you getting hysterical on us."

"So then why isn't there a desk for you, Paul? If your project—your *only* project, if I'm not mistaken—is so far behind, why haven't you been here working where the problems are?"

"Fine, if you know so much, then you also know it's the most international project the company has ever undertaken. Japan isn't the only piece, and since I can't be everywhere, I manage from the place that best facilitates liaison with specialized resources in Portland."

"You mean Portland is best for face time with upper management, best for projecting your PR about how wonderful the chip will be and what an amazing job you're doing, best for claiming every good idea as your own. It's a place to stay far enough from the actual work that if it all comes apart, you can blame it on the local manager. You know, it has always surprised me that David can work with you. He doesn't suffer fools, and he's been known to lose his temper. Odd he never has with you—"

"Get out of the chair."

Kelly jumped up and stepped into Paul's face, blocking his path to the desk. "What did you ever accomplish on this project, Paul? What part of this chip did you design?"

Paul attempted to step around her, but she moved with him at every step and proceeded to review the project for him and how David was its only chance of salvation. She had listened well when David talked about it week after week. As her review went on and she got more animated, more people looked. By the end, most were watching discreetly, and a few had turned around to get a better view.

Paul said, "Sounds like you know David's accomplishments better than he does."

"I might. I tried to teach him the self-promotion you seem to think makes a career, but David's never been much good at it. It's a shame too. Unlike you, he has something to back it up with."

"I think it's time for you to leave, Kelly."

"No!" Kelly could read people, and even with her voice beyond strident, *you've gone too far* was on no one's face but Paul's. "I'm here for a reason, Paul, and do you know what that reason is?"

"No, pray tell, enlighten me."

But with that, Kelly's voice showed barely controlled rage. "I'm here because my husband is missing! *My husband!* And do you know why?"

Paul's eyes were narrowing.

"He's missing because you put him in an impossible position, demanded an insane deliverable, and refused repeated pleas for backup. David's missing," she said, choking on the last word, "because you're too proud to admit that the project is dead in the water because of your incompetence. He's missing because you needed a scapegoat!"

Paul looked ready to drag her from the room. "Shut up and get out."

"No! Look around, you unctuous, self-serving bastard!" She jerked his arm so he was facing most of the people in the room. "They all know it!"

Paul yanked his arm away, stuck his finger hard into Kelly's chest and yelled, "No, Kelly! David's the incompetent one! They all saw his little nervous breakdown! What a lunatic! You know what? I hope he did 'off' himself!"

It was the first time in her life, but Kelly swung with everything she had, a backhand aimed right at Paul's mouth. Unpracticed, though, she was too slow. Paul saw her windup and went to step away. But seething at Kelly, Paul couldn't see Takahara, sitting just to the side and behind him, place his foot behind Paul's. Paul tried to catch himself, but his back hit hard on the corner of the desk behind him on his way to the floor.

Kelly was as surprised as everyone else in the room, but the look on Itō's face as he buried his mouth in his sleeve broke the tension for her and she laughed out loud.

Takahara, on the other hand, was quite solicitous as he scrambled to help Paul up. "Oh, Paul-*san*! So sorry! Are you okay?"

There were subtle looks of satisfaction and barely perceptible nods toward Takahara from many in the room. Not only had he cleverly intervened in the unseemly scene, but by innocently standing over Paul, he effectively ended it; for to strike back at Kelly, Paul would have to go through Takahara, and diminutive though Takahara was, that was *not* going to happen.

68

"TIRED?" ASKED DAVID.

"Not so tired yet."

"Bored?"

Shōko smiled. "Talk to me and I will not be bored."

His eyes on the sketch, David asked, "What about? Your hand that I'm drawing?"

"Tell how you will paint me."

He picked up a tortillon to blend the color in the shadow of her arm. "We start with a finely gessoed canvas, a smooth painting surface. I'll outline everything in charcoal, detailed but no shading, and then start on the underpainting. We'll build you up in layers."

"Not direct, like pastel or acrylic?"

"Nope, very old-school. We'll start with a monochromatic version of the painting. Probably in olive. If you look at yourself in the mirror, at your skin, you'll see there's a greenish caste, especially in the shadows. I'll do the whole underpainting with that one color, no mixing, all the lights and darks done with different thicknesses of paint over the white gesso. With that done, I'll add medium transparencies that will be the basic colors and textures. Your skin will be the most important element. I'll use transparent dark layers for shadows, and thin transparent washes of color to show reflections of the surrounding colors. Opaque highlights will shine where light reflects most brightly. Last of all, I'll add the finest details of your hands and face."

"Layers will need many weeks, I think," said Shōko.

"I'm in no hurry," he said, looking over the pastels on the table.

He worked for a few more minutes before he said, "Maybe I won't use olive for the entire underpainting."

"*Sō?*"

"Gray might be better under your pajamas, which will be whites in the painting. It needs an unadulterated white, almost absolute."

"Absolute?"

He worked for a little while longer before he stopped and said, "I look at the whiteness and I see your innocence. The white in the painting will suggest a purity beyond what others experience, a purity that brings you both simple peace and a profound . . ."

"*Nani?*"

"Almost a pain."

"*Ē?* I think you see too much in pajamas."

69

DETECTIVE KIKUCHI TURNED ON THE HEADLIGHTS AND HIS PARTNER Nakagawa appeared out of the dark, hurrying toward the parking lot. Kikuchi locked the doors, though, as the young detective approached. Nakagawa looked at him expectantly as Kikuchi pulled out, so he rolled down the window and told him, "Find a ride in another car. Or catch a taxi home. Anyway, looking like that, you're not riding with me."

"But—"

"How did you get yourself so muddied? It's all up in your hair and everywhere. What did you do, jump in headfirst?"

"I slipped in the dark, that's all. I was just trying to lend a hand as we wrapped things up."

"For all the good any of this did us."

"I'm sorry, sir. I know you were hoping we would turn up a body and have this finished."

"Yes, but now, to be honest, I'm having my doubts."

"So you think . . . what?"

"Maybe—I'm not saying it's likely, but *maybe*—he's alive."

Nakagawa's eyes widened.

"Anyway, I'll see you Monday."

"We could talk about it on the drive to the station," said Nakagawa with a plaintive smile, but Kikuchi's eyes were on the road, and he rolled up the window as he drove away.

70

DAVID AND SHŌKO WERE BACK AT WORK BEFORE SIX ON SUNDAY morning. Although it was Sunday, Shōko did not have to meet with the middle school English students this week. Still, she and David could not work through the entire morning. The angle and color of the light would start going wrong by eight and be useless by ten. He would spend the afternoon working on her hands and other details. There was one thing, though, where the morning light was essential: Shōko's pajamas. They took on a multitude of shades, not only the shadows in the folds, but because the white reflected every nearby color.

As they worked through the morning, Shōko insisted on long drawing sessions and often took her pose after only five minutes of walking and stretching. David assumed she was pushing hard because it took so long to arrange her pajamas each time she lay down. When he finally mentioned it, though, she told him his own stamina the day before had inspired her. That energized him all the more, and he sketched through many of her breaks.

A maddening problem arose, though: clouds began to roll over the sun. At first, he simply waited a few seconds for the shadow to pass. But soon the clouds were stealing so much time he had to sketch through them, adjusting light and dark to match areas he had completed earlier; until suddenly the cloud would be gone and he had to break himself from adjusting; only to have another cloud pass over.

David closed his eyes and stretched his neck. "Let's make this the last break before you call it a day and get dressed."

"I can go longer."

"No, we've only got time for one more session before—"

Their eyes darted to each other's and widened in alarm as they both heard the footsteps on the stairs. David jumped up, but the pastels were spread over the table in such disarray he could never gather them up in time. He looked at Shōko in dismay and whispered, "What do we do?"

Shōko had leapt off the bed, said, "She can't see me like I am drawing pastels in these pajamas," and was grabbing sweatpants out of her dirty clothes. She flopped onto the floor, slipped her feet in, and kicked her legs into the air as she pulled them on. A quick roll and she was onto her knees, where she whispered, "Turn the clean page. I do like I am drawing!"

David flipped to an unused page and dropped the sketchbook on the table. He yanked the cardboard out of the western window and turned to see whether Shōko was ready—but she had no shirt! She looked back, covering herself with her hands, panic in her eyes. Faster than he could even think, David stripped off his T-shirt and smock together and threw the T-shirt at Shōko as he dove under the bed.

David's view was blocked at Shōko's waist, but he saw the fabric of his T-shirt dropping over her pajama pants, still sticking out of the top of her sweatpants, as the door opened. He did his best to silence his breath and watched her mother's tiny feet shuffle into the room. Shōko spoke to her in a loud voice and David realized that the sound of his breathing would go unheard. Her mother seemed surprised at something, probably that the table had been moved across the room, and then excited . . . that Shōko was drawing? Shōko laughed in return. The conversation was beyond him, but there was more laughter in the middle. Her mother left after only a couple of minutes.

When the door closed, David peeked out with an inquisitive look.

Shōko whispered, "Tonight there is neighborhood meeting, but I don't go. So smoky," and she made a disgusted face and waved her hand in front of her. "I say take father, like a date." Shōko smiled. "But she does not think my joke is so funny."

"Everything's okay?" asked David as he slipped out.

"Yup."

"Ooh, very American response. Okay, we work more?"

Shōko looked at him and nodded, so David walked back to the table and opened the sketchbook to his last page. He looked over at Shōko and smiled. "That was a close call."

Shōko just nodded again, and David realized that she was waiting for him to look away. His T-shirt landed at his feet a few seconds later, and he turned around to see her shining once again, pure white.

CURLED UP AGAIN on the bed, Shōko opened her eyes after a few minutes and was surprised to find David just sitting, staring at her. She asked, "Are you tired? We can stop and you rest."

David gave her a brief smile before he stood and wiped his hands as he stepped closer.

"Are you okay?"

David nodded, then looked down at her body.

"*Nani?*"

"I . . ." He tossed the rag back onto his chair, shoved his hands into his pockets, and frowned.

"Tell me, please."

"I was remembering that sketch when we were young, the last one, where we . . ."

Shōko felt herself blush.

David sat next to her. "It was very . . . private."

Shōko met his eyes and nodded once.

"You weren't nude."

She did not respond.

"So, I was sitting over there, thinking. . . . " As his voice trailed off, he smiled apologetically and looked away. Finally, he looked at Shōko again sheepishly and said, "Sorry. I was going to ask whether we could try a sketch that was a little like that one."

Shōko patted him on the hand. "I think it would be hard to—" But before she could draw her hand away, David laid his other hand on top of hers. Shōko felt her face go flush. As he squeezed her hand, she tried to smile. "I could not do it then without Yuki-*chan*."

David pursed his lips and nodded, seemingly resigned.

Shōko felt . . . disappointed? She looked away.

David suddenly smiled. "I don't suppose you know anywhere we could get a cat."

She was looking at her free hand but didn't see it. All she could do was feel the other, so warm in David's hands, and after a few seconds, she turned her eyes to him. He returned her gaze, and ever so slowly, she lowered her face, still holding his eyes, until she was peeking out at him past solemn brows.

His smile faded. "What?"

71

DETECTIVE NAKAGAWA HAD NOT SEEN HIM COME IN, SO KIKUCHI dropped his bag on the desk and watched Nakagawa pop up in his chair. "You come in on Sunday mornings now?" asked the older detective.

"I was going to review more of the security camera files," said Nakagawa

"After you read *manga*."

"Just this one. But I'll get started on the files right away, unless you have something else for me to work on."

Kikuchi frowned. "Not today."

"Is there anything I can do for you?"

Kikuchi stared at his desk for a few seconds before he pulled out his electronic dictionary and said, "Yeah, get me those letters of his. It's time I got to know S a little better."

72

KELLY THOUGHT THE DETECTIVES WOULD BE HOME ON SUNDAY morning, but what might they be doing? They wouldn't be mowing lawns. She had yet to see a house with grass, and the little in public spaces was some anemic variety that didn't actually seem to grow. A trip to the police station to call on absent detectives, though, was better than her apartment alone. Besides, it might spark an idea, some suggestion she could make to move the search ahead.

As Kelly entered the station, a young female officer in a neatly pressed uniform and a woefully unflattering hat bowed and asked her something unintelligible. Kelly smiled. "Hello. I'm Kelly Reese. I was wondering whether Detective Kikuchi is in today."

"Excuse me. Please to say again."

"Detective Kikuchi," Kelly enunciated clearly. "Is he here today?"

"Kikuchi?"

Kelly smiled. "Yes, please."

"Thank you. Please to wait one moment."

The young woman looked as if a leaden weight had been lifted from her shoulders as she picked up the phone and called someone. To Kelly's surprise, Kikuchi came trotting down the stairs.

"Hello Mrs. Reese. How may I help you?"

How indeed? "I was . . ." *I was what?*

Kikuchi looked at her expectantly.

"I was wondering . . . whether . . . you could update me on the case."

"I am sorry to tell you no change since I call to you last night."

Kelly looked away, back at Kikuchi, and away again. On her next glance at him, he had his head cocked to the side.

"Mrs. Reese—"

"Please, call me Kelly."

"Mrs. Reese, I think maybe you are wanting to do something."

Yes! But what?

"You want to search, but you have no place to search."

She was wringing her hands, so she forced herself to stop.

"I think you are frustrated like we are also."

Looking down, all Kelly could do was nod. They were both quiet. Finally, Kelly asked, "You are working on another case today?"

"No, case of missing David is my full-time case now."

"Your only case?"

"Yes."

"May I ask what you're doing today, then?"

"You remember so many letters from S? I read them today to look for new clue."

"I see." Kelly felt a knot in her stomach. *But given the choice of a hundred knives in the back or that apartment alone . . .* "The letters are all in English?"

Kikuchi nodded.

"Maybe I could help you read them?"

Kikuchi pursed his lips and thought about it for a few seconds. He studied Kelly's face. As he turned to head for the stairs, he said, "Please follow me, Kelly-*san*."

73

"WHAT?" DAVID ASKED AGAIN, NONPLUSSED BY A LOOK IN SHŌKO'S eye that he had no hope of deciphering.

She didn't answer.

Should he let go of her hand? The seconds passed. He didn't know what to say, so he stood and took a step back toward his chair on the other side of the room.

Shōko said softly, "My shirt buttons were . . ."

He stopped and turned back toward her.

Shōko sat up, paused for a long moment, and stood.

David picked up a rag and wiped his hands again as he hesitated. He dropped the rag and took a short step back in her direction. She looked down, and he took another.

They stood a handbreadth apart, both of them looking down, for a full minute before he reached out tentatively.

Shōko stood perfectly still.

He took the bottom button of her pajama shirt in his fingers and just held it.

She brought her hands to her face.

David reached out with his other hand, pulled on the smooth linen, opening the buttonhole far enough for the thin white disk to slide through, and let it go. He did the same for the next button. Shōko still did not move, so he undid another. He could see the soft, smooth skin of her stomach, the depression of her navel. As he lifted his hands to the last button, Shōko held her arms closer to her chest. It popped open, and they stood still for another minute. David reached out with both hands, slipped them into the open space, and took hold of her waist. She lowered her hands from her face, held her shirt to keep it from opening too far, and raised her eyes to look into his.

Shōko looked scared, so David smiled and asked, "Shall we try your pose again?"

She looked back toward the bed, and David turned around to give her a chance to get settled.

After a minute, she whispered, "Okay."

Although Shōko's shirt was open top to bottom, she had it draped so that her breasts were not completely exposed. David smiled reassuringly and asked, "May I?"

Shōko nodded in reply, and he said, "Hold the top so it doesn't pull open too far."

She did, and he reached down and carefully pulled her shirt open to reveal the skin of her stomach, peach smooth.

Shōko let go of the shirt tentatively, made an adjustment, and returned her hands to their posed positions, the weight of her top arm keeping her shirt in place.

David stood back and appraised her for a few more seconds before he stepped close to the bed and gave her a look as if asking permission. At her nod, he undid the bow on her pajama pants, tugged to loosen them, and pulled them down off her left hip to below the leg seam of her underwear, short and snow-white.

He stood back and looked again. He realized he was staring, but he could not glance away. She was staring back. He whispered, "Close your eyes." She gave the merest of smiles, only a moment, and shut her eyes. He watched her body relax into the pose. This was an entirely different painting! He worried that it could be seen as Shōko asleep after a sexual encounter, though. Even a nude would have been less sexual.

"Is a pose okay?" She had opened her eyes.

David nodded and smiled. "But it needs . . ." He slowly perused the room. He stepped over to the bookcase, pulled out a small book, opened it, and set it facedown on the bed below her hand.

"You were reading."

She smiled softly and closed her eyes. "Yes, I was tired. Did I fall asleep?"

David's eyes stayed fixed on Shōko, trying to see past his own desire to what a museum patron might assume from her unbuttoned repose. "Asleep . . . maybe. We'll try it both ways. Then we can decide together."

The clouds stacked up unbroken to give David steady, subdued light. His studies of Shōko with her pajamas open, none completely revealing, had kept him disconcertingly aroused. Although posing and painting a pretty woman included attraction at the beginning, it rarely surfaced once the work was underway. Gazing at Shōko, though, he had to compel himself to objectify her, and all too often he lost his focus on drawing altogether.

Finally, anything approximating the proper light was gone for the day. As David wiped his hands on a rag, his gaze stayed fixed on Shōko. He had often wondered what would have happened if he had gone to her on the bed instead of finishing that sketch in her apartment so long ago. He imagined it now, the look in her eyes as he approached, the feel of her lips soft and warm, the arch of her back as she gave in to his touch . . . but it was too soon.

"I think we're done for today."

Shōko opened her eyes. "I am okay. Are you tired?"

"Yes, but we've lost the light."

"Ah," she said, but did not move.

"You want to see?"

She nodded, carefully got off the bed, and grabbing her pants with one hand to keep them from slipping off her slender hips and her shirt in the other to keep it from flying open, she walked in baby steps over to the table.

"Mmm, nice" was all she said, but she looked for a long time.

74

"YOU'VE READ ALL THESE?" ASKED KELLY AS SHE LOOKED AT THE LARGE stack of S's letters.

"No, I ask others to read," answered Kukuchi, his voice somber. Kelly didn't ask why, but the look on her face still begged the question. Kikuchi must have felt it too, because he continued: "So many letters . . . is like another thing for me."

Kelly waited. Kukuchi looked at her for a long time, as if gauging whether or how much to tell. Finally, he said softly, "My wife wrote letters but did not give them to me."

"Why?"

"She wanted to tell me things to help me after she was gone."

"I'm sorry."

"One every day from the day she hears about her cancer until she could not write. Two hundred forty-eight letters."

"I'm so sorry," said Kelly, wanting to tell him he could stop; he didn't have to put words to his pain.

"Then my wife speak, and her sister write for her. Nineteen more letters." He went on almost whispering: "Then I held her hand for a few days."

"How long ago did she pass?"

"I read one letter each day since she died. One letter is left. I could not read it yet on that day. I am waiting two hundred thirty-nine days to read it."

"I'm so sorry for your loss."

"But to have something is to lose something, no? You say in English they are two sides of one coin. We cannot love something with joy and not have great pain also."

"You know, I can read these and just tell you whether there is something you should know."

"Staff already did for me. But now I must know S myself. Best way is read her letters."

"But they're so old. Is there anything in them that will help?"

"Personality does not change so much with time, I think." Kukuchi was about a quarter of the way through the stack. He picked up the letters he had read and placed them in front of Kelly. "These are high school letters. S and David were . . . we say in Japanese, 'Penparu,' from English. Do you know David when teenager?"

"No, we didn't meet until we were both out of college."

"Then you will know younger David more when S answer questions of him."

Kelly sat up in her chair and unfolded the first letter, dated 1 April 1973. It had cherry blossoms pressed in it. The English was hard to understand, but Kelly saw a girl embarrassed at writing a letter to a total stranger. More than anything, she talked about her cat, Yuki. If this was what S's letters were like, perhaps Kelly didn't need to be jealous after all.

An hour later, Kelly had been through all the high school letters and was into college. She had seen photographs of S's paintings, some with ribbons or other signs of acclaim. The girl was talented; that much was obvious. Her English had also improved. While the college letters were much more personal than the high school letters, though, they were not love letters. They also didn't hold Kelly's attention. She was already on her second cup of bitter, office-quality coffee, trying to stay focused.

At length came letters as David's trip to Japan was approaching. Full of anticipation, Kelly sensed a climax coming—and then the letters stopped for six months. Finally engrossed, Kelly felt cheated not to know what was happening while David was in Japan. She had seen the Japan sketchbooks, though, so it was not a total blank.

When the letters started up again, Kelly was reading about a very different S, and Kelly realized she should have been keenly jealous. The letters were not explicit, no gushing expressions of love, but there was an intimacy born of a profoundly deep common devotion to art. For all the ways Kelly and David were soulmates, they had never shared this. Kelly loved art, particularly David's, but she had never dedicated herself to it as S had. Kelly felt cowed. But as she read on, she thought more about the things she shared with David that S never had. She read S had never modeled for David for anything more than sketches—which likely meant he had never done a nude of her, since there were none in his sketchbooks, including his precious book number twelve. They had also never lived together. S had not borne his children. They had not shared decades of each other's lives.

Had they shared a bed, though?

They had clearly loved each other. S never mentioned marriage, but Kelly found allusions to a future together. They were understated, though, like this brief January 1980 letter when David was studying in Amsterdam:

Dearest David,

How are you in the winter of Amsterdam? Tokyo is cold now,
but I think Amsterdam is colder very much. I hope you have warm
places to study and work and sleep. Do you have a good coat and
warm shoes? I do not want you to be cold and sick in a wintertime.

You asked what I am painting now and wanted a photo, but
sorry no photo today. I am working so hard these days on my
final project for graduation. It is very large canvas, 160 cm each
side, acrylic of a small child lies in the field of flowers. I work hard
on it, but it makes me smile always, even when I am very tired,
because a child is so contented (that is my new word for today!)
to lie in the flowers. I think I wish I could lie in flowers like a
small child.

Will you send me a photo of what you are painting now—
or a photo of you and your painting? When you were here, I can see
you painting each day. Now I miss your painting. (And miss to see
you.) But some day we will see painting each day again. I think I will
be very contented in those years of a future.

How is it possible to become so used to a person in only a few
months, and without live with a person? I ask that question to myself
often. I miss the person who was a part of every day. I think he
becomes a special existence for me.

I am sorry this letter is short. I will send another soon with a
photo of my painting project, even if not finished. Please take care
in the cold and snow and ice.
Love,
S

Or there was this from a much longer letter a few months later showing the future dreams were mutual:

I think it is hard to be alone after not to be alone. I agree with you.
I miss the you I can touch. But as you wrote, someday will come
and we will not be alone ever again. For now I have Yuki-*chan*
for holding. But you are right that holding a hand is much better.
Japanese do not hold a hand so much (I think you know),
but yours is my special memory that I want to feel it again.

And this plaintive excerpt was from the last letter before S's beloved
cat died:

Oh, David, I miss you. Yuki is sick and I am so scared for her.
It makes me to have a selfish wish that you could be close again.
I wish that future was now and we did not need letters again.
You write wonderful letters, but those months without letters
were so close when you were here. I want that again today very
much. Maybe a selfish wish will end when Yuki is healthy again,
but maybe I will feel this selfish until someday in future together.
I hope our day is so soon.

As subtly tender as S's letters were, they eventually became less fre-
quent and less moving. Kelly could sense them drifting apart . . . because
they never met again? How much time apart does it take to squelch a
love? How much to damage it? Could it be little enough that Kelly and
David had made a mistake in being apart for—

"You look like you decide your question," said Kikuchi suddenly.

"My question?" asked Kelly. She showed him a wan smile. "Which one?"

Kikuchi smiled in return but said nothing.

Kelly sighed. "I guess the big question is whether S has anything to do with David disappearing."

"Does she?"

It took Kelly a while to respond. "I don't think so. She's not the answer to any of this."

"Do you think he found her?"

"I think he would have told me."

"But you worry."

Now it was Kelly's turn to be silent.

Kikuchi showed her a sympathetic face. "Do not worry too much, Kelly-*san*. Letters are very old. People keep old thing. It does not always have strong emotion."

Kelly nodded even as she frowned.

"Tell me, how did you meet David?"

Her frown disappeared, but she still felt a sadness in the smile she showed the detective as she said, "I loved art—not like S, not as a cre-ator—but I loved going to galleries and museums. That's where I met David. And I guess more than anything, we liked to talk. The first time we talked, a few weeks after we sort of met—a few months after the last of these letters—we sat in a diner and talked all night." She smiled. "They fed us breakfast in the morning, no charge." They both chuckled. "By that time, I was over the moon."

"Over the moon?"

"Totally in love. You can't imagine how beautiful David was over blueberry pancakes. I guess talking was what drew us together more than anything. It seemed like we had everything in common; talking was so easy."

"Maybe that is your strength."

"It's what I do most in my work. I guess it's what I do with people in general."

"It is what my wife did too."

Kelly gave him a sympathetic smile.

"Thank you for read letters with me today and explain many words. I think I know S and David young time now." He smiled. "And I know Kelly-*san* just a little."

"Oh?"

"I know she is not quiet as me. I know she reads much faster. And I know she does not like our coffee." Kikuchi laughed. "But I do not too."

75

DAVID WAS EXHAUSTED FROM TWO SOLID DAYS OF DRAWING, SO HE enjoyed the evening sitting on the bed with Shōko, watching television he didn't understand. Now, the television off, he lay on the floor in his pajamas trying to unravel his spine as Shōko admired the pastel sketches once again. She made soft exclamations in Japanese as she turned the pages. He understood a few words, and for the rest, the tone of her voice was enough.

At length she asked him, "How can you be so fast and be so good too? This is *so fast!*"

"It wasn't easy for either of us."

"No, I like posing. It feels lazy."

David smiled and rolled over. "You know, a few marathon days in an actual studio and you'd start to see your real skin."

"You are ready to start the painting?"

"We need a few more studies. I still don't have your jammies draping right. I'm not sure how long they'll take though. We'll only have mornings before you leave for work."

"You want one more day like today, maybe . . . tomorrow?"

"That would be heaven." *And I could put off facing my disaster of a career for another day.*

"Okay."

"What?"

"I said 'okay.' You have me all day."

"How?"

"Tomorrow is holiday!"

"All day...."

"No, just half-holiday."

"What?"

"Of course, all day! What country has holiday not all day?"

"Oh, no, I mean you, mine all day."

She smiled softly and nodded.

SURPRISED TO FIND DAVID still on the floor after she finished the day's final chores downstairs, Shōko stood him up, took him by the shoulders, and steered him to the bed. "Lie on your front," she said and pushed him gently down. He did as ordered, and Shōko sat by him and massaged his back. She could feel the muscles through his shirt, and she rubbed hard. She smiled at the little noises that came out of him when she put all her strength into it.

As she worked her way down his spine, though, suddenly she was back in Masaru's house. Their shanty of a relationship was near toppling over—she had not heard a civil word in over a month—so she was surprised when he politely requested a back rub. Still the dutiful wife, she acceded. She even reluctantly complied when he told her to move over and sit on him. It wasn't long, though, before he was aroused and his demand, disgustingly explicit, was nothing she was prepared to do for him anymore. With her refusal came the tirade—but with a twist: he cited her expenses and said he was due "services" in return. Incensed, Shōko screamed back at him—forgetting her precarious position. Masaru turned over, knocking her hard to the floor, where she lay for a few seconds, disoriented, as Masaru stood over her, leering, undoing his clothes.

Shōko knew she had only one chance, and she waited for Masaru to drop his pants to his ankles before she bolted for her room and locked the door. As she cowered there, terrified that the door would give way under his incessant pounding, Masaru finally screamed the words that made her flee: "I should just strip you naked and tie you down! And leave you that way! Then I'll take it any time I please!"

He had never physically attacked her, sexually or otherwise, but his belligerence had been escalating for weeks, and with the psychotic edge she heard in his voice, Shōko knew it was no idle threat. She slung her purse over her shoulder, messenger-style, threw her coat out the window, climbed out after it, and ran barefoot through the chill December darkness until she was sure he couldn't catch her. One night in a hotel, twenty minutes of frantic packing after sneaking back the next day, and she was gone.

Now, sitting by David, she trembled. He had never gotten especially aroused, but she never massaged him. What if he—

David was snoring quietly.

Shōko's hands roamed up and down his back before she leaned down and kissed the nearly bald spot on the top of his head.

I should have married you, just bought a ticket to America and proposed.

Shōko kept rubbing for the next few minutes as she considered what to do. With David sleeping soundly, Shōko had no bed. He seemed to be able to sleep well underneath it, but she had no wish to try. Besides, if he found her on a *futon*, no matter her protests that it was all right, he would feel awful.

She could not bear to wake him, though. He worked so doggedly, hour after hour, drawing with an intensity she could scarcely believe. She finally started forcing him to rest, though not enough.

She looked at him, unconscious, muscles weary, fingers clean but stained with pastel, in every way the most beautiful man she had ever met. Rubbing his head, she felt his hair velvety soft. He looked so peaceful. . . .

David was easier to roll over onto his side than Shōko expected. It was also an easy decision to change into the white pajamas and sleep in them for the first time. She savored the linen, cool against her skin, as she slipped in front of him and nestled up close. It took a few minutes, though, to overcome her final reserve, pull his arm around the front of her, and hold it tight as she dropped off to sleep.

76

IT RAINED HARD IN THE NIGHT, AND NOW SHŌKO LAY IN BED LISTENING to water dripping from the roof and trees. From the light, she knew it was still early. She could check the alarm clock, but that would mean moving and David might wake up, or move the arm that was holding her close, or his legs that were pressed into the backs of her knees. She could not help yawning, though, and as she felt him move, rubbing her back into him. Then his arm did move—

Shōko held her breath as David's hand slipped up into her shirt, rubbed her stomach, and pulled her closer.

"*Ohayō*," he whispered.

"*Ohayō*," she whispered back, trying to sound calm and sleepy. Too inexperienced at waking up with a man to know what to say, she whispered, "Did you sleep well?"

"Mm-hmm." He slid his hand up to her ribs and held her tighter.

Shōko suppressed a gasp and quickly rolled over—away from his arm, for fear the other way might push his hand higher into her shirt. Now facing him, she nuzzled her head against his neck.

David soon had his hand inside her pajamas again, rubbing her back. They lay there, occasionally talking, until the room was fully light.

"So, what holiday is it today?"

"*Umi no Hi*, Marine Day."

"Military?"

"No, 'marine' like 'sea.' We are thankful to the sea for take care of us. And we go to a beach."

"So, do I have to go to the beach and sketch the ocean or may I stay here and draw you?"

"You don't want to go to a beach?"

"I'd love to, but . . . ," he said and pulled the curtain away from the window over the bed and looked out. "The clouds could turn into rain. So, if my model's okay with it, I'd prefer to do more studies of her."

"All drawing. The man under my bed is so boring."

"The man *in* your bed is so boring."

"*Sō desu ne.*"

After a minute of quiet, David whispered, "Shōko . . . ?"

"*Nani?*"

"Why didn't we ever meet again?"

The question had been a fishbone caught in their throats ever since they first met on the levee, but she responded playfully, "You were too young and foolish."

"No arguments there. Still, that's not much of a reason."

She was silent for a long time, and then serious when she whispered, "It was my turn, and I was scared."

"Your turn?"

"You visit Japan, so next I should visit you when you were in Amsterdam or after that in America. You remember I planned a trip after graduation but was so busy."

"Mm-hmm."

"But not only busy." She paused, and whispered, "Also I was scared."

David pulled her closer.

"So, when I had a chance at New Year holidays, not busy, still I did not go."

"We were both scared." David kissed her head. "But I'd rather draw you than talk about that."

"Okay, we draw maybe one hour and then I make fast breakfast." Shōko rolled over onto her back, yawned, and stretched. She expected David to climb over her and off the bed, but instead he kissed her ear, soft and slow. She squirmed, but David draped his leg on top of hers.

She lay still.

Still kissing her ear, he laid his hand on her stomach and caressed her.

But as he moved his fingers to her pajama shirt's bottom button, she said, "*Ara!* What do you . . . ?"

He opened the first button and raised his hand to the second.

"*Dame!*"

And the third.

She grabbed his arm but did not pull insistently enough that he let go of the button. It popped free of the buttonhole.

His face was in front of hers now, and she looked into his eyes and whispered pleadingly, "We can't."

He undid the last button.

"David . . . ?" Her voice quavered.

He undid the tie on her pants. With his face so close that his nose brushed against hers, he whispered, "Shōko, I realize we have to wait, but there's something you need to know."

"What?" she whispered back, almost too soft to hear.

"We were both young and scared, but it was my foolishness not to come back. And my mistake when I didn't marry—"

Shōko shook her head to stop him. It was her foolishness too, but she couldn't tell him; not that she lacked the words, the feelings were simply too intense. She might never be able to confess that she had feared seeing him again would ruin her, plunging her so hopelessly into an uncertain love that coping without him would be impossible. Twenty-two doesn't certify a dive that deep. As much as it hurt, it was easier to suppress her love than to let it grow any stronger and risk losing it. Just as it was easier now to pretend that she was not facing the same risk of drowning that petrified her thirty years ago.

77

"ANYTHING NEW ON THE PHOTO SEARCH?" ASKED DETECTIVE KIKUCHI.

"Nothing positive," answered his partner Nakagawa. "Of the five original candidates, they've contacted and ruled out all but one, including the local one. That leaves Shōko Kawasaki. She's been living in Tokyo for over twenty years according to the household registry, married a year and a half ago to Masaru Ōta, Setagaya-ku address. There's no answer despite repeated phone calls. Probably away for the holiday weekend.

Although the *kōban* officers are apparently following up with the local family."

"Anyway, don't worry about it for now. Our missing foreigner isn't in Tokyo."

"They got four new candidates and already talked to three."

"Okay, follow up on the Ōta thing tomorrow. If there's still no answer, go by the family house here, if there still is one, and ask about her. No loose ends on this one."

"Would you like me to go by personally?"

"No, have the *kōban* do it. Just stay on top of it."

Kikuchi was almost back to his desk when he stopped, stood still for a few seconds, and slowly walked back to Nakagawa. "That sketchbook you looked at when we searched the apartment, you said he was good?"

"Very."

"And there are drawings of a girl?"

Nakagawa sat up, eyes wide. "Perfectly recognizable. We could reduce a few onto a single sheet of paper and put it up all over town like a 'wanted' poster!"

"Or be a little more circumspect and let the *kōban* officers make inquiries."

Nakagawa shrugged. "I suppose that would work too."

"You suppose?" Kikuchi closed his eyes and rubbed his forehead before he looked at Nakagawa sternly. "Just get the sketchbook from Reese-*san* and make it happen."

<hr>

78

THIS MORNING THE WEATHER COOPERATED, AND AS SHŌKO RELAXED in her pose, David did one finely detailed study of her full body. He talked to her about it as he went, explaining that her skin would be the central element of the painting. It would form a strong line that ran up her leg to her knee, then arced from her bare hip and stomach, up through her open shirt, to her face.

As Shōko listened to David's voice, soft and deep, she dissolved toward unconsciousness. How could she be this relaxed lying in bed in front of a man, scandalously improper, even erotic? At least, that was how it felt when she was twenty-two, how it felt even yesterday.

She opened her eyes enough to peer at him sitting across the room, a few short steps away. She could feel him as if he were inside her head, her body, as if they were joined. She thought of the first letter she wrote to him thirty-six years ago. Her high school English teacher wanted everyone in the school to become a pen pal with someone who shared their interest. So she found each club (a compulsory element of high school) a companion group in America. Everyone in Shōko's art club had to write to a student in David's high school art class. She had no idea how the teacher found that class, or why every other girl in the club got to write to a girl. Maybe writing a boy was what kept it going, though; none of the others made it past three letters. Or maybe it was just David. He wrote long, funny letters that took hours to read as she thumbed through her dictionary. She wrote back, telling him about Japan, her family, her friends, and the fun they had. Soon after each letter she sent, another would arrive from David, full of questions, always interested. At first, she wondered how he made sense of her English, but it got better. Eventually, with all the practice, she had the best English in her class. As her ability to communicate improved, the letters also got more personal. They sent each other photos of their paintings and shared their dreams of the future as artists, but it took eight months before they were brave enough to send photos of themselves. David's was taken in front of a Christmas tree, a photo she still kept in one of the boxes under her bed.

It wasn't until the next year that they promised to meet someday, and four more years before it happened. She kept the reins on her heart throughout—until he stepped out of immigration and customs at Narita Airport and she saw that smile in real life. In the following weeks, her heart ran ever faster, as he sat and listened to her broken English (if only the letters had helped her speaking), never showing the slightest impatience. It was strange how she could talk to him so easily. Love should have tied her in knots, but he would smile, his green-gray eyes would focus on her as if the rest of the world had disappeared, and somehow her tongue worked, the words flowed out, and he understood. She used to lie in bed and dream it was magic. Lying on her bed now, closer to undressed than any man except her husbands had ever seen her, at ease, safe, content: maybe it *was* magic.

Would they be together today if she had gone to America? She might have ended up back in Japan, but she didn't think so now. If only she had not been so young and scared and stupid. Or was something missing, her love or commitment somehow inadequate?

DRAWING TODAY was more exciting than the previous two days. The studies were progressing better than David had hoped. In fact, with today's pastel, it was almost as if he had never stopped painting. He was thinking of taking a trip to Shōko's art supply store tomorrow to buy a canvas, and he wondered at his reformation: how much arose from his captivation with her skin and how much from her relaxed air. Kelly's life was one of constant motion, so posing had made her so tense, even impatient, that they never managed sessions this long. But there lay Shōko late in the third morning looking as if not a moment had passed.

Shōko had always soothed him, though, even when they were teenagers. It was the letters that hooked him. He read them over and over, imagining Japan. When he saw that first picture of her with Yuki, he knew he had to meet her. The chance finally came in college. When people asked why he was going to Japan as an exchange student, he said what a great art school it was, never confessing that he was going solely for her. Then he saw her, quiet and shy on the surface, tantalizingly bubbly underneath. She was everything he loved in her letters but animate and wrapped in a beguiling cuteness. He fell for her completely. When he went back to America and then Amsterdam, it didn't go away; not that year, nor the next. If only he had married her then. The next step, though, meant one of them moving to the other's country, and he was too scared to do it, and too ashamed to ask something of her that he was unwilling to do yet himself. Being that scared, was it merely courage he lacked, or something else? Faith?

As he pondered it, though, he was sobered to realize what his disappointment over the years spent without Shōko said about his loyalty to Kelly.

"It is break time. You will be so tired," said Shōko in her girlish voice.

David smiled back. "I'm doing okay."

"I bring a treat."

David lay down on the floor to rest his back, and in a few minutes, Shōko returned with melon slices and little spoons. David, though, stayed on his back and just picked his up with his fingers. He was sore enough he was beginning to think losing Shōko to her job tomorrow might be a good thing. He would be all right for a day alone—but more?—a week?

He grew somber again as he thought of his last day with Kelly, and her words, the coldest he'd ever heard. He could not sense the slightest love remaining. How long was she a stranger, hating him, before she finally left?

David was glad his eyes were closed.

How will I ever stop the tears when divorce papers arrive, though?

Oh no! What if they already have?

I need to call the kids—tomorrow. They need to hear I haven't abandoned them.

DAVID LOOKED SORE, eyes closed, lying in the middle of the floor, his long legs crossed at the ankles.

If he wasn't so tired, I could mention that sitting up and using a spoon would be more civilized. Or should I keep him, exactly like this, let him lie here and eat melon with his fingers forever?

Shōko took a bite.

It will take a divorce, though.

Two, actually. No problem for me, but . . .

79

SHŌKO HAD LOOKED MORE RELAXED FOR THE LAST TEN MINUTES. Was she asleep? Now, as he heard her breathing slow, he stopped shading her pajamas and just stared at her. To another it might have seemed a sign of overwhelming boredom, but David sensed only contentment, seeing her comfortable enough posing before him to fall asleep.

She rolled flat on her back, losing the pose completely. David considered what to do. He did not want to lose the light, but he hated to wake her when she looked so tranquil.

Then Shōko moved again, only her left arm, which had been on her stomach, but as it slid off her onto the bed, it took that side of her unbuttoned pajama shirt with it.

David sat utterly still as he gazed on the gentle line of her neck where it met her chest, her little rib cage, her bottom ribs showing, and her skin soft and smooth. It was amazing, as if she'd hardly aged since she left college.

He thought of turning to a fresh page to capture the moment, but it would be too disrespectful to sketch parts of her as she slept that her modesty otherwise concealed. Somehow, even with all the nudes she must have done in art school, she maintained a straitlaced, childlike bashfulness.

David stood, stepped silently to the bed, and pulled his blanket from underneath it. Looking down on her, he knew that covering her was the right thing to do, but it felt wasteful. She deserved to be adored. He hesitated, yearning to touch her. It was sublime, the way her caramel skin swelled gently, a simple curve perfectly smooth, the form classic, however slight in volume. *And her idiot husband was dissatisfied?*

Two idiot husbands; whom she never would have married if I had done the right thing thirty years ago.

David carefully laid the blanket on her and stepped back to his chair. He sighed as he sat and rested his chin on his hand. *Our language and cultures are so different, when talking and understanding are the keys to making a marriage work.* Such was his fearful reasoning at twenty-two. If he could have looked into the future and seen her now, serene and loving, he could so easily have chosen this, and everything would be different.

Different didn't necessarily mean better, though. Even with Shōko's tender solicitude, there might still have been times he was so emotionally overwhelmed that he shut down. With all the other problems of trying to make a living at art, could he say with certainty that Shōko would not have left him?

He looked at her sleeping face and thought back to that first night under her bed, her feet walking softly around the room. *No, she wouldn't have left, not ever. I could have loved her completely—*

It knocked him straight up in his chair.

I do love her completely! I always have. And seeing her again, feeling this, I'll never be whole without her. I don't know where we'll live or what job I'll find, but one thing's for certain, nothing will keep us apart—

And if I could bring Kelly back?

David's mouth fell open. He wrapped his arms around himself as he doubled over. Flush and sweating, dizzy, he shut his eyes. His thoughts, devoid of words, were all pictures, snippets so short he could barely identify them: Kelly's tears as he slipped a ring onto her finger; her breath warm on his ear as she whispered that she was pregnant; holding Melissa tight to his chest, her elbow shattered, as Kelly raced them to the hospital; comforting Kelly through the long night when her mother passed; the hours of painting Kelly, Melissa, Ben, time and time again; and on it went, emotions so intense they left him trembling.

Everything that's mattered is Kelly. Life without her will be agony.

It is agony!

Raising his head and looking at Shōko, thinking of Kelly, the loves were altogether different, except that each beat with his whole heart, each a perfect dream, two sirens' songs, never to fade, ever to tear him asunder. He could not imagine a day without Shōko, yet he burned for Kelly to return and love him forever; these two loves, inseverable, irreconcilable, impossible.

David stared at Shōko as he gasped for breath.

I'm damned!

No matter how joyful his days with one, he was doomed to grieve the rest of his life for the other. His soul, cloven in two, would bleed forever.

Shōko slept peacefully, seemingly floating in his tears, as David pulled his knees tight to his chest and measured the lifetime of misery that lay before him. He saw only one precious bit of consolation, useless as it was: the choice between them was already made.

80

KELLY PERUSED THE SHELVES OF THE CONVENIENCE STORE LOOKING for something familiar enough to be appetizing. There were probably tasty things, but it was all so chancy. She still remembered her first trip to a Japanese grocery store, when she bought what she guessed was cooking oil and it turned out to be *sushi-su*, sweetened vinegar. She did not know until she was heating it up to fry chicken and the apartment started to smell like Easter egg dye. She had little appetite since she got back, though, so finding food was not much of a problem.

Perhaps I should start with something to drink.

She looked at the refrigerated soft drinks.

They can't be serious: she had her choice of regular American-looking Pepsi or sea-foam-green Ice Cucumber Pepsi.

Why not live the adventure?

To go with her drink oddity, she chose an egg salad sandwich—at least, she hoped it was egg salad; time would tell. She topped it off with a bag of potato chips. She was sure about those because there was a big potato character on the bag. (Although she wasn't sure whether the finger he pointed upward showed number one market share or whether he'd realized something of great import, perhaps the meaning of life, or potato life, anyway.)

Carrying her white plastic bag into the muggy afternoon air, Kelly felt the gray sky weigh on her shoulders like a mass of wet concrete. The air was warm and thick with the scent of chestnut trees in bloom, but she was oblivious. She ambled toward the apartment but stopped.

I don't want to go there, not without David, ever.

She looked around, then turned and headed to the levee. She twisted the cap from her soda and was about to take a drink when she noticed it indeed smelled like cucumber. A quick sip eased her fears: it was Pepsi— but the aftertaste as it went down was cucumber. Oh, this was *not* good. It was what she had, though, so she continued sipping it as she walked, thinking about what David would have chosen, grapefruit juice.

We used to do everything together, living and dreaming as if we were one person. How did we turn into two?

The more she thought back on it, the more she thought David could have been collapsing when she left and crumbling for weeks before that. But he could never kill himself! *He loves the kids too much to make them live the rest of their lives with that pain.*

Kelly climbed the stairs to the top of the levee, opened the potato chips, and started down the path. She looked at the potato character in his almost disco-like pose. Why did everything in Japan have a cute mascot character, even the police? *Perhaps if they spent a little less effort on being cute, they could find a missing foreigner.*

As she walked along, Kelly traced with her eyes the channels of the river, engorged with last night's rain. She studied the big cedar trees and stands of bamboo behind the far levee. Visions of David popped in and out of her aimless thoughts, until finally, she saw the day she left. She wasn't the only one who said awful things that day. Was he serious that he was only here because she pushed him into it? All she told him was that he would never get into top management at Micron. It was true! And it was all his choice. Accusing her of pushing him into this job and then abandoning him, that she had no reason to stay now that his career was over; more than a lie, it was cruel! It was frustration and loneliness that drove her back to America, and David was supposed to go home too. She should have talked it out, but he was ignoring her, and nothing made her angrier. She would gladly swallow that anger now, though, and every one of those horrible words, especially telling him to put her bags in the car. She had never done anything that stupid.

Kelly stopped and stared out at the water flowing past her fast and powerful.

Their last minutes together were too strange. He was as angry as she had ever seen him, but as he drove her to the station, not a word; no anger, no sadness, no goodbye. He set her bags on the sidewalk, got back in the car and drove away.

It was as if he was a robot, or dead inside—

Her thoughts, until then a leisurely afternoon drive, swerved hopelessly quickly, no signal, no braking, into a dark alley to hell. Her mind simply took another step, but an unspeakably horrid one: *If he did it, how—?*

She tried to dismiss it, but it was too late; the question finished itself and the answer followed in an instant, striking with such force she could not stop her mind from reeling toward the water. It was undeniable; they had talked about it!

Kelly turned her back to the river and looked toward the little houses by the levee, but the sound of the rushing water carried her away, an entire river pushing her into a vision of David drowning himself. The potato chips poured out of the bag as she watched him bind his ankles and wrists, hesitate, then throw himself into the current. She saw him struggle helplessly as his air ran out and panic gripped him; and finally, going limp, he sank.

He killed himself. Oh, Lord, no! Please no!

Raising her face to the heavens, she opened her mouth to scream, but what came out was a long, mournful wail as she convulsed in tears.

"KELLY-*SAN*, what happened?" asked Detective Kikuchi, worry creasing his brow.

Kelly whispered, "I decided to go home."

Kikuchi was silent. He had wondered when it might come to this, but what should he say to a woman who had finally, justifiably, abandoned all hope? It was not his place to reinstill expectations, despite his own sliver of optimism that remained.

After sitting silently with Kelly for a few minutes, though, he had to say something. And even if David was somehow still alive, more searching would not turn up someone who did not want to be found. "Thank you for tell us. So if I understand, we have your permission to end our search?"

Kelly didn't make eye contact. Obviously exhausted, conclusively beaten, she merely nodded her head.

There was paperwork to do, after which Kelly followed Kikuchi out to the street. He bowed one last time. She bowed too, awkwardly, before she turned and walked away. She moved aimlessly, like a leaf blowing down the sidewalk. *But that's how it feels at first*, thought Kikuchi. *She'll pull out of it, eventually. She's a strong one. She'll recover—as much as anyone ever does.*

81

MOST EVENINGS, SHŌKO WAS STRIPPING OFF EITHER OFFICE CLOTHES or casual clothes as she got ready for the bath, but she had been in her white pajamas all evening. In fact, apart from the time she spent downstairs with her parents, the whole day was pajama time. They were so comfortable she wished she could wear them all the time.

Maybe I can. Maybe David and I can just live in pajamas. What did he call them? Like jam, but not fruit.

She almost giggled.

Jamus? Jamamas? Jammies! Mmm, jammies.

She smiled at herself in the bathroom mirror as she undid her pajamas, and her skin appeared, button by button. It looked smooth and soft. She ran her hands up and down her chest and stomach, then opened her shirt and pulled it off her shoulders. Extending her hands down behind her, she relished the smooth linen as it slid down her arms. She looked at them in the mirror. They were nicely toned for a woman her age. Looking at her chest, her stomach, then turning to try to see her back, she looked quite fit. She especially liked her trim waist. She looked at the gentle curve and thought how feminine it looked in pastel, even with her pajamas on. It was also nice to have breasts this firm after fifty. *Maybe there are advantages to being small.*

Making eye contact with her smiling self, Shōko blushed. It was bath time. She slipped off her pajama pants and panties together in one smooth motion and stepped out of them. Her legs were still firm. She turned. Maybe her bottom could use a little work, but it was a nice size. She was glad it was round and not flat or boney like so many—

She smiled as she realized she was looking herself over like a schoolgirl.

Shōko cleaned herself methodically, starting with her hair and ending with her toes. She gave herself a good scrubbing, trying to get off as much of the used-up Shōko as she could. She knew it was a lost cause, but it wasn't a cause she really needed to win. David liked her skin. He even said so. In fact, she had to tell him to stop saying so. He talked a lot. It was embarrassing when he said something that was better simply felt. He would say it again later, though, and then again. But he was American, and that was their way, all emotionally oozing.

One thing David managed to make clear without words, though, was wanting to be with her. Three days of drawing with no makeup, no hiding, no covering up—well, he hadn't seen her naked, but he had seen enough of her to know what she looked like, and he wanted what he saw. She could see it in those leaky American eyes. He wanted her body, her soul, all of her. Three days of perfect intimacy, and he wanted more.

She smiled. It would be joyful to grow old with a man who liked dried apples.

She gave herself one final rinse and then stepped into the deep, compact tub and felt herself melting. She had loved the bath since she was a little child. Then, she bathed with her mother and father, the whole family sharing bath time, not uncommon with small children. She had never bathed with her husbands, though.

Maybe this one . . .

82

THE APARTMENT WAS NEVER DARK; THE CITY LIGHTS GLOWED THROUGH the curtains even when they were closed. Kelly left them open tonight, though, and the clouds, low and thick, seemed to reflect the glare of the entire city into her bedroom. She saw the stark shadow of each item in the room as she looked at it in turn, as if taking a final inventory. Not a single thing was hers. There wasn't even much of David's.

So little left behind . . . made it easier for him to leave? And if I had been here, could he have left me behind so easily?

She wiped her eyes. Tomorrow she would deal with it: packing, throwing things away; tomorrow, in the light, not in this awful pale.

She needed to sleep, but there was little chance of it tonight.

Perhaps if I have a shower, wash off the day.

And how do I wash off the guilt and—

No. A shower; that's all I need to think about.

Dragging herself into the bathroom, there seemed to be a dull ache everywhere, but it was worst in her neck and shoulders.

David rubbed them when they hurt like—

No! I don't want to think about him anymore! I don't want to think about anything!

There was a large mirror in the bathroom, and for a long time she simply stood, staring at herself. She had always been pleased with how well she was aging, but tonight, for the first time in her life, she felt faded, used up, as dry as forgotten toast.

She pulled off her pants and began unbuttoning her shirt. When she was younger, she took her shirt off first, but David once commented that no pants was sexier than no shirt.

Kelly stepped into the heat of the shower, her mind swollen with an unending stream of things she could never share with him again, thoughts to drown in.

The walls outside the shower were damp with condensation before her tears flowed in earnest, but once started, there was no stopping them. Her breathing now just gasps between the moans, Kelly's shoulders heaved uncontrollably as she sank to her knees and curled into a ball on the shower floor.

Oh! Oh, dear Lord, no! I have to call Melissa and Ben!

83

SHŌKO EXPLAINED TO DAVID A FEW DAYS AGO THAT A JAPANESE BATH is not only about getting clean, it also renews the spirit as you calmly soak in the hot water, the day wholly washed away to prepare for a peaceful night's sleep. You wash outside the bathtub, so there is no need to draw fresh bathwater for each person. The order of bathing in Shōko's house was the same almost every night. Shōko's mother was first, then her father, after which they went to bed. Shōko bathed after her parents, and these days David bathed last. She tried to hurry her time in the bath, as did David, so that her parents wouldn't notice the change, and Shōko made sure all was clear before David hurried down the stairs.

It didn't take David long to wash, and thoroughly rinsed, he lowered his foot into the bath. It burned for the first couple of seconds. In went the other foot, and then he lowered himself into the water up to his neck. He sat still, steeping in the potent heat and breathing the dense air, as he waited for the tension to leach out of him as it had on other nights. He thought of the last sketching he did that afternoon, adding richness and texture to the crimson gradient at the bottom of the page. He also traced in hard pastel the red yarn where it dangled from Shōko's finger to the bed and disappeared into the gradient as it fell to the floor. He thought of the brush he would use when he made the line in paint.

His contented thoughts, though, soon gave way to darkness. A lifetime of soaking would not begin to ease his tearing pain. No matter the love that might drench him in a lifetime with Shōko, he had lost Kelly's. Never able to jettison his guilt or grief over driving her away, he would spend the remainder of his life being dismembered, night upon night.

But I have Shōko. I'll fill our years with all the love she's ever hoped for.

David wiped his face, leaned his head back, and closed his eyes. He tried to clear his mind of everything but her. She would be his solace.

He felt the water soften him.

I can't have them both, but I have one. I have Shōko.

If I lost her, though, this world truly would be over—

And without the slightest warning, the world ended. As he heard the door open, he had only enough time to open his eyes and see Shōko's tiny mother standing naked in the doorway before he heard the scream. It was the loudest he'd ever heard, and as he recoiled, his only thought was wonder at how such volume was possible from someone so small.

She was gone as quickly as she had appeared. At the sound of doors and running feet, David leapt from the bath and wrapped himself in a towel. He expected Shōko or her father to burst in, but soon realized they were running to her mother.

Shōko appeared a minute later with a look of utter panic. "I could not stop her. She called the police! I hurry downstairs but she is already talking to them!"

"The police?"

"Yes, David, yes! *Kōban* is only a few blocks away. They will come so fast! What will we do?"

David wasn't even half dressed before he heard the first officers arrive.

VI

Skinned Alive

生きたまま皮を剥ぐ

84

DAVID LAY ON THE FLOOR, WATCHING THE COLORS FLOW IN PSYCHEDELIC patterns on the insides of his eyelids. He tried not to think, but his mind had no lock, and with each thought bullied out, another slipped in through the open door. Still, thinking about not thinking kept at bay the thoughts he dreaded most. He longed to sleep—

"It's not as bad as you're making it out to be."

He maneuvered himself onto his back and covered his eyes with his arm.

"You know there's always a way out."

She'd go away.

"Davey, you answer when you're spoken to. We respect people and our words show that respect. And you answer when I speak to you, because I paddle your little behind if you don't!"

"No, you don't."

"Yes, but you're talking now, aren't you?" *There was a self-satisfied smile in her voice, although he couldn't see it.*

"Yeah, I guess."

"Now is that how you answer me?"

"I'm sorry, Miss Roselda."

"That's better. Now, child, it's time for you to sleep."

"It must be four a.m., but I don't know because they took my watch. Is there any way to make it darker in here?"

"Is there a switch on the wall?"

David uncurled enough to look at the door and saw a switch next to it. He crawled out, turned out the light, and crawled back under the bed.

"Can we make it quieter? All the footsteps are driving me crazy."

"No, David, I don't think so. But I can give you something nicer to listen to." With that, Roselda began singing, her alto voice soft and rich. It was a hymn she sang to him countless times as a child: "Though swiftly falls the eventide, it bears no fear or sorrow. There is a light that e'er guides me along. . . ."

David awoke with a start as he banged hard into the bed above him, but it wasn't Shōko's, and there was no *futon* on the floor beneath him. His door was closed, but he heard noises from the hall: voices, doors, footsteps. The slit of a window showed it was still dark outside. He must not have slept more than a few minutes.

He closed his eyes, but he could still see things. The first couldn't have lasted more than a second, the memory of the ceiling above the entryway in Shōko's house. David puzzled for a moment before he remembered himself in a fetal position on the floor near the *genkan*. One of the officers shook him and turned him over so he was looking at the ceiling before he curled back up. He remembered voices too. There must have been people everywhere.

The next scene was a little longer: Shōko's mother screaming at her as Shōko knelt, crying, her face bowed to the floor. He wanted to stop it, to protect her somehow, but he was powerless, and as he had then, he curled up tighter on the floor and covered his head with his arms.

But the next was worse: Shōko's mother crumpled onto the floor. Her father knelt, his face in his hands, while Shōko, still kneeling, panic-stricken, held her mother and sobbed.

The image of her collapse quickly ended, but the next one went on and on, as the police and then the team from the ambulance worked on her. As he gasped for breath, he tried to focus on his knees, but he was compelled to watch, to see whether his weakness and selfishness had killed Shōko's mother.

By the time the ambulance pulled out, he was so sodden with shame he could not let go of his knees. He held them fast, coiled up tight, as two officers carried him to a police car. Flashing lights bathed everything in red: cars, houses, people—so many people, a whole neighborhood, some staring, some merely glancing, but everyone talking and everyone looking. He wanted to disappear—until he heard Shōko following, crying, telling him everything would be all right. With all that was happening, Shōko was somehow thinking of him.

THE DOCTOR REFUSED to let anyone in, even the police. As Kelly pressed her face to the small one-way mirror in the door of David's room, hoping for any glimpse of him, she heard the bang. *He must have hit his head—lying on the floor under the bed!*

SHŌKO, STANDING NEARBY, knew better. It was his shoulder hitting as he turned over suddenly in his sleep.

85

ALIVE! AFTER DETECTIVE KIKUCHI'S MIDNIGHT CALL, KELLY COULD finally breathe. She waited forever, though, before he called back to tell her he was sending a car to take her to the hospital where David was being admitted. Kelly gripped the phone, her other hand pressed to the wall to steady herself, expecting to hear that David had been in a terrible accident. But then Kikuchi said it was the psychiatric ward, and she trembled as she set down the phone.

The officer in the car could not speak much English, but he told her that David had been staying with a local woman. Kelly broke out in a cold sweat, her stomach wringing itself into a knot, as the officer tried in vain to give her a coherent explanation.

The hospital offered no relief. Kelly's few glimpses into David's room, more like a prison cell than a hospital room, made her cringe. The walls were covered with something soft and there were no sharp corners on any of the surfaces. Other than the narrowest of windows, it had nothing but a toilet and sink in the far corner behind a low partition, and a bed that was built into the wall. Oddly, David wasn't in it. Then the doctor explained, and Kelly turned away until she could compose herself.

The nurses monitored David with a camera mounted in the ceiling of his room, and Kelly longed for an excuse to plant herself near them. After the doctor turned her away, though, he ushered her into a dull, stark waiting room. So she sat, clinging to what the officer had said, that it was a woman and her parents.

Who goes to stay with his lover and her parents? So perhaps it's not an affair. But all this time in Japan, ignoring me, refusing to leave, with no apparent reason. . . . Damn it, it's not fair! David alive should be joy, not a knife in the gut!

Unable to read even the captions of photos, it took Kelly thirty minutes to leaf through every magazine in the waiting room. So she went to peer again through the small window in David's door. He was out from beneath the bed. His back was to her, stepping away as he paced. They had him in a hospital gown and a lightweight robe, but he had none of the sickly or injured look of a hospital patient, and as he turned, the intensity in his face unnerved her. *Good heavens! What happened to him in that woman's house?*

Kelly returned to the waiting room dazed. Images assaulted her as if punctuated by a ghoulish laugh track: David mentally shattered, institutionalized—and there was nothing she could do but wait. So, exhausted, helpless, and alone, she curled up sideways in her chair, held herself, and cried.

WHILE HER MOTHER'S doctor stopped short of saying Shōko caused her mother's attack, he suggested that she wait at least a day before visiting. He hoped it was merely syncope brought on by hyperventilation, but he wanted to keep her for observation.

So, though it was the middle of the night and far outside of visiting hours, Shōko went upstairs to the psychiatric ward. Kelly was already there, trying to convince the doctor to let her see David. Shōko realized immediately who she was but did not introduce herself. What was there to say to David's wife? *And why did the demon come back?* Shōko looked away, not wanting to be caught glaring.

Shōko listened to the doctor's conversation with Kelly, but he was not going to relent, so Shōko walked out to the waiting room, sat, and stared at the doors to the ward.

Soon, though, Kelly followed. Shōko looked away as Kelly came in, but Kelly sat in front of her. Shōko gripped the arms of her chair and stared at Kelly, the woman who pushed David away from painting, abandoned him when he was too weak to make it alone, drove him to the brink of suicide. She should have stayed gone—forever!

At length, Kelly went back into the ward, but shortly returned, sat in the first chair by the door, and broke down completely.

Watching Kelly disintegrate, a shiver ran up Shōko's spine. She tried to look away, but her eyes kept returning to Kelly, so she retrieved her handkerchief from her purse, pressed it to her face, and went to see what was happening.

It was her first glance into David's room, and she gasped into her handkerchief as she saw him pacing. In all the days with her, he never looked this haggard. There were blue-gray shadows beneath his eyes, and his skin hung on his face like the hospital gown did from his shoulders. She watched as he circled the room once, twice. As drawn as his face appeared, there was power in each fluid step, tension in every movement.

David suddenly stopped and turned toward the door. Shōko stared at him. She watched him breathing slowly, standing as if every muscle in his body was taut, even his fingers. And with her own fingers trembling against her lips, Shōko backed away from the door.

KELLY WAS SURPRISED when Detective Kikuchi came striding back through the waiting room with a young detective and gave her no more than a quick bow before entering the ward. She followed to see whether the doctor would let them into David's room. The Japanese woman who was in the waiting room earlier was standing near David's door.

She must belong to a patient in one of the nearby rooms. For her sake, I hope the person's in better shape than David.

At that point, the doctor approached Kelly and she asked, "What can you tell me?"

"His behavior is abnormal. Maybe he has psychological trauma."

"May I see him?"

"No, he must sleep."

"May I see him tomorrow?"

"Maybe tomorrow, maybe next day or day after."

"Can I wait here, just in case?"

"No, go sleep home is best. You rest and be ready to see him."

The doctor was right. There was nothing to do, and Kelly was exhausted. The doctor kindly had someone call her a taxi while she made her way to the night entrance, and soon the taxi dropped her off.

She was standing in front of the apartment door, fishing in her purse for the key, when it dawned on her: *The Japanese woman the detectives escorted out while I was talking to the doctor, that was her! I should have recognized her from David's sketches!*

By the time she found her key, she was shaking so badly she could barely get it in the lock.

86

"DAVID, CALM YOURSELF."

"How? I need to get out of here. Look, there isn't even any toilet paper. They're afraid I'll stuff it down my throat and choke myself to death."

"You'll get out. What difference does a day or two make?"

"Shōko needs me."

"And she knows you're here. She needs you well more than anything."

"I'll be well as soon as I see her."

"And the calmer you are, the sooner they'll let you. You think they'll let her in here with you pacing like some wild animal?"

"Maybe I am. I've ripped her life apart. She was already in hiding from her psychotic husband, and I came charging in and destroyed the little sanctuary she'd found."

"Don't make it sound so black."

"Isn't it? How's she supposed to go on after our escapade killed her mother?"

Roselda's voice softened. "Now, you don't know that her mother died. Did she look dead when they carried her out?"

"No, but she looked close."

"She's a tough little lady. She'll be fine; just you wait and see. Now try to sleep. You know you'll feel better after some sleep."

"I don't deserve to feel better."

"You don't remember that's what you were telling imaginary Shōko two weeks ago?"

"I deserve every bit of pain and guilt, today, tomorrow, and the rest of my existence for what I've done to her."

"You aren't getting a little carried away?"

"You ever obliterate someone's happiness?"

"Why don't we wait till tomorrow to find out whether her happiness is all destroyed."

He paced.

"David, sit."

He stopped and stared at the door. She was right, of course; he needed to sleep.

David heard the lock in the door moving. A doctor and nurse entered and turned on the light. The nurse gave him a pleasant smile and said, "You drink medicine now," as she held out a small paper cup with a pill in it, and a bigger paper cup with water.

"What is it?" asked David.

The doctor seemed to understand but was searching for the English. "This is for relax. Calm medicine. You drink now."

"You're calming down just fine on your own. You don't want them pumping you full of pills. Tell them, 'No.'"

"No."

The doctor regarded the nurse as if to say, "Your turn." She thought, then smiled. "Medicine help to sleep, be good health."

"I don't need it."

There was a short conversation in Japanese, the doctor turned to go, and the nurse bowed to David and followed the doctor out.

The lock clicked and David shrugged. *"That was simple."*

"You don't need a sedative. They're worried you'll hurt yourself, but you won't."

"Because Shōko needs me."

"Because I won't let you. Now you lie down."

David turned off the light and crawled under the bed.

He listened to her sing for a few minutes before he said, "Miss Roselda?"

"Yes, child?"

"Am I crazy? I mean, I'm talking to someone who's not here."

"Not the picture of mental health, I don't suppose."

"That's what I was afraid of."

"Now, slow down and think about it before you go deciding you're insane. You said you know I'm not here."

"Yes."

"Are you talking out loud? Do you hear my voice?"

"No."

"Then you be forgetting that worry and get some sleep."

<hr>

87

KELLY WOKE UP LATE AND LAY IN BED, WISHING AN EARTHQUAKE would buckle the walls and bring the apartment above pancaking down on top of her. It would be better than having to think of David at that woman's house. She tried to hold on to the fact that it was a whole family. Although too horrid to think, as much as it had hurt believing David was dead, the chance of an affair now seemed harder to live with.

The little bitch even had the gall to come to the hospital!

But every time she asked, "How did we get to this?" the answers failed to fit, a jigsaw puzzle made up entirely of single pieces from other puzzles.

To dwell on it, though, would only hack away at the calm, loving feelings she needed to show if they let her visit David today. So Kelly got out of bed and focused on getting to the hospital as quickly as possible. She had a glass of milk, showered, and put on a diaphanous sundress, light peach, one of David's favorites.

THE HOSPITAL was busier than last night, but it was not long before the doctor sent for Kelly. He was waiting at the nurses' station, a different doctor from last night. After the briefest of introductions, Kelly went straight to the matter at hand: "How's David?"

"Last night Mr. Reese sleeps—sleeped after you go home until one hour ago. That is good."

"I looked in the room, but I didn't see him."

"He is under a bed."

"Asleep?"

"No, awake, but stays under a bed."

Belying that blow, she put on her calmest voice. "May I visit him?"

"First, he must come out. We must be patience. Even if he has bad trauma, he can recover." Glancing away, Kelly saw the Japanese woman enter the ward. She was coming down the hall . . . talking to the nurse, who nodded toward the doctor . . . walking over . . . standing behind the doctor . . . listening?

Get out!

No, I mustn't look at her. Talking with David's doctor is too important. Concentrate on his eyes.

"First, we should wait. He does not hurt himself. He is quiet and sleeps. We can wait. We have time."

With that, the doctor excused himself—but the Japanese woman followed and started talking to him.

She has no business talking to David's doctor!

But they kept talking. The conversation continued for five minutes before the doctor walked back over to Kelly and asked, "Mrs. Reese, she is friend, yes?"

No!

But even more than Kelly wanted to tear the woman's throat out, she wanted to find out what they'd been saying. "If she says so."

"She says to try give Mr. Reese a paper and pencil."

"What for?"

"She says if he can draw, he comes out."

Kelly looked over at the woman and stared, her jaw slack and her eyes wide in amazement at the woman's audacity, and the woman averted her eyes and shrank back behind the doctor.

At least she's embarrassed to be seen. She should just leave!

But it's David who matters, not this . . . whore!—who has no right to be here suggesting anything! So she thinks she knows him? Fine!

Kelly answered in a measured tone, "I'm not opposed if you think it's a good idea."

"He is ill to behave like he does. I do not diagnose him yet—that takes time—but we must be careful he does not injure himself and pencil is sharp. I think no."

The woman stepped to the doctor's side, bowed low, and said to him, in English, "Please, he needs to draw. If pencil is too dangerous, please allow crayon. Anything. Please. Small child use crayon. Not so dangerous at all. Please! He will not hurt himself. I am sure. He just needs to draw!"

Her pleading tone stunned Kelly, but then Kelly's neck and shoulders tightened. The woman was imploring out of more than friendly concern, much more. Kelly asked, "Is a crayon safe?"

The doctor looked back and forth between the two women and finally said, "Yes, I think so. And we watch."

Kelly took her place at David's door, and the Japanese woman waited across from the nurses' station. It was twenty minutes before the nurse entered his room. Kelly watched her put the paper and crayon where David would have to leave his hiding place to get them. Kelly wasn't sure what to hope for, the infinitesimal chance that David would show himself, or that paper and crayon would go untouched and this woman who thought she understood David so well would learn that real intimacy comes with years together, not two weeks of—

David crawled out and sat in front of the paper. He picked up the crayon, put the end in his mouth, and held it there for a minute. He took the crayon from his lips and rolled it between his fingers as he stared at the paper, and finally, he bent over and started to draw.

Kelly swallowed hard. She ran her hands down the front of her skirt to smooth it as she took a deep breath, and she turned to study the woman.

Is this really S?

She was small, shy looking, altogether ordinary, not some young skirt David was chasing (and he was not one to stray), but no casual acquaintance either. She was clearly special to David, quite close—and tremendously dangerous.

Kelly walked toward her.

Be polite. Avoid emotionally charged phrases like "my husband." Offer sincere thanks for what she accomplished just now. And find out whether she's who I think she is.

The woman seemed anxious as Kelly approached, so Kelly smiled and held out her hand. "Hello, I'm Kelly Reese. I wanted to introduce myself and thank you for suggesting the crayon."

The woman bowed. "I try to help." She looked at Kelly's hand before she reached out and took it, not firmly. "Nice to meet you. My name is Shōko Kawasaki."

88

"MR. REESE, I AM HAPPY YOU FEEL BETTER AND YOU ARE COMFORTABLE on a bed. I show picture you draw to nurse and doctor. Everyone so impress your much talent," said the doctor.

David said nothing in return. He simply sat with his crayon and paper, the third piece they allowed him since morning.

"You have visitor. She waits night and today."

For the first time, David stopped drawing and made eye contact.

"Medication is good for you. You must drink before visitor comes."

"Miss Roselda?" he said to her in his head.

"I heard."

"I want to—I have to see her, but they want to medicate me."

"You don't need it."

"Yes, but I do need her. If meds are the only way—"

"Calm down. Didn't I say she'd be waiting to see you? She's not going anywhere. If you're out from under that bed and happy for a day or two, they'll let you see her without medication. Have a smidgen of patience, for heaven's sake."

"You can't ask me to wait. I want this—" He paused. "Miss Roselda, I want this as badly as I wanted to die two weeks ago."

Roselda was quiet for a few seconds before she answered, "All right then."

"All right, Doctor."

The doctor left, and the nurse appeared a few minutes later. David looked the pill over and asked, "What is this?"

"Medication for you. Please drink now," and she handed him the cup of water.

He did not want to swallow something without knowing what it was, but he did it for Shōko.

"Thank you, Mr. Reese."

"You're welcome, Nurse . . . Nurse-*san*."

She covered her mouth as she laughed. "My name is Suzuki. Two other nurse are also Suzuki, so it is easy to remember. I am here to help you every way. Please let's be so cooperating together." She bowed.

David bowed in return. "It's nice to meet you, one Nurse Suzuki of three. I'll try my best to be a cooperative patient. How long before I can see her?"

"Oh, David, don't be so anxious."

"Maybe one hour or maybe less. Do you need a new paper?"

"No, I'm not quite done with this one yet. Although . . . I don't suppose I could get an actual pencil."

"Please say again?"

"Could I have a pencil?"

"*Etto* ... I ask doctor, but today maybe crayon is good for drawing. I can bring more colors, maybe. You do so beautiful picture with crayon. I want to take home and see on my wall." She smiled broadly in admiration.

"Thank you, you're too kind."

"I come back soon." She bowed politely as she left.

David sat on the bed, too excited to draw. *"I feel way better."*

"Trouble is the doctor's gonna think it's that pill. That's why I didn't want you to take it. Anyway, it'll all come out in the wash. He'll see you're better, and it won't matter how you got that way."

"Yeah, I suppose you're right."

She laughed. "Of course I'm right. And you don't need to be all jumping up and down inside either."

"Seeing her again after staring at these walls. I hope she's okay. And her mother. I just hope everything's okay."

"It's gonna be fine. You just be calm when she comes in and don't be all excited or crying or anything. You need to show them all some emotional control, so they'll let you out."

"Cool, calm, controlled; I can do that."

He lay on the bed—to relax and to show he was relaxed—but in the next few minutes, he journeyed far past relaxed. This wasn't just some mild anti-anxiety medication. He felt ... wonderful. He didn't need to draw. He didn't need to do *anything*. He could be just fine feeling like this for ... forever. *And wooow! How'd they ever make the ceiling tiles so ... full of little holes?*

Without the pills, David would have hopped to his feet when the door opened, unable to contain himself, but he and the bed were such friends he thought he'd simply stay melted into it. He didn't even turn his head. He just waited for Shōko's little form to appear before his eyes, all that warm sunshine and—

"Hi David," came a voice, quiet and tentative.

Why is Shōko using Kelly's voice?

"How you feeling? May I sit?"

Why does she look like Kelly? What was in those pills? "Sure, you sit and let me get my head on straight."

"Okay. Take all the time you need. I'm not going anywhere."

David watched her sit, still looking every whit like Kelly.

If I close my eyes, maybe she'll look like herself in a minute. "I feel terrible about your mother. Is she gonna be all right?"

"My mother?"

"Uh-huh."

"David, Mom passed away three years ago. Are you okay?"

David looked at her again. She wasn't sounding or looking the least bit Shōko-y. *What kind of hallucination . . . ?*

"She doesn't look like herself," he said out loud to Roselda.

"I know. This is so strange."

"David, who are you talking to?"

"Doesn't sound like herself either," said David.

"David?"

"You think she's real? Or is she in my imagination too?"

"You can see her, right?"

"So, she's a hallucination?"

"Prob'ly."

"David, are you okay? Who are you talking to?"

"Yes, she must be."

"So, hallucination wife, what gives you the right to come barging into my medication? You hated me and left me and wanted me to die. Isn't that kinda final?"

"David! I never hated you. And I didn't leave *you*, I left *Japan*. The idea was for you to leave too."

"You said you hated me."

She choked up. "I know, David. I'm sorry. I didn't mean it. I was angry because the project was killing you and you wouldn't leave. I didn't mean it. Really, I didn't."

"Sure sounded as if you meant it. Then you pack your bags and leave. I'm falling apart and you fly away."

"I know. I'm sorry. I made a terrible mistake."

"You didn't bother to call and say so."

"I was so angry. Why did you ignore everything I was saying? That's not like you. It was as if there was something else going on. Was there?"

"Yes! My project going down the drain and my career with it!"

"That's all?"

"What, you need more?"

"Why couldn't you just quit and leave?" She was sobbing.

"Because I wanted to succeed! I wanted you to be proud of me! Isn't that what you wanted?"

"Of course, but this project was a lost cause from the start."

"So you leave me? You couldn't help? You had to break me instead?"

"Oh, David!" She was crying too hard to speak any more.

The door opened. It was the doctor.

"And your lawyer calls the same day! How long did you plan it, leaving, divorcing me, without a word? Just your lawyer calling while you're still on the plane!"

"No, David! No, I swear!"

"Mrs. Reese, I think today is short talk. You meet again soon."

Kelly put her hand to David's cheek, but he batted it away.

The doctor escorted Kelly from the room. David rolled over and was silent for a long time before he said to Roselda, still out loud, "There. She finally got to hear what she did to me."

"Yes, David, but the real Kelly did that, not the hallucination."

"Yeah, but hallucination Kelly can tell real Kelly. I mean, they talk, right?"

"They talk?"

"Of course, Miss Roselda, like you and I talk."

"Oh, I hope not. I surely hope not."

"NO, ŌTA-*SAN*, you're not under arrest. Neither is Reese-*san*. As much trouble as you caused, neither of you broke any laws. But do you have any idea of the time and resources we expended trying to find him?"

Shōko did not respond, but the way she hung her head, Detective Kikuchi understood: she had bowed so low, apologized so many times, her shame was so complete, there was nothing left to say.

"So our part in this is finished. You're free to go. There is no plan to deport Reese-*san*, although I doubt Fuji-Star will want to keep him, so it looks as if he'll be going home."

"Thank you."

"If I may offer a personal comment . . ."

Shōko did not meet his gaze, so Kikuchi leaned forward in the waiting-room chair. His voice was softer as he continued: "First, I'm glad your mother is all right. As far as Reese-*san*, I know how close the two of you were when you were younger. I read . . . or that is, I got to see . . . he was . . . special. I can understand how you feel, better than you may realize. I know you were trying to help him these last few weeks, but you must understand, he's quite ill. He needs medical attention, the kind he'll get back in America from a psychiatrist he can talk to in his own language. So I hope you'll let him go, cut the ties completely and permanently. It's best for everyone."

She nodded and whispered, "I understand."

As flat as she looked before his advice, she now appeared crushed. Witnessing her anguish, Kikuchi wondered for a moment whether it had been his place to pop what few bubbles of hope she might have had left.

But grief is a process. So is loss. At some point, you have to let go of the thing that causes the pain. Even if you love it.

He sat up and looked away.

Even if it's the only thing in the world you want to hold.

SHŌKO STARED at the floor tiles, worn and chipped. The police were done with her, and she could not visit her mother yet.

Shōko shut her eyes and sighed.

I ought to at least peek in on David before I go home.

As Shōko entered the ward, the doctor was huddled with the nurses watching a monitor, but as Shōko approached, he suddenly ran to David's room. Shōko hurried behind the nurses' station while the doctor escorted Kelly out. She was crying so hard she could hardly speak: "He didn't . . . know it was really me! He was . . . so angry!"

Shōko waited for the doctor to leave the ward with Kelly before she ran to David's room, but he was lying there, looking quite calm. After a minute, though, he started talking. She pressed her ear to the door.

Roselda? Who worked for his family in Chicago and cared for him when he was growing up?

Leaning hard on the door, Shōko bowed her head.

89

AS SHŌKO WALKED FROM THE BUS STOP, SHE KEPT HER EYES ON THE street, lest as she passed some doorway or garden, she spy a neighbor. Every one of them had been visited by the police, shown David's picture, asked whether they had seen the missing foreigner. But with the next turn, her house would be in sight, and the full shame of last night.

Shōko stopped and looked toward the river.

If I wasn't there, would he have drowned himself?

Shōko had thought of taking her own life after her first marriage, and she knew it took incredible resolve. It was almost more tempting now.

Shōko forced herself to walk again.

She had not been home since they put her into the back of a police car in front of the entire neighborhood. Most kept a discreet distance, but they watched. Now as she hurried for her front door, the memory of it forced her head down until she viewed only the pavement.

Shōko slid the door closed behind herself and stood in the *genkan*, staring at the shoes. David's were still there, where she put them when she brought them downstairs last night, before the police took him away in his bare feet.

In a somber, restrained voice, she called out, *"Tadaima!"*

It was generally her mother who answered, but she would not be home for a couple of days. When her father did not respond, she searched for him. He was sitting on a *zabuton* pillow at the low table in the living room.

"*Otōsan*, are you all right?"

He looked up at her for a moment but did not answer.

Shōko glanced down at the table, where an old photo album lay open. She stepped closer and saw they were pictures of herself in the old house the summer she was five.

"*Otōsan*, I'm so sorry." Tears ran down her cheeks.

He said nothing; he just pulled a *zabuton* around and placed it next to his. She searched for the handkerchief in her purse and sat. He continued to gaze at the pictures for a few minutes but never turned the page. It was obvious he had something to say, and she dreaded it.

When he finally spoke, he did not turn to her. She could not see the emotion she heard in his voice: "Shōko-*chan*, you cannot stay here."

Hardly unexpected, Shōko choked, nonetheless. She had already decided to leave regardless of whether her parents suggested it. She had brought shame on the whole family and staying would only perpetuate the odd looks and whispers. With her father's words, though, it was real. She closed her eyes tight, trying to keep control. There was nothing to discuss. "Yes, I understand."

He was silent for a long minute before he spoke again: "Your mother was upset last night. Her words came from shock and anger, and they were . . . too harsh." He fell silent. "You know we do not want you to go. It is what must be done. And I hope you may return soon. You are welcome here. But for now . . . "

Shōko squeezed his hand, communicating that she understood, that he could stop.

"You tried to help your old friend. He is special to you. I have often wished you had married him instead of that rich fellow. You did not tell us much about him, but I could tell your feelings. I've always blamed myself for that. I should have talked to you about it. I could have saved you from such pain."

"No, *Otōsan*, it was all my—"

"Shh, quiet. A father knows his responsibility, however difficult it may be, however he might have failed."

"*Otōsan* . . . "

"Just know, leaving is a temporary thing. You will be back. And . . ." They were both silent for a long time as he collected himself. "Shōko-*chan*, you must be happy. That man, Ōta, has not come looking for you in months. I think you are safe now. But you must divorce him. You must make a happy life for yourself. I trust you to do that."

"Thank you, *Otōsan*."

"So understand, you cannot take what happened here last night with you when you go."

"*E?*"

"You must leave here happy and confident. You cannot leave with the shame you carried into this room just now. You will leave it here. You have no choice in this. Going is something I request of you. Leaving your shame is something I order you to do."

"Yes, I understand. *Otōsan*, I understand," and as she buried her face in her hands, he patted her gently on the shoulder.

CICADAS HAD EMERGED in force in the last few days and their singing reminded Shōko of how loud they were at the old house when those pictures were taken. It was enormous in her memory, but she returned one day as a teenager and wondered how they ever lived in a place that small. Feeding the chickens was her responsibility. They did not make the trip to the new house, and Shōko missed them at first, but then came Yuki and she forgot the chickens.

Too bad they don't make cats with such power for grown-ups.

They make people like that, though, sometimes, and she found hers. Was it fate that had brought him here? She wasn't sure there was such a thing, but David coming here had made it easy to think so. Even now she wanted to believe it. If it was fated, somehow it did not seem as . . . evil? But that was what it would be to steal David from his wife and take him away to Tokyo. She had lived with mistakes, even their shame, but never guilt. David and Kelly might never completely reconcile if she did not let him go, and she could never pretend to be guiltless if she ended their marriage.

What if she wasn't stealing him, though? What if he wanted to go to Tokyo? Was she duty bound to force him back to a wife who could not understand his true heart, even after all their years together? David was healthier here. Sick as he was, he might never recover with Kelly.

For now, though, all Shōko could do was wait. It would be David's choice.

90

"GOOD MORNING, MR. REESE. YOU HAVE VISITORS TODAY," SAID THE doctor.

"You want to medicate me again before they visit?"

"No, not today."

"Good, I don't need another hallucination."

"Hallucination?"

"Yesterday, I thought my wife was here."

"Yes, your wife was here."

"What? That wasn't . . . ?" David closed his eyes and rubbed his temples. "No medication, please."

"You are better last twenty-four hours. Today we try visit no medication. Two visitors today. Your wife and Ms. Kawasaki."

"Shōko is here?"

"Yes, she is waiting."

"You want me to see them at the same time?"

"That is you decide."

"You want me to see them both?"

"That also is you decide."

David sat quietly for a minute. "I'd like to see Shōko now. And Kelly . . . maybe tomorrow. I don't know."

"Today, only Ms. Kawasaki?"

"Yes, only Shōko."

The doctor left and David lay down on the bed. He had been confused and anxious ever since the police found him, but this was—

"You're not gonna see her?" asked Roselda.

"Not today," he responded in his head.

"Why?"

"I'm too angry."

"You mean you're lost, embarrassed, ashamed—"

"I mean she left me. And now she's come back? Just like that? No phone calls, nothing? She simply appears at the hospital?"

"Did you call her?"

"No."

"Then how do you know she just arrived? And why does she have to be the one to call?"

"Because she's the one who left."

"And you had nothing to do with it?"

"We were fighting, yeah, but I didn't tell her to go."

"And before the fighting?"

"I had a project disintegrating around me."

"And she was . . . ?"

"Offering no help."

"None?"

"All she did was tell me to quit."

"Should you have? You told plenty of people that the project was hopeless. Why not quit something like that?"

David didn't answer.

"Would you have quit if the job was in India?"

"Probably."

"Then her advice wasn't so bad."

"But this isn't India."

"And what's the big difference?"

After a few seconds, David silently replied, "You know."

"Yes, but I want to hear you say it."

He hesitated before he whispered aloud, "Shōko."

Roselda's voice softened. "Did Kelly understand that?"

"No," he responded silently.

"Why not?"

"I was afraid she'd be jealous."

"Of what?"

"An old girlfriend she never liked."

"What's so bad about meeting an old girlfriend? After all, Kelly won, didn't she?"

"Shōko wasn't in the picture then. We'd drifted apart by that point. They weren't competing."

"And if they were?"

"I'd have chosen . . . Kelly, maybe . . . probably. I'm not sure about now."

"Now in the hospital, or when Kelly first arrived here?"

David didn't answer.

"You think maybe you should've told her? You think maybe then none of this would've happened? Maybe she wouldn't have gone stir-crazy watching you as your project crashed, unable to help you or even comprehend your seeming devotion to it? You keep pitying yourself, mercilessly abandoned. But didn't you abandon her before she left?"

"Maybe."

"And you aren't gonna see her?"

David heard footsteps. He sat up and said out loud, "Not today."

"KAWASAKI-SAN, moshi yoroshikereba, Rīsu-san ni o-ai-dekimasu ga . . . "

Kelly did not understand what the doctor was saying to Shōko, but the result was clear enough. As the nurse interrupted him, Shōko got up and turned toward the door to the ward.

*So David chose the one who hid him, who's doing her best to steal him—*she clenched her jaw—*who understood him well enough to know a crayon could lure him out from under a bed, Shōko, with a little line over the first o.*

Kelly watched Shōko approaching the door. She was powerless to fight Shōko's insidious influence if they would not even let her visit David. Shōko, the snake, was poisoning him by degrees, and they were letting her in to inject another dose. As Shōko opened the door, Kelly had a violent urge to run up to her, grab her by the hair, throw her against the wall, and tell her what kind of woman she was. *Would she understand that kind of English? Even if she could, would she care, a woman who wedges herself between a husband and wife? To face old age alone would be scary, but to take a married man!*

It was self-serving to dismiss her that lightly, though. David obviously loved her when he was in college—still did, for all Kelly knew. All the times he told Kelly how sweet she was, how kind and thoughtful—and cute and innocent and childlike and trusting—always protective of her, as if she was still the same girl he knew in college, even though he hadn't seen her in years. *It's how you feel about a pet bunny, not a woman you loved. To be competing in his mind with a pet bunny for the qualities of an ideal woman!*

How much of his ideal was still Shōko: thin, exotic, untethered to any past troubles, his salvation of the moment, still untested, still perfect?

So I have to outshine long-lost love and win David back from a person who isn't even real?

Was it the pet bunny playing on his paternal side, though, or the other thing rabbits are known for? She didn't look like a seductress, but some women are . . . skilled. And she was trim.

The doctor, finally free from the nurse's questions, sat next to Kelly. "Mrs. Reese, I think you must wait another day. You may be here, but you are more comfort at home, I think."

Kelly's mouth dropped open. "I can't visit him today?"

"I am sorry. Maybe tomorrow." He sat for a few seconds, smiling reassuringly, before he walked back into the ward.

ANXIOUS AS SHŌKO WAS to see David, she felt sympathy for Kelly. She seemed absolutely lost. It was obvious she still cared for him.

But does she love him? She left him in a horrible state. What I was seeing could be guilt, or just concern for a man she loved long ago.

Or she could still love him. This could all be a huge, tragic misunderstanding.

Shōko's path seemed clear to her when she came to the hospital today, but now she was wavering. Approaching David's door, she slowed. In a moment, she would have to smile.

The nurse reached out to take her purse. "I'm sorry, but you're not allowed to take anything into the room with you."

The nurse unlocked the door, then smiled and bowed. Shōko reached out, put on a pleasant face, and pushed on the door.

David immediately stood, looking excited to see her, but at the same time mortally embarrassed. It was little wonder, wearing that awful hospital gown. She looked around the room, and as her throat started to close, she realized she did not retrieve her handkerchief before she gave her purse to the nurse. *I'll never make it through this. He's so sick!*

"Hi," he began.

"Hi."

"Thank you for coming." He sat at the foot of the bed.

There was ample room for Shōko to sit, but she stood close to the door and tried valiantly to look pleasant. "I am sorry. If I take you to a doctor at a start, everything is fine now. But I like to not be alone. I let you stay and now there is so much trouble."

"I could've left anytime, gone back to the emptiness. You made me well again."

Shōko blinked. "But you are not well. You are in hospital now."

"True, but I'm not suicidal."

Shōko lowered her head.

"Shōko, you understood why I was at the river that day."

She turned her head and stared at the door, her chin crinkled and her lip quivering.

"When you let me follow you, you saved my life. You let me draw, let me share your life, and my life was bearable again."

David stood and took a step toward her, but she put out her hand to stop him.

"What's wrong, Shōko? I'll be out of here soon. Just spend a little time with me and I'll be fine and they'll let me go."

Shōko turned to him and asked, voice thick with emotion, "Then what will you do?"

"I'm not thinking that far ahead."

"Please think far ahead. What will you do?"

David sat back down and rubbed his temples as he thought. "Well, I don't suppose I'll have a job here anymore, so I guess I'll have to go back to America and find one."

"Yes, that is a good idea. We will say goodbye here and you will go back. That is best."

David looked at her, eyes wide. "Goodbye? I didn't say anything about goodbye. What's to stop you from going to America too?"

Shōko stood tall and looked him in the eye. "Kelly."

HER ANSWER, a bucket of ice water in the face, left David leaning on his knees, staring at the floor. After a minute, he said, "I don't think I can go on without you."

"You must. You have her. You can go on with her."

"But I need you."

Shōko looked at him, her eyes narrow, but said nothing.

"David, you're pushing too hard. Back off," warned Roselda.

"Shōko . . ."

"Don't you say it, David!"

"I love you."

"Oh, Lord."

"You don't have to say. I know. Some things, many things, don't need words. Learn this and you will be happier."

"But what's wrong with putting into words what you've already felt from me?"

"It is not only you say your heart, feelings running out of your mouth. It makes pressure to me to say too, right?"

"Shōko, maybe not pressure . . . but I see your point. A statement like that begs a response."

"David, you do not want to go there," said Roselda.

"So, the question ...," said David.

"David, don't you ask her. You do not want to hear the answer."

"Shōko, you can tell me what's in your heart. We're that close, aren't we?"

"David!"

Shōko looked up sternly. "What is in my heart?" She paused. "You are my friend. This was nice two weeks. You helped me decide I will get a lawyer and divorce my husband. That is what I feel."

"You mean you don't love me?"

"David, stop, for heaven's sake! Just stop this!"

"No, I do not love you."

David sat still, no tears, no tension in his hands or face, nothing.

"David, you need to say something. She's waiting."

He stayed silent.

"David, you need to say something to show her you're all right."

"And if I'm not all right?" David snapped at Roselda, aloud.

KELLY'S CLOTHES were tearing off as she sat there, alone, afraid, naked, for everyone to see how miserably she had failed. She had seen David blue more times than she could count, even paralyzed to the point of needing medication, but nothing that required hospitalization. She did not understand how to help him out of this.

But I can't fix this sitting in a waiting room. I have to talk to him.

Kelly opened the door. As she looked down the hall, to her surprise, no one was at the nurses' station. She could hear animated voices in a patient's room just ahead, so she hurried to David's room at the end of the hall. She couldn't see David. Shōko was standing too close to the door, blocking her view. She felt like a child peeking into her parents' bedroom, but she had to hear what they were saying, so she held her ear at the door. David was too far away to make out clearly, but she could hear Shōko ... telling him to go back to America? She listened on. Telling him she doesn't love him?

"Mrs. Reese, you cannot be here! Please go waiting room," said the nurse with obvious displeasure.

Kelly looked blankly at the nurse, said, "I'm sorry," to no one in particular, and wandered up the hall.

DAVID SAW SHŌKO draw back in astonishment at his outburst to Roselda. She held her arms tight to her chest, her fingers pressed to her cheeks, and after a few seconds, in a tentative voice, she asked, "Who do you talk to alone here?"

David stared at the floor.

"Do you talk to Roselda?"

He nodded. "A little too crazy for you, I suppose."

"Do you talk to her when you are at my house?"

"No."

"Do you talk to her before that?"

"No."

"This is first time?"

"Yes." He hesitated before he went on, "But in the first days at your house, before I started drawing . . . I talked to you."

Shōko looked around the room, as if searching for reassurance he was not insane.

David stood and took her hand. He sat her on the bed and tried to explain. "I'm not crazy. I know she's not here. I don't see her or hear voices or anything. It's just in my imagination. I guess . . . she helps me work things out, or the conversation does, or . . ." Unable to go on in an explanation this lunatic, he looked down for a few seconds. "It really is just . . . weird. Sorry to freak you out."

"I am not freak out. You told me about Roselda long ago in letters. She was kind, I think. It is nice to have someone kind to talk to." Shōko tried to smile, but her chin was still crinkled.

"I'll be out soon and I'll be better. I'm sure I will."

She shook her head as she looked at him.

"Shōko, we can work this out."

"How? You are married. You love Kelly. I know that when you are in my room. You never stop loving her. I don't want to be alone loving a married man, I don't want guilt if he divorce his wife, and I don't want him to marry me and always love her still. So I do not love you. Can you understand?"

He stayed silent, looking at her, wanting her, terrified.

"David, don't do it. Back off."

"Shōko, just tell me. . . ."

"Don't you ask again whether she loves you. What's wrong with you?"

David answered Roselda silently now, "I won't. But there's something I have to know."

He collected himself and asked, "Is this goodbye? I mean, no relationship anymore, ever? It's over?"

Shōko didn't make the slightest response, and as she kept her head bowed, fear ushered reason out of David's mind. His eyes flitted desperately around the room.

"You must go back to your family. You are a husband and a father." She stopped, her eyes still on her lap. He could hardly hear her when she went on, "And you are my old friend. We can . . ." She was still again. "Maybe over is best."

"You can't mean that."

Shōko was quiet. She looked at the door, and after a few seconds, she nodded and stood to go.

David whispered, "Don't leave me."

Shōko looked at him, obviously on the verge of breaking down, before she turned her eyes to the door and said, "You should rest. I need to check on my mother."

"The doctor told me she's doing well."

She nodded. "And I should go home. *Otōsan* is alone now."

"Come back tomorrow," he said as she walked to the door and knocked. Shōko nodded, facing the door. When the nurse opened it, she turned, and without making eye contact, bowed to David.

David bowed back, and then he watched the door slowly swing closed on the rest of his life, punctuated by the lock's metallic click.

He lay down and closed his eyes. He had not handled it well, but at least he controlled himself at the end. Shōko hadn't recognized that he'd lost all hope. Neither had the doctor if he was watching via that camera in the ceiling, or they'd already be strapping him to the bed.

"David, talk to me." Roselda waited. *"You know she didn't mean what she said."*

"Then why'd she say it?" he silently replied.

"You know very well why." Again, she waited. *"And what if she'd told you what was really in her heart, told you she loves you and wants you to stay, would you?"*

"Yes."

"You sure about that?"

"Probably. I don't know!"

"Exactly. You want her to put her heart on the line for you and you're not even sure whether you're ready to take it."

"I'm ready."

"But you're not willing to give up on Kelly."

"I love her."

"Which 'her'?"

He didn't answer.

"All right then, love them both."

"But . . . ? There is a 'but,' right?"

"But—you cannot expect them both to love you."

"Why would either of them?"

"Oh, don't you go feeling sorry for yourself. I can't abide that. The height of selfishness is all self-pity is."

David was silent again.

"Imagine loving a married man you can't have. Would you wish that on anyone? Now imagine your husband in love with another woman. Imagine facing each day knowing he's missing her so badly he can hardly bear it. Can you even begin to fathom that pain?"

He stayed silent.

"David, do you remember how I came to work for your parents?"

"Only what I've heard. I wasn't even born yet."

"That's right. Your momma was pregnant with you."

"And your boyfriend was working for my folks as a driver and handyman and living in the carriage house. When they found out his girlfriend was pregnant and he wouldn't do what they felt was the right thing, they fired him and hired you as a housekeeper."

"That's right. They tossed him out, and I moved into the carriage house and lived there for over thirty years. Your parents placed great stock in doing the right thing. They taught you to call me 'Miss' out of respect"—she paused, and seemed even more serious when she continued—"and you did, child, always. You were raised like that. It's part of you. You can't ever escape it. You can ignore it for a little while, looks like, but not for long. And David, you know what that right thing is. You can feel it in your soul. It burns in you; I know it does. You have to talk to Kelly and work to fix things. You haven't even tried. Only a fool would throw away a real life with a woman he loves for a dream of someone else."

"And what about Shōko? I abandon the woman who saved me? You know what pain she's been through. All these years I never stopped loving her. Now that I've seen her again, lived that again, I'll never be able to pretend it's not there. And you know as well as I do it'll never go away."

"Yes, I know. But you can't do the same thing with this that you did with your art, blaming Kelly that you weren't painting and all the while knowing she pushed another career onto you because you were falling apart. It's like you have two views of things and you go with whichever makes you feel better at the moment. Painting as a livelihood, for you, was an impossible dream. So is Shōko. But you have them tucked away in your back pocket, and you pull them out and gaze at them and sigh, pretending you could've had them, if only."

He was silent.

"Fine. Act like a child. But sooner or later you're gonna have to face that there's no 'if only' in real life."

91

THOUGH DAVID HAD REFUSED TO SEE HER, KELLY WAS NOT ABOUT to leave as long as Shōko was there. But even after Shōko hurried out of the ward, through the waiting room, and out the door, Kelly stayed, hoping: that with Shōko gone, David might want to see her; that perhaps, somehow, she could fix things; that she could do better than yesterday. It wasn't long before she was hounding the doctor. "I have to see him!"

"Yes, but you must think he is sick. We always must do best thing for him. Now, best thing is quiet."

"Can't you simply ask him? Please. He needs to see me too. Please, Doctor."

The doctor relented, and Kelly followed and waited across the hall. As he left David's room, though, Kelly saw the answer on the doctor's face and cried before he even spoke.

"Mrs. Reese, he says no. You maybe go home now. You rest. Come back tomorrow, yes?"

Kelly looked up at the ceiling, at heaven, but no words came.

A nurse checked on David, and looking into the room as the door opened, all too desperate to follow the nurse, Kelly realized there was no hope for today. At the thought of no hope forever after, she doubled over and bawled.

Two nurses hurried down the hall. It took a few minutes—and the third nurse, who had been checking on David—but they got Kelly back on her feet. They tried to stop her from taking one more look at David through the little window in his door. Her brief glimpse, David disappearing under the bed, left her barely able to stand, and they helped her down the hall to the waiting room.

"DAVID, you need to get out from under the bed. They'll never let you out if you keep hiding."

He had his eyes shut tight, hoping to block her out.

"Might as well say it. I'm in your head, so it's not like you can hide what you're thinking."

David stayed silent for a minute, then with deep emotion he said, "She looked so . . . ," before he fell silent.

"What did you expect?"

He didn't answer.

"I'm sure it was a shock to see her crying there in the hallway, but come now, David, how did you expect her to look?"

"More like she did the day she left."

"She left out of frustration, and that passes. It's been nearly three weeks."

"Seeing her crying like that . . . "

He choked up as he lay there, his hands folded and pressed between his knees.

Roselda said quietly, "Suddenly she was your wife again, your dearest friend, the woman you've loved for nearly thirty years."

"It hurts. And it'll never stop!"

"I know. I can feel what you feel." She was quiet for quite a while before she offered, "It won't always hurt this bad."

David started to cry.

"David, keep control or they won't let you out."

"Yeah. I'll be okay soon. Give me a minute."

"Okay, but at least get out from under the bed."

David stood, then walked in little circles around the room.

"That's better. Now why don't you lie and rest."

As he lay down, she went on: "David, you've got to face this now. As much as you hurt, they're hurting even more. Different—they're not in love with two people—but each is in love with a man who, although he loves her, also loves someone else. Put yourself in either of their places. Try to comprehend that pain."

"I don't think I can." He paused. "I've mutilated the two most precious . . ." He was still for a minute. "What do I do? How do I fix that?"

"You can't. There's no point trying. It's time to make a choice. There are three hearts in this, all terribly hurt. You finish one off, break it completely.

Another heals over time, you hope. And yours, maybe it heals someday—but likely not—so you just do your best to forget about your own. You dedicate your life to healing that one heart. It's the only way."

"That's a choice? I choose to stop loving one? How?"

"You may not see a choice in who you love, but you certainly have a choice in who you hurt. And if you try somehow to keep them both, you force a life of unimaginable heartache onto all three of you."

"No. There has to be something else, some other way. There's no way I can do that to either one. And I can't make it without them."

"Break one or break both."

"You have to give me another way."

"I can't give you the impossible."

"Then lie to me!"

"No. You do a fine enough job of that all by yourself." And Roselda walked off in disgust.

All alone, David watched Kelly not merely crying in the hallway, but flying home alone, discarded. He saw her enter their house, go to the bedroom, fall on the bed and cry—for days and weeks and longer—crushed by the same mountain of pain that drove him to the river three weeks ago.

He opened his eyes, hoping the reality of his hospital cell would extinguish both the image and the burning coals lodged in his chest. He got up, took a few deep breaths, and splashed water on his face in the sink in his room.

Kelly stayed with him, though. He thought of two years ago, an autumn evening. They were arm in arm against the nippy twilight, as the stars winked on one by one. They were talking about Ben, who wanted to apply to college a year early, and they weren't sure whether he was ready to be on his own. They walked along, understanding each other perfectly, most of the conversation known without ever being said, as if the two of them shared one mind.

He had ached to have her back since the day she left, and now she was here: not the cold, angry woman who abandoned him, but his soulmate. Yet going back to America with Kelly would mean throwing away the love he unthinkingly sheltered for even longer than he had loved Kelly. He would shatter the most innocent person he had ever known, just as she was becoming the spirited Shōko he knew so long ago, discarding her when she most needed him. David stumbled to the bed, where he curled up again. His stomach cramped as he struggled to ignore the vision of himself forcing in the knife, finishing what even her husband in his vilest abuse could not do.

92

KELLY HAD BEEN IN THE SHOWER FOR AN HOUR, SITTING, WAITING for some ray of hope to obscure the grief. She kept tracing the timeline, watching herself ignore all the signs, inevitably arriving at David's hospital door, locked out of his life while he and his new love talked of the future. Kelly wanted to break the door down and choke the life out of her! As she looked at her fingers taut with rage, she realized that if she had the chance at that moment, she might actually kill her.

That's . . . psychotic.

She shuddered, then stood and put her face in the spray.

It was true, though; she was that desperate. She had looked David's death in the face, felt the numbness of going on alone, and it terrified her. And the vision was too fresh: the sorceress begging the doctor to give David a crayon. Kelly opened her eyes and leaned on the shower wall. Shōko may have denied it to David, but the bony little *geisha* still loved him. The whole scene in his hospital room was self-serving, the requisite words to assuage Shōko's guilt, so she could tell herself it was David's choice.

And what if Shōko was sincere? Was Kelly to feel grateful to her for trying to give her husband back, thank her for sacrificing what she was never supposed to have in the first place?

Still, telling him to go home to America, however half-heartedly, should earn Shōko a grain of respect. If she was desperate enough to go after a married man, though, she'd never have the nerve to go through with it and give him up. Even if she could, the prospect of losing Shōko forever might be so daunting that David would ignore her and stay. If he stayed, the woman who wrote him 118 letters would never let David suffer alone.

If Kelly could make going back to America even slightly less onerous, though, once back, away from Shōko's influence, it might take time, but David would come to his senses. He would be Kelly's, never again to stray.

If Shōko let him go.

But Shōko . . .

As it occurred to Kelly what she had to do, she shook her head violently. "No. I can't!"

She pounded the shower wall with her fists. "No!"

"Please, no," she begged.

But she knew it was her single best hope, even as it sent her back to her knees.

93

SHŌKO'S MOTHER WOULD COME HOME THE NEXT DAY, AND SHŌKO WAS pleased that this morning's visit went well, with none of the anger she had to endure in yesterday's visit. Not having to worry she might set her mother's recovery back, Shōko stayed and talked. They never approached David, what happened that night, or Shōko leaving home. They stayed at wading depth: her father's inability to cook anything for himself, Shōko's responsibility to make sure he took his medication, and wondering why all the doctors looked like children.

Now, approaching the psychiatric ward, the hallway was like a pool of molasses growing thicker with each step. She had agreed to come back and talk things over again today, but would David ask her to come back tomorrow, and the next day, talking and talking, accomplishing nothing but giving words to their pain? They had to make a choice.

Shōko left her name at the nurses' station, to be called when David was ready for visitors, and took a seat in the waiting room near the air conditioner. Sitting in the cool with her eyes closed, dabbing the sweat from her temples and neck with a terrycloth handkerchief, she tried to steel herself. She did it by imagining her guilt when she traveled to America with David to visit his children, their hate for the woman who drove their parents apart, and David's dejection at their refusal to visit him in Japan. As it began to have an effect, though, her mind, escaping the pain, pictured a rosier future. They weren't in Japan; David was working in America, successful, happily adjusted to life with his new job and his new wife; and he was making time for painting, breathtaking pieces, enough that his show would open soon at a respected gallery.

Shōko could sense her heart quickening, so she decided to force her mind into one of the old magazines that was lying around. As she opened her eyes, though, she blanched: Kelly was walking into the waiting room, looking directly at her.

Kelly's jaw looked tight as she turned her back on Shōko and stepped over to the nearest seat. After she set down her purse, though, she stayed standing. Shōko watched with apprehension, and saw Kelly look up at the ceiling, then hang her head and pick up her purse. But their momentary eye contact as Kelly entered the room was more than enough for Shōko, so she quickly picked up a magazine to look at while Kelly left.

Kelly turned, though, stared at her, and started to walk over.

Devil! You destroyed him once. Are you here to finish the job? Go home!

Shōko turned a page, affecting nonchalance, as she waited for Kelly to take a seat, but she was walking straight toward her. Shōko raised her head and showed Kelly a polite smile of discomfort. Any woman, even an American, would understand it and turn away. But she was approaching too purposefully. There was nothing Shōko could do. If Kelly insisted on making things uncomfortable, Shōko would have to endure it politely. It made Shōko's skin crawl looking at Kelly as she approached, but looking away would cast her as David's lover, and *no one* could impute such a base character to her.

Kelly stopped in front of the empty seat next to Shōko.

Is she going to say something? Do I need to stand for an exchange of greetings or is she going to sit quietly?

Kelly broke eye contact to look at the empty seat, then looked at Shōko again and bowed awkwardly. Shōko returned another smile that politely hinted at her discomfort and annoyance, then bowed her head in resignation.

Every seat in the room is available. The only reason to sit here is to talk. But why? What is wrong with Americans?

Kelly took a few seconds to position herself sufficiently sideways in the chair to face Shōko. She fiddled with her purse, set it on the next chair, and sat still.

Shōko waited, her eyes on the magazine in her lap.

Kelly said nothing.

Does she expect me to start? I'm not the one who ignored all decorum and strode across the room like a cowboy. It was unnerving. What if it turns into an argument—or a fight?

Shōko glanced at the door into the ward, where the doctor and nurses could come to her aid. She had an unobstructed path.

At that moment, though, looking Shōko up and down as she spoke, Kelly said, "I wanted to thank you for taking care of David while he was sick."

"I am sorry that he has relapse so bad now," replied Shōko as she tried to keep her hands from fidgeting.

"Using drawing to bring him out . . . that was . . . insightful." Her tone was even but seemed forced.

Shōko saw Kelly studying her, but Shōko, determined not to let her distaste for Kelly show, wiped her face clean of all emotion and looked down at her hands.

"It seems he stayed at your home for most of the time since I left Japan. He stayed with—he stayed for about two weeks?"

It was a direct question; she had to respond; so Shōko looked at Kelly apologetically and said, "Yes. I should have telephoned to his company to say he was sick. It was a bad mistake."

"I take it the two of you are . . . you and David are close, obviously."

Shōko looked down again and bit the inside of her lip, hoping Kelly would be polite enough not to ask.

"Shōko—oh, I'm sorry, may I call you Shōko?"

She looked at Kelly and smiled politely. "Yes, please call me."

"Please call me Kelly."

Insincerity leered out from behind Kelly's forced smile, and her voice was so thick with it that Shōko could almost hear the thought that followed: *I'm David's wife!* But Shōko smiled demurely and said, "Thank you, Kelly," as she strangled the handkerchief in her lap.

"I'm glad we're getting a chance to talk today. I wanted to ask what your intentions are at this point."

"Intentions?"

Shōko understood the word. Kelly must have guessed so too; her lips drew tight at Shōko's evasion. "I mean, I'm not sure whether you and David . . . not sure whether you . . ."

Kelly looked down as she fell silent. Was she all right? When she saw Kelly's shoulders fall, as she saw the pain, so close, she wanted to reach out to her—but she knew Kelly's sole aim was to take David away.

They sat in silence for two minutes before Kelly looked up, fighting back tears, and asked, "Are you and David lovers?"

The question, jarringly direct, was not entirely unexpected, but Shōko heard an undertone that belied Kelly's pathetic appearance. Shōko wanted to jump up and run, but she merely recoiled, letting a look of shocked insult be her answer.

Kelly just sat there, though, eyes wet, looking at her. Both her mother and the police had asked Shōko the same question. And she knew from her own heartbreaking, humiliating experience with her first husband that the pain of asking such a question was like staring into the sun. Pity required a vocal response, so she looked Kelly in the eye and said, "No."

"You never slept together?"

I said we're not lovers! Why is she asking again? Intolerable as it was to be interrogated, though, she answered the first question, so she had no choice but to answer this one—and they *did* sleep together. Shōko was careful not to look away, not to do anything that would imply guilt, as she desperately searched for words that would be truthful but not sound evasive. As much as it galled her to speak crassly, a direct response was the only way. In her most reassuring tone, she said, "We never had sex."

Shōko waited for a moment, then looked off across the waiting room. What she said was true, but Kelly wasn't responding. In fact, she looked as if she expected more. As Shōko considered what to say, though, it occurred to her she never even kissed David, and it left her with an echoing hollow. She thought of his lips, of his fingers caressing her under her pajamas, of his body, warm and strong, pressed tightly to hers in the bed. She fought to focus, searching for something she could say, something truthful but unrevealing. Shōko tried to control her breathing as she looked at Kelly again and said, "He is a good and close friend in the last two weeks. He is a good man and I am lucky to . . . have his . . . caring. I hope he will be well." *That was awful!*

Again, silence.

And more silence, until Kelly asked, "Do you love him?"

What? How dare she ask something that personal? I didn't confess my feelings even to David; I'm not about to tell his wife!

Shōko sat up straight and replied coolly, "I worry he is more sick and need medication now. I wish for him to be happy again. I care for him . . . for his happiness."

KELLY IGNORED THE WORDS. The real answer, defiance, showed in Shōko's posture and even more in her eyes, that narrowed ever so slightly as she spoke. Shōko loved David and would keep him if he chose to stay. Her sitting here waiting to visit him confirmed it beyond any doubt.

At least they hadn't—

Or so she said. How was Kelly supposed to believe it? When she asked the police if David was so sick that Shōko had essentially kidnapped him, they said the two of them cooperated in keeping his presence a secret from her parents. Two whole weeks together, alone in a Japanese bedroom, loving each other. How could they not?

Stop it! Stick to the plan!

But, dear God, how I hate her!

Kelly's shoulders were drawn up so tight it felt as if her head would pop off. Glancing down, she saw her knuckles were white, so she closed her eyes and focused on David—but the thought of him in Shōko's bed-room—

She clenched her jaw. *No!* Kelly forced the image from her mind. What replaced it, though, was too pitiful: David under the bed in that padded cell down the hall. *And Shōko put him there! He wasn't this sick when I left. I have to save him—and that means keeping a lid on my feelings.*

Control . . . for David . . .

I can do this.

One more deep breath, and unthinkingly, she sighed.

SHŌKO DREW BACK as she saw rage pass over Kelly's face.

Is she capable of violence? Has David had to live with this? And what was that sigh?

Shōko was feeling nauseated.

Go away! This is intolerable!

"Shōko, thank you for answering that question. I am concerned about David's health too. He needs to go back to America right away."

Shōko nodded slightly in understanding.

"We have to think of David, do whatever is best for him. I'm afraid that what he feels for you, be it friendship . . . or something more, might be strong enough that he won't want to leave."

It was like a diving bell imploding on Shōko. With those far too simple words, Kelly tore the cover from Shōko's deepest, most disturbing, most cherished hope. Losing control for the briefest moment, she winced—before she realized that next would come an appeal to relinquish that hope forever. All morality and propriety dictated that she bow and step aside, but Shōko was silent as she sat, straight and tall as she could, and stared at Kelly through cold, narrowed eyes.

David is the man I should have married, fated to be mine all these years, and late as our start might be, I will not lose my only remaining chance at a life filled with genuine love. I've felt it from him. I brought him back from the brink and rekindled his greatest passion. I am what he needs, not you. He is mine now!

———

THE CHANGE IN Shōko's demeanor was frightening. *Why isn't she saying anything? Does she mean to keep him?*

Kelly thought of David's anger two days ago, and his cold determination as he took her bags from the car, before he drove off without a word, without even making eye contact. She thought of Shōko's letters and the sketchbook David brought to Japan. *He could stay—he will, if she holds on. I could lose him. Perhaps I already have!*

Kelly, usually the master of every encounter, shifted nervously in her chair. She had to go on, but realizing she was at the point where she needed to say it, she balked. It was too awful to even imagine, let alone speak aloud.

But I have to. There's no bargaining from a position of strength this time. Shōko holds the high ground.

She looked down and saw her hands clenched tight again.

I have to say something.

"So . . . ," she whispered, and stopped.

Smile at her. Swallow your pride and say it!

With a wan smile and her best try at a normal voice, Kelly began: "So he should go back, but he won't want to." She paused. "We have to get him well, have to get him help."

She's just looking at me.

"Going back is what's best for him, but he might not leave . . . if it means losing you."

Oh no, my hands are shaking. She closed them tight.

"So—" Her voice caught. The tears were coming.

No, I can't cry in front of her.

Kelly took a breath as she encouraged herself: *You're the cool one, always. Stay poised, the imperturbable—*

But there was no way. Looming up till it was all she could see was the vision of herself flying home alone, living alone, without David for the rest of her life. She saw, as clearly as this room, the waiting room in an American hospital weeks from now, waiting for Melissa to deliver her first grandchild, waiting alone.

As Kelly started to cry, decorum and restraint failed her completely. Unable to stop, she whispered between sobs, "I know you love him . . . and he loves you. But I love him . . . so much!" She fought to take a breath. "Shōko, please let him . . . go back to Amer— . . . America with me. I can't . . . live without him!"

KELLY'S emotional explosion stunned Shōko. Watching Kelly's panic, Shōko's heart sheared open, horrified at the sight of her own hidden dread acted out by the woman in front of her. But there was sympathy, too, and it grew, knowing Kelly's lifelong pain or joy was incumbent on Shōko's decision. Stealing a man from his wife was the most abhorrent evil she could imagine, and she shuddered, seeing herself as the same loathsome creature who stole her first husband. Duty and virtue demanded—

But then the agony would be hers! Shōko felt tears on her cheeks and realized she was crying. But she couldn't speak.

Kelly paused for a moment before she said, "I have . . . have a pro— . . . proposal."

Shōko discreetly wiped her tears as Kelly stopped to compose herself—two eternal, silent minutes—before she went on: "You may be in love with David, I don't care. You may stay close. Be . . . close friends, from his side. Close like these two weeks, kind of. Write and talk. And everything. Maybe we could be friends too. Maybe, if you want." She paused, obviously on the edge. "Just please—" And she choked as the tears burst out again. "Please! You have to . . . make him go back . . . back with me!"

It was too much to witness. Too much emotion, too much pain, tragedy, fear—too much sacrifice. Shōko looked down. Tears, an entire flood, were only a word away—

NEITHER OF THEM noticed the nurse approach, and Kelly was surprised when she heard her say to Shōko, quite tentatively, *"Anō, Rīsu-san ni menkai dekimasu kedo . . ."*

Kelly didn't know what it meant. Shōko straightened up, eyes still in her lap, but then just sat there.

"*Daijōbu desu ka?*" asked the nurse.

"*Hai,*" answered Shōko, and without looking at Kelly, she reached over, squeezed Kelly's hand, stood, and walked into the ward.

94

SHŌKO HAD HARDLY BEEN GONE A MINUTE AND KELLY WAS STILL struggling to regain control of herself when someone entered the waiting room. He didn't look Japanese, which caught her attention, but it took her a second, glancing through her tears, to see it was Paul. He was headed for the ward—and David, who was too weak to deal with him. Kelly sprang to her feet, grabbed her purse, and entered just behind him. She jogged the last few steps and grabbed his arm.

Paul feigned surprise at the sight of her but said nothing.

"What are you doing here?" asked Kelly.

"Probably the same as you. Just here to see David. How's he doing, anyway? From the look of you, not too well."

Kelly narrowed her eyes and was about to speak, but Paul turned, stepped over to the nurses' station, and got the attention of one of the nurses watching the monitor of David's room with the doctor. She stepped over to the counter with a smile. But as Paul asked, "What room is David Reese in?" Kelly looked at the nurse in alarm. She noticed. She bowed, stepped back to the doctor's huddle, and said something to him. He shook his head, whereupon the nurse stepped into the hallway, stood in front of Paul, and said, "No visitor."

"It will only take a minute," said Paul as he looked up and down the hallway, seemingly trying to guess which room was David's.

The nurse looked over at the doctor, who furrowed his brow and said something to the other nurse. She made a brief phone call, then joined her compatriot in the hallway. They were both positioned between Paul and David's room, one on each side of Paul, as if to prevent him from stepping around them and up the hallway.

Paul looked at the two of them, then back at Kelly. "You know what? Forget it."

He turned and walked past Kelly, at which point the door to the ward opened and a man rushed in who had to be the biggest Kelly had ever seen in Japan. He took a few steps toward Paul and stopped.

Paul stopped too. After a few seconds, he turned back to Kelly. "Fine. I tell you what, I'll fill you in and you can pass it on to David. First, let me say I was relieved when they found him, alive and all."

Kelly cocked her head to the side.

"I know it hasn't been long since his little . . . hell, I don't know what to call it, nervous breakdown? And I don't want to set his recovery back, but I'm leaving in the morning, so . . . well, I'm sorry, but David's got to face up to the music and admit to himself the trouble he's in. I don't need to explain to you that David had a whole multinational project team depending on him. It's bad, Kelly, *super* bad. I mean, they're already telling stories back in Portland."

Kelly didn't respond.

"And you know who's dealing with it all, who will have to clean up his mess."

Kelly said, "David's mess?"

"That's who the Japanese are blaming."

"Oh? I've met the head people on the Japanese side. Which of them is saying that?"

Paul looked surprised. "Who?" Then he smiled. "Hell, I'm supposed to tell the little buggers apart?"

Kelly shook her head.

"So, I'm sorry to spring this on you while he's still in the hospital, but I'm afraid we'll have to let him go." He looked behind himself at the man who blocked his way. "So, anyway, I'm done." He gave Kelly a shrug. "Sorry again. David can call personnel about getting back to America whenever he recovers . . . or if . . . or whatever."

Paul turned to go. The big man looked past Kelly at the nurses. The older of the two looked at Kelly, who gave a small nod. The nurse nodded to the man, and he stepped aside.

Paul waited for a couple of seconds, gave an awkward head bow to the nurses, then slipped his hands into his pockets and walked up the hall and out of the ward.

Kelly pouted as she watched him go.

But then, with a sardonic smile, she fished her phone out of her purse. No matter which of them David belonged to now—even if he was Shōko's—Paul would *not* have the last word.

"Hi, Kelly. What can I do for you? How's David?"

"Hi Leon. David is . . . to tell you the truth, he's been better. But I need something. You said some bigwig is coming in from Portland?"

"The COO, Bill Dietrich."

"When does he arrive?"

"Yesterday."

"I suppose he's in meetings all day today."

"I don't know his schedule, but I'm sure that's so."

"Leon, I need you to get him out of whatever meeting he's in."

"Excuse me?"

"I need to talk to him."

"Gee, Kelly, that'll be—"

"Leon, Paul is trying to fire David. You know where I'm calling from? I'm at the hospital, Leon. David's in the hospital and Paul showed up here to fire him."

"Wow. That's . . . just cold." Leon was briefly silent before he said, "Kelly, keep your line free."

Kelly answered her phone before the end of the first ring. "Hello."

"Kelly Reese?" asked a voice with a mild German accent.

"Yes."

"I'm Bill Dietrich. I understand you have a matter of some urgency."

"Thank you. I know you must be terribly busy today."

"Yes, I am."

Kelly's heart was racing. She knew she had to pique Dietrich's interest with her first line, so she did her best to sound apocalyptic: "The chip

Fuji-Star is developing is fatally flawed and needs a complete revision. My husband proved it."

"Ms. Reese?"

"Yes?"

"I am woefully short of time here, so I must ask, this doomed microchip, what business is it of yours?"

"My involvement...," said Kelly. "You might say I was deputized today."

"I'm afraid I do not know that word."

"I was given a formal task today by Paul Salazar, David's boss."

"So you are working for Paul, in a sense."

A shiver ran up Kelly's spine. "You could put it that way."

"Well then, you work for me. So what is this task that is so urgent?"

"Paul came to the hospital where David is now a patient—"

"Oh? I'm sorry to hear he's in the hospital."

"He came to the hospital to lay all the blame for the failed microchip on David. He came here to fire him. I stopped him from getting to David's room, but Paul told me David is fired anyway. He said it's my responsibility now to tell David."

"Deputized indeed," he said softly.

"David has tried everything to save the chip, but the embedded processor IP that Paul bought is junk. Now Paul is trying to pin the chip's failure on David. Whatever you've been hearing—"

"Let me stop you there. I've heard echoes of this already."

"Please understand that David created none of the problems that—"

"That's the other thing I have heard."

"You have?"

"Ms. Reese, did you tell David he's been fired?"

"No, he's not well enough."

"Then for now, don't."

"Yes, but—"

"I need to go."

95

AS SHE NEARED DAVID'S DOOR AND THE NURSE BOWED, SHŌKO WAS dizzy with thoughts of the waiting room. Seeing Kelly's pain all too real, Shōko could not cause any more. She could never live with that guilt. And Kelly's proposal! How brave was she to do that? How desperate? Shōko was still on the verge of tears thinking about it. She shrank, though, at the lifetime of longing that awaited her if she stepped into David's room and did the right thing.

Shōko reached out to open the door and noticed her hand trembling. She stopped and closed her eyes.

A choice . . .

But choosing is a process. As awful as the consequences will be, I'm near the end—certainly further along than David.

A process—I can hold tight to that. That and a little patience.

Shōko knew her eyes must be red, but she showed a sunny smile as she stepped into the room. "Do you feel better today?"

Yesterday, when she entered David's room, he was instantly on his feet. Today, he withdrew silently to a back corner of the room, looking at the floor.

Shōko bit her lip as she wrung her hands. *I've brought David out before. I can do it again.* She smiled, stepped over to the bed, and said, "Will you sit with me?"

David took a heavy breath and blew it out slowly.

Shōko sat and smiled again, and to her relief, David walked over to the bed. He just stood there, though, looking at the floor.

Shōko placed her hand on the bed and said, "Please sit with me?"

David sat, his eyes still downcast.

How is he ever going to make a choice? But it's a process, and first he has to speak. "I hope you are feeling better today."

He nodded.

Maybe good news would help. "I visited my mother today. She is so much better. She will go home tomorrow."

David said, "I'm glad. And I'm sorry—"

"No sorry. All is okay."

"I was afraid I had . . ."

Shōko smiled. "Imagine her surprise to open a door and see a stranger in the bath."

David brightened slightly. "I should've known she'd be okay, known she was strong, by the volume of her scream."

Shōko laughed.

David smiled ever so briefly, but his eyes remained on the floor.

She said, "I am sorry it was such a shock for you."

"I'm sorry I handled the shock that badly." He glanced around the room before his gaze dropped again. "This badly."

"I think it is a difficult time these two weeks."

David nodded.

After a few seconds, Shōko put her hand on David's and said, "You recover much in my home. You show so much strength. Just like *Okāsan*, my mother, you can go home soon, I think."

David turned his head and looked at Shōko for the first time. He was still for a few long seconds before he asked, "Where is home?"

Shōko pondered how to respond. At length, she picked up where they left off the day before. She smiled again and asked, "Did you think about what I said yesterday, about what you will do?"

David frowned. "May I speak directly?"

"Do you not ever?" joked Shōko.

David looked stung. "I try to be careful and not hurt your feelings."

A process . . . and I am further along in it. I need to calm him.

I need to calm myself.

"Yes, you do. I am sorry. Please tell me."

David gave a deep sigh and looked down for a full minute before he said, "Shōko, I don't need to tell you how I feel about you. And I think I understand your feelings."

Shōko consciously tried to relax her hands.

"You said yesterday I should go back to America."

She nodded.

"But I meant what I said yesterday. Whatever strength I showed, whatever recovery I made these last two weeks, was because of you."

Shōko nodded again. "You thought about other things I said yesterday, about Kelly?"

David hung his head.

Shōko laid her hand on David's once again. "Yes, I understand what you feel for me. I also know from last two weeks what you feel for her." She squeezed his hand until he looked at her. "I know it is impossible choice for you."

She saw tears.

Maybe I can shoulder the load for him while he's still weak.

"I can choose for you," she said.

"Don't you see, Shōko? No, you can't," whispered David. His eyes were filling. "It's my choice, and we all have to live with it. All the pain that's coming, it's all because of me."

David had something to say, so Shōko steeled herself to hear it as she wrung her handkerchief almost to the point of tearing.

"I made a choice yesterday. It's killing me, but I had to decide. And even with this decision, please understand I need to share your life somehow," said David.

"Share?" David was quiet and after a long minute Shōko asked, "What do mean to share your life?"

David glanced at her before returning his gaze to the floor. "Maybe not living here with you, maybe not married . . . but sharing . . . something, no matter where we are."

Shōko's breath caught in her throat and she looked away. *Maybe I'm not as far ahead of him in making this choice as I thought.*

Shōko—having rehearsed to herself all morning that David returning to Kelly was the right and proper thing, the guilt-free thing, what Shōko wanted—was shocked by the sudden aching in her stomach. Deep down, though, she knew all along that her rehearsals were a lie.

Shōko closed her eyes and said, "I do not understand. What do you mean by sharing?"

David blew his breath out slow and long again. "It's hard to define or explain. We'd be talking . . . not every day, but often. And visiting . . . sometimes. We'd be . . . friends, though we might have to hide our—"

"I will not be 'another woman.' I am not *hikagemono!*" *Was it possible Kelly meant this?*

"No, no, not an affair," said David.

"Then what? How do we not? Man and woman can't be friends. They always become an affair," answered Shōko.

"Not *always.*"

She could not help frowning.

"We can feel what we feel and be . . . something."

"Friends?" she asked, trying to be polite in her incredulity. "You can be just friends and not love me?"

"I . . . my feelings will be mine. If 'just friends' is what we need to be to have you in my life, then that's what we'll be."

Shōko spoke softly, trying to help David realize what he was suggesting. "But you can't hide your feelings. You say 'friends,' but you show your feelings always. Kelly will see. I . . . we . . . you can't hurt her more. She feels too much pain."

David softened his voice to match. "Shōko, there's something between us, some tie—fate? *Something.* We can't cut it even if we try. We can say it's cut, but that won't make it so. We let go once before, and the tie remained." She saw frustration on his face as he paused. "Okay, complete honesty: I want to be more than friends. Not . . . what's 'affair' in Japanese?"

"*Uwaki.*"

"Okay, *not that,* but something closer than 'just friends.' I want to be part of your life and have you be part of mine. Shōko . . . " He was tearing up again and his voice quavered. "I can't imagine living the rest of my life without you. I just—"

Shōko put her fingers to his lips to stop him. She wanted everything he was suggesting and more, but here! Knowing he wouldn't be hers, the thought of being close—the strain, controlling her feelings, knowing she couldn't have him . . . yet losing him completely—she was staggered by the loneliness, and he wasn't even gone yet.

David said, in a mild voice, "So, something, more than friends, but not an *ukiwa*."

Despite the tension, Shōko laughed out loud. "'*Ukiwa*' is 'swim ring.'"

"Oops. What did I want to say?"

"*U·wa·ki*," said Shōko with a smile. But she still shied away from thoughts of where she might end up. It had left her speechless in the waiting room. What did Kelly expect her to say? Kelly could not possibly be seeing the consequences. Still, Kelly was right that it was all about David, and if he needed Shōko to steady him, how could she abandon him? Shōko was hopelessly lost. "I think it is hard to be your friend only. And it is hard to lose a friend. I am on a wall, maybe."

"On the fence."

"Yes, on the fence."

"You know, you could jump off. I could catch you."

"What if you drop me? You are a sick man and too weak. I think it is not safe."

"You are so mean!"

Shōko smiled. "So, you go back, like I tell you yesterday?"

"Yes, that's what I decided yesterday after we talked. I'll go back."

"And make Kelly very happy?"

"Whether that's possible anymore."

Shōko's eyes opened wide. "You don't want to make her happy?"

"No, no, you misunderstood." As David began to tear up, he stood and walked over to the window in the outside wall.

Shōko's feelings were too knotted up to deal with someone this fragile. But seeing him shattered, leaning on the wall, illuminated by the thin beam of light through the strip of frosted, wire-reinforced glass, she was precariously close to tears herself. She had to try again before she broke down: "I am not angry. Please, tell me about 'possible anymore.'"

He didn't respond, so Shōko got up, took his arm, and sat him back down, but he still looked broken, sitting hunched over, staring at his hands. Finally, he said, "I meant I'm sure she's hurting, her heart's broken too, and I can't see how she'll ever be truly happy again. I don't know what she feels anymore."

"Then I tell you." He needed to see her eyes to understand, so Shōko rested her hand on his back until he sat up and met her gaze. But then she saw the same green-gray eyes that looked back at her from under the bed, pleading to be wanted.

If Kelly can be brave, so can I.

I have to.

Voice thick with emotion, she said, "She loves you"—Shōko blinked and swallowed hard—"more than anything ever in her life. She wants you happy even more than she wants happiness herself."

"You're assuming—"

Shōko shook her head. "Not assuming. I know. We—"

No, that was not hers to tell.

"She wants you happy." Her voice cracked. "She is not angry for us to be friends. All she wants is . . . David healthy again and happy. She is strong woman . . . and right wife for you. You must be trying so hard from now." She whispered, "If you make her happy, I am happy."

Her eyes were brimming, and David answered with a reassuring tone, "Okay. I don't know how you're so sure what she's feeling. Women are *not* all alike. But if I could make you both happy, that would be a life well lived. I'll do all I can."

It took a few minutes for them to settle down, but the conversation turned to Shōko's mother, each of them finding a new job, and other friendly topics. After half an hour, David brought up her art: "Shōko, I asked before about painting, and you said you drifted away from it. But have you thought about going back?"

"It is too long time."

"But you loved it."

Shōko sat still, but David looked worried that he had broken the back of their conversation, so she told him, "I think you want to know why I stopped painting."

He waited.

"I stopped because you are so talented."

He gave her a puzzled look.

"In all high school and college years I took all awards. Everyone tell me they love my painting so much. I am the painting star. Not so popular as volleyball star, but I liked it." She smiled. "In college, I met a handsome exchange student who was a painter like me. I knew him before in high school, but only letters. I saw pictures of his paintings then and he was *very* good, but I could think I might be better. But when we met in college"—and her voice lost the playful edge—"he was *so* good."

"Oh, Shōko, don't be—"

"Shh. Let me tell. I never saw painter like you except in big show or museum. I thought I was great painting talent, but I met real painting talent. I never saw painter my age who was better than me. Many good and many style so different, but you were not just different, you were better. So much more talent."

"Even if you thought I was better, we all have someone we think is better."

"But I start to doubt myself. I worry more about my painting, and about a painting career, worry about selling paintings. So I found an office job after university. Then I have no time and it was hard to be painting."

"But Shōko, you were good—no, more than good. There was a reason you won all those awards. I loved your paintings. You should paint again."

"Now you are silly. It was too long ago."

"Talent never goes away. Pick up a brush again and you'll see. Besides, the things we love stay with us forever."

"Then maybe I get a cat to love."

"And name him Botero?"

She laughed. "I can't feed so much. I give a skinny name."

96

ALL KELLY KNEW ABOUT SHŌKO'S MEETING WITH DAVID WAS THAT IT lasted over an hour. Shōko smiled at her when she bowed on the way out, but that might have been nothing more than politeness. Visiting hours ended shortly after that, and as much as Kelly ached to see David, after what happened yesterday, she would not ask the doctor. Still, she was in no hurry to get back to the apartment, so when she left the hospital, she decided not to take a taxi.

As Kelly walked along, she stopped into little shops to distract herself. She considered going into a restaurant and checked the plastic food on display in the front window. It looked amazingly realistic. After a minute, though, she walked away, not hungry enough to go to the effort of try-ing to order. Passing another, she was surprised to see their display food faded and dusty. *Who would ever want to eat there?* As she looked up, she saw her reflection in the glass superimposed on the forgotten food.

Kelly jumped at the sound of her phone ringing. She almost dropped it in her hurry to get it out of her purse. "Mushi-mushi."

"Hello. Mrs. Reese? This is Suzuki, nurse at Chūō Hospital."

"Is David all right?"

"Yes, he asks for you. You come hospital now?"

"Yes, immediately!"

Kelly was already in the taxi before she realized she hung up on the nurse without thanking her or saying goodbye.

They stood silently for a few moments before David motioned to the bed. Kelly wasn't sure how close to sit. She wasn't sure of anything, except that her nervousness showed.

"How are you feeling today?"

David was quiet for a while before he replied, "Pretty well. Much bet-ter than a couple of days ago. I'm sorry for what I said then. I really didn't know it was you."

"I know, baby. It's okay. I meant what I told you, though, if you can remember. I was leaving Japan and all the frustration, not you. But I handled it horribly. I'm so sorry. I never should've left. You needed me and I shouldn't have tried to manipulate you into leaving. I should've just stayed with—"

"No, it wasn't just you. I wasn't doing anything to support you here. I was so wrapped up in things."

"And that lawyer was calling about the sale of the Boise house. I'd been trying to work it all out for weeks and was sick of it but didn't tell you because you were already under so much pressure. David, I wasn't leaving you, I swear."

David looked down, clearly grieved, so Kelly explained in more detail that the lawyer was opposing counsel, not Kelly's attorney. With each bit of explanation, she watched his head rise and his shoulders relax.

Even with that misunderstanding illuminated, they were both reserved, but a conversation developed in fits and starts. Kelly didn't ask and David didn't state it, but everything implied he was going back with her. Kelly fought hard to control her emotions, no tears of joy or loving embrace, for David, although conciliatory, remained coolly unemotional. As they moved beyond the realization they were going home together, though, rambling through the family and events at home, they became more themselves.

Eventually they got to David's psychological state, and that was their vehicle for explaining the last few months to each other. Kelly told him how much she had looked forward to sharing Japan with him, and how she collapsed under the loneliness and isolation. David told her how he lost himself in the project, how it dragged him along as it spun out of control, about meeting Shōko on the levee, and how Shōko saved him. Thinking of him that despondent, Kelly had to turn away lest he see her misting over, and as thankful as she had been that Shōko gave him up, Kelly realized her debt to Shōko was infinitely deeper.

Talk about Shōko naturally led to how he fought off his demons with drawing and painting. "I was working on a sunrise over the river, acrylics, very bright. But I don't suppose I'll get to finish it."

"Why not? You could ask her to bring it to the hospital with all the paints and stuff. I think you've graduated from crayons."

"How did you know about the crayons?"

"I'm not entirely unplugged."

They smiled, still awkwardly.

"Kelly, the painting helped. In fact, I guess I hadn't realized how much I missed it or . . ."

"What?"

David shut his eyes and raised his shoulders as he lowered his head, as if drawing into himself.

"What? Tell me, even if it might hurt. I need to know."

David opened his eyes, but kept his head down as he went on, "I found myself blaming you that I wasn't painting."

Kelly was quiet.

"I know you never asked me to stop, but I sometimes got the feeling you thought it was a distraction from what I ought to be doing, merely a hobby."

"I love your paintings. You're an amazing painter, David, truly awe-inspiring. I never wanted you to stop." She considered her words carefully before going on. "You're right, though, I did always worry that painting might jam you up again and send everything, both our lives, into a tailspin. You were so passionate about it."

"I still am."

Kelly waited for David to look up and meet her gaze. "Then paint."

David looked down again.

"What?"

"And figures?"

"What do you mean?"

"I'd like to feel free to paint anything I choose."

Kelly was silent for quite a while, mindlessly fingering her tissues. She took them from her purse before she entered the room, but they were long since reduced to a single tiny ball. Finally, she gave a little sideways smile and asked, "Can you paint only old, ugly ones?"

David smiled.

"Could you paint them at the house? I think that would help me feel more comfortable with it."

"Let's just take it a step at a time and make sure we're both comfortable."

"We could turn a room into a studio."

"It would have to be big, with good light, that we can close off, so the house won't smell."

"We'll look things over when we get home."

David nodded. They were quiet for another minute before he said, "Thank you for coming back."

A response would come with tears, so Kelly stayed quiet until she was under control. "Shōko seems very nice."

"You met her?"

"It's a small waiting room."

David was quiet.

"More than nice. She seems . . . guileless?"

David nodded again. "It's amazing she still is. Her marriages should've left her cynical and bitter, but somehow she stayed . . . *kiyoi* fits better than anything in English."

"Your Japanese has gotten that good?"

David rolled his eyes and Kelly laughed. She leaned over and hugged him, and David put his arms around her and pulled her close.

They sat holding each other for a long while before David said, "I suppose I'll have to find a new job."

"Leon told me the COO is here to sort everything out, so I wouldn't be so sure," said Kelly, and then she whispered into his shoulder, "Anyway, we'll think about that later."

97

THEY MOVED DAVID TO A REGULAR ROOM LATE THAT AFTERNOON. He was sketching that evening when Kelly arrived with an older gentleman.

"Hi, David. I brought someone to meet you, Bill Dietrich."

David rose and extended his hand. "It's nice to finally meet you, Mr. Dietrich."

"Call me Bill. I'm sorry we haven't met before and sorry we put you in this situation. We have not served you well, David, and I intend to change that."

"Thank you."

"I had gotten a disturbing report from Fujitsu, but the people I asked to follow up on it turned out to be the ones who created the problems in the first place. It was a grave mistake on my part. I've been on the road for weeks and when I got back to Portland and tried to call you, that was the first day you were gone. I asked Leon to brief me and he told me what you found. You were right about the chip needing an all-layer revision. We met this morning with the Fujitsu people and agreed it's not worth it."

"So . . ."

"It's done. Fujitsu still sees a long-term opportunity and we'll have future discussions, but this project is done. Leon will shut it down from our end. After Kelly's phone call this afternoon"—David looked at her in surprise—"I had another talk with Paul. I told him that people see through self-aggrandizement, even if it takes an embarrassingly long time, and he swore the problems were all on you and said he was after your resignation."

"So, I'm—"

"No, David, you're not fired, and I hope you don't resign. Actually, Paul isn't fired either. He has some valuable management talents if we can break him of a couple of bad habits. Anyway, there are going be big changes in Portland and we need you. Take some time and when you're ready to come back to work and the doctors sign off, call me."

"Thank you, Bill. I appreciate you taking the time to come and tell me personally."

"I'm just sorry I didn't intervene sooner. Oh, and I hear you're an artist, and quite accomplished. Why hadn't I heard that? We have some talking to do when you get back. So were you drawing something when we came in? May I see it?"

98

Before, David had always enjoyed the sensation of an airplane taking off, the realization he was actually flying as his body was pressed into the seat. It was late afternoon, clouds hanging dark and low like smoke, and as the ground vanished and they swallowed him up, he closed his eyes. *Nine hours. If I had one of Nurse Suzuki's pills, I might sleep.*

Kelly took his hand, and he squeezed hers in return. She leaned over, took his arm, and hugged it. He appreciated the load she carried the last three days, working with Leon to have their things sent back to America, and then packing everything up before he even came home from the hospital. There wasn't much to pack, but even a simple thing such as finding boxes can be daunting in a foreign country. She was solicitous, too— almost uncomfortably so—but with all that had happened, it wasn't odd to be walking on eggshells. David knew that getting back into a routine would help, especially going back to work. He would find a psychiatrist as soon as they got home. A few visits, maybe a month or two, should convince the doctor he was ready.

The plane broke through the low clouds and David opened his eyes at the brightness. As he watched the puffy white expanse fall away, he saw Shōko lying on the bed in her white pajamas, smiling at him, perfectly relaxed, as if she had found peace at last. *Peace that was a mere mirage . . .*

Stop it. You'll cry. The last thing Kelly needs is her husband sobbing as she takes him home.

Alone, later.

Someday, it might even stop.

DEAR GOD, please don't ever make me go back there.

David will want to, though. . . .

Kelly looked over at him. His eyes were closed, but she knew he was awake; even in business class he never slept. She reclined both of their seats, leaned close, and rubbed his shoulder. The muscles she was kneading were perfectly familiar, but she couldn't help feeling that something inside him was off. There was the same silliness, the same forgetfulness and being lost in whatever he was doing, even the same gentleness, but these last three days he hardly talked. She expected distance—they each had big hurts to get over somehow, someday, but it was more than that. Might he never be as open as before, as if he'd turned Japanese?

Deeper than the quiet, though, there was something about him that was, she didn't want to think *scary*, but *unsettling*? She couldn't see through him. He seemed unpredictable, even feral, as if something inside him snapped and might never be restrung.

She gently rubbed his neck, and then his head. She loved the feel of his short hair, freshly cut, velvety in the back, like fur. For now, she would smile and focus on that, not the anxiety, not the pain.

99

THE PRESIDENT OF THE TRADING COMPANY WHERE SHŌKO WORKED for twenty-five years before marrying Masaru had been genuine in his offer to help if she ever needed anything. Still, she had not wanted to call. She did not want to do anything but lie on the bed. She should have been elated at being told they had a job for her, but relief was all she could muster. She knew that her lack of enthusiasm could devolve into something more debilitating.

David only left town this morning. I'll pull out of it.

Someday.

Maybe.

Shōko collapsed on her bed and buried her face in a pillow.

SHŌKO CHOSE the levee for their final meeting yesterday. It brought them full circle, and breakdowns were less likely in a public place. As they walked in silence, Shōko realized it was up to her to get a conversation going, so she asked, "Are we alone?"

David looked around. "People can see us, but nobody's close enough to hear."

"What about Roselda?"

"Oh, that kind of alone." He smiled. "She left the evening after you first visited. Didn't even say goodbye. Kind of rude, don't you think?"

"She is probably very busy."

He nodded. "Or it could have been that I got an actual pencil the next afternoon when they moved me into a regular room."

Shōko chuckled. After a minute, she asked, "Do you have your tickets?"

"Mm-hmm. Kelly worked with Fuji-Star and they set it all up."

"It will feel nice to go home."

It took him a long time to answer. "Yes and no."

"You focus on 'yes,' yes?"

"I'll try, but right now all I feel is—"

Her shoulder accidentally bumped into his arm. David took hold of her hand, and despite her embarrassment at such a public display and all her conviction to show no emotion and keep things arm's-length friendly, she clasped his hand in return.

They walked on, unhurried, hand in hand, as they made a big loop, crossing the bridge downstream, up the path on the far levee, and crossing back on the bridge upstream. As each brought up topics—painting, work, plans for the immediate future—conversations limped along and then died. At one point, David pointed out a family of ducks swimming single file and struggling to stay near the bank, the river flowing fast and high after rain for most of the previous day. Shōko, in turn, called his attention to the distinctive call of an *uguisu* hiding in a nearby thicket of bamboo. They even saw a *kiji* run into a dense growth of *susuki*, and David reacted with glee: "The bird on the money!" They were isolated bits of distraction, though, in an hour and a half of pain and longing.

Shōko knew when they got to the street where he would turn off to his apartment that she might never see him again, and her feet slowed involuntarily as she fought off panic. David got quiet too, and pulling on her hand, he led her down off the levee toward the river, to a stand of old willows where they could not be seen as easily.

Shōko looked up into his eyes. He was doing his best not to cry. She could guess what was coming, and though she knew her voice would be choked with tears, she said, "We can't."

"I know."

"You are married and Kelly . . ."

"You're married too," he said softly.

"*Sō desu ne,*" she whispered back.

David smiled and wiped her tears away. Shōko could still imagine a pastel stick in his slender fingers, though, and the world grew bleary and disappeared again in flood. This time he kissed her weeping eyes. Feeling his lips on her cheeks, a soft kiss on her nose, and then his beautiful hands lifting her face, there was no reason to let him go. She raised up on her toes and kissed him, eyes shut tight against the tears.

The torrent that flushed Shōko's levee away would have yielded to anything David's lips or hands insinuated, and she expected his mouth to press on hers, manic and coarse, as her husbands' had. But unhurried, at first, he barely grazed her lips, and even as the passion in his kisses grew, the touch of his lips stayed delicate, as if unfolding the most intimate of stories. The love in her true husband's kiss left her tingling, from her lips, through her neck and back, to her knees. Fated to be his, she held him as if reality could be reset, thirty years of steps untrodden, to touch for more than minutes in the willows. But long before either was ready, one of them broke the kiss—she wasn't sure now who—and she clung to him as his tears wet her hair, rolled down past her ear, and disappeared into her shirt. It was as if she was pressing him into her memory, to feel the embrace forever. To do that, though, was to abandon all hope, so she let go and they stood close, listening again for the *uguisu* as they watched the roiling water. Finally, with smiles of resignation, they clasped hands and he led her away from the river.

Back on the levee path, David tugged on her hand to have her walk up the street toward his apartment.

"I can't."

He was quiet for a minute before he replied, "Okay." He squeezed her hand. "Shōko, you know what I want to say."

She glanced down.

"But I won't. I'm trying to learn what you teach me."

"Thank you. My other husbands—"

She looked down as she blushed, but David let it pass. He promised to contact her as soon as he got home, she promised to respond, and they parted. She looked back once and waved but lacked the strength to look back again.

SHŌKO GOT UP and looked at the sketchbooks on the table. She reached out and touched the large one but did not open it. She would not pull away from David—she loathed the thought—but if this longing went on, she would lose her mind. So she pulled one of the boxes from under the bed, put the smaller sketchbooks inside, and stowed it away. She retrieved a roll of parcel wrapping paper from the spare room, got scissors and tape, and went about the agony of wrapping up the large sketchbook. As she placed it carefully under the bed, she took some small solace in the knowledge his vision of her, barely concealed in pure white linen, skin of soft pastel, was pristine, and always would be.

VII

Winter

冬

100

DAVID TURNED OFF THE ALARM AND SAT UP, WAITING FOR THE ROOM to come into focus. It was quarter to five a.m. on a Tuesday, but only early mornings ensured uninterrupted time at the easel. David paced briskly in the hallway to warm himself, the house unlit and altogether silent in the January darkness. He remembered the blackness of the first days under Shōko's bed that he thought no light would ever penetrate, and pain beyond hope, like a terminal disease without the final blessing. He was lucky, though: he remembered only that it hurt, not the actual pain, and he could vanquish this darkness with the flick of a switch.

David squinted in the light as he entered the room he now used as a studio. He donned his smock. While his eyes adjusted, he looked at his latest painting—looked, but did not see—as he imagined walking up the narrow path through the rhododendrons to her house, where he quietly slid open the door, slipped off his shoes, and climbed the stairs. He opened her door with practiced stillness, stole into the room where she lay sleeping, sat next to her on the bed, and gently brushed the hair from her face.

Love under separation: people think ardor will never disappear. But then comes the ceaseless light of time, day upon day, through weeks and months and years, until what were saturated crimsons show hardly a blush, faded into shades so dull no one would bother to name them. For some few, though—lucky, perhaps?—and others all too unlucky, the color never bleaches; quite the opposite, it seeps into all they think and say and do.

So David painted—far less than he wanted, but enough that he saw himself once again as a painter who designed computer chips. In fact, he could not imagine working at the company longer than about five more years. Life's tenuousness pressed upon him, and in five years their finances would be secure enough that there would be no reason not to have a brush in his hand every day. In fact, with not too painful belt tightening he could quit now; he was working mainly to reassure Kelly.

Still, as much as David longed for it, could he and Kelly ever regain the unguarded closeness they once shared? He loved another woman, and Kelly knew it. He could call his feelings "friendship," submerge them so deeply they made nary a ripple, and show his ardent love for Kelly, giving her tenderness and attention she had not known in years, but Shōko would always be with them. Cutting off contact might eventually ease Kelly's hurt, but Shōko also gave him confidence—and Kelly knew that too.

So, while David loved Kelly as completely as ever, he finally realized that the depth of his love was not the issue. Kelly used to have it all. She alone was enough. She had lost the oneness with a soulmate that was the anchor of her life, and restoring it would require a break that might always be beyond him. So David used painting to pick his way through limbo: never wholly belonging to one person, always longing to be closer to both the one he could touch and the one he could not.

101

KELLY ROLLED OVER IN BED AND FOUND HERSELF ALONE. IT JERKED her far enough out of the warm sand of sleep that it was hard to burrow back in. She checked the clock: 5:48. Shivering in the cold, she found her robe, then stole down the hall to check on David. The studio door was ajar, like always, but she did not intrude when he went to such effort to make time for his art.

Finally understanding the depth of David's need to paint, Kelly was staggered by the sacrifice he had made. She also saw a darker side, though, even in the large oil painting that hung in her office, one of his last before the long hiatus. It was the finest of his few self-portraits. He stood somber and indomitable, luminous highlights starkly set against deep shadows that merged into the profoundly dark background. But these days she saw defiance in it, perhaps even anger, the artist implacable as he was pressed to drop his brushes and disappear into the blackness.

David's therapy was going well. In fact, he was more confident than ever. He was more thoughtful too. He looked for ways to be helpful, asked Kelly out on dates, and turned off the television and spent evenings talking—and mostly listening. He had told her more than once why he was home with her, how deeply he loved her, and she'd felt that love, ever at least smoldering, at times an open flame. She caught him gazing at her, the way he used to years ago. He had asked her to model for him again too—thankfully, not nude—and they were exploring poses and compositions.

But David could also be quiet and withdrawn, as if someone had spirited away her mate of nearly thirty years and left an attractive stranger in his place. Sometimes, when he didn't hear her speaking to him, Kelly sensed someone in the room with them. She chose this, though: David's mental health at the price of a boarder in their marriage. She precipitated the crisis by leaving in the first place, so she had no choice but to muster patience in like magnitude to the original insensitivity.

Still, she missed the old David who had been open about everything—except his resentment over painting. Hiding his feelings for Shōko did little to dull the pain, something she doubted he would ever comprehend. So now she had a hidden side too. He didn't show he loved another woman, and she didn't show how much it hurt. Their own little North Korea, peace without resolution.

Kelly sometimes questioned her duty to uphold the desperate compromise she put into place that afternoon in the hospital waiting room, but there was no denying David still needed Shōko. She rescued him from a moment darker than Kelly had ever seen. It was probably the painting as much as Shōko, and David did not dispute it, but it was Shōko who made him paint again after Kelly herself was the main reason he stopped. So her husband was, to some extent, Shōko's creation; a metamorphosis in only two weeks. Shōko's unremarkable exterior veiled an astounding power over him. Perhaps that was the biggest disappointment, not that Kelly had lost her sway or her ability to hold

David together emotionally, but that she never had Shōko's ability to move him.

102

SHŌKO RETURNED TO HER OLD TRADING COMPANY AT THE BEGIN-ning of September. When she got to Tokyo, she looked up old friends, joined a gym, and started weekly visits to museums, trying to be active and forget the shame of her banishment as her father had adjured her. Still, she could not ignore that she was abandoning her duty to her aging parents—over a man.

Far worse, though, was letting herself back into Masaru's house a few days before she started work. There were things she wanted to retrieve before divorce papers revealed she was back in Tokyo, but a pass through the house staggered her with grief at what little remained. He had dis-carded every book. The novels weren't important; the cookbooks were more valuable. Losing her collection of art books tore at her, though. Few would be available even in Jimbōchō's remotest used-book haunts. She was even more devastated at the loss of her paintings, her four most favorite creations, including the large acrylic of a child lying in a field of flowers that had won awards her last year in college. Most tragic, though, was losing her photo albums. She moved almost everything to her par-ents' house when she married Masaru, he made so little room for her, and as she chose most judiciously what would go to Masaru's house, she picked *all* her photos; boxed them up and carried them merrily into hell, where he burned them.

Shōko mused sometimes how her life might be easier if she had not walked home on the levee path that day she first ran into David. She tried to dull the guilt at intruding into his marriage by remind-ing him that their friendship depended on Kelly's happiness, but every time David mentioned Kelly was like a punch in the stomach. Even at her strongest, Shōko was intimidated by the years ahead. The work that filled her days would be over all too soon. No family meant no safety net in case of financial trouble. She would turn to strangers for care as she grew frail. The fantasy of a third marriage, though, only made Shōko feel pathetic. The real shock came one weekend when, tired, alone, and deathly bored, she wondered how long Kelly might live. It was perverse! David had made his choice, and it was time for her to stand on her own.

No guilt or newfound assertiveness, though, could alter the reality that she loved David and always would. So as the months passed, Shōko was dropping her love into a memory, not discarded, yet severed from daily life, another keepsake under the bed. Of course, she could never tell David. Still, even an American like David would understand—eventually.

103

"MOSHI-MOSHI."

"Hi," came David's voice, soft and low.

"Hello," Shōko replied, her tone suddenly tender.

"It's been a while since we talked."

"Not so long, I think. Christmas is not even three weeks ago."

"Seems like longer."

Shōko was quiet for a second. "Thank you for flowers today. They are so beautiful."

"I'm glad you like them. Did you have a nice birthday?"

"It was quiet."

"Hmm . . . sounds as if your package didn't arrive yet."

"Package?"

"I couldn't let your birthday pass without a gift, could I?"

"Flowers are such a kind gift."

"There's something else on the way."

"Something else? Americans do too big birthday, I think."

David's grin showed in his voice: "Probably. But for you . . ." He paused and said more quietly, "Just know, when it gets there, I realize it's not enough."

She was quiet for longer this time. "Oh, I got a divorce form and took it to the town office after New Year. It is done now."

"So, that's it? The divorce is final?"

"Yes, all final at town office."

"Wonderful! I know it wasn't easy. So do you feel freer?"

"'Freer' means 'more free'?" She paused to think. "No, I feel free already. But I feel I am single again, finally."

It took him a second to respond. "I'm happy for you."

"Thank you. I was single many years. It suits me, I think."

He was silent for a while. "What are you painting now?"

"A self-portrait, still. I love the paints you sent so much."

"Hey, Shōko is a painter, and a painter needs paints."

"But I can't paint every day."

"Still, you'll show me soon? I don't have to wait till it's done, do I?"

"Maybe."

"Maybe you'll show me or maybe I have to wait?"

She laughed. "Those two are only one 'maybe' together."

It wasn't long before it was time to go. As often happened, David's voice got steadily softer. "You know I miss you."

She was quiet but finally said, "I know."

"Talk to you soon."

She was quiet for a few seconds before she said, "Okay."

"Bye." His voice was soft, deep, like a bedtime story.

"Bye," came her reply, childlike, almost whispered.

A FEW KILOMETERS AWAY, two men moved the wooden crate, a meter tall and wide and twenty centimeters thick, off the truck. Busy with their night's work, neither took any thought for what might be inside as they scanned it into the tracking system and set it aside for delivery tomorrow.

Contacted by phone the next day, Shōko would arrange for delivery in the evening, and when the time arrived, a man would load it onto a truck and drive to her building. Barely able to fit it into the small elevator, he would be thankful he did not have to heft it up the stairs to her fourth-floor apartment. He would appreciate her shock at such a large package, and even more at the careful crating. She would fret she had no way to open it, and he would hurry back to the truck for a pry bar. After he opened the crate and the box inside, he would pull out the large, flat item, remove the bulkiest of the padding, and after slipping off his shoes in the *genkan*, carefully carry it through her hallway. She would help to remove the last of the padding, the inner box, and the paper covering. Finally, he would inspect the oil painting and its frame, but only to check for damage, paying no attention to its classically detailed figures and modern style. He would be long gone, of course, before she cried, and it would be days before she wrapped it with the greatest care and placed it under her bed, unable to face such a pure reminder of her loss, despite knowing it was not at all intended as such.

The painting portrayed a woman, perhaps a deity, certainly immortal, and a pitiful beggar, barely conscious, on the rocky skirt of an ancient road. She stood in the earliest morning sunlight, arms outstretched over the man, lifting him off the ground with unseen power. He was awakening, a light appearing in his eyes as he hung in midair, still half reclining, his limbs draping limp except for one hand reaching out, seemingly trying to grasp the red binding of her sleeve. The rest of her open, hooded gown, her only covering, was the sheerest white tulle. She glowed white as well, but it was not the gown. The light shone from her milk-caramel skin, hardly concealed, along with the gentle curves of her slender body, by the almost transparent fabric. Her bearing, one leg slightly bent, her arms and hands extended in subtle grace, bespoke confidence and power, yet her earnest expression showed not regal detachment, but Heaven's own solicitude. And while she may have been divine, her gaze betrayed that this was no messenger's errand. His eyes were opening to intimacy that glowed warm, deep, and true in her ageless face; a face that, obscured by both the glow and the gown, might not be recognizable to some, but would be obvious to Shōko, as would the man's, even through tears.

Japanese Words and Phrases

PART TITLES

I   *Noraneko* › stray cat › 野良猫 (のらネコ)

II   *Shima, aruiwa muchiuchi* › stripes, or lashes
› 縞、あるいは鞭打ち

III   *Sōsaku* › search › 捜索

IV   *Kegawa ga atta nara* › if (we) had fur › 毛皮があったなら

V   *Shiroi neko no shūsaku* › studies of a white cat
› 白い猫の習作

VI   *Ikita mama kawa o hagu* › to skin while still alive
› 生きたまま皮を剥ぐ

VII   *Fuyu* › winter › 冬

NAMES OF JAPANESE CHARACTERS

Itō › senior Japanese manager at Fujitsu-Star Microchips › 伊藤

Kikuchi › lead detective › 菊池

Kuniko › Leon's wife › 邦子

Murakami › police officer from the nearby *kōban* › 村上

Nakagawa › detective › 中川

Ōbuchi › supervisor of detectives › 大淵

Masaru Ōta › Shōko's second husband › 太田勝

Shōko Kawasaki/Ōta › Shōko › 太田/川崎昭子

Suzuki › nurse › 鈴木

Takahara › number two Japanese manager at Fujitsu-Star
Microchips › 高原

WORDS AND PHRASES

"Ā, sō ka?" › "Ah, is that so?" › 「ああ、そうか?」

"Ā, sō ne." › "Ah, that's so." › 「ああ、そうね。」

Akita Komachi › a premium variety of Japanese rice › あきたこまち

"Anō, Rīsu-san ni menkai dekimasu kedo . . ."
  › "You may see Mr. Reese now. . . ."
  ›「あのうリースさんに面会できますけど . . .」

"Ara!" › exclamation of surprise (feminine) ›「あら!」

"Atta!" › "Found it/them!" ›「あった!」

"Bikkuri!" › "What a surprise!" ›「びっくり!」

-chan › title of familiarity, similar to "*-san,*"
  but for children/cute things › ちゃん

Chip Star *(chippu sutā)* › a brand of Japanese potato chips
  › チップスター

"Chū-san wā . . ." › "Third year of middle school [ninth grade] was . . ."
  ›「中三はあ . . .」

"Daijōbu desu ka?" › "Are you all right?" ›「大丈夫ですか?」

"Dame!" › "Don't/No/It's wrong!" ›「駄目!」

danna-sama › master (long ago it also meant "husband") › 旦那様

dojin › indigenous inhabitant, esp. dark skinned (offensive) › 土人

e / ē › expression of surprise or wonder (esp. with rising pitch), "Huh?"
  "What?" "What did you say?" › えっ/ええ

ētto › expression used when thinking or hesitating,
  like "uh," "um," or "er" › ええっと

"Ētto . . . otoko no pantsu-tte . . ." › "Um . . . [what do you call] 'men's
  underpants' . . . ?" ›「ええっと . . . 男のパンツって . . . ?」

futon › mattress filled with cotton batting,
  placed on the floor as a bed › 布団

geisha › woman professionally trained to entertain
  (mostly men) › 芸者

genkan › entryway (generally one step below floor level)
　　　where shoes are removed › 玄関

genki › feeling well, spirited, happy, cheerful, energetic › 元気

gochisō-san › informal version of the traditional expression of thanks
　　　for a meal › ごちそうさん

"Guradēshon! Jojo ni henka suru koto ne. Sō datta wa ne!"
　　　› "Gradation! Changing gradually. Of course!"
　　　›「グラデーション！徐々に変化することね。そうだったわね！」

hai / hāi › yes › はい/はあい

hamanashi › Japanese rose › 浜梨

hikagemono › "shadow person," one who avoids social contact or is
　　　hidden away (e.g., a mistress), an outcast › 日陰者

hirugao › small pink flower similar to morning glory;
　　　it closes at night and opens at midday › 昼顔

"Hoippu kurīmu-tte nan te iu no . . . ?"
　　　› "What do you call 'whipped cream' . . . ?"
　　　›「ホイップクリームって何て言うの … ？」

hoteru › hotel › ホテル

"Hoteru? Hoteru ni ikun desu ka?"
　　　› "Hotel? You are going to a hotel?"
　　　›「ホテル？ホテルに行くんですか？」

irusshaimase › welcome (commonly called out by store personnel
　　　when a customer enters) › いらっしゃいませ

"Irasshaimase. Ētto . . . Nihongo wa . . . ?"
　　　› "Welcome. Um . . . [do you speak] Japanese?"
　　　›「いらっしゃいませ。ええっと … 日本語は … ？」

Isetan › high-end department store chain › 伊勢丹

itadakimasu › polite expression said before eating › いただきます

iya › no (very informal) › いや

iya da › expression of dislike or disgust › 嫌だ

Jimbōchō › an area of Tokyo known for bookstores › 神保町

kabocha › Japanese winter squash (also known as Japanese pumpkin)
› かぼちゃ

kaki › persimmon › 柿

kanji › Chinese characters (about two thousand are commonly used
in written Japanese) › 漢字

kawa › river › 川

"Kawasaki-san, moshi yoroshikereba, Rīsu-san ni o-ai-dekimasu ga . . ."
› "Ms. Kawasaki, if you are ready, you may see Mr. Reese now."
› 「川崎さん、もしよろしければ、リースさんにお会いでき
ますが . . .」

kiji › Japanese pheasant (national bird of Japan, along with the crane;
pictured on the back of ten-thousand-yen banknotes until
2004) › キジ (雉子)

kimono › clothing; garment; esp. traditional, long, loose robe with wide
sleeves, tied with a sash › 着物

kisu › Sillago (Japanese whiting), a mild whitefish › 鱚

kiyoi › clean, clear (water), pure, innocent, chaste › 清い

kōban › neighborhood police box, a very small building
commonly occupied by one or two officers who focus
on local policing › 交番

komaru/komatta › to be troubled, distressed
(present tense/past tense) › 困る/困った

"Komatta nā." › "[We're] really stuck/in trouble." › 「困ったなあ。」

Koshihikari › a premium variety of Japanese rice › コシヒカリ

manga › Japanese comics › マンガ (漫画)

Meiji *(Meiji jidai)* › the Meiji period, 1868–1912 › 明治時代

mejiro › Japanese white-eye, a songbird marked with green,
about the size of a sparrow › メジロ (目白)

miso › a traditional seasoning most commonly made from fermented
rice and soybeans › みそ

"Moshi-moshi." › "Hello." (used only when answering the telephone)
› 「もしもし。」f;icmfori

nā › sentence ending that tacitly suggests that others in the
conversation do or should agree with the speaker › なあ

"Nan da be, Shōko. Hari doko sa oitan da be?"
› "That's odd, Shōko. Where did you put the needles?"
› 「何だべ、昭子。針どこさ置いたんだべ?」

"Nani?" › "What?" › 「何?」

"Nan te iu kana . . . " › "What should I say . . . ?" or "What's the
word . . . ?" › 「何て言うかな . . .」

nē › expression used to get someone's attention, start a new topic
of conversation, etc. (feminine) › ねえ

neko obasan › middle-aged or elderly woman who has many cats
› 猫おばさん

nemu (nemunoki) › Persian silk tree or pink siris
› ネムノキ (合歓木)

nori › [a sheet of] dried laver (an edible seaweed) › 海苔

obasan › aunt, middle-aged woman › おばさん

ohayō › good morning (informal) › おはよう

"Ōi! Bāsan, doko sa itta?" › "Hey! Where are you?"
› 「おおい!ばあさん、どこさいった?」

"Ōi! Bāsan, in no ga?" › "Hey! Are you here?"
› 「おおい!ばあさん、いんのが?」

Okāsan › Mother › お母さん

o-kaeri-nasai › welcome back › お帰りなさい

o-nigiri › rice ball, often with *umeboshi* or salmon flake or other savory
thing in its center and wrapped in *nori* › おにぎり (御握り)

orenji › orange › オレンジ

Otōsan › Father › お父さん

o-tsukare-sama › an expression of appreciation for or acknowledgment
of work done, like "good job" › おつかれさま

penparu › pen pal › ペンパル

rāmen › "ramen," Chinese noodle soup › ラーメン

-san › polite title, equivalent to Miss, Mr., Mrs., or Ms. › さん

"Seijitsu-tte . . . " › "What's [the word for] 'true' [or 'faithful'] . . . ?" › 「誠実って . . .」

sen-giri › finely chopped ("thousand-cut") › 千切り

Shibuya Crossing (*Shibuya sukuranburu kōsaten*) › Hundreds, even thousands, at a time cross the iconic scramble street crossing at Tokyo's Shibuya Station, a favorite of foreign media to show Japan's techno-sea-of-humanity image › 渋谷スクランブル交差点

shima › island › 島

Shinkansen › high-speed "bullet" train › 新幹線

shītake › a variety of Japanese mushroom › 椎茸

"Sō?" › "Is that so?" › 「そう?」

"Sō desu ne." › "Yes, that's so." › 「そうですね。」

"Sō ne." › "Yes/yeah, I guess so/that's true." › 「そうね。」

sugoi › amazing, wonderful (also terrible, horrible, awful) › すごい

sushi › rice, flavored with *sushi-su* (sweetened vinegar), spiced with *wasabi* (Japanese horseradish), and topped or rolled with various ingredients, such as sliced raw fish › 寿司

sushi-su › sweetened vinegar used to flavor *sushi* rice › すし酢

susuki › Japanese pampas grass › 薄

tadaima › I'm back › ただいま

takushī › taxi › タクシー

"Takushī desu ka? Hoteru e no takushī?" › "Taxi? A taxi to a hotel?" › 「タクシーですか?ホテルへのタクシー?」

tempura › lightly battered and fried seafood and vegetables › 天ぷら

"Te-narashi-tte . . . " › "What's [the word for] 'practice' [or 'training'] . . . ?" › 「手慣らしって . . .」

tentsuyu › *tempura* dipping sauce › 天つゆ

uguisu › Japanese bush warbler (a symbol of early spring in Japanese poetry, it sings most distinctively in late spring and summer) › ウグイス (鶯)

ukiwa › swim ring, life ring › 浮き輪

ume › deciduous tree, relatevd to the plum and apricot, with winter
blossoms in colors from white to red; also the sour, fleshy
yellow fruit of the *ume* tree › 梅

umeboshi › a pickled *ume* fruit › 梅干し

un › yes (very informal) › うん

Uonuma-san Koshihikari › Koshihikari-variety rice grown in the
Uonuma region of Niigata prefecture › 魚沼産コシヒカリ

uwaki › (extramarital) affair › 浮気

wasabi › Japanese horseradish › わさび

yakuza › Japanese mafia › やくざ

yukata › traditional, summer-weight, unlined *kimono*,
usually made of cotton › 浴衣

yuki › snow › 雪

"Yūkōkyā-tte nan darō . . . ?" › "I wonder what '*yūkōkyā*' is . . ."
(his mistaken hearing of "you call cab")
› 「ユーコーキャーって何だろう . . . ?」

zabuton › pillow/cushion used when sitting/kneeling on the floor
› 座布団

Acknowledgments

I wish to thank my wife, who cheered, critiqued, and edited throughout the writing process. Keiko Homma's ideas and encouragement were invaluable, as was her help in the drawing and painting sections and all things Japanese. Kuniko Nagano and Satoko Fujii helped localize Japanese conversations, Tom Rugh and Jeffrey Rugh advised in the painting sections, and David Mayhew and Shane Harker advised on the microchip problems. Fran Lebowitz helped me shorten and tighten the manuscript, and Sadie Rittman helped me see where the story needed to be filled out. Tricia Callahan did a final copyedit. Laura Duffy designed the cover, and Karen Minster, the interior. Friends read drafts and gave me what I needed most from them: more feedback. The writing changed based on what they said.

Lastly, this story was inspired by someone who would be most upset if named but whose life, pain, strength, and patient care have lifted me. 親友、ありがとう。

FOR MORE FROM M. HARMON WILKINSON,
VISIT WWW.MHARMONWILKINSON.COM.